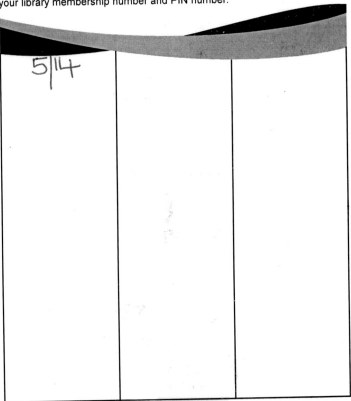
'A deep profundity . . . it is rare that
of its own conventions – *Depths of*

'An ambitious and convincing w(
essentially the pretext for a d
– *La Va*

'Intellect(

Depths of the Forest

Eugenio Fuentes was born in Montehermoso, Cáceres, Spain. His novels include *The Battles of Breda*, *The Birth of Cupid* (winner of the San Fernando Luis Berenguer International Fiction Prize), *So Many Lies* (winner of the Extremadura Creative Novel Award) and *Blood of the Angels* (Arcadia) also featuring private investigator Ricardo Cupido.

Paul Antill works as a translator from the Spanish and French. His translation of *La Tempestad* by Juan Manuel de Prada was listed for the *Independent on Sunday* Best Translation Prize out of over 70 submissions.

EUGENIO FUENTES

Depths of the Forest

Translated from the Spanish by Paul Antill

Arcadia Books Ltd.
15–16 Nassau Street
London W1W 7AB

www.arcadiabooks.co.uk

First published in the United Kingdom by Arcadia Books, 2002
This B format edition printed June 2007
Original Spanish edition published by Alba Editorial, s.l.u., Barcelona,
as *El interior del bosque*
Copyright © Alba Editorial 1999
Translation copyright © Paul Antill 2002

A catalogue record for this book is available from the British Library

ISBN 1-905147-48-1

Typeset in Monotype Ehrhardt
Printed in Finland by WS Bookwell

Arcadia Books Ltd acknowledges the financial support of la Dirección General del Libro,
Archivos Bibliotecas del Ministerio de Educación, Cultura y Deporte de España.

Arcadia Books supports English PEN, the fellowship of writers who work together to promote
literature and its understanding. English PEN upholds writers' freedoms in Britain and around
the world, challenging political and cultural limits on free expression. To find out more, visit
www.englishpen.org, or contact English PEN, 6–8 Amwell Street, London EC1R 1UQ.

Arcadia Books distributors are as follows:

in the UK and elsewhere in Europe:
Turnaround Publishers Services
Unit 3, Olympia Trading Estate
Coburg Road
London N22 6TZ

in the USA and Canada:
Independent Publishers Group
814 N. Franklin Street
Chicago, IL 60610

in Australia:
Tower Books
PO Box 213
Brookvale, NSW 2100

in New Zealand:
Addenda
Box 78224
Grey Lynn
Auckland

in South Africa:
Quartet Sales and Marketing
PO Box 1218
Northcliffe
Johannesburg 2115

Arcadia Books is the *Sunday Times* Small Publisher of the Year

There's always a problem, and it's still there after killing
J. C. ONETTI

One

She knew there was nothing to justify that sense of dread, but couldn't stop herself looking back. No shadow, no inexplicable sound or smell intruded on the tranquillity of her walk, and yet something she couldn't pin down had frightened her and made her turn her head. *For those alone in the forest there's always a wolf lying in wait*, she reflected, surprised by her own fears. It was the first time this had happened on her many rambles through the Paternoster Forest. She knew this part of the Reserve well, and although she had previously experienced some minor mishaps in it – a fire that nearly got out of hand when she and Marcos were there one windy day, injuring one of her legs as the result of a fall, and the discovery of a hanged stag with a dog licking up its semen – all these had been the result of chance, carelessness, or the brutality of local customs, and never because another individual had intended to harm her. She stopped walking, breathed deeply for a few seconds, listened to the profound silence that penetrated the forest, and spoke aloud for the first time since walking out of the hotel an hour and a half earlier.

'There's nothing there, nobody. There's nothing to be scared of.'

Her voice sounded unconvincing even to herself. She was surprised to feel her heart beginning to beat faster, and the word *terror* was becoming fixed in her mind like an undesirable lodger she couldn't evict. She recalled what she had written in her diary three weeks before: *But fear isn't an innocent emotion* – and she knew that in the solitude of the forest she would not find it easy to suppress.

She had begun her walk after breakfast, having worked out the time it would take to get up as far as the ledges on Yunque Mountain with their cave paintings, to eat the cold meal she was carrying in a small knapsack which the hotel had prepared for her, and to study the last details she needed to finish off her pictures. Before returning, she would still have time to think calmly about her relationship with Marcos as she looked down on that unique view which made it possible to believe that there are no such things as contaminated rivers, or smoke-blackened skies, or fields polluted with rubbish. Before setting out she had put on a pair of comfortable Gore-Tex boots, linen trousers, a light-coloured shirt tailored like a man's, and a cap. Everything was as good as it had been on other occasions so she mustn't allow herself to be affected by this absurd fear. She knew that completely alone in the middle of the forest it is possible to feel frightened, but she was a strong-minded girl, she told herself, independent, and had lived alone in Madrid since her father died; she was always ready to open her front door without first asking who was there, and had proved herself free of the sort of cowardice that insists on double locks and creates a fear of shadows; nor did she show any sign of that mistrust and defeatism common to many women who lead sad, lonely lives and believe that every ring at their doorbell portends menace. She had been walking for ninety minutes and could turn back without too much regret if she decided to, but somehow she guessed that if she did return to the hotel, she would never again dare go out and walk alone in the forest, because she knew something about the poison that memories can generate. She adjusted the straps of the knapsack on her shoulders, drank a little of the water from her flask, and set off again with a firm step.

Five minutes later, the path which up to that point had been a forest track made to take motorized vehicles, led into a clearing. From there it split into two paths. The one on the left, the wider of the two, dropped down towards the reservoir. With no hesitation she took the one on the right that led up to the caves with the paintings. Once she had left the clearing and had started on the steep, narrow path she became aware again of the silence, the tingling sensation on her neck, as if someone close by was watching to be sure that she took the path she had intended following since leaving the hotel. Again she wondered whether she should turn back, but again quickened her pace up the slope even though she knew that from here on it was highly unlikely that she would see or pass another person, that very few people, and then only occasionally, took that difficult and lonely route because they preferred to roam around the lower ground and gentler slopes in order to view the Reserve's prolific game that grazed in the vicinity of the reservoir and, being almost domesticated, allowed itself to be photographed from some way off without being easily startled. A bead of sweat dripped from her forehead, ran down between her eyebrows, and on to her nose. She brushed it away with her sleeve and, without knowing why – possibly to observe the position of the sun – looked up at the sky. There, in the clear blue of the morning, two kites, high above, wheeled slowly and contentedly as they digested their prey – mice, snakes, or carrion – that they had consumed early that morning. She had always loved and been astonished by the richness and variety of the birds: the kites with their fantails and deceptive languor, majestic pot-bellied eagles, neat Egyptian vultures with the white bibs round their necks, elusive black storks with their beaks full of frogs, Griffon vultures that made an epicurean feast of every piece of carrion, picking it clean; iron-beaked falcons that always attack the skulls of their prey, fast and elegant swifts, cheeky magpies, silent goshawks cutting through the gauze of the sky with their scissor-sharp wings, golden orioles with their bell-like song, partridges whose wings creak as if the act of flying breaks their bones... She loved all the birds of the forest, much more than the flowers or the animals. She had always considered them the best evidence that this area was the one that survived as the most unblemished, the purest in spite of everything, and the least polluted. Nobody could confine them up there in the sky, and if they stayed in the Paternoster Forest it was because it still offered a habitat of a kind that had disappeared almost everywhere else. It was possible to create artificially a reserve for wild boar or deer by wiring off an area, but nobody could fence off space for birds of prey to live and hatch their young in. It was fortunate, she reflected, that it was not yet so well known as to be packed out with sightseers every Sunday, although at that very moment she was still gripped by fear and would have liked to hear other voices nearby, children shouting, laughter, even the babbling of a radio broadcasting a football match. She had heard that the forest was about to be declared a nature reserve, or something like it, and wondered whether amongst its future benefits they would still have the privilege of being able to walk along its paths, freely and alone, without too many restrictions or obligatory routes. She caught a slight noise behind her, and felt the sense of dread increasing. It had sounded like a dry twig snapping, but she repeated to herself that that was no reason to believe she was in danger. On the contrary, the forest became menacing only when it was shrouded in silence, not when it was alive with sounds. Her throat was dry again, and she stopped to have another drink from the hip flask she carried at her belt. She felt the water that was still pleasantly cool slip down her throat and wash away the dust she had swallowed during her walk. Of all the wonders of the forest that was certainly the best: the way in which all her senses, dulled by city life, came alive again, making her aware once more of every part of her body, even the smallest and most intimate. While she was closing the flask, she recalled that

nowhere else had she enjoyed making love so much as she had
in the middle of the forest, on the grass, or in the tent pitched
near one or another of the half-hidden inlets of the reservoir in
which she would bathe naked afterwards, every pore dilated in
the cold water. She remembered him, and his refusal to come
with her that weekend so that they could talk undisturbed about
what was going wrong between them, with no reproaches, and
without looking for sympathy. She lowered her head in order to
replace the flask on her belt, but raised it again as she saw the
figure that sprang from her terror hurling itself towards her,
knife in hand – one of those black shepherds' knives that always
look as if they have just been sharpened on a whetstone, and
which in the course of time lose their straight edge and become
curved in the part that has seen the most use, acquiring as a
result a terrible capacity for injury. She cried aloud, and tried to
defend herself by raising her forearms. The searing pain in her
wrist reached her brain one tenth of a second before the pain in
her left breast where she clearly felt the steel thrust into it,
rending the tender, spongy flesh. Anguish and terror made her
quiver and shudder violently. The knife was pulled out of her
breast to give one more thrust, and it now sought the base of her
neck. She heard the metal grind against the tendons and carti-
lage of her windpipe, and was aware of how its fibres were
slashed at the very moment when her second cry turned into an
animal-like gurgle. She was surprised by the warmth flooding
over her, soaking the skin of her breast, and scalding her throat
as if she had swallowed something hot and viscous, very different from the water she had drunk a moment before, and which
provoked an unbearable need to vomit. She knew then that she
was going to die, and had known this since she left the clearing
and took the path up towards the caves. She stretched her arms
out towards her executioner and clutched at his clothing in one
last effort, even though by doing so she left her breast utterly
exposed to further knife wounds. The pricking of a pin in the

middle finger of one hand hurt her, but, without knowing why, she pressed even harder against it, as if that tiny, sharp pain would make her forget the greater pain in her throat. She sensed that she was falling backwards and was sinking into a scarlet river. Then she felt nothing.

It had heard a shot that morning and since coming to live in the forest knew that shots meant blood. From its burrow it had also heard a woman's cry and, a little later, the laboured sound, growing fainter, of one of those machines in which human beings move about. After this, it had stayed still, probing the silence and the absence of vibration in the surface of the earth. For several hours it had remained motionless in its dark lair, curbing the hunger caused by the knowledge that there was meat not far off.

The rat put its black snout out of the hole, spying out the empty terrain with its tiny pupils. Everything was in its usual place: the trees, the sun, the insects, and the dust. It took one step forward and raised its head. The delicate and sweet odour of blood it had dreamed of since hearing the shot reached its nostrils. However, it still didn't decide to go further. There was a distinct echo of human voices from the clearing further down in the forest, but these were too distant to bother it. It feared humans because of the killing machines they used, but wasn't disturbed by their presence. Unarmed, they were the most sluggish of all predators, blind as moles, with little sense of smell, and ridiculously slow in their movements. It remembered a dog in the city which had always been faster than most of the rats, and used to break their necks with a sharp blow to the ground. And it didn't even eat them. So long as the rat was not spotted by the humans in the clearing there was no reason to worry.

It looked around again, and then up at the sky, knowing that its main enemies were up there – the vultures that were quick to find corpses, and the raptors that were always famished. However, nothing was flying overhead. On a sudden impulse, it left the burrow and crept towards the trunk of a pine. It couldn't wait for nightfall. Like this rat, a host of other nocturnal predators would have heard the shot and smelled the blood, and would be in their lairs waiting for the darkness of the night before pouncing on the remains of the catch or on the smaller animals that would have answered its call.

The smell became stronger, carried on a gust of wind. But now, mingled with it, came the aroma of a thousand flowers that it had smelled before on some of the clothing and other leftovers abandoned by humans on their passage through the forest. It looked up at the sky once more before running swiftly closer to the food. Crouched in a clump of cistus it looked at the body lying there, huge and succulent, enough food for a whole year – if human bodies didn't decompose so excessively quickly, giving off a stench that even rats couldn't stomach. There was not a quiver to suggest it was alive; it couldn't be a trick. Flies, the most reliable heralds of death, were already swarming over the lips. At the sight of so much food and the intense smell of blood, its hunger became uncontrollable. It approached the body with confidence and ran all round it consumed by greed and delight, like a beggar invited to eat in a palace who cannot decide where to begin on so many delicacies.

It raised itself on its hind legs and rested its front paws on the forehead of the body until its whiskers grazed the cold pupils that were dilated with horror, but immediately drew back, frightened by the unbearable fixity of those open eyes so close to its own. Its three minute toes left traces of earth on the woman's skin.

Crouching near the neck, it again looked round, fearful of the approach of stronger rivals. Then, convinced at last that it would not yet have to share this prize, it ran down to the feet that lay slightly apart, stopping near the soles, and turning its nose up at the lizard smell that they gave off. It climbed on to one of the boots, and gazed up at the length of that immense body which, for now, it had all to itself. Given greater strength it would have dragged it away and hidden it in its burrow. For a moment it envied the ants, not for their strength, but for their tenacity and the co-ordinated efforts that enable them to fill their larders. But the custom of rats is the fierce struggle between them for territory and food. With a leap it reached the knees and advanced slowly, sensing beneath its paws the smooth, fleshy thighs that it would have sunk its teeth into had the strong linen cloth not prevented it. The odour of urine drew it upwards. It moved on a few steps and sniffed the crotch where a dark stain made it salivate even more. There had been the same smell in the old house in the town where it had lived before being driven out by the fierce dog and the steel machines. It licked the dampness on the trousers and rubbed its belly against it, drunk with delight. Then it continued its tour arriving at the breast where it steeped its snout in the blood of the first wound, and lifted its head to savour it to the full. Deer's blood was thicker, but this was sweeter. About to begin its feast it caught sight of the knife stuck in the neck a little higher up. Blinded by greed, and without looking at anything else, or obeying any call other than the insistent pangs of hunger, it sank its sharp teeth into the torn flesh near the blade and bit off a small piece. Never had it tasted such soft, such tender meat. Swallowing without chewing, it continued to tear lumps off like any carnivore, supporting itself on its bloody front paws in order more easily to rip out its meal. For now all this belonged to the rat: it had found it, and owned it. It felt a glutton's hatred for the flies that settled on the wounds cheating it of minuscule portions of food. But suddenly it heard footsteps, and without ceasing to chew, raised itself on its hind paws. From the time it had left its hole it had heard voices a long way off, but now one of them was coming near. It saw the enormous, hostile figure, which was unsure where it was going and stood there with head bent; almost certainly it too was searching for something to eat. But then it looked to its front, and continued to approach. Now there was no doubt about it: the figure was coming nearer; the rat would be forced to flee and abandon its feast. It was always the same. Like the struggle for food, this was the eternal fate of its race: to find paradise and then immediately be expelled; if only they could live safely like the eagles or the moles. Greedily, it bit off two pieces to fill the cavities in its cheeks. Then, with bulging jowls it leapt down and ran off, to hide again underground.

The group of twelve- to fourteen-year-old boys arrived at the clearing on their mountain bikes. Here they stopped, threw their bikes on the ground that was parched from four years of drought and, laughing and shouting, sought the shade of the pine-trees to eat the sandwiches they carried in their small, brightly coloured satchels. October was well advanced, and there remained few long afternoons for this type of excursion through the forest. They swapped jokes as they ate and drank – concealing their dislike of the rough, heavy wine that one of their number had helped himself to at home. Having finished their picnic, another of them took out a packet of cigarettes and a few of them smoked, swallowing hard to avoid coughing. They spent a few minutes discussing whether to start off again immediately to try to get as far as the caves, or whether to wait for a while to digest their lunch. And as, all things being equal, idleness usually triumphs, the more active among them agreed to half an hour's rest and to devoting this time to those childish amusements that so often combine cruelty with play. They took out a tube of glue they carried for repairing punctures, and three of them went off to look for two forked sticks, while the others cleared the grass and stones from a circle with a radius of half a metre and ringed it round with more grass and dry twigs.

Only then did they separate to hunt for scorpions hiding under stones. It was early afternoon, a good time to find them, but also the most dangerous if one of them was stung, because the heat increases the virulence of the venom. A short time later they brought along the first two scorpions inside the glass jars they had emptied during their meal, and threw them into the middle of the ring. The scorpions, more frightened than angry, began to race around crazily trying to get out of the arena that had been cleared of stones and grass, and in which it was impossible for them to find shelter from the sun or protection from those enormous figures that stared at them from above. Their attempts to flee were futile because, using the forked sticks, the boys pushed them back time and again into the centre of the ring. And then, in spite of the signs clearly forbidding it, one of the boys set fire to the little barrier of grass and dry twigs they had constructed round it. Frightened by the smoke, the creatures stayed still, in an attitude that was misleadingly submissive. But it was easy to imagine the entire systems of viscera and glands inside their stationary bodies working frantically to stimulate the production of huge doses of venom.

That was the time to start the game. The two boys with the sticks held the scorpions fast against the ground with their forked ends. A third one removed the cap from the tube of glue and with great care – but with a precision and a steady hand that showed it wasn't the first time he had done it – squeezed drops of glue on to the sharp, curved points of their tails, which quickly hardened. They removed the sticks, and let the creatures free. These remained in their immobile, spider-like state, considering what strategy they should adopt, but still frightened by the movements of those gigantic figures and the smell of burning from the barrier surrounding them. No doubt they still had confidence in the strength of their venom and their unshakable determination. The boy who had applied the glue then extended one hand towards them. The two scorpions placed themselves in the defensive position, sting next to sting, to protect their backs against an enemy who was both immense and held together by bones and tendons a thousand times stronger than their fragile shells. As the finger came near they raised their bellies off the ground and aimed their stings at it, but like those strange implements with a heavy ball at one end used by some shepherds, they couldn't inflict an injury with their points, and could only strike as if with diminutive fists. They struck several times against the finger drawing nervous laughter from above them, before stopping to rest, bewildered by the hard blob that hindered their jabbing. Some of the other boys then ventured to tease them with their fingers, to stir them up, and to taunt them, until they lay exhausted one beside the other, aware of the practical joke to which they had been subjected. Two of the boys picked them up and holding them in the palms of their hands drew them close to their faces, and then dropped them on the ground and stamped on them to make them burst. Still not satisfied with this game, as if they had confronted two not particularly ferocious adversaries, they went to look under stones for another pair. They spread out round the clearing, and two minutes later the forest resounded with a yell from one of them followed by his hasty dash back to the safe refuge of his group of friends. The others thought he had been stung putting his hand under a stone, but as he ran up, he said:

'There's a dead woman.'

He was so pale they all knew it wasn't a joke.

Then, raising his hand to his neck, he explained:

'She's got a knife stuck in her throat.'

It was some time since the sun had set behind the crest of Yunque Mountain, and the darkness had made it necessary to switch on searchlights. From time to time camera flashes lit up and froze a colourful and unreal scenario, startling the birds awake in the middle of their night. A dozen men, most of them in Civil Guard uniforms, who had been informed three hours before by the boys who had found the body, moved backwards and forwards between the trees observing every detail, every dry blade of trodden grass, every broken branch, every dislodged stone.

A man in sergeant's uniform approached a taller and younger man, a lieutenant wearing plain clothes, who was talking to the investigating magistrate and the forensic surgeon who had come up for the removal of the corpse.

'We've looked all round three times, sir, but we can't do much more in this light.'

The lieutenant looked at the magistrate waiting for his approval; he nodded agreement, and it was only then that the sergeant allowed the two stretcher-bearers dressed in white to approach. The ambulance had remained lower down at the point where the path forked. They lifted the body with great care and placed it on the canvas stretcher. Its round aluminium tubes gleamed brightly reflecting the searchlights.

'It's as if somebody had been waiting for this moment to do it. Until the end of last week a surveillance helicopter was flying around here,' said the lieutenant, as he looked down at the livid face and the knife with its wooden handle buried deep in the neck that no one was allowed to touch before the experts from Madrid were able to examine it, the tiny bits of earth and the bloodstains that the rat in its meanderings had deposited on the forehead and the light-coloured shirt.

The stretcher-bearers quickly covered it with a cloth. Even they, accustomed as they were to pick up dead bodies mangled in road accidents, seemed stunned by the cold-blooded and appalling brutality of this murder.

'Just a moment,' said the investigating magistrate, leaning over the stretcher. 'I think we can open her hand.'

Twelve hours had gone by, and rigor mortis had set in through every limb, as well as in the joints of the fingers which had become stiff and clenched into a closed fist. The knuckles, rather whiter than the rest of the skin, indicated that there was something caught in the hand.

'A clue; just one clue; something at least,' muttered the lieutenant, as if he was talking to himself.

The forensic surgeon began to force the fingers apart, one by one, starting with the little finger. When he reached the middle finger they could see, stuck in the tip, a small metallic object that gleamed in the light of the torches pointed at it. It was the pin of a badge. The sergeant removed it with tweezers, and showed it to the magistrate and the lieutenant before putting it in a small plastic bag. It was round, and encircled by a red 'forbidden' sign. In the centre could be seen the word MURUROA beneath a drawing of the tiny Pacific atoll, above which rose a huge nuclear mushroom cloud. The badge represented a protest against the atomic tests carried out a few months earlier by the French.

The lieutenant bent over the corpse and looked at the two sides of the blood-stained shirt, searching for the mark it would have left in the material, although he guessed he would find nothing.

'I think we've got something here,' he said.

'Yes...' replied the sergeant, who was old and sceptical. 'Something...'

At a sign from the surgeon, the two orderlies picked up the stretcher and made their way down to the clearing where the ambulance was waiting. The photographer took a few more shots of where the body had lain on the dry grass and crushed twigs, its silhouette marked out by a fine line of white chalk.

'I think we can go,' said the lieutenant. 'I want three men to stay here. Tomorrow morning we'll have to look it over again in daylight. Thoroughly. We'll need a metal detector to search all round.'

They headed down towards their four-wheel drive. The ambulance had left. The lieutenant took the victim's documents out of the glove compartment, having already had them picked up from the hotel, the Europa, where she had spent the previous night. From the tiny identity card photograph an attractive, smiling girl with fair hair that fell across her forehead, looked him straight in the eye. He read her name once more, Gloria García Carvajal, and the date and place of issue. He thought with relief that this time he would not be the one having to choose the right words to inform her parents of the tragedy; their names appeared on the reverse, next to her address in Madrid. This time it would be his stuck-up colleagues in the capital who would have to doff their caps, lower their heads, and phrase the necessary expressions of condolence. He didn't let the sergeant drive. He took the wheel himself, and they began to descend the unmade track.

Two

Cupido was a quarter of an hour early for their meeting and he watched as the other man approached him at the Chico Cabrera fountain, the starting point for nearly all local mountain treks, partly because it was the spot where paths from several different parts of Breda converged, and partly because hikers came there to fill their flasks with the pure water that was believed to be good for soothing aching muscles and treating various health problems. He was surprised to see that he had walked the more than two kilometres from the town that could be seen lower down on the southern slopes surrounded by holm oaks and olive trees, and spreading so far along the main roads radiating from it that it was difficult now to make out its ancient and original shape of '*a dove that time had flattened against the earth*'. Walking was a habit that most local people had given up, and every man he knew would have come by car, even if it had been only half the distance. The habit and the pleasure to be obtained from walking, he reflected, was only now being reinvented by groups of visitors from the big cities who came down at weekends attracted by the varied scenery of the region and the abundance of animal life, or to indulge in that age-old recreation nowadays known as rambling or hiking.

Their meeting place had been chosen by the man who was walking towards him and was now only fifty metres away. He had been the boyfriend of the girl murdered three days before, and had left a message on Cupido's answerphone to the effect that he wanted to hire him for something connected with her death.

As he came nearer he saw that he was young, tall and powerfully built, much like those who made long treks through the mountains, that new generation of tourists and visitors who, 2,000 years later, had rediscovered Julius Caesar's advice about the benefits of very long marches. They were also doing their best to rescue from oblivion the names of trees and shrubs that nobody less than forty years old knew, and were learning not to overuse the term 'oak' for each and every type of *quercus*. They had nothing in common with the noisy family groups who also came from the cities to sully the countryside on Sundays, led by overbearing, chain-smoking individuals who had never practised any sport but who inflicted the nerve-racking hysteria of football commentaries on everybody round about. This new type of visitor, accustomed to walking and to leading a healthy life, was a match in terms of physical strength and fitness – two qualities until recently the prerogative of country people – for the strongest village lad brought up to heavy work in the fields, and nobody would have bet on a certain winner in the event of a trial of strength. Cupido had welcomed them: he recognized their respect for the environment, the fact that they were spruce and polite, and that most of them were quite as tall as he was; they didn't succumb to the temptation of showing off the presumed superiority of their urban lifestyles and ways of speaking compared with the deficiencies of rural life; nor did they mythologize the salubrious quality of country life and local produce – another way of expressing contempt. They came well equipped, with expensive footwear that was ideal for the terrain and the weather, and clothing that was both light as well as protective when it rained and was cold. From the first he had looked upon them favourably, while keeping his distance, because they came from an attractive world that he had got to know too late in life, and to which he would never belong.

The man came up to the detective kicking up the dust from the ground, parched from the prolonged drought, with every one of his lengthy strides. Seen close to when he stopped beside the fountain, with the sun shining directly on his freshly shaven face and revealing the fine lines round his eyes and mouth, he was not as young as he had appeared at a distance. He was about thirty, but gave the impression that he would look the same without much trouble for another ten years.

Cupido was so used to older clients – mostly between forty and sixty, uncertain of themselves and often tongue-tied or too weak and cowardly to sort out their own problems and misfortunes – that he was surprised to find this man who was so young and forthright wanting to make use of his services.

'Ricardo Cupido?'

'That's right.'

'Marcos Anglada,' he said, as they shook hands. 'I don't know if this is the best place to talk, but I'd like to see where it happened.'

'Yes, it is the best place,' replied the detective. He also preferred to have their meeting there. He didn't like using his apartment as an office. He knew it gave potential clients the impression of being makeshift and amateur. He had nothing to create the right impression: no big fan revolving slowly overhead, no solid metal, lockable, filing cabinet, not even a well-endowed secretary with painted nails and plenty of free time. As he'd given up smoking three days before it didn't even smell of tobacco. And although he knew very well that none of these things was strictly necessary, the fanciful ideas people have about private detectives were so deeply rooted in the minds of those who wanted to engage him that he always noticed their first glance of surprise or disappointment when they failed to find any of the trappings they expected.

Cupido looked up towards the north-east, to the blue slopes of the Volcan and Yunque Mountains with their cave-paintings, and the area where the girl had been murdered.

'You know this place?' he asked.

'Yes, I came here with her on a couple of occasions. Once, we went for a very long walk and stopped first at this fountain because we'd been advised to fill our water bottles here,' he replied, gesturing at the black metal pipe through which the water ran, and then flowed into a deep, granite basin below.

'Which route did you take?'

'We followed a path she already knew that went up towards some caves with ancient paintings in them.'

The detective nodded, remembering the path he had frequently followed many years before.

'Was it on that path?' asked Anglada, looking up.

'Yes, the same one.'

Anglada crouched down beside the black spout of the fountain and put his hand in the stream of cold, clear water.

'I think you're the right man for this job,' he said, without looking at Cupido, but with no hesitation. 'You're from here and you know the area and the people who live here.'

'What job exactly?'

'Who killed her. I want you to find him, and I want to find out why he did it. I want to know his name before the police do,' he said. His voice was low, cool, calm, and decisive, the voice of a man, it was obvious, who was accustomed to giving orders, to drawing up plans of action, and choosing the right people to carry them out. Only a desire for personal revenge and no faith in the normal machinery of the law could justify such a cold tone of voice. He also seemed to possess all the patience needed, however long it took to get revenge. Even so, Cupido was surprised by the nature of the assignment.

'Private detectives like me are usually engaged to look for missing persons, and even more trivial matters, but not to find out who committed a major crime. That's police work.'

Anglada raised his eyes from the stream of water and looked curiously at Cupido.

'You're right. In this country we get worked up about people who disappear, especially young women. And finding them makes us feel heroic. But detecting the person who's committed a murder makes us feel we're sitting in judgement and that's a job nobody wants. It gives us the shivers every time we hear the words *trial by jury* because we think it might involve us one day. I'm a lawyer,' he concluded. 'Maybe that's why I've lost confidence in the police.'

'If they can't find the murderer, it won't be easy for me to do so.'

'I'll pay you well if you'll only try. Tell me how much you charge,' he went on, his voice friendly but firm, and with that self-confidence that comes naturally to a man who holds a commanding position over another.

'Thirty thousand pesetas* a day, all costs included. Plus a fixed sum if I'm successful irrespective of the time I spend on the case.'

'OK. Thirty thousand a day it is. And I'll give you a million on top if you find him,' he added quickly, as if anxious to move on from that topic and to concentrate on what really mattered.

Cupido nodded agreement. He still hadn't got used to talking about money in his work. Having to agree terms with somebody who has an urgent problem to solve still seemed to him a cold-hearted and disagreeable process. He couldn't avoid an equivocal sense of blackmail. But he knew that if they didn't agree on the price right at the start his client would feel even more awkward and anxious than he did.

'Do you know the exact place where it happened?' asked Anglada.

* Approximately £115

'Yes,' he said. He had gone up there the day before after listening to the message on his answerphone.

'I'd like to go there. If it's all right with you we can talk as we go.'

Cupido was pleased the other man was making it easy. Anglada was the first person he would have to question, and the time they would take going up the path would be ideal. There was just one difficulty.

'There may be other people there,' he said.

'Still?' Anglada seemed surprised.

'Yes. In this type of crime the place where it happens becomes front-page news. There could be individuals with a morbid curiosity, or some photographer who's arrived late. Besides which, the Civil Guard have still got the area taped off.'

'It doesn't matter. Let's go.'

'What exactly was your relationship with her?' Cupido asked as they got into his car.

'We were planning to get married. We'd talked it all through about wanting to live together and how to organize it, although we hadn't actually fixed on a date.'

The detective looked at him in profile. He was good-looking, sun-tanned, with a small nose and short, dark hair. He found it odd that such a young man should harbour such powerful feelings of revenge, which would have come more appropriately from an older man who had been deprived by death of everything he lived for, and at an age when he no longer had the strength to begin again. He felt it would have been more reasonable to forget, not to want to know more, and to try to remake his life, with the long future he had before him. To probe the pain was as absurd as it was fruitless.

'Why did she come on her own this time? You said you sometimes came with her.'

'I suggested it, but she didn't want me to come.' He fell silent as if it was too soon to talk about that. 'She's been a bit strange lately, and she told me she wanted to be on her own for a few days. She's done that before. Her parents came from Breda, and although Gloria was born in Madrid she used to say she still had roots in the place. Before her parents died they spent several summer holidays in the area, so she knew it well and got a lot of pleasure from coming here. I didn't share her enthusiasm. There are other places that are more beautiful and with better amenities. But apart from that, she was working on a series of paintings of the countryside round here and especially on the old cave-paintings.'

'So she was a painter?'

'Yes. She was a professional artist.'

'Did anyone else know she'd be coming into the Reserve last weekend?'

'Anyone who happened to ask her would have known. Gloria liked talking about how beautiful all this is…' he said, with a vague gesture that suggested he didn't share her taste.

'Who did she know here?'

'Almost nobody. She didn't come to be with people she knew. A few distant holiday acquaintances. She'd say hello to them but didn't even remember the names of most of them. She knew one of the forest rangers. I think he's called Molina. He helped her get a permit to enter the restricted areas so that she could paint there. I also went with her once to visit an uncle and aunt and a teenage cousin, the only family she had left.'

'Do you remember their names?'

'Clotario. He was her uncle on her father's side. The boy's called David.'

'Didn't she have any other relatives?'

'I don't think so. Gloria still hung on to a little house here that was uninhabitable – it had been abandoned since her parents died. That's why she used to stay at the Hotel Europa whenever she came. But she'd been having some work done on it recently – the roof and the kitchen and bathroom – and was renovating it little by little. Her relations here advised her about choosing local workmen, and she was also bringing down a few small items of furniture and cooking utensils that she didn't need in Madrid.'

'And now?'

'How do you mean?'

'Who will get the house?'

'There's the house here, plus her apartment and studio in Madrid. I've never heard her mention a will. It's not something you think about when you're twenty-eight.'

'All together it must add up to a tidy sum,' Cupido ventured.

'Yes. She wasn't exactly a millionairess, but she was quite well off. A large part will go in tax, but there'll still be a respectable amount left. According to the law her closest family will inherit.'

He didn't need to be more explicit. Those words were charged with meaning. Or possibly it was normal lawyer's language. But if it could be proved that her relatives in Breda had had something to do with her death, they wouldn't get their hands on her inheritance.

'Apart from you, is there anybody else in Madrid who might have come here with her at any time?' he asked, forcing himself to persist with this first interrogation – what he thought of as the disagreeable aspect of his work – stacking up information, dry facts, often routine or boring, but always essential.

'A few of her friends. Camila and Emilio at least…'

Cupido waited for him to continue, but Anglada remained silent.

'Who are they?'

'Gloria and Camila owned an art gallery in Madrid.'

'Were they partners?'

'Yes. They'd known each other for years and made a good team. Camila's efficient, well organized, and calculating – she concentrated mainly on the management side. Gloria contributed her knowledge of art. They used to say she had an intuitive feel for it. I don't believe in that, but it seems they were able to make it work, besides which the gallery's opening hours left her time for painting.'

'And Emilio?'

'She only recently got to know Emilio. What brought them together was their dedication to art.' He spoke it in a tone that was mildly ironic, or possibly concealed the fact that he was ill-at-ease and uncomfortable using words he seemed not to understand.

'Is he also a painter?'

'No. A sculptor. He has a country house here in Breda that he inherited from his grandparents, I believe. It's a big house, and he spends time here whenever he's tired, or has a commission and needs to be alone. Emilio pretends to be the angry, mis-understood artist, the outsider, but in reality he'd like to be famous and acclaimed by the critics. In that respect he's a fail-ure,' he added, and the detective noted the clear hint of contempt in his voice. 'For years he's been swaying backwards and forwards between different projects without ever finishing one of them. Recently, he's been working on the cave-paintings up there as well,' he motioned towards the Yunque. 'It was Gloria's idea they should work together on something, using different materials and techniques. He's also got an exhibition in her gallery, but I can't tell you much about it. I haven't been there since...' He seemed to hesitate as if trying to choose the least painful words. '... since she was killed. The fact is it never interested me much. I knew that Gloria was happy with her gallery, her painting and her friends. I had no problem with that, although it prevented the two of us being much on our own. I didn't fit into that milieu. We all went out together from time to time, but I never really got to understand them. They were too Bohemian for me. I have to keep fixed hours in my office, and they don't. They're not responsible to anyone for the way they spend their time. When I was out with them I had to make an effort to be relaxed. Gloria on the other hand might be with me or with them, but she was always Gloria. This question of her friends was the only one on which we didn't see entirely eye to eye.'

'We're nearly there,' said Cupido when Anglada fell silent, implying he had nothing more to say. He had listened carefully and without interrupting, rather surprised that a man who seemed so sure of himself was able to talk so freely about such personal matters and his own weaknesses. These conversations often turned out to be the most important, even the most decisive, in his work.

They reached the clearing and Cupido stopped the car. On the far side, where the trees began, a yellow tape looped round a number of their trunks, and this prevented them from going further. Contrary to what he had feared, there was nobody else there. Perhaps nobody would dare walk up that path on their own for months to come, in the same way that nobody likes to shelter under a tree from which a man has hanged himself.

'Was it up there?' asked Anglada.

'Yes, but we shouldn't find anything, there isn't anything to see. The police have worked it over thoroughly.'

Anglada remained standing near the tape, not attempting to go further. Then he looked down at the ground, deep in thought, and resisting the temptation to squash a line of processionary caterpillars that was proceeding slowly and invasively towards the enclosed area. Cupido stayed a few steps behind him, and from where he stood asked:

'Who could've wanted to kill her?'

'Kill her? Nobody!'

'All of us have an enemy somewhere,' he said evenly.

'But no one who would dare go to this length.'

The detective didn't reply, recalling faces and names of individuals who had had the courage to commit murder and hadn't lost the opportunity to do so on the day they thought they would get away with it.

Three

Cupido strolled through the small city that Breda had developed into in the course of only fifteen years. The reopening of the old thermal spa and an increase in tourism to the Reserve had provided a powerful boost at the same time that a dozen or so medium-sized companies had started up in the town. These didn't have more than 300 or 400 employees in all, but they'd become established and well run businesses. His apartment was at a convenient midway point between the old town entrenched in its ancient customs and rural origins, and the new town that was the hub of most of the city's amenities and the favourite residential area for its elite.

Following his return five years before, he had worked his way through various jobs during the first three without discovering one that he enjoyed, either because he couldn't stand the constraints imposed by rigid, work-place hierarchies, or because he was too old to get back into the habit of getting up early every morning in order to put in eight hours of boring, repetitive work. He had always done his best to avoid tedium. Eventually, he had obtained a licence that allowed him to put a plate on the door of his apartment that read: RICARDO CUPIDO. PRIVATE INVESTIGATOR. In common with other private detectives he knew he was well aware that he hadn't entered the profession out of a sense of vocation. Like them, he had stumbled on it after leading a restless, aimless life doing jobs he was no good at.

He had reached the conclusion that this was a profession made for those who fail at everything else. But it was a profession for which the town would never forgive him. It was a long time since he had stepped out of line, and he knew that in Breda he could never atone for taking on a job that risked bringing to light matters that many people would prefer to keep in the dark. Alkalino once said to him: 'You'll never get rich in this town doing that job. It's not considered respectable, and the only person who might do well in it is someone who's respected for his own sake. And you aren't – not since that other business.' But he didn't care. He had begun to take it for granted that the only sort of life now open to him was a lonely one. The work itself was varied, and he earned enough to live on. At first he was surprised by the diversity of people who engaged him and the range of problems he was asked to solve. They constituted a vast compendium of hatreds, anxieties, reprisals, and mean, insignificant offences: from discovering who was guilty of stealing a couple of cows to tracking down a relative who had disappeared to Costa Rica thirty years before; from collecting debts from recalcitrant debtors to obtaining sad and often squalid proofs of adultery; from dealing with minor personal threats to locating teenage girls who had run away from home – quickly and secretly – before news of their disappearance gave rise to shame and dishonour. He had also got used to the lonely condition of his small apartment where – without knowing quite why, or exactly what was appealing about him – from time to time a woman would appear on the scene, only to move out shortly afterwards when she realized that he rejected any form of commitment and was incapable of offering anything more than affection and sex, that neither his thoughts, nor the body she held in her arms would ever belong completely and exclusively to her.

Without noticing, he found he was already near the headquarters of the Civil Guard. By one of those ironies that can result from urban expansion, this building had been put up on a vacant lot just outside the city and next door to one of those old-fashioned houses of ill-repute that has one table and a heater underneath it in the main room, and wardrobes with mirrors in the bedrooms. As soon as they started on the foundations, the brothel was summarily transferred to the other side of town, as far as possible from its new neighbours in uniform. This had happened several years before, but Cupido smiled as he recalled Alkalino's well-chosen words late one night when he had insisted on taking him there and then complained bitterly that it had been moved so far away. 'The girls should never have left that house. The first and second oldest professions in the world ought to stick together. After all, they entered to the world more or less at the same time. The first one came about so that everybody could satisfy their need for love; and the second so that nobody might take it upon himself to satisfy his hate!'

He saw in front of him the solid, ugly, red-brick structure, built in the mid 1980s, and couldn't help wondering what percentage of the money allotted to its construction had disappeared into the pockets of Luis Roldán, the little man who had been made responsible for the work – how much he had siphoned off on every brick, every bag of cement, and every one of those spikes he had had set in the ground around it to prevent vehicles parking there as a precaution against a highly improbable terrorist attack, so very far from the north and the centre of the country. He recalled the old headquarters when Breda was merely a largish town with a shape extraordinarily like that of a dove, with a beak, and with its wings spread. It had been almost in the centre, in a not very wide road, and had had stables spacious enough for all the horses on which the Civil Guards made their rounds and pursued smugglers who came over the border from Portugal; but it had been much too small for the fleet of motorcycles and cars that they now used for controlling the traffic in the centre and patrolling the Reserve. The old head-quarters had been knocked down and the site turned into a pub-lic car park that nobody could avoid using. This had shattered the silence of the street, where previously it had seemed as if its inhabitants spoke more softly than the rest of the population, and barking dogs were not permitted. Twenty-five years before, even the local children had been awed by a combination of fear and respect that the building and its occupants inspired. If at times the whole of Breda had resembled a large children's play-ground, without a word being uttered or a formal prohibition announced this street had remained off-limits, a no-go area, like a bubble that nobody dared touch, and where young people were forbidden. Cupido assumed that the basic reason had been the reluctance of their parents to have any contact with its occu-pants, a fear they transmitted to their children – and it applied equally to the children of all ages of the Civil Guards themselves who lived there, and who went in a tight-knit group to the local school as if they were members of a sect that banned friendships outside their own circle, possibly because of the aura of exclu-siveness that emanated from them and was evident even in the games they played.

The impeccably uniformed guard at the door, a youngster barely twenty years old, raised his right hand in salute.

'I'd like to speak to the lieutenant,' said Cupido.

'Let me have your ID?'

Cupido handed over his identity card and the young police-man went into his cabin. He watched through the window as he picked up the phone and read out the details on the card. He was made to wait a few minutes until a sergeant emerged who, without a word, led him inside. It was a meeting he would have preferred to put off. He had absolutely no enthusiasm for it, but he knew that if he wanted to draw on the support and goodwill of the official agents of the law he had to talk to them in the first instance, and before they learned by other means that they were investigating the same crime. They had always been sensitive to outside interference. Besides which, so far he had no real information, and this could be a way of getting at the preliminary facts of the case. The courts had recently begun to pronounce many cases *sub judice* – a secrecy that was usually violated the very next day by a collaboration between the media eager for dirt and officials who were easily suborned, or even by the accused themselves who had an interest in creating confusion in the public mind by glossing over their offences with half-truths which were quite as suggestive of guilt as they were of innocence. However, in this case he had heard nothing.

The lieutenant was waiting for him, seated at a wooden desk, his hands clasped together and resting on a black file, his wedding ring very visible on his third finger. A white telephone, a computer, and a diagram of the ranks and symbols of the Civil Guard completed the scene. The office had an air of neatness and efficiency that went with the appearance of the lieutenant, one of the young officers fortunate not to have been faced with a picture of Franco on every wall of his training school. His face was tanned and his hair dark, although it was beginning to thin, and baldness was creeping up his forehead leaving a horseshoe of hair. At first sight it looked as if he wasn't wearing uniform, an uncertainty caused by the ambiguous front that this honourable body of men had developed in the past twenty years: grey functionaries when out in the street trying to melt into the background, but in full uniform – and proud of it – in their military parades and in barracks. It was difficult to imagine the lieutenant in a three-cornered hat. Cupido tried to remember his name but, although he had heard it several times, he failed to do so. Nevertheless, there came back to his mind a story told about him. It seems he had been on the point of throwing up his whole career less than a year before because of an incident that had occurred during his previous posting in Campo de Gibraltar. It was said that one night when he was not on duty he went into a disco for a drink. From where he stood at the bar he noticed how several very thin youths with that evasive look he knew so well approached, one after another, an individual accompanied by a very young girl, almost a child, seated at a table almost hidden in a corner. Every time one of the youths went over to him the man stood up and indicated that he should follow him to the washroom. It didn't take the lieutenant long to guess what was going on. It was not in his character to observe drug trafficking without doing something to prevent it. He went over to the table in the corner, identified himself, and told the individual that he was going to search him. The man made no objection, nor did he comment on the fact that the lieutenant was out of uniform. He simply imposed one condition: that he should not be searched there in front of the girl, but he was prepared to go to the local police station. The lieutenant looked at the girl; she was very young, and he could read the fear in her eyes. He hesitated for a moment out of decency, and not wishing to make it harder for her by having to attend a search that would be carried out strictly by the book, followed by an arrest. Convinced he had caught the man red-handed, he took him down to the station without a second thought. Somehow, possibly as they walked there – unless it was not he who carried it on his person but the frightened girl – he managed to get rid of the stuff he was selling, because when they searched him in a cell, he had nothing on him. He was clean. He had to be released without charge or other formalities, although his name and a note of his arrest went on the record. Five days later, the lieutenant was summoned to an interview with a senior officer from the Ministry of Internal Affairs who had been extremely annoyed by a malicious press report and by public reaction to it: the lieutenant faced a formal complaint on the grounds of illegal detention and ill-treatment. Everything pointed against him: he had acted on private property without a judicial order, there were no other witnesses to the alleged trafficking, and the man had no drugs about his person. It wasn't long before he heard what his provisional punishment would be: a month's suspension without pay for having exceeded his authority. The lieutenant had appealed, and in the end the whole affair was reconsidered and the penalty revoked. However, his promotion had been blocked, and he was posted elsewhere.

Cupido looked at him and wondered what he had learned from that episode, how much it had led him to be more circumspect and mistrustful, and how much it had convinced him that he needed a professional success to rebuild his good name with his superiors.

The lieutenant stood up as he came in, but didn't come round the table to greet him. He stayed at 'duelling' distance, shook hands, and invited him to sit down.

'Well?'

'My name's Ricardo Cupido.'

'We know that,' he interrupted. 'We've never spoken to each other but we've seen you around trying to solve the pathetic little problems that people try to keep under wraps. As if we don't know all about them!' he added, banteringly, almost insolently.

'A man came to see me yesterday called Marcos Anglada. He's the boyfriend of the girl who was murdered in the Reserve,' said Cupido, ignoring the lieutenant's words.

'Yes, the lawyer. He helped us identify the body.'

'He's contracted me to find out who killed her,' he explained.

He was afraid of an angry reaction from the lieutenant, but he observed that Gallardo – his name suddenly came back to mind – nodded approval as if to confirm what he had already guessed as he saw him come in.

'He didn't tell us that, but *you* have come here to do so,' he said drily, as if reluctant to concede that Cupido was collaborating whereas Anglada hadn't.

'That's right. I could start by asking at the hotel where she was staying whether they'd seen anyone hanging around. Or the game wardens on the Reserve. But I'd never get more out of them than you must have done already.'

'What exactly is it that you want to know?'

'If you've got hold of something definite. I don't want to waste my time on a case that's already been solved.'

'We do have something…' the lieutenant replied, and left the sentence in the air to make Cupido wonder what that was. 'Suspects!'

Cupido smiled, registering the irony.

'I've been reading that in the papers for the past three days,' he replied.

'Why should I give you information that I don't give to journalists?'

'Because I shan't publish it.'

Gallardo thought for a moment. Cupido feared he would point to one or another official rule to bring the conversation to an end, so he offered the only thing he had to offer, knowing quite well that it didn't add up to much:

'I shall pass on to you everything I find out on my own account.'

'There's no deal. You couldn't sell us anything we can't get for nothing elsewhere. You and your local friends with their rumours and their old stories of petty hates have nothing to do with this. This is serious crime.'

The telephone rang at that moment. The lieutenant picked it up and listened, swinging round in his chair so that he sat sideways to Cupido, hiding the earpiece as if the detective might have been able to guess what was being said. It was obvious that he disliked what he was hearing because he stiffened, and Cupido could see the tension in his face.

'One man? Only one man?' he asked, with exasperation. 'What do you expect me to do? Leave the station and go and question them myself?'

He looked up and waved a hand at the detective who had got

to his feet and was on his way out of the office. Cupido walked down the corridor without seeing anyone, and crossed the yard where he noticed that one of the doors of the garage where they kept their cars was open. He reached the cabin at the entrance and heard the telephone ring as the guard was handing him back his identity card.

He had not gone more than a few steps when the young policeman called him back.

'The lieutenant wants to talk to you again.'

Gallardo was drumming his fingers impatiently on his desk.

'You've got yourself a deal,' he said.

Cupido guessed that this sudden about-turn had something to do with the telephone call, but he didn't dare ask. He waited to hear the proposition.

'I asked Madrid for help in the work we have to do there, but all they offer me is one man,' he explained, as if to make it clear that his change of mind wasn't merely capricious – and nor was it motivated by personal liking but by bureaucratic obstruction. 'They claim that even they can't manage with all the men they've got. That's a lie. They believe the only things that matter are those that happen in the capital – and a provincial murder is a second-class murder which doesn't concern them, and isn't a threat to their families. So I want to do a deal,' he repeated.

'Yes?'

'You want to know the facts we're holding. I need someone who can talk to those friends of the victim who live in Madrid. You've been hired by the girl's boyfriend, and they'll feel under an obligation to answer your questions more honestly and more accurately than they would if we talk to them. I want you to tell me everything they tell you.'

'No problem so far.'

'At the same time, you belong here in this city,' he said, gesturing vaguely towards the window.

'Yes,' replied Cupido. Through the glass he could see a large satellite dish on a roof with two pigeons perched on it.

'I want you to tell me everything they're saying out there – the sort of gossip that everybody knows except us: the scandals and the rumours that don't get reported to the police. The people in this city have never been prepared to work with us; they've always looked down on us as foreigners. They always lie, and what's more, they think we believe their lies!'

'No problem,' the detective repeated. He saw immediately that their working in harness would suit him because it fitted in with his own plans. Even so, he was aware that Gallardo could more easily cheat him than the other way round.

'I need to know all the details before I go to Madrid.'

'Have you talked to anybody yet?'

'Only Anglada.'

'You can forget him,' he said, taking some papers out of the file on his desk. 'He was in Madrid that morning acting for a client at a court hearing. We've already checked, and there's no doubt about it. What you ought to do is start your search with the girl herself. Although she knew a lot of people, her circle of close friends – those who might have known she was intending to come to the Reserve last weekend – was very small. There is one friend, Emilio Sierra, an odd character. He's a sculptor.' He added this as if his profession alone was enough to make him a suspect. 'He was here in Breda over the weekend, as well, living in a big old house that used to belong to his family.'

'Anglada's already mentioned him to me,' said Cupido.

'He told us he was working on some sculptures, although nobody actually saw him. You'd better question him again.'

'I'll do that.'

'There's also a woman who worked with Gloria. They were partners. Maybe she'll let you know more than she's told us.'

'I find it difficult to imagine a woman wielding a shepherd's knife,' said Cupido. Of the facts published, that was the one on which the local newspaper had laid most emphasis, allowing itself to be carried away by the most bloody and sensational aspect of the murder, in common with the rest of the regional media. A photograph of the weapon had been printed on the front page to show that it was the type of curved knife that serves equally well for cutting bread as for slitting the throat of a lamb.

'I've seen more incredible things,' retorted Gallardo, giving him an ironic look as if he was an amateur too naïve for the job he was taking on. 'We also learned that some time ago the girl had a relationship with a man quite a lot older than herself, a schoolteacher – and not long afterwards he broke up with his wife,' he continued, adding to the catalogue of disasters and reasons for suspicion – anything in fact that appeared out of the ordinary, or likely to have caused distress. 'His name's Manuel Armengol. You'll get more about him from the papers I'm going to give you to read.'

'The girl had relatives in Breda. Anglada suggested that they'll inherit her properties.'

'We'll take care of those people. In any case, I wouldn't bother about them because we found something the victim had in her hand that points in a different direction. The press doesn't know about what I'm going to show you because we regard it as an important clue.'

The lieutenant stopped, waiting for Cupido to ask a question – which he did not do, although he was extremely impatient to know. Everything they had discussed so far was routine, facts he could have dug out for himself without much trouble.

'The victim was holding one of those little badges that are all the rage with teenagers. We know that a thousand of them were produced for a protest campaign against the French atom bomb tests on Mururoa in the summer of 1995. They were sold in Madrid by one of those ecological groups that collected signatures on a petition and organized demonstrations against the tests.'

'Couldn't it have been hers?'

'No. There's no sign of it having been pinned on her shirt. And there's nothing else to indicate that she might have been wearing it. The forensic lab people are categorical about that. Nor could she have picked it up off the ground because there wasn't a trace of earth on it. Everything suggests that she grabbed it from the person who attacked her – the pin was firmly stuck into the tip of her middle finger. It isn't much to go on, and by pressing it so hard she may have obliterated a fingerprint, but it's our only clue. There wasn't a diary or a single piece of paper that might have given us more information in the few bits of luggage she left in the hotel. Her personal documents were in the bag she was carrying along with a receipt for various painting accessories, two metro tickets, a little money and her credit cards. She wasn't raped, and there were no signs of violence having occurred before she was killed. She wasn't pregnant, and there was nothing to show that she smoked or took drugs,' he continued with his report making it clear how difficult the case was. 'She must have been one of those girls who look after themselves.'

'Can I see the badge?'

'Yes.'

He opened one of the table drawers and took out a transparent plastic bag containing the badge. Cupido looked at the design of it through the bag: in the centre of a circle with a red 'stop' sign, he could make out a green background on which he read the word MURUROA and, above that, the surface of a blue sea and the atoll, from the middle of which rose the nuclear mushroom cloud.

'When will you go?' asked the lieutenant, as he took it back and replaced it in the drawer.

'Tomorrow.'

'I shall look forward to hearing from you,' he said. He stood up, came round the table, and accompanied him to the door of the office. They shook hands quickly and firmly.

Cupido left the premises that were still closed to the outside world. Even if they no longer inspired fear, there lingered an underlying distrust and suspicion. He believed the lieutenant had been sincere in proposing that they combine forces, but only because of the exceptional circumstances and their mutual interest. It wouldn't be easy to get along with them. Cupido felt alienated by their strict concept of discipline and their sense of belonging to a select group governed by unswerving adherence to a set of rules – ties that he, with his love of independence, could never have accepted. Nonetheless, as his work had developed he had learned the benefit of being able to count on their collaboration.

Before returning to his apartment he went to the Casino. The girl's death had occurred only three days before and was bound still to be the main topic of conversation among the groups that met there. Alkalino would certainly be there, and he would be able to question him about the theories being bandied about, which would range between the fantastic, the rational, the illogical, and the grossly extravagant – everything the locals had been able to dream up about the crime. From the names of the numerous likely murderers that would be mentioned he might obtain one reliable fact, one certainty; or, just possibly, a clue based on what a shepherd or a hunter might have seen but was reluctant to reveal to the Civil Guard; or perhaps a passing motorist who may have noticed somebody who happened to have been in the vicinity of the hotel that Saturday morning.

The Casino occupied the ground floor of a big, but otherwise empty, old house. Facing the city's main church, all the windows on the upper floors were closed. Founded by a Society of Friends of the Countryside, for a hundred years it had been the most prestigious meeting-place for the local bourgeoisie to play cards or dominoes, but now its art deco tables with their alabaster tops and their wrought iron legs of an exclusive design with the letter C prominently featured were almost empty. The deep, built-in bookcases, in which hundreds of dusty old books slumbered, were never opened even to be cleaned. In an extension to the rear of the house there was another room, with not such a high roof and more informal in style, but with a door giving access to a garden with three palms and plane trees. It had been fitted out in the early 1970s by some of the older members who had tried vainly to ensure that their children – with their long hair and curious habits, and who reeked of substances never before smelled in the Casino – would continue, if not with the same games, at least with the same attachment to this centre of entertainment. However, it had been abandoned soon after by the next generation that had gone looking for brighter lights and more colourful interiors, and wanted to be able to slouch comfortably in ways that the rigid chairs in the Casino made impossible. It was only on Tuesdays when what was termed the 'livestock market' was held, a title that was much too pompous for the get-together of three dozen local cattle farmers swarming around four or five middlemen who had already secretly plotted how to get the prices of the animals down, that the Casino enjoyed an atmosphere of bustle that was unknown during the rest of the week.

Alkalino was playing dominoes with three elderly, obviously retired, men. Always alert to everything that happened round about, he caught sight of Cupido as he entered, and gestured to him to wait a moment. The detective ordered a coffee to find that it was as good as ever, the best in town, combining standard roast with the exactly right measure of Portuguese dark-roast. It was not long before he saw Alkalino pick up a few coins at his table, invite another man to take his place, and come over to where he was sitting.

'They're the ones with most of the money,' he said, pointing over his shoulder. 'Everything's turned upside down. Now it's the old who support the young.'

Cupido smiled. Alkalino never changed. He was so garrulous

he could have carried on talking even if he'd been held under water. That was why the detective had come looking for him.

'Did you want to see me?' he asked.

'Yes.'

They had always got on well because Alkalino's tireless chatter and unusual notions matched Cupido's talent for listening. He was a small, dark, nervous man, with bad teeth and lively eyes that gleamed through short lashes seemingly scorched by so much peering around. Everybody called him Alkalino because, like the batteries, he never ran down. Once he had accepted the nickname he had insisted that it should be written with a K as a way of asserting his individuality. He could drink any other man under the table. He was capable of staying awake for three full days without showing a sign of fatigue. He could talk for a week without ever running out of words, and what was even more remarkable, without boring his listeners. He held strong views about everybody and everything, but never imposed his opinions. It was said of him, at times admiringly and at others with fear and even enmity, that he knew all that happened in Breda, and could remember the name of every outsider who had ever lived in the city. He didn't conceal his sympathy for the Communist Party of which he had been a member for years, but even so he kept up his friendships outside the party and was quite at home in the traditional, even decadent, atmosphere of the Casino.

'I've landed a really big job,' said Cupido, when the waiter had served the invariable glass of brandy.

'Congratulations!'

'I've been hired by the boyfriend of the girl who was murdered.'

Alkalino looked at him without surprise, and took a sip of brandy before replying.

'So that you find the man who did it? Here in Breda?'

'In Breda, or in Madrid.'

39

'If what they say's correct, you're going to have a tough job.'

'What do they say?'

'Everybody's got his own version and draws his own conclusions. In this city every man's convinced he'd make the best detective, and given a free hand would find the guilty party in a matter of hours. Some of them claim that the boyfriend himself is the murderer, others that it was her lover, and others – '

'Her lover?'

Alkalino raised his eyebrows, astonished that the detective was beginning his investigation with so little information.

'The sculptor. The Sierra family. Haven't you ever been to the house?'

'No.'

'Whenever he comes here he keeps open house, and now and then he's invited a few of us in.'

'I've heard him mentioned.' Rather an outrageous character, Cupido recalled, and known for organizing parties for friends from elsewhere – parties at which anything might happen in his beautiful, big family house on the right bank of the river. Once or twice when passing by he had seen cars parked there and the front door open – but Cupido was accepted in many fewer places than Alkalino. 'Are you sure he was the girl's lover?'

Alkalino made a gesture to express uncertainty; he couldn't be absolutely sure. In a small provincial community like Breda there were certain forms of behaviour that would always be misinterpreted even when there was nothing unusual about them.

'It's said they were lovers because they were occasionally seen together, but I wouldn't put my hand in the fire about it. Round here we're in the habit of believing that if a man and a woman go alone into a house they do so in order to leap into bed as soon as they're inside the door. That's because we don't get much sex, and therefore we're always thinking about it!'

Cupido smiled, though Alkalino had spoken in all seriousness.

'There are others who say it's a family affair, all to do with inheritance,' he continued. 'But then there are a few among us who are looking in a totally different direction.'

He took a large gulp of brandy, smacked his lips, moved closer to the detective, and whispered:

'Some of us think that Doña Victoria may be involved.'

'Doña Victoria?'

'Yes, that's right. D'you know her?'

'Who doesn't? But they say she's a bit touched.'

Alkalino raised his elbow and poured the rest of the brandy into his mouth. It seemed as if the glass didn't even touch his lips. He signalled to the waiter for a refill.

'No, she's not mad. Unless you call madness fighting for twenty years against a much more powerful enemy who's bound to win in the long run.'

'That's also a form of madness,' insisted Cupido.

'You were away for some years,' said Alkalino gently, without referring directly to where he had been. 'That was when the battle between her and the new independent administration was at its fiercest. They had passed a law that formally created the Reserve and allowed for its enlargement. It was a vicious fight, and the lady conducted it with real courage. Didn't anybody tell you about it?'

'A few rumours reached me. But I'd like to hear about it right from the beginning.'

'It's a long story and it's rather bizarre. The battle began more than twenty years ago, in Franco's time, when one of the last ministers of the so-called "technocrat" government decreed that all the land of the Volcan and Yunque Mountains, down to the reservoir, should become a Nature Reserve. I don't think the decision he took at that time would have complied with the ecological principles that are fashionable today. Just imagine, not even the Communist party – and we were in the vanguard of progressive thought – had any such idea in our programme,' he said with a touch of irony. 'It was really more a matter of wanting to keep it as virgin territory for certain privileged hunters. I don't know if you remember that Franco hunted here at least once.'

'Yes, I do. I remember the occasion – they took us out of school and gave each of us a little Spanish flag to wave as a row of enormous black cars in which it was impossible to see the passengers went by.'

'It's always said that Franco very much approved of reservoirs. It's a lie. He didn't give a damn about the desperate need for water in parts of this country. Otherwise he'd have piped some of the surplus up in Asturias down to the deserts in Almeria. He could have done it, because nobody would have dared object in the way the north with its petty greed puts obstacles in the way today. But what made Franco really enthusiastic were the reserves that were created for hunting, in the catchment area above the reservoir. As you know, of course, from the dam downwards, there's electricity and an irrigation system, and above it there are game reserves. Now, Doña Victoria had a number of grazing areas in some of those deeper and more fertile gullies, but these were expropriated when they were flooded by the waters behind the dam. At first she accepted the fact, and didn't protest. All of us have to make sacrifices at times for the common good. But as the bigger animals need extensive territories for breeding purposes and the original reserves were too small, they extended the expropriated area by means of a decree that was legal according to the law of those days. Doña Victoria didn't accept that second decision, nor the shoddy way in which it was done. She was the last descendant of a family whose name had always been associated with that land, and she bore a historic responsibility on her shoulders – if I can put it that way as we used to do in the party. It's said that she even refused to accept the substantial sum of money they offered her once they realized how stubborn she could be. That sum corresponded exactly to the market value of the land that had been taken from her. The fact is there was also a sentimental element in the conflict. Do you know El Paternoster?'

'Yes,' replied Cupido. El Paternoster was a tiny village that had given its name to the Reserve, and the waters of the dam had flooded most of it. There remained a sort of peninsula of dry land, a hillock, on which there was a small and ancient cemetery which people were allowed to visit on one day in the year – All Souls' Day.

'There were already very few inhabitants, most of them had left in the 1960s, and they sent the last ones to live in Breda and work the irrigated land that was given to them in compensation. Doña Victoria was already a widow, getting on a bit, but she was rich and attractive for her age – a good catch that more than one man tried to lay his hands on. But Doña Victoria is a very unusual woman. Her husband, who died not long after they married, was buried in that cemetery, as well as a baby son who died before he was a year old. He was her only child. On one hand the law says you can't open a grave until I don't know how many years have gone by; on the other, they were in a hurry in Madrid to get the game reserve ready for the General. They all knew it would be one of his last whims, and for that reason they had to sort it out quickly: the last supper of the damned! With every year that went by his aim must have been getting less sure, his hand shakier, and he would have needed bigger and bigger targets, closer and closer, to aim at. They couldn't wait for the full legal term to elapse, and they wanted to fence in the boundaries. But Doña Victoria wasn't going to let them stop her visiting the graves of her husband and her son, nor would she let hunters in their big boots trample all over them. Apparently, it was a macabre sight watching her go to the little cemetery every Sunday to put flowers on their graves and stand there next to them for a while, whispering to herself...'

'Macabre, and also moving,' said Cupido. He remembered having seen her always dressed in black, her head held high, with gleaming antique gold ear-rings and a pendant at her throat which emphasized even more the sombreness of her mourning clothes.

'Yes, maybe it seemed moving twenty-five years ago. That sort of thing doesn't happen any longer. Widows don't remain widows for long. What's certain is that she started an action against the Ministry itself to have the second expropriation of her land rescinded. It was claimed at the hearings that there was, besides, a serious technical fault, namely that the stipulated period for giving notice of eviction hadn't been observed, and she made skilful use of this error on the part of the Ministry. Without any doubt, she was resting her case on the correct pro-cedures in which these matters should have been carried out, and the docile way in which they were actually done locally, in order to drag things out – which meant that the case went from one tribunal to another until all the deadlines had passed. In Madrid they must have hoped she'd get tired of the affair and give up. Or that she would die. But the lady wasn't prepared to die. On the contrary: she knew that Franco was thirty years older than she was. She knew that perfectly well because she personally had served him his coffee during his first short stay in Breda in the early days of the Civil War as he was on his way to Salamanca. She was a young teenager in the Falange, and she and several other girls were chosen to look after him during his brief visit. I've even seen a photograph of it. Provided nothing out of the way occurred, she knew his turn would come before hers. And she must have guessed that without him, the dicta-torship and all its decrees would fall off the bough like over-ripe fruit. There were many voices already being raised against him, and I'll just mention in passing that the loudest voice of all belonged to us – the Party. Once the process had been halted the lady prepared to take her revenge. She knew that a young, orphaned boy was one of those who had been expelled from El Paternoster; he was about nine or ten, and was outstanding at school for his extraordinary intelligence. When he was four, the old folk used to gather round while he read the newspapers to them, and at seven he was giving lessons to boys twice his age. She went and talked to his surviving relations, asked if she could become his godmother, and then took him off to Madrid to study in one of those very expensive colleges where half the deputies in our present Parliament were educated. She knew very well she was in for a long battle, and if she was not to lose it she would need to have the very best weapons to hand.'

'It's quite extraordinary that degree of calculation for such a long-term plan,' said Cupido.

'But she wasn't wrong,' replied Alkalino, putting a hand on his arm. He too was moved by his account. 'What Doña Victoria had predicted with absolute accuracy actually came about. Franco died soon after, the dictatorship collapsed and in the referendum we voted for democracy. But her case hadn't been solved even eight or nine years after the change of government; it was passed from judge to judge in the expectation that new laws would provide a way out of the dead end. Not all that unusual in this country. Just think how many years it took the courts to sort out the rapeseed oil scandal, or the Tous kidnap case.'

'And the Rumaso case is still up in the air,' added Cupido.

'Meanwhile, the lad she had taken under her wing graduated as a lawyer. There was a photograph of him in the local newspaper because he came top of his year as well as being the youngest. He had only one aim both in his work and in his life: to recover for the old lady the land that had been confiscated, and also that patch of ground where her husband and son were buried. She had infected him with her own obsession, and she would be able to rest a bit after so many years of uncertainty. I don't know all the ins and outs of the story, but once the democratic government came into power I know that some of the earlier decrees were overturned. So they were able to make a fresh start. Doña Victoria was now able to take advice from her brilliant new lawyer – he's called Octavio Exposito – and must have believed that from then on it would be easy going, that they would give her back everything they'd grabbed from her illegally, and that it had been worth while holding out for so long. But this time she was wrong. For two or three years the affair was deadlocked, until the transfer of powers to the autonomous regions was arranged. Amongst these powers were those relating to the environment. They must have breathed again in Madrid when they got that hot potato off their hands. But when it came to the point, instead of a change, Doña Victoria was to discover that the new politicians had the same ideas as the old ones, reminding her that nothing had changed. So at that point she embarked on direct action, openly and fearlessly, adopting the habit of walking in and out of the Reserve where the wardens, who were so strict with trespassers, didn't dare stop her, terrified of that woman carrying bunches of flowers to put on the old graves, and who used to show them her ancient title deeds which in the end it had been found impossible to invalidate.'

'I remember her at that time,' said Cupido. 'We wanted to make an amateur documentary film about the Reserve, complete with the cave-paintings and the animal life. One day, while we were looking for suitable places for filming she turned up with one of her employees, asked us what we were doing, and there and then told us that she was the one we should have got permission from, not the regional authorities. After that, and once we said we recognized her authority she was very pleasant.'

'You'll also remember that about that time, when she realized that the democratically elected government was going to deal with her in the same way as the dictatorship, she set fire to one of the game wardens' four-wheel drives. Nobody saw her strike the match, but everybody knew she had done it. At last,

less than a year ago, it looked as if the proceedings would be
wound up: the Supreme Court finally ruled that the disputed
land had been correctly expropriated after all and Doña
Victoria would no longer be allowed to wander around it freely
as she had been doing. Neither her efforts nor all Exposito's
legal skills had achieved anything. After fighting for twenty
years the two of them were utterly defeated. But they still
wouldn't give up, so then they appealed to the European
Supreme Court in Luxemburg. The final verdict should come
through quite soon.'

'But what has all this got to do with the murder of the girl?'
asked Cupido, although he guessed what the answer would be.

'Since the Spanish Supreme Court decision the authorities
have gone ahead with plans for developing the potential of the
Reserve. They had held back from exploiting all its possibilities
for a long time. But now they started a new project to stimulate
rural tourism: bridlepaths and footpaths were opened up
through previously restricted areas and people were allowed
into those that are not of vital ecological importance; they also
set up new observation posts for watching the birds of prey and
the deer. The fashion for rural tourism was knocking at the door
with a fistful of money, and the Reserve is so beautiful, and so
full of interesting things that the number of visitors is going up
every weekend. They go crazy to photograph the deer, the sun
setting over the reservoir, and the old tombs in the abandoned
cemetery,' he said, in a scornful tone. 'It seems the girl was murdered on one of those paths. Do you think Doña Victoria will
shed many tears over her death if it serves to frighten away the
people who are invading the property that she has always considered her own?'

'No, she won't have many regrets. But neither can I imagine
her arranging a murder to stop the invasion.'

Alkalino shook his head as if faced with a well-known but
incorrigible flaw in Cupido's character.

'You young men have very little imagination,' he protested – although he wasn't so very old, and Cupido wasn't particularly young. There were only seven or eight years betwen them.

'Maybe you're right.'

'I am. I am. Time will tell,' he concluded, draining the rest of his glass of brandy.

It occurred to Cupido that if he went on drinking like that it wouldn't be long before he ruined his liver. He paid for their drinks as he watched him return to the table where the game of dominoes was in progress.

Four

Although Cupido had told the lieutenant that he would leave for Madrid the next day, he decided to delay his journey by twenty-four hours in order to gather more information in Breda first. He had spoken to Gallardo and Alkalino, but neither of these two had known the dead girl personally.

The next morning – not particularly early, in keeping with his usual habits – he drove to the Hotel Europa where most travellers who came to see the Reserve put up. It had links with a chain of travel agents specializing in rural tourism which made it easy for visitors to make reservations from other parts of the country.

He drove through the barbican arch, beneath the crenellations that surrounded the whole forecourt of the ancient palace which had been converted into an hotel, and parked in front of the door. He remembered it well, but even so he couldn't help admiring once again the arms of the De las Hoces family that had been carved into the granite lintel five centuries earlier: a menacing pair of sickles grasped in two strong hands shielding an ear of corn.

It was a three-storey building, and the windows, each with its forged iron grill, combined with the Cordovan-style crenellations to make it look like a fortress. Above the central vertex of the door and the shield was the central balcony which opened out from what was now the best suite in the hotel. The owner, who still bore the 500-year-old family name had leased it for thirty years to an international chain of hotels which was investing in rural tourism. He had agreed to the deal, not so much for the trifling rent he received, but because of the restoration work his lessees had agreed to carry out. It was the only way he was able to maintain the property which was subject to laws on the conservation of historic monuments. These buildings give as much pleasure to visitors as they give vexation to their owners, who have to modify them without excessive expense, because complete restoration would be more expensive than knocking them down and rebuilding.

The hotel company had had all the stonework cleaned, those parts of it that were penetrated by damp chipped out and repaired, and the rust on the ironwork removed; they had put a new roof on the building that was an exact copy of the original with its four sloping sides for draining off rainwater. However, in the process of removing the patina of antiquity and decay, they had stripped the palace of its true character, and had wrenched it out of its historical context and grafted it on to an age that welcomed it rapaciously, in the same way that a nouveau-riche family welcomes the last penniless heir to a noble lineage simply because he will enhance their prestige in the eyes of the world. Cupido recalled with nostalgia the lovely, neglected Italian garden, overgrown with moss, in which the radiantly white and delicate marble statue of a nude Andromeda whose breasts and pubic area had been riddled with bullets had formerly stood. He wondered what had happened to her. Where was she now that the space she had dominated was occupied by an ostentatious swimming pool?

When he reached the reception desk, a young girl clerk addressed him with a forced, professional smile.

'Good morning, sir.'

'Good morning. I want to speak to the manager, please. Tell him Ricardo Cupido's here.'

The girl spoke on the internal phone, and a matter of seconds later Teo – Jose Teodoro Monteserin – appeared.

'I can guess why you're here,' he said, as they shook hands. They had been friends since childhood and had grown apart only because of their different types of work and diverging career paths. Cupido had been jailed for cigarette smuggling; Teo had risen to become manager of the best hotel after it had been converted from the most ancient stone building in town. But years before, they had often climbed together over the barbican at the rear of this same building in order to meet up with the Dutch woman who had put the final touches to their sexual maturity. 'You want to talk about the girl who was murdered in the forest.'

'Dead right!'

'I can still remember clearly the answers I gave the lieutenant. So you can start straight away. Would you like something to drink while we talk?' he asked nodding towards the bar.

'Coffee, please.'

'Fine.'

They sat in the deep, wide armchairs beneath a lofty, coffered, timber ceiling and next to a window through which they could see the gleaming blue-green of the oval swimming pool and the wall put up to hold back the slope of the land behind, in which there was a series of embrasures, now empty, which had formerly housed statues.

'The lieutenant came here to interrogate us – me, and those of my staff who were on duty that day,' he said, when the waiter had gone away. 'The same girl you saw just now was in reception. Shall I call her in?'

'Later, maybe. Tell me what you knew about the murdered girl.'

'Not much. She was very reserved. She'd stayed here several times before. The first time her name appears in the register is two years ago, just a few months after we opened. She would take a single room, and always at weekends or public holidays. She reserved a double room on only two occasions because she came with a man who apparently was her boyfriend. But we didn't actually register him because we already knew her quite well,' he stated, by way of explanation. He raised his hands, palms open, to indicate that that was all he knew. 'Nobody remembers anything special about her, except that she was always pleasant, and was extremely good-looking. Perhaps a bit sad too.'

'When did she get here last weekend?'

'On Friday, pretty late. Around midnight.'

'Were there any messages for her?'

'No written message. But the receptionist remembers transferring two phone calls to her. It was a man's voice on the line.'

'When was that?'

'On the Saturday morning before she went out.'

'Nothing else?'

'Nothing else. She knows it was a man, but she didn't recognize the voice nor how long the calls were. When a guest is on an outside line they can hang up without having to go back through reception.'

'What time did she go out that morning?'

'At nine. She'd asked for a call at eight. At nine, our cook and his assistant who were just arriving for work saw her go. Their shift begins then. At the same time as our receptionist. Would you like me to call her in now?' he repeated.

'Yes, please.'

Teo stood up, and returned in less than a minute with the girl. He invited her to sit down, but she preferred to remain standing.

'Did she go out alone?' asked the detective.

'Yes, sir. She gave me her room key to put in its pigeonhole.'

'Did you notice anyone following her, either then or just after she'd left?'

52

'No. At least, not immediately. I think I would have noticed because I was wondering whether she wouldn't be afraid, walking on her own up the mountain.'

'How did you know she was going to walk there?'

'Because of the clothes she was wearing and the picnic lunch I gave her,' she replied unhesitatingly. 'She wore mountain boots, and was carrying a small knapsack in which she put the food we'd prepared for her.'

'Guests can request a cold lunch to take with them on excursions. They just have to ask for it the night before, and then pick it up in reception on their way out,' Teo explained.

'Did you notice whether she was wearing any accessory of any kind?'

'Accessory?'

'A badge, for example.'

'No, I didn't notice anything. At least, I don't remember doing so.'

These were the replies he had feared. He hadn't been very confident of learning anything useful at the hotel, but he had had to confirm it and leave nothing to chance, because there had been times in the past when he had obtained useful bits of information from caretakers and porters that the clients who were paying him hadn't known about.

Teo nodded to the receptionist who returned to her post in the lobby.

'Who engaged you for this?'

'The girl's boyfriend. He wants me to find the person who did it.'

The hotel manager raised his eyebrows and sighed as a way of expressing his doubts about him succeeding.

'You're going to find it difficult, because it looks like the work of a madman. I recognized the girl as soon as the lieutenant showed me the photo on her identity card. It would have been difficult not to recognize her after seeing her just once. She was too beautiful to go off walking up there on her own. But only a lunatic could feel an urge to destroy a woman like that. If the boyfriend hadn't engaged you I would have done. A death like this is bad for a business which is just getting under way,' he said, waving an arm to embrace the whole of the magnificent setting that surrounded them.

Cupido realized that that was another reason why he had answered his questions with such good grace. If the news got around the travel agents that there was a murderer on the loose in the Reserve, the hotel that had been created specifically to benefit from its tourist potential would have to close down because of lack of custom. He couldn't help thinking of Doña Victoria, and Alkalino's words.

'Don't hesitate to call on us for anything we can do for you,' Teo added.

'Thanks.'

'And the best of luck.'

The first feature to be seen on arriving at the Base Depot of the Reserve was the high surveillance platform used as a lookout for fires. It was fifteen metres tall, constructed entirely of tree trunks, and it dominated the country on all sides, well above the roofs of a number of scattered buildings and the tops of the trees. Below it were sheds for the patrol cars and the firemen's water tankers, a warehouse for storing tools, and a small building which occasionally served as an office, although the main administrative centre was in Breda. A little way off were the large pool from which, in emergency, the helicopters could take water on board, the heliport which the last of the machines had left ten days before, and the three houses available for use by those employees who chose to live there. Only one of these was occupied – by Molina – the game warden who had been on duty in that sector of the Paternoster Forest on the day of the murder. The other employees preferred to live in Breda rather than in that place that was isolated for much of the year, except during the hunting season, at weekends and holiday times, in spite of the fact that by doing so they sacrificed free accomodation, and had to travel in from Breda every day.

A woman with a small baby in her arms came out of the house when she heard the sound of the car. Another child of four or five appeared behind her, and it occurred to the detective to wonder whether he wasn't already of school age. The woman looked at Cupido as he got out of his car, without coming nearer, but with an air of nervous curiosity: aware of his presence, but without knowing who he was, or why he was there.

'I'm looking for Molina, the warden. They told me he lives here.'

'I'm his wife. He's coming out now.'

Cupido observed her closely while they waited. She was probably not more than twenty-five, but her dirty, unkempt appearance made her look older. Her hair was of that sad, straw colour, that doesn't even seem to be a colour. It was cut to mid-length, and through the strands that fell across her face he could detect the submissive and wary look of one who has lost all confidence in herself as well as in other people. She wore a mannish shirt which was too long in the sleeves for it to have been bought for her, and a sloppy pair of brown trousers. She had made no effort to improve her appearance by brushing her hair or tidying her clothes, as if she had long since resigned herself to slovenliness and to creating a poor impression.

Molina appeared at the door. His hair was wet and had just been combed; the detective guessed he had been taking a siesta, and had got up when he heard the noise of the car. The contrast with his wife could not have been greater. Cupido remembered having seen him in town from time to time. He took note of his dark, leathery face, the head that seemed too small for his body, the few grey hairs among the head of thick black hair, his lean physique, and his bearing which had something of the gipsy about it: the grace with which he walked in his high boots and wide-ribbed black corduroy trousers which he wore in preference to the pale green uniform of the other wardens on the Reserve. He looked about forty, which made him considerably older than his wife, but he gave the impression of being one of those men who are harder and stronger at forty than at twenty-five.

Molina approached the detective. He certainly knew why he had come there.

'What d'you want?' he asked.

'I'd like to ask you a few questions.'

'What about?' he answered without attempting to conceal his distrust; tall and dark, he tossed his head back in a gesture that looked like a challenge.

'About the day the girl was murdered.'

'Police?'

'No.'

'Journalist!' he deduced.

'No. I'm a private investigator.'

Molina looked at him with growing curiosity as he pondered this unexpected reply.

'Go and talk to the Civil Guard. I've already told them all I know.'

'I've already done so. They told me that you were the only man on duty in this sector of the Reserve that morning. So you must have been on the lookout for anyone entering it or going beyond the permitted limits for camping and hiking.'

The warden gave him a hard look, wondering what else they had told him, and to what extent the detective was able to rely on the lieutenant's goodwill for his information.

'Two thousand hectares is too big an area to see everyone who goes in and out every moment of the day,' he said quickly, as if he had learned that response off by heart, and had always found it effective.

Cupido could see he wasn't going to get much out of him. Molina was one of the suspicious types, midway between crafty and cautious, and skilled at concealing information. He had to make it clear that he wasn't a beginner at this game.

'You knew the girl,' he said, and noted how the warden immediately became tense; his words also provoked the woman to look up sharply.

'Who told you that?' he retorted. He was trying to look cool, but Cupido knew that he had got under the man's skin.

'Marcos Anglada, the girl's boyfriend.'

'Is it the boyfriend who's got you working on this?'

'Yes.'

'It's true I knew her,' he explained, as if he was relieved to learn who Cupido's client was. 'I saw her once or twice.'

'When?'

'On one occasion when she and her boyfriend had lit a fire that was threatening to spread. And on another I had to guide her to certain parts of the Reserve where she wanted to paint. It was just the same sort of job that I do when I take a hunter to a hide, but in her case it wasn't that she wanted to shoot anything. She'd asked for and had got permission from the management of the Reserve.'

'Did you see her last Saturday?'

'No. And I had no reason to. At the time she was killed I was still in the sector that's free for anybody to enter, and we don't bother to exercise the same vigilance there. Besides which, it isn't easy to detect a person who just walks in on his – or her own.'

'Did you go anywhere near that path at any time during the morning?'

'No,' he repeated. There was a note of irritation in his voice. 'I took a different route that morning.'

'Did you meet anyone at all? A car, perhaps?'

'I've already told you, I didn't see anybody.'

The warden looked at his watch to indicate his impatience. Then he looked towards the forest, as if someone was waiting for him somewhere up there. He said:

'Have you finished with your questions?'

'For now, yes. Those are all I have at the moment. Goodbye,' he said, addressing the woman as well.

On his way back he asked himself whether Molina was capable of killing the girl, and wasn't surprised to conclude that he was. He gave the impression of being the sort of individual more likely to be involved in petty thefts or taking small bribes than murder, but he also looked brutal enough to go further if a suitable opportunity came up. Cupido had learned that murder can result as much from an innate capacity for it as from favourable circumstances, and Molina seemed to him the type of man made for violence: he would kill provided he had an alibi – or was draped in a flag, and would be what they call a good soldier! But there was something about the death of this girl that didn't square with the image he was forming of the man: if he had been the murderer he would have imagined him raping her before killing her. His physique would make him attractive to many women – those who prize virility above any other attraction – but he was sure that wasn't true of this girl from Madrid. He was probably jumping to conclusions, but the picture he was building up of Gloria was that of a young, beautiful, independent-minded woman, who would have admired gentleness more than brute strength, and deliberation rather than drama.

The woman dressed in black had told him where he would find her husband: on a small olive and vegetable farm three kilometres from Breda, halfway between the city and the Reserve. On his way there he foresaw that this interview was likely to be difficult. He needed information, but he wouldn't be able to chivvy the old man with a routine interrogation such as the Civil Guard could do. What were you doing that day? At what time? How did you get on with her? When was the last time you saw her? Who might have had a motive for killing her? He had known Clotario since he was a child, and twenty years before had frequently watched him riding his docile old mule that was covered with sores along the ancient track across the common land, the same mule that had carried him on the long search for his errant daughter, the expedition that had led to the final loss of pride in himself. Clotario had been a soldier in his youth, but he hadn't done well in the French Foreign Legion, and had returned to Breda to open a bar and cultivate his not very fertile plot of land at a time when half the local country folk were abandoning theirs. At that time he thought of himself as a legal expert, was violent as well as proud, used to boast of his foreign travels, and would come out with a couple of dozen words in execrable French. He was known locally as the *legal eagle* – with more than a hint of mockery that he never caught on to. His younger brother, Gloria's father, had also served in the armed forces but with much greater success. He had volunteered for the Spanish Air Force, because even then he had had the sense to foresee which arm of the services was most likely to advance in the course of the century as a result of technological change, and which were destined to lose public respect. Although he attained the rank of squadron leader, it used to be said in Breda that he always ended up terrifying those who flew with him, and that it was inexplicable how he managed to keep a plane in the air and land it without destroying both himself and the plane. One young conscript sent to the squadron leader's unit many years before had recounted to Cupido that on one occasion when he was piloting a two-seater fighter to demonstrate its capabilities and advanced technology to a senior officer from the air force of an Arab country, he pressed the wrong button by mistake and ejected his terrified co-pilot into space in an emergency bail-out, complete with his seat, from which he was able to escape only by his parachute opening automatically. Whether or not there was any truth in this and other anecdotes, he reached the very top of the promotion ladder. Thus, the paradox to be found in many families happened in this one: the younger brother was destined to be triumphantly successful while the elder one was doomed to failure, in spite of the fact that both had seemed to possess the same flair, to have had the same upbringing, and the same opportunities.

Clotario had swapped arrogance for resignation when the painful affair of his younger daughter Rosario occurred. Cupido smiled nostalgically as she came back to mind. All the boys had been in love with her during their last year at school. Now her cousin, whom he had never known, had been murdered, and he wondered whether she still had the same smile, the same beauty, and the same attractions that had made men run in circles round her in the way birds flock round belfries. That summer Rosario ran off with a young bullfighter who had arrived in Breda to take part in the heady excitements of the town's annual fiesta. From then on, Clotario finally lost his pride and any gift he had possessed for getting on with people; he had shut down his bar, and taken refuge in a humiliated and rancorous silence. Perhaps he might have wished to leave Breda at that time and go to the big city where nobody knew him, and where he had a brother in the Air Force who was continuing to move up the promotion ladder. But he didn't do so, and it must have been then that he began to be resentful, a sentiment that always risks turning into rank jealousy. A brother triumphing in a sphere in which the other has failed; a brother flying – quite literally – high, while the other is condemned to survive on the income of whatever he is able to squeeze out of his miserable crops of vegetables, cereals, and oil, tied to a land that would never allow him a rest from his labours, working an arid soil. While the rest of the world was calculating in hectares and tonnes, Clotario continued to use acres and bushels, linked to old-fashioned production methods that he was never now going to change. By night he did a bit of illegal hunting with the old shotgun he had brought back from Africa, shooting the wild boars that from to time came down from the safety of the Reserve as far as his farm, lying in wait with his finger on the trigger guard, not so much for the value of the meat, nor for the pleasure of the hunt, but because the animals laid waste the scant crops he got from his ground. Marcos Anglada had suggested to Cupido that they would inherit all Gloria's property: the apartment in Madrid, her studio, the small house in Breda, her car, her paintings. Did Clotario know the financial value of all that?

He stopped his car near the gate the woman had indicated, and continued on foot up a path. Before he could see anybody he heard the rhythmic sound of billhooks lopping the branches of olive trees, and from the frequency of the blows he deduced that there were two people engaged in the task. He was able to get near them without being seen, and he watched for a minute or so as they struck powerful, precise blows on the rough, grey, knobbly trunks. The sun gleamed on the cutting edges of their blades each time they raised them before striking, and the detective admired once more the skill and craft of the countryman who could create perfect tools that were so well adapted to his purposes. They had welded to the blunt, outside curve of a sickle another piece of metal shaped like an axe, but with a finer, sharper blade that was set in a wooden handle about forty to fifty centimetres long. It was a terrible weapon, that could easily kill, whichever edge was used. He mused on the fear that everything to do with the country often provokes – above all, the cold brutality latent both in the work and the tools.

It was some time since Cupido had seen him, but he hadn't changed much. He wore the same harsh and surly expression, but he stooped more and his face was more lined. His son of about sixteen or seventeen – who had been a late and unexpected arrival – closely resembled the father, similarly lean and sinewy. Seen together, hacking away the new growths, they created an effect of synchronized power, force, and efficiency of effort. Both of them noticed him at the same time, and both ceased cutting with their knives.

As Cupido came nearer they looked at him without a trace of curiosity, knowing full well what had brought him there, to their field of olive trees, looking for them.

'I'd like to ask you a few questions,' he said to the old man. It was the second time in two hours that he had used those same words, and he wondered how many more times he would have to repeat them, and how many lies he would have to listen to before arriving at the truth.

Clotario nodded, with the look of resignation that he had adopted twenty years before when he had returned to Breda after pursuing his runaway daughter, and with nothing to show for it other than what he considered the greatest possible disgrace when, even at that time, the younger men saw it as nothing more than just another ridiculous tragedy caused by an antiquated rural inflexibility that warped all the customs of the town.

'I've been commissioned to find out who killed your niece,' said Cupido, and hoped they wouldn't see his words as a threat, but as a straightforward way of presenting his credentials. Clotario knew him, and also knew the nature of his work.

'Who asked you to do it? That character who says he was her boyfriend?' The boy cut in before his father could speak.

'Yes,' he replied, surprised by the weight of contempt and defiance in his tone, and by the nervous, adolescent quickness with which he had responded.

The lad turned back to his tree and continued attacking it with even more violent slashes. The detective had to raise his voice in order to be heard.

'You don't like him?' he asked.

Clotario raised his head; there were splinters of wood in his dirty, wiry hair, but once again it was the son who got his reply in first.

'No, we don't like him. He's a rich city type!'

The detective waited quietly for the lad to continue, but caution now induced him to keep his mouth shut. He turned again to the old man.

'Tell me about Gloria,' he said. He was surprised to realize that this was the first time he had spoken her name out loud, and by such simple means he began to sense that he was getting closer to her. He felt that until then, all other words had merely been a necessary but so far unproductive prologue leading up to this moment.

'There's not much to tell you. We didn't see much of her, although in the last few months, since she began to do up her house, she came to us more often. Perhaps she would have been a better niece if her father and I had been better brothers.'

'Did you fall out?'

'Let's say we kept our distance. He used to visit us when he came to Breda, and he'd phone at Christmas. He had a very good position in Madrid. The rift between us happened years ago, and had nothing to do with his daughter. We had nothing against her. But her father could have helped me when he was already established in Madrid and I was still in Africa. He could have pulled me up with him. But he did nothing,' he said in a subdued, but resentful tone.

Cupido was discovering once more how long spite can fester in a certain type of countryman who's addicted to rough red wine and corduroy trousers, and who can keep the memory of a minor snub alive for decades – just as they hang on to old tools in the loft whose purpose nobody remembers, or big, black, iron keys that will no longer open any door. In the capital, he thought, everything moves faster, there isn't enough space to hang on to things, nor the same capacity for keeping alive the memory of insults.

'And Gloria?'

'Gloria didn't want to know anything about all that. She never referred to it with us. She'd come to see us from time to time and did her best to be pleasant, but we didn't have much to say to each other.'

'Gloria was different,' his son interrupted again, as he walked towards another tree. The obvious admiration in his voice surprised the detective; it didn't seem to come from the same person. This young lad was beginning to worry him.

'Did she come to see you the day before?'

'The day before what?'

'The day before she was killed.'

'No,' said the old man. 'We didn't even know she was in Breda that weekend. We were out here on Saturday morning doing the same sort of work as today. We didn't know she was dead until the next day.'

The detective would have liked to ask whether anybody had seen them working there at ten-thirty in the morning, but decided against it. He wasn't the lieutenant.

'Did she ever mention being afraid of anything?'

'No,' said Clotario. 'Not to us.'

'Whoever killed her must have come with her,' said the boy. For the first time, his father gave him a look which was clearly intended as a warning to keep quiet.

'What d'you mean?'

'Gloria was also going out with that sculptor who owns the house near the river. Everybody knows that.'

'David!' shouted his father; and then turned back to Cupido. 'You'd do better to talk to the others. We don't know anything,' he repeated.

Cupido took from his pocket the piece of paper on which he had made a sketch of the design on the badge, and showed it to them.

'Have you ever seen this design?'

Father and son looked carefully at it.

'No,' they replied.

He put it back in his wallet, said goodbye, and began to walk back down to his car. Behind him the sound of dull thuds made by steel on the twisted branches of the olive trees started up again.

'They told me your name is Ricardo Cupido. They told me you are investigating the death of that girl. And they also told me you are very clever.'

'They got the last bit wrong,' replied Cupido. 'I don't think too much praise is good for me. The only people we usually praise are the dead,' he joked.

The old woman gave just a hint of a smile; it was scarcely visible on her lips, but it deepened the lines on her face. For a moment she seemed to him even older than she had looked when he had leant forward to shake her hand and had noticed the little oval gold watch on her wrist. She must have been about seventy, and sitting in her deep armchair with its very high back she gave the impression that, when young, she had been a very attractive woman. Her pale face contrasted with the dark cloth of the chair, and she had an elegance for which Cupido could find no better word than aristocratic. Her hair which was grey and as fine as cobweb was drawn back in a chignon high on her neck to make it look less severe. Her necklace and matching earrings were made of old gold and elaborately worked in a style no longer fashionable. The detective remembered having seen his mother wear similar jewellery that she had inherited and which she took out of the deepest recesses of her chests where they lay with the traditional heavy dresses, only to be worn on the most special festive occasions. But for Doña Victoria, this was everyday wear, and their value wasn't a matter for either concern or calculation. She wore black, but this didn't make her look like a woman in mourning.

'Can I offer you something? Port? Or a glass of brandy?'

'Thank you. I should like a brandy.'

'Octavio. Would you please pour the gentleman a brandy?'

After greeting him briefly on his arrival, Octavio Exposito had sat down a little apart from them, in a sort of middle distance. He now stood up again, and went over to a dark sideboard at the far end of the spacious drawing-room. He poured some brandy into one glass and port into two others that were small and decorated with gold filigree, and placed them on a tray covered with an embroidered cloth. Cupido noticed Doña Victoria's initials in one corner of the cloth. Everything in that house, every utensil, every ornament, seemed to be valuable in its own right, irrespective of the nature of its use: from the geometrically cut granite stones in the façade of the house to that drawing-room where the antique furniture was kept in impeccable condition under its satiny, shining surfaces produced by frequent applications of beeswax; from the great chandelier with its bronze branches which had not lost a single one of its crystal drops, to the marble staircases, of which he had heard it said that every step bore the name of a long deceased person on its concealed underside.

They waited until he had raised his glass of brandy to his lips before beginning to sip their port. Now, Exposito sat in front of a high window, and by its light Cupido could see that he had cold sores on his lower lip, a sign of herpes. It was the first thing he noticed about him, which was surprising because he usually looked straight at the eyes of the person he was talking to; it was only when faced with an animal that might be dangerous that he looked first at the mouth. He was tall, slim, and rather pale. He wore heavy, metal-framed glasses which, combined with his pale complexion, inevitably gave him the joyless look of a young man preparing for the priesthood, devoted to his studies and lacking in the social graces.

'I imagine they'll already have spoken about me as one of the first who might have killed that girl,' said Doña Victoria, replacing her glass on the table.

The detective thought for a moment, wondering whether to lie.

'No,' he replied. 'Not in those exact terms.'

Again Doña Victoria gave her half-smile, as if that was what she had expected to hear. She briefly revealed her teeth through her thin lips; they were too white not to be false.

'You are also very polite, and nobody told me to expect courtesy. But I beg of you that in this conversation you won't allow kindness to conceal the truth. I know this city well,' she said, nodding towards the window, 'and I know that half its inhabitants are pointing the finger at me. They never understood me. They'll have told you already that having dared to do all the other things I've done I wouldn't hesitate to commit a murder, especially now that, at last, after twenty years our long dispute is about to be resolved.'

'Resolved?' asked Cupido. He had to admire the pride and fierce determination of this woman who had fought for twenty years against two national governments to prevent them taking away what she believed to be rightfully hers, to keep at all costs the land on which she had been born, and which had nurtured her ancestors for twenty generations. Perhaps, he thought, pride mounts up over the generations in the same way that wealth does, and both are passed on to their descendants.

'Yes, it'll soon be over,' she said, turning once again to look out through the window.

The afternoon light was reflected off the whitewashed walls of the street, and it filtered into the room through the white lace curtains, lighting up the face that the detective was watching in profile. She must have been a very beautiful woman in her youth to have retained that complexion and those gleaming dark eyes.

'But they don't know that we are going to lose,' she added. 'Twenty years – and we are going to lose. If they knew it out there, nobody would have come out with those ridiculous accusations. They're waiting to see us beaten so that they can turn us into martyrs. It's always been like that. This city will never change.'

'Don't say that,' Exposito interrupted. 'It's not at all sure that the verdict will go against us.' He stood up and went to stand next to the old lady's chair. Doña Victoria took one of his hands in hers and looked up at him lovingly, grateful for his loyalty.

'We've never had such a good chance of a favourable verdict as we have now. For the first time ever our case is being heard in an unbiased court. Do you understand the law?' he asked Cupido.

'No,' replied the other, although he remembered every detail of the trial that had led to his conviction.

'The European Court in Luxemburg accepted rather more than a year ago to hear our appeal, on the grounds that the original process of expropriation was flawed in law. In view of that, all the earlier hearings and the final judgement were legally invalid, not to say criminal. There's only one possible verdict,' he said, his sore lips moving fast as he brought out his legal jargon.

As she listened to him Doña Victoria gave the sad smile of one who knows that to be in the right does not always mean being the winner. Then she turned back to Cupido to ask:

'Did you know that I knew your father?'

'No. No I didn't,' he replied, in surprise.

'He made a special journey on my behalf in that wonderful German lorry he had repaired bit by bit. He was a very good man. And discreet. I asked him not to tell anyone about it, and now I know that even his own son never found out. I'm still grateful to him.'

Cupido remained silent. Now he understood why Doña Victoria herself had summoned him to her house before he had even tried to speak to her.

'I invited you here to tell you something that I don't think you would have dared to ask. You don't need to investigate whether anyone saw us that morning, or where we were when she was murdered. I shall give you our alibi. That's what it's called, I believe.'

'That's right.'

'It's an ugly word. And so easy to create one with just one small lie! We were in our house in Madrid. Octavio went out in the morning to have a blood test done in a clinical laboratory. It will be easy for you to verify that. We were 250 kilometres from the Reserve, so I shouldn't like you to come back to interrogate us in the way the lieutenant did. But for any other reason the doors of this house will always be open to you.'

Cupido nodded, but he knew he couldn't give any such undertaking.

'It may look as if this girl's murder is a piece of luck from our point of view – in terms of our interests, that is to say – but I assure you we had nothing to do with it,' said Exposito.

The detective reflected that this could well be the case. He had learned long ago that the best question to ask for discovering the author of a crime was not always '*Who profits most from the death of the victim?*' To do so risks ignoring the irrationality that often surrounds murders, and relying on the simplistic logic of cause and effect. He watched Exposito put his hand in the inside pocket of his jacket and take out a black leather wallet.

'I left the house a little before ten without eating breakfast, and drove to the laboratory. They made me wait about fifteen minutes before taking a blood sample,' he explained, pointing out the clinician's report with his name, blood group, the types of analysis to be done, and the time – 10.43.

'Were you ill?'

'The week before last I felt a bit sick and dizzy. Our doctor in Madrid wanted me to have the tests done.'

'He didn't look well, and had to stop working for a time,' interrupted Doña Victoria. 'But I had to push him to make him go.'

'Have you had the results yet?'

'Yes. I got them this morning before leaving Madrid. Nothing serious. I don't have a virus. When I left the clinic I bought a newspaper, went to a café, and ate a good breakfast to get over it. I can't remember how long I was there, but I should think it was about half an hour. Then I did some shopping. I paid with my credit card,' he said, showing Cupido the Corte Inglés receipt. 'Probably, if it hadn't been for the lieutenant interrogating me so soon afterwards I wouldn't have kept this receipt. Then I picked up my car and went back home. That's all I did that morning.'

Everything stacked up perfectly. The time of the blood test and the personal identification proved that he had been a very long way from the place where the girl was killed.

'Did you know her?'

'No.'

'No.'

Both replied together, and although the lawyer's voice was less firm than the old lady's, Cupido had a fleeting sensation that they had prearranged their response to this question. The perfect timing of those two syllables, spoken too quickly in that house where everything moved so slowly – the unhurried atmosphere, the light filtering through the lace curtains, the movements of the pretty maid who had shown him in, and their replies to his questions – aroused for a second or two an instinctive sense that he was being tricked; there was something there not far removed from a lie.

'I don't think there's anything more I need to ask you,' he concluded, standing up to go.

'You have a lovely name,' said the old lady, looking deep into his eyes. 'Ricardo Cupido. I hadn't imagined you as you are.

You're not a bit like a thug, or an alcoholic, as I'd always thought men in your profession are.'

Cupido smiled. A long time had passed since a detective who didn't smoke or drink like a fish was regarded as a discredit to the profession. He was about to tell her that it was only five days since he'd given up smoking, but kept quiet about it assuming that, like most people who've never smoked, she wouldn't appreciate the effort it was costing him.

'You're too nice to be doing such an nasty job,' she added.

'It's the only one I know how to do properly,' he said.

He walked to the door and left, retaining in his mind's eye a clear picture of the old woman in her chair and the reticent young man, tall and pale, with cold sores on his lips.

By 10.30 that evening, the detective had eaten his dinner and had no wish to talk to anyone. It had been a day of listening to too many words, and he was sure that some of them were lies, but he didn't yet know which. He took off his shoes and collapsed on the sofa, refusing even to think. He had already made notes of everything he had heard and that had happened during the day, and comparing it with the lieutenant's reports he was unable to find any contradiction. Although at first he was tempted to re-read it all and to try to picture the face of the murdered girl – a face that in the end would become as familiar to him as a lover's – he finally picked up the remote control and flicked across all the TV channels without finding any programme that would help him relax. Even so, he wasn't pleased when he heard his front door bell ring, not once but twice, as if whoever was there was either very anxious or in a great hurry.

Silhouetted in the open doorway stood David, Gloria's teenage cousin. He had cleaned himself up and combed his wet hair, flattening it down on one side with a perfectly straight parting. He also wore new clothes, indicating the importance with which he regarded this visit. He stood stock still, shy, his uncouthness quelled, but not daring to ask if he could come in – perhaps he was embarrassed because of his brusque manner that afternoon – even though he knew that what he had to say could not be said standing on the landing.

'Come on in.'

He invited him to take the armchair, and the lad did so, but sat on the very edge of it, without leaning back, still unable to master his timidity.

'Would you like a beer?'

'Yes. A beer, please.'

Cupido went to the kitchen, took out two bottles and opened them very slowly to give the lad time to relax, to look around the room and the walls until he felt more certain of himself in that unknown setting.

He handed him one of the bottles, and sat himself down opposite, waiting for him to speak.

'I wanted to talk to you,' he said at last, almost genially, as if to make up for his surliness earlier that day. Cupido was wary of this sudden change of mood and the youngster's state of trepidation.

'Is there something your father and you didn't tell me?' he prompted.

'Yes.'

'What was it?'

The lad drank deeply from his bottle of beer.

'It's about the drawing you showed us. The circle with the island and the bomb. I couldn't tell you this afternoon... not in front of my father ... but I *had* seen it before. He can't stand me talking about painting and drawing.'

The detective felt a tingling sensation in the tips of his fingers, suspecting for the first time in this investigation that he was about to get hold of something solid, a real fact that wouldn't be a fabrication.

'Where did you see it?'

'In her diary.'

'So Gloria kept a diary.' Nobody else had mentioned it. Neither Anglada, nor the lieutenant. If they knew about it they hadn't thought to tell him.

'Yes.'

'When was this?'

'About a month ago, the last ...' he started, then corrected himself. '... the last but one time she came to Breda. I saw her car outside her house and went in to see if she needed anything.'

'And you saw her diary?'

'Yes. I knocked on the front door which was open, and although she didn't answer I assumed she was busy and hadn't heard. Just inside, on the left, there's a small room, and I saw this book open on a table. I called Gloria again, but she still didn't reply. I went towards the window, and when I looked down I saw it was a diary and that the page was dated that day. Then I read the one sentence which looked as if it had just been written, because there was a pen without its cap lying on it, as if she'd been interrupted.'

'D'you remember what she had written?'

'Yes. I haven't been able to forget it because I didn't understand it, and I thought about it for days. It said: "*He frightened me yesterday. But fear is not an innocent emotion*".'

The detective became thoughtful. Those words taken out of context didn't mean much, except that the two sentences implied a vague and anonymous threat.

'Is that all? Wasn't there a name?' he asked. For a moment he thought that the boy could be lying, but instantly rejected the notion; he couldn't imagine him inventing those words that were so difficult to interpret divorced from the rest of the diary.

'It was all she had written under that day's date. I flicked back over some of the earlier pages, but when I realized it was her personal diary I didn't want to go on reading. But I couldn't help noticing a few pages before that one the design you showed us this afternoon.'

'Are you sure it's the same?'

'Yes. I could draw it now.'

He looked around, and seeing a biro and the notebook in which Cupido had been writing his notes on the investigation on a shelf he went over and picked it up. Sitting at the table he sketched the design of the badge on a blank page without omitting a single one of its details, without a mistake in the layout, and only altering slightly the proportions and sizes of the different elements. The detective was surprised to see the skill with which he executed every stroke of the pen, each one perfectly shaped, and without a moment's hesitation. He wondered whether this gift for drawing may not have had the same genetic origin as the one that had enabled Gloria to live professionally from her art.

'You've got it absolutely right,' he confirmed. 'Do you paint as well?'

The young man bowed his head in a mixture of embarrassment and pride. Either the unusual circumstances in which he found himself, or the delightful subject of painting, had finally eradicated the aggressive and uncouth behaviour he had displayed in the olive orchard.

'A bit. I paint landscapes from time to time, and an occasional portrait.'

'Watercolour?'

'No, oils. I have a complete set of paints and brushes. She gave them to me as a present.'

'Gloria?'

'Yes. Nobody knows that. My father would never have let me accept anything like that from her. He's too proud. My parents are too old to understand.'

'Did Gloria teach you to paint?'

'Teach me? No. I'd have liked her to, but she never said

anything about teaching me,' he answered, and once again Cupido detected a trace of resentment floating to the surface. 'She was always too busy when she came here, walking in the forest, or going to that sculptor's house. But I often stood next to her while she was painting a landscape near the reservoir. Or the deer. I helped her carry her easel, and just stood and watched how she mixed the colours on her palette. Then, when I got back home I tried to do what I had seen her do. Gloria didn't teach me to paint. I taught myself.'

The detective imagined him standing motionless, just behind her, dazzled twice over, first by her painting skill, and secondly by her beauty, his eyes wide open, watching her hands at work, or staring at the back of her neck, her shoulders, her hips, and stopping only at the point where the inability to resist desire takes over.

'Did you often see her in her house as well?'

'Not often. A few times. I looked at her art books, or asked her about things in Madrid. I loathe farmwork, and I'd like to leave here. Even my father has travelled. But the problem with fathers who have travelled is that if they came back empty-handed, they don't want their sons to follow in their foot-steps,' he said, with a lucidity that was surprising in a boy of seventeen.

'Didn't you ever ask Gloria to help you?' He put the question gently.

'No.'

Cupido was sure he wasn't wrong in his assessment of the boy's feelings: blind admiration for the cousin some years older than himself who was also disturbingly beautiful, rich, and able to enjoy all the types of pleasure that he would never know; and all this was combined with a deep resentment for the slights that had caused the family rift. He must have been horrified when he realized he would become a born-again version of his father in a repeat performance of the contempt of the wealthy urban family for the poor country relation whose destiny is to remain chained to a perpetual round of hard physical labour.

David finished his beer, left the empty bottle on the table and continued to sit there, his head bowed, staring at his hands that had started to tremble. Cupido guessed they were both thinking along the same lines: four or five more years of working with heavy farm implements, and those fingers which possessed the skill for more pleasant tasks would become useless for ever after, incapable of handling a brush with the delicacy and precision that painting requires. He began to wonder whether this teenager sitting there in front of him may sometimes have stopped to think that Gloria's death would allow him to achieve all his ambitions.

'Did you see anything else written in her diary?' he persisted.

'I can't remember anything else. It was only a moment or so. Gloria came in just then and found me looking at it. She wasn't cross; she just smiled, shut the notebook, held it close, and said: "*This is secret. My life is written in here.*"'

Although the existence of a diary was an important fact, Cupido didn't feel too optimistic. He never liked it when an investigation turned on finding a physical object, because he knew how easily guns can disappear in the deep waters of a reservoir, and how quickly paper burns.

'What did your father think of these visits?'

'He never knew they were so frequent. He agreed that I could help her carry things around or move her furniture about, but he would never have accepted the idea of anything to do with painting. I'm his only child still here in Breda, and he can't accept the idea that I might go away one day.'

'Thank you for everything you've told me,' said Cupido. 'If you remember anything else to do with Gloria, don't hesitate to come and see me again.'

'Thanks. I will.'

Five

It was one of those tall buildings made of steel and glass in which the top executive and the high-class prostitute live side by side, separated only by a thin wall. The marble floor of the corridor looked like that of a hotel with its numerous doors on either side that opened into apartments in which every square centimetre had been skilfully exploited. It is a style of architecture that resembles a beehive but without quite reducing its human inhabitants to the level of insects.

Cupido pressed the door bell, and immediately heard resolute footsteps approaching; his arrival had been anticipated since he had called from a public phone box. Anglada opened the door without bothering to look through the peephole, and with a couple of words and a wave of his hand invited him in. He wore a bathrobe and a pair of elegant leather slippers that flopped across the parquet floor. His hair was wet as if he had just emerged from the shower.

'I'll get dressed straight away, and then we can go. Make yourself at home,' he said, before disappearing again through a door.

It was a medium-size apartment with a lounge that looked out on Comandante Zorita Street. Through one open door he could see the kitchen, but there wasn't a single plate in sight; it was immaculately clean, without even a crumb of bread on the worktop, all the electrical appliances were switched off and gave the impression of being seldom used; they looked cold, metallic, and spotless – typical of homes where there are no children, and characteristic of people who do little cooking and are in the habit of eating out.

In the lounge, and next to one of the two double-glazed windows set in PVC frames and with close-fitted blinds, Anglada had arranged an area to serve as his office or study when working at home. A computer occupied a small table beside his desk. There were hardly any books to be seen, but the walls were covered with pictures. Glancing at them, Cupido picked out two engravings, a portrait of Anglada himself that was excellent, and several watercolours on which Gloria's signature could be easily made out, written in a clear, round hand, which, without knowing quite why, didn't seem appropriate, as if an artist capable of that quality of work shouldn't have possessed such a simple, childish signature. In the space between the two windows there was just enough room for the graduation photograph of his university year and, beneath it, his official law graduate certificate, clearly visible to any visitor.

Anglada was soon ready, and they went down to the street. After waiting ten minutes, they managed to get a taxi to take them to Gloria's apartment in Cea Bermudez. The traffic was terrible. A strike by the drivers who had refused to accept the basic minimum service imposed by the city council had paralysed the metro. As a result the city seemed to have gone car mad.

On their way there, Anglada told him something about the area where Gloria had lived. Her father, like all military men, had felt the need to look to the future – possibly importing into their domestic lives what they learn in their military academies about the art of predicting an enemy's next moves in battle, in an attack, or in any other type of emergency. In consequence, he had bought one of those spacious apartments which were on sale very cheaply at the time in that particular area, and which many other officers bought who were being posted to the barracks not far off in Moncloa. Later, with her first earnings, and almost certainly helped by her father, thought Cupido, Gloria had rented and later bought in the same building one of those attic rooms that had been converted into studio apartments from their original purpose of storage areas and roofed terraces. They went there first.

'She used to come up here to paint. Or when she wanted to be on her own,' said Anglada, letting Cupido go in first.

The studio was a large, bright room, rectangular in shape, with two load-bearing pillars in the centre. It was lit on one of its two long sides by three circular windows which gave it a certain Bohemian appearance. Through them could be seen a landscape of reddish roofs, and beyond those the extensive green background of Dehesa de la Villa. Facing the door, on the opposite shorter side, could be seen two closed doors that must have led into a bathroom and a small bedroom. Between these doors there was deep shelving, each shelf piled high with tins of paint, brushes, portfolios, sketchpads, and a few books, all muddled together in that delightful disorder that Cupido had seen in numerous photographs of painters' studios. Pictures hung on the fourth wall, or leant against it, facing the wall, revealing the reluctance of the artist to let anyone see the pictures she hadn't known how to finish, but couldn't bring herself to paint over; when all's said and done, he thought, every unfinished painting is the tale of a little failure in the same way that for a writer every incomplete idea, plot, or story, every novel abandoned halfway through, is evidence of a lack of skill or an error of judgement in respect of his own powers or talent. He also knew that, for a detective, every problem he is unable to solve is a defeat.

In full view, on the two thick pillars, in the spaces between the windows, and on two easels turned towards the light, could be seen the last pictures Gloria had painted, or had nearly finished. There was a series of oil paintings of the Reserve and the harsh landscape of the Yunque and the Volcan mountains. Some of these depicted the inlets hidden between their slopes and the reservoir; others featured groups of stags drinking at the water's edge at dusk; and others suggested fallow deer concealed behind cistus shrubs with only their scuts occasionally visible. In some smaller canvasses, there were variations on the cave paintings that Cupido, twenty years before, had often looked at. A series of photographs of the actual cave-paintings were pinned to the walls, scattered about in no obvious order or sequence that he could understand, but which possibly had held a strict and secret logic in the mind of Gloria. It seemed to him that in spite of being two sets with distinctly different subject matter, they complemented each other: the earth, and its living occupants, in a delicate balance somewhere between narrative and poetry, as if those magical drawings, executed in iron oxide – that twenty years before adolescent boys had tried to brighten up by urinating on them – found their justification in this land-scape that combined harsh prehistoric life with the echoes of a lost paradise. Those delicate images, at the limit of figurative representation and reduced to their basic, minimum forms depicted, not just the concept of men struggling for food and survival, but placed them in their natural setting. Gloria had given them faces, and had incorporated in their dark, ruddy countenances the emotions of fear, desire and happiness. She had expressed her need to discover how we had been then in order to arrive at what we are today.

Cupido went over to the shelves. There were several portfo-lios tied with red tape and bulging with notes and sketches. The rest consisted of note pads, exhibition catalogues, and mono-graphs on different painters and their styles.

Anglada had not spoken, looking at the pictures and moving round the studio with which he was obviously familiar, but doing so respectfully, and without touching anything – like a parent who refuses to change any detail in the room of a daugh-ter who has died tragically young.

'Did you know Gloria kept a diary?' asked the detective.

'Of course, the diary!' exclaimed Anglada, slapping his forehead. 'Of course I know, though I never actually saw it. She mentioned it several times. Is it important?'

'It could be. It might clear up one or two things. Gloria took it to Breda once, but not last weekend. At least, it wasn't among her belongings.'

'Who told you?'

'Her cousin, David. He saw her writing in it one day. I think we ought to look for it.'

He noticed Anglada become tense, as if alerted to something he hadn't foreseen. It was more than likely that Gloria would have written down her opinions of him as well as intimate matters that concerned them both, things she was pleased about, or little slights, petty disagreements, erotic activities that she had enjoyed, and he must have feared the detective digging into all that and penetrating private matters that had nothing to do with the investigation. Even so, he didn't object: 'In the circumstances I'm sure Gloria would have agreed.'

'Where might she have kept it?'

'I remember telling her one day that I would read it secretly. It was just a joke, but she said I'd never find it, because she kept it carefully hidden behind closed doors,' he said. He looked thoughtful.

They looked around the whole studio, assessing all the possible hiding places.

'I don't believe it's here. It must be somewhere in her apartment – as soon as you see it you'll understand why!'

'You were right,' Cupido agreed when they had gone down to it.

It was a large apartment with unusually high, panelled ceilings that were embellished with extensive plaster mouldings. From the hall they entered a spacious living-room that was divided by a central partition into two symmetrical halves with two sliding doors between them. It didn't look at all like the home of a young woman, but the fact that she had inherited it not so long before from her dead parents explained why it looked cluttered. Gloria hadn't wanted to get rid of their excellent furniture, nor their collection of ornaments and photographs, but neither had she missed the opportunity to bring in some of her own furniture and hang some of her paintings in the few remaining spaces on the walls. The result was an extensive apartment full of every conceivable type of object and potential hiding place.

'It would take a whole day to go through all this properly. Look at this for instance,' said Anglada pointing out a sideboard of an unusual design that combined a main section containing small, flat drawers similar to those used in printing shops with two other sections consisting of large and shelved spaces for glassware. 'Gloria designed this, and it could have a hiding place built into any corner of it.'

'Between the two of us we could do it in half a day,' suggested Cupido. Even if the diary was hidden, he didn't believe it would be in a secret compartment of a piece of furniture, but in some place that would be difficult to visualize but easy to gain access to.

He imagined that Anglada would have preferred to find it and read it on his own, but it was too late now for him to refuse. He was paying for the investigation, and he couldn't delay its progress by raising objections.

'I agree. Let's look now. In a few days time it may not be possible for you to get in here,' he said. He sounded disheartened to a degree that Cupido hadn't heard from him before, even at their first meeting when he had engaged him for this job. 'But before we start, I must make a phone call.'

He picked up the phone, automatically dialled a number, and gave instructions that his office shouldn't expect him for some hours because he had things to do. He hung up, and looked at the detective.

'We'll start in the bedroom.'

It was a long, meticulous, systematic search. Every corner, every space between the boxes and clothes hanging in the wardrobes, every shelf with its innumerable books on painting, treatises on aviation and military biographies, every pile of magazines was carefully checked by the two men. Anglada would stop from time to time as if trying to recall something, and the detective did so too with the disturbing thought that he was committing an offence. The apartment was just as it had been when she had been living there, and the suddenness of her disappearance had left everything as if it had been caught unawares in its normal daily routine, waiting for its owner's return to find all her everyday objects ready to hand: tweezers next to a little magnifying mirror, the last newspaper crossword half completed, an empty Coca Cola bottle she had forgotten to remove, a disc of popular classical music in the CD player. All her more intimate garments that Cupido tried to avoid touching and let Anglada be the one to handle, every perfume he detected on a handkerchief or in a handbag that had become unfashionable and that she had given up using, every comb or lipstick that had slipped behind a cushion told him something about her, her tastes, her whims, her habits, what had given her pleasure, and what she had discarded, presumably because she had grown tired of it. All these details were beginning to build up a picture of a woman imbued with a high degree of sensuality, in particular her senses of sight and smell – the two that most stimulate nostalgia. In one corner of a wardrobe he found a dried sprig of thyme, in the drawer of another piece of furniture he discovered some of those small perfumed fruits carved in wood, or an inlaid 'thousand flowers' box which at one moment emitted a scarcely detectable aroma, and at another an intense combination of perfumes. Where her artistic vision was concerned, all her clothes, every handbag and item of personal use was of those strong and brilliant colours that invite stunning combinations.

From time to time, Cupido would put a question to Anglada about a particular object, or a detail that had caught his eye. Occasionally, it was Anglada who would bring something to his attention – a figurine she had kept as a holiday souvenir, or a photograph album featuring the two of them. The detective had the impression that in every one of their photos they seemed to be separated by a third person or by some object such as the table in Anglada's apartment where they sat on opposite sides, holding hands, but under the impertinent gaze of the hundred tiny faces in the photograph of his last university year.

The detective was surprised to find in a ceramic pot full of small items of jewellery a badge similar to the one Gloria had held, gripped tightly in her hand, when she was murdered.

'What's this?' he asked.

The lawyer took it from him without paying it much attention.

'It was the symbol of one of those ecological protest campaigns that never get anywhere. Gloria designed it, or at least she collaborated in its design. Later, she made everyone she knew buy one. I must still have several of them at home somewhere.'

They searched very thoroughly, but failed to find the diary in which Gloria had written: '*He frightened me yesterday. But fear is not an innocent emotion.*' – those words that Cupido was unable to elucidate, and had no idea to whom they applied, but which obviously reflected a deep sense of distress. He looked at Anglada who at that moment was sitting on the floor next to a hi-fi unit, glancing one by one through the discs they must so often have listened to together, remembering songs that possibly were already beginning to sound old and distant. The lawyer suddenly raised his head and looked around, as if for a few minutes he had forgotten where he was, what he was looking for, or how he had got there. He stood up and replaced the discs in their rack. The lounge was the last room to be searched, and by

the end they were both convinced they had examined every centimetre of it. Anglada shut his eyes and rubbed them, very
aware of the fatigue produced by three hours of intensive
search. They had phoned out for sandwiches when they felt
hungry and could see how much remained to be done. They
stood up, disheartened, and left the apartment to return to the
studio. With renewed hope they moved all the paintings around
and examined the few possible hiding places, given the absence
of furniture and the plain walls until, disappointed, they came
to the conclusion that the diary wasn't to be found in either the
apartment or the studio.

'The only place left is her office,' said Anglada. 'It isn't likely
she kept it there, but there isn't anywhere else.'

'Her office?'

'Yes. In the gallery. I can't spend any more time on this. Let's
have a coffee, and then I'll take you over there and leave you
with Camila. She'll help you search. She can also tell you more
about Gloria.'

'How long had you known each other?' asked Cupido when
they had ordered coffees in a local café.

'About three years. Three years,' he repeated.

'Was she afraid of anything that might have occurred in her
life before meeting you? Somebody she might have hurt – even
if unintentionally?' he asked. He knew how often after some
unpleasantness a person discovers that there had been genuine
reasons to be fearful, and could have taken precautions against
it.

'No,' he replied categorically. 'Gloria was a very transparent
person. She may not have been easy to understand but she
would have been incapable of hiding something sinister from
her past – if that's what you mean. She was still too young to
have any skeletons in the cupboard!'

Anglada was leaning forward over the counter, concentrating
on stirring his coffee that was still too hot to drink. The

detective wondered what Gloria might have written about him in her diary. Any woman might fall for a man as attractive as he was – so sure of himself, with a good professional situation, and probably sound judgement in the way he spent and enjoyed his income. He was surprised when, with an abrupt gesture, Anglada dropped the spoon, and banged his fist down on the counter.

'I should have gone with her,' he said despondently, as if blaming himself for negligence, while at the same time subtly acquitting himself of a possible charge of murder.

'Where were you that morning?' asked Cupido, trying to ensure that there was no hint of suspicion in his tone.

'I'm surprised you haven't asked me that question before now. It surprised me that you could interrogate people without starting with me.'

'Do you ask that sort of question of people who come to your office when they need your services?'

'No. Right from the beginning I make a point of believing whatever I'm told by a paying client. That's part of my professional duty. However, from the first day I spoke to you I knew you were a good detective, but that you'd have made a bad lawyer. You need to know the truth as part of your work. We lawyers only need to work whether we know the truth or not!'

Cupido smiled to himself, imagining that Anglada had to be a formidable adversary in those types of trial that turn on quick exchanges of question and answer. It left him without a reply.

'It was a quiet morning,' said Anglada. 'The lieutenant in Breda has already asked me that question so I've committed everything I did to memory. I arrived at my office at nine – '

'Do you always start so early on Saturdays?' Cupido interrupted.

'Almost every Saturday. Starting early is one of the first conditions for becoming a good lawyer. If you don't get to court half an hour before the judge you've already lost the case!'

86

The detective nodded; it sounded convincing. His own inability to get up early in the morning was the second reason why he would never have made a good lawyer. He was also impressed that a man accustomed to asking all the questions was prepared to accept so many from him.

'In the office I finalized some papers with my secretary so that half an hour later I could hand them over personally to a judge on behalf of a client. I left the courthouse, stopped for a coffee, glanced through a newspaper, and went back to the office to sort out my work for Monday. Apart from the judge himself, there are half a dozen witnesses in my office who can vouch for this.'

It wasn't necessary. The detective had no doubt about the truth of what he said because it tallied exactly with what the lieutenant had established.

Anglada insisted on paying for their coffees, and they left the café. They were lucky, and didn't have to wait long before getting a taxi. Half an hour later they reached the gallery. Two men were busy removing some metal sculptures from their pedestals, the remains of a recent exhibition. After a quick glance Cupido realized that there was something about their style that he recognized.

They crossed the room to the open door leading into an office that had various cupboards, a few exhibition posters on the walls, and two desks. On one of these there was a sealed cardboard box, and a heap of files and portfolios. At the other desk a woman who was reading some formal documents raised her head when she noticed them, and stood up to greet Anglada with a polite kiss on the cheek. Then, the lawyer introduced them.

'Ricardo Cupido. Camila.'

The woman shook hands with him, giving him a speculative look as she did so.

'He's a private detective,' added Anglada impassively, without a hint of either approval or disapproval.

Camila was unable to conceal a look of mild surprise. Cupido's appearance did not accord with what she had expected from Anglada's words.

She was some years older than Gloria, about thirty-five, and compared with the unconventional flair they had found in the younger girl's wardrobe, Camila gave the impression of being a sophisticated and well-groomed woman – helped by the generous use of expensive creams and regular depilation, immaculate make-up that was just a little heavy thus creating a barrier against the world, but with a discreet touch of perfume calculated to make her seem not too distant and, finally, an air of being well organized and in control. The sort of woman, however, who may raise doubts about the happiness of the husband.

'I rang you several times both at home and at your office, but couldn't get hold of you. I'd put all Gloria's things aside thinking you'd want to take them away,' she said to Anglada, pointing to the cardboard box and the files on the other desk.

Unable to conceal his impatience, the lawyer made as if to open the box.

'D'you know if the diary's in here?' he asked.

'Gloria's diary? No, it wasn't here. I've been through all her personal things, but the diary wasn't among them. I think she kept it at home.'

'Have you ever seen it?' asked Cupido.

'Yes, a couple of times.'

'Here?'

'No, in her apartment.'

'D'you know if Gloria wrote in it very much?'

'I believe she wrote very little, but she would make a note of anything important that was happening to her at the time, and how she felt about it. She told me that once, although she never actually showed me what she'd written. She probably wrote about the sort of things that women never admit to anyone,' she said, looking closely at the detective, and involving herself in that sisterhood of secrecy, determined not to be left out of it.

Anglada looked at his watch, and gathered up the portfolios and the cardboard box.

'I've got to go,' he said. 'I have to get to the office to prepare a number of things for tomorrow. I'll be there for the rest of the afternoon. Call me if you need anything.'

Then he added, turning to Camila: 'He wants to talk to you.'

'Of course.'

'Right. I'm off.'

'Did you come on your motorbike?' asked Camila, as she accompanied him to the door.

'No.'

'It'll take you an hour to get to your office. With this strike it's impossible to get around.'

'We came by taxi, and it didn't take too long. I just hope I'll be as lucky now.'

The detective and the woman remained alone. Cupido wasn't sure how to begin his questioning, and she was unprepared for the difference between the two stolid policemen who had already interrogated her and this good-looking private investigator who didn't wear a suit and seemed polite. One thing at least, she was unable to detect any sign of a pistol tucked in his armpit as he moved.

As for Cupido, he was suddenly aware that he needed a shave, his hair was a mess, and his clothes were not too clean after the hours spent looking for the diary in Gloria's studio and apartment. He was also aware that these feelings only affected him in the presence of women to whom he felt attracted, and he had to make an effort to remember the job he was being paid to do and the information he had to get from her.

'Please tell me about Gloria,' he asked. She was the first young woman he had met in this job and he was interested to know what light she might throw on the truth.

'Gloria!' she murmured. 'Nobody ever really got to know her.'

She continued to look at him for several moments without speaking, and without knowing how to deal with a question that had such a wide scope. Then she went to the door, and said: 'Come with me.'

Cupido followed her as she walked purposefully and proprietorially into the main gallery. The workmen had nearly finished packing the last of the sculptures, and were placing them in a corner near the door to the street. The large, empty room with its long, bare walls, its spotlights switched off, the pedestal bases empty, had lost all the appearance of an art gallery, and could have been taken equally well for a bar, a shop, or an office.

'Gloria set up this exhibition. She was very personally involved in it. And suddenly, now she's gone it's as if the sculptures and their sculptor had also vanished because they haven't anybody else to lean on. Gloria was indispensable. There are those people who disappear and nobody notices they've gone,' she said, as she glanced over the empty, useless stands. 'But everybody will miss Gloria. She leaves a void in all of us who were close to her.'

These vague words were not what Cupido had expected. But he knew they too were important because every time someone talks he or she risks letting something important slip out. Discovering who had wielded that brutal shepherd's knife was going to be a slow task, and every conversation would let in a little light. It would be vital to ensure that every single word that referred to the murdered girl, however trivial it might seem, didn't fall on sterile ground but quickened the rich soil of memory until it brought the whole truth to the surface. Besides which, every new fact he acquired, every separate piece of information, when linked together with what he already knew, would make its contribution to elucidating what had happened in the past, in the same way that learning a new language improves one's ability to master others.

'Who's the sculptor?'

'Emilio Sierra.'

'Gloria's friend?'

'Yes.'

He understood now why these twisted, stylized iron figures had seemed familiar; he recognized their connection and their debt to the drawings he had been looking at just a few hours earlier.

'They look similar to some of Gloria's pictures.'

Camila smiled for the first time, both surprised and impressed by his observation. She took one of the sculptures out of an unsealed box; it was about fifty centimetres high, made of metal tubes and plates evoking the figure of a hunter armed with a bow, and placed it on the floor.

'Now just look at that. She was even able to influence Emilio,' she said. 'Gloria used to say they were working from completely different points of view to create two different interpretations of the cave-paintings. But when you see the results you can easily guess which one of them possessed true creativity, and which was the plagiarist. Gloria's figures come alive; Emilio's are static. Gloria's figures have defined features, whereas his only have masks. It was always the same with Gloria: her influence pervaded everything and everyone. I've seen women who, after a meal or working alongside her for a few hours, would begin to imitate her way of speaking, and when they smiled they'd try to copy her smile in spite of the difference in the shape of their lips.'

'But if it was she who put the exhibition together,' said Cupido, pointing at the sculpture, 'she can't have been upset by what he was doing'.

'No, of course not. Actually, she was flattered that someone as full of himself as Emilio let himself be carried away by her influence and originality because, quite apart from being a painter, Gloria was able to break away from time to time in order to reflect on the significance of art. I imagine the same happens with all great artists. In recent months, she'd entered on a new stage in her development. She'd become more introspective. The fact that Emilio copied her indicates that hers was the real driving force. Besides which, I don't imagine it will come as a surprise if I say that there were other, more personal, factors that brought them together. Am I right?'

'Were they lovers?'

One of the workmen overheard this question and turned round to listen to the answer. But he immediately turned back to what he was doing when he noticed the look of disapproval on Camila's face.

'Shall we just say that they played at it?'

'Did Anglada know?'

'Things like that – although they may not be known for certain – really are known, don't you think?'

'I do,' replied Cupido. He had a feeling she was trying to suggest something else that he wasn't quite grasping. 'Even so, her relationship with Anglada seems to have been a stable one, and they'd talked about getting married in the not too distant future.'

Camila gave a cynical little smile.

'Marry? Don't believe everything Marcos tells you. Possibly they did talk about it, but I don't believe Gloria would actually have taken that step. Not for some time at least. She was one of those very passionate people who can't look on life with another person only as a matter of convenience or as a mutual compact against loneliness. She often used to say: "*If your partner's unable to raise you up to paradise and you have to go on living with him, in the end he'll drag you down to hell!*" She also used to say that in all the couples she knew one of them was the leader and the other was the laggard, one went ahead fast and the other dawdled behind. Although they were in love with her, both Anglada and Emilio were laggards in her opinion.'

Cupido wondered what type of person Gloria was, given that somehow or other she fascinated everyone around her. He wondered whether, had he ever met her, he too would have been captivated by the appeal she had exerted in her lifetime.

'When did the exhibition open?'

'Nine days ago. On Wednesday of the week before last.'

'Was Sierra here all the time?' he asked, although he knew the answer because the lieutenant had told him that Sierra had been in Breda over the weekend.

'If you want to know if he was here on Saturday, no, he wasn't. We're closed at the weekend. I was here on my own all the morning getting our accounts up to date. Gloria hated that type of work, and it was I who dealt with it. Nobody else came in,' she replied, falling neatly into one of those clumsy traps that Cupido would set, although they always made him feel uncomfortable because he was sure the other person could see through them. But to his surprise they were often effective. In this case he was able to deduce from Camila's words that nobody had seen *her* in the office that morning.

'Did Gloria have any enemies in the art world?'

'There isn't a single artist who doesn't have a host of enemies among his fellow artists,' she said firmly, and with a malicious smile. 'They all detest each other. You should listen to them tearing each other to pieces as soon as backs are turned. But if you're thinking that one of them killed her, I think you're wrong. Not because they wouldn't have liked to, but because art makes cowards of artists: too much thought and not much action. The history of art is as replete with suicides as it is decently devoid of murders. Besides which, the way in which she was murdered was so...' She faltered, searching for an appropriate word. '... so savage. Only a depraved brute would have been capable of that.'

Cupido doubted her words, but he didn't contradict her. He took the paper with the drawing of the badge out of his wallet.

'Do you recognize this design?'

Camila stared at it for just a few seconds, with the air of an expert, half-closing her eyes like someone who needs glasses but, possibly from vanity, refuses to wear them.

'Yes.'

'Where have you seen it before?'

'Come in here,' she said, returning to the office. She opened a cupboard door and rummaged through a wooden box before holding out three of the same badges.

'We bought them from Gloria. She collaborated on the design. It was the logo of an ecological campaign. In my view the design's rather bland and simplistic; it isn't bold enough to have an impact on anybody. In any case, I don't believe the French were bothered in the least by the protests. But while they lasted there were people who went round wearing these badges.'

The detective did not allow his disappointment to appear as he listened to her. They all gave the same story about the badge, and everyone seemed to have at least one. It was useless as incriminating evidence against anybody.

One of the workmen came into the office to ask Camila to sign his worksheet confirming that their job had been satisfactorily completed, and Cupido took advantage of the interruption to leave.

The traffic had again become horrendous at that late hour of the afternoon when a million people were returning home by the same routes made impossible by the strike; but reconciled to delay, it now moved more slowly. It took Cupido half an hour to walk to the sculptor's apartment in Las Vistillas. He went up to the fourth floor of an old, but renovated, apartment block, and pressed the bell. Its ringing sounded distant, but he didn't have to wait long before the door opened.

'Emilio Sierra?'

'Yes.'

'My name's Ricardo Cupido – '

'Yes, I know,' he interrupted, in order to cut short any awkwardness he might have felt in explaining his visit. 'The last time I called Marcos he told me about you. You private detectives all seem to go in for names that aren't easily forgotten! Come on in.'

The apartment was a duplex in which the lower floor was arranged as a living-room. The upper floor consisted of an extensive and well-lit room that was being used as a workshop, although it was not here that the metal sculptures scattered around could have been welded. A partially sculpted block of wood was placed prominently on a pedestal where it was being roughly hewn into a sinuous figure that seemed either African or prehistoric. A candle burned in a candlestick on a table littered with papers.

'I was working. If you don't mind, I'll carry on while we talk,' said Sierra.

'Of course.'

The sculptor sat down on a high revolving stool that looked as if it had been stolen from a bar, and facing the block of wood, picked up his mallet and a small chisel, leaned back slightly in order to obtain the correct angle, and began to chip away at the wood with sharp, precise blows.

'I don't imagine Marcos will have had anything good to say about me,' he said, in a condescending, even disdainful, tone. 'Now that Gloria's no longer with us, he hasn't any reason to maintain the courtesies. When he told me he'd engaged you, I didn't know whether he was giving me information or a warning.'

'All he told me was that you and Gloria were good friends,' Cupido replied.

The sculptor stopped work for a moment. His hands remained suspended in the air as if they were doing the thinking, before starting again to cut into the wood, a task that was somewhere between pruning and three-dimensional geometry. The detective admired his strong forearms and the powerful hands on which the veins stood out as he gripped the tools, giving an impression of enormous strength.

'And were you?'

'Were we what?'

'Were you good friends?'

Instead of being annoyed, Sierra gave him a tolerant, good-humoured, but mocking smile – possibly he was flattered at being the object of that type of suspicion.

'I don't know why, but whenever a young and beautiful woman is murdered everybody imagines there's a third party and an eternal triangle behind it!' he said ironically.

Because very often it's the triangle that causes the murder, the detective thought to himself, but he didn't dare say it out loud. He didn't like the sculptor. He seemed to him a conceited, arrogant individual with an acid tongue, a type he had met not infrequently in artistic circles who curls his lip and sticks his jaw out when he disagrees with other people, as if about to settle somebody's hash with violence.

'Were you lovers?' he insisted – because that was the type of question Sierra seemed to be expecting.

'Yes,' came the unhesitating reply. 'Did Camila tell you that?'

Cupido didn't answer. A detective should never reveal his sources of information. Sierra struck a few more quick blows at the block of wood, and then dropped his tools on the pedestal. He seemed to have lost his inspiration.

'Don't you get on with Camila?'

'Gloria was the only person who did get on well with her. She was jealous of every little thing that Gloria had to do with me. She did nothing to help when it came to putting on my exhibition, and she's waited barely four days after her death to close it down.'

'She told me it hadn't been very successful,' he ventured.

'Successful? Successful?' Sierra's reaction was one of deep irritation. 'She took good care to make sure it wouldn't succeed. She invited all her little friends who were bound to dislike my style, and conveniently left out those critics who might have approved of it.'

Cupido watched him closely as he washed his hands in a small washbasin set into the wall. He was about thirty-five, but dressed as if he was still eighteen. His hair was cut very short, his head almost shaven, but with long sideburns. He was no longer in that period of early youth when fervour and over-weaning confidence justify vanity, bumptiousness and arro-gance. If it was true what Camila had said about him, he lacked talent and worked in the shadow of Gloria, but if he was con-scious of his own limitations, he gave no sign of accepting or recognizing the fact; and possibly that was the reason for his aggressive reaction to Cupido's words. *The sort of artist who tries to hide his mediocrity by being irascible – only really in his element when he's caused a violent argument*, he judged. He also sus-pected that the lieutenant wouldn't have liked him at all because, like all military men, he would have hated his eccen-tricity and his pretensions.

'Did she also inform you that now that Gloria's dead she's the sole owner of the gallery?' he asked suddenly in an accusatory tone, while continuing to wash his hands.

'No, she didn't say anything about that,' Cupido replied. Nor had Anglada mentioned it when, at their first meeting, they had talked about who would inherit from her.

'Where were you on Saturday morning?'

Sierra smiled, dried his hands on a towel, and went over to the untidy table. He took a cigarette from a cigarette case and offered it to the detective.

'Would you like one?'

'No thanks,' he said. He had now gone six days without smoking and still found offers of cigarettes galling.

Sierra lit the cigarette in the flame of the candle which he then blew out.

'I've been waiting for you to ask that question ever since you rang my bell. I was in Breda, in my house there. I had to weld some sculptures that had been commissioned. I can't do it here and I go there whenever I have to. They let me use a forge.'

'Were you in the forge all day?'

'Only the afternoon. I spent the morning in my house getting things ready.'

'When did you arrive in Breda?'

'Friday afternoon.'

It didn't seem very logical to Cupido that an artist who has just inaugurated his exhibition and ought to be there for promotion and sales should have abandoned it on the second day, unless he was certain in his own mind that it was going to be a flop and didn't want to be a witness to his own failure.

'Did anyone see you that morning?'

'No, I don't think so. I don't have much to do with people there. With just a few exceptions they're not very welcoming to someone with habits that are very different from theirs.'

The detective smiled. Sierra was right in that respect.

'Do you know what they did when my grandfather brought electricity to the town?'

'No.'

'Half the population ran off into the woods on the day it was switched on because they thought the lamps were going to explode and send showers of glass everywhere.'

It all came back to Cupido's mind. The sculptor was the last heir of a famous man who had been exiled to Breda for several years before 1920, but having been reinstated in office as a result of a political upheaval, one of his first gestures had been to have electricity brought to the town out of gratitude to the group of people who had helped him there during his exile and hadn't treated him as a pariah. Later, he had built the big house near the river.

'Did you know that Gloria was also going there for the weekend?'

'No, I didn't. She must have made a last-minute decision, as she did about so many things. Two days before we'd been together at the exhibition and she didn't say a thing. I never saw her again.'

'Do you recognize this design?' He showed him the piece of paper that by now was very crumpled.

'Yes. I have a badge with that design.'

'Can I see it?'

'Of course.'

He went back to the enormous, untidy table, and scrabbled around in a drawer among the muddle of small objects that had accumulated there.

'Is it very important?' he asked.

'No,' lied Cupido.

'Here it is,' he said at last, showing him the badge with the silhouette of an atomic mushroom cloud above a small green island.

Six

It hadn't been a good day. Although term had begun little more than a month before, his students had been particularly fidgety, argumentative and lazy; their work had been careless, because all they thought about was what they would be doing at the weekend. By the time May came they would be utterly bored, and would have lost all remaining interest in the course. Not that they had much now. Art wasn't a subject they regarded with respect as they did languages and mathematics, but it did require a minimum effort that most of his pupils weren't prepared to make. He had begun to hate his job once he realized that the key to teaching these adolescents didn't lie in the teacher's professional knowledge, but in his capacity for inspiring them. It was possible to be an artistic genius and yet be incapable of developing ability in others. He had needed only two or three years to realize that the barrier to communication between him and his pupils was not due to inexperience on his part, nor ignorance of the complex processes by which a child or an adolescent succeeds in acquiring the knowledge that society considers necessary for its future, but in their fundamental lack of interest in Van Gogh's ear! The difference between animals and human beings, he believed, is that each generation of an animal species has to discover everything for itself – which is why they always occupy the same rung on the evolutionary ladder – whereas human beings are able to transmit to the next generation what has already been learned, and to help young people evolve beyond the point to which their ancestors have led them in the relay race we call *civilization*. The microscope, penicillin, Don Quixote, *Las Meninas* by Velázquez, Roman Law, the lever, writing and fire are the springboards that enable humanity to rise even further. But in the case of pupils like this lot, mankind would start moving backwards! Disappointed in all his efforts to motivate them, it was years now since he had opted for indifference, in the hope that they would at least behave themselves politely in the way people do who don't know each other. But that method hadn't succeeded either. The adolescents had reacted with insolence; it seemed as if they had a compulsion to fight with their teachers and resented his contempt for them even more than discipline. In the end he had concluded that it was impossible to get through to them.

He opened the door of the small apartment where he lived. He wasn't hungry but knew he needed to eat something to assuage the pains in his stomach. All he had eaten during the entire day were the *tapas* that had been served with the glasses of wine he had drunk that afternoon in the four or five local bars where he was becoming a regular customer. He had observed that, as good professionals, some of the barmen served his drink before he even ordered it, and he found this disturbing because he preferred to remain an unknown.

He looked around at the tiny living-room, the open bedroom door through which he could see the unmade bed, and the work top of his fitted kitchen littered with dirty plates and glasses as well as scraps of food, its edge chipped from opening innumerable bottles of beer by striking their caps against it. The dirt was eloquent of his loneliness, degradation and loss of self-respect. It all needed to be thoroughly cleaned. The apartment was small and had little furniture, but he was incapable of mustering the necessary energy to do it. In the first months after his separation he had sworn he would maintain the conventional standards that would prevent him from sinking into the slovenly habits he had often seen in people who lived alone; he would keep a tolerable level of hygiene and cleanliness in the apartment, which, even if not very comfortable, would at least look decent. But, little by little, he too had succumbed, until he had fallen into that slovenly state that became more difficult to get out of with every day that passed. There were nights when he woke up in the dark and thought back on his previous life, the modest comforts he had enjoyed, his marriage which had been neither more exciting nor boring than most, with a tolerable wife and two children for whom he felt progressively less affection as the months went by without seeing them – as if love itself was a habit that grows with familiarity and dwindles with distance. Everything had gone overboard when he got to know Gloria. From that moment on, all other women had begun to appear boring and insignificant, as if their only purpose had been to provide him with an apprenticeship for the time when he met her; it had been a valuable apprenticeship that helped him to begin his relationship with her, but, in the event, insufficient for holding on to her. After she left, other women were pathetic imitations. When he slept with a prostitute who was not too fat or too dirty, or when he had some other chance encounter, it always ended with him wanting to kick them down the stairs. After Gloria, every naked woman seemed a fraud, and the degree of his obsession was such that he was incapable of hiding his aversion. His marriage had fallen apart in the brief space of two months. And barely one month after his separation he found that Gloria had begun to lie to him.

He sat down in the grubby armchair that was covered in crumbs and opened the newspaper to read all over again the brief article that gave the news of her death on the page dealing with crimes and accidents. It was four days since he had spotted it by chance in the porter's lodge at his school as he handed in his key. There were no photographs or information about the victim other than her name and age, but there were full details of the weapon used in the murder: a shepherd's knife that had inflicted a lesser wound on one breast before the deadly one in her neck, the most vulnerable of all the vital parts of the body because it has little or no bony protection, but through which pass the windpipe and artery that are critical to life. The same shudder ran through him that he had experienced that day, when in spite of the agonizing pain in his heart he had felt himself avenged.

Driven by thirst – his mouth was dry and his stomach on fire – he went to the fridge and took out an almost full bottle of wine. Glancing around but failing to find a clean glass among the dirty crocks, he drank straight from the bottle. It was a long, deep, noisy gulp, like pouring cold water on to hot stones. He felt the fumes rising in his throat, and as they reached his head they quickly diffused the feeling that he was cohabiting with a corpse.

It had been so long since anyone had called at his apartment that he was startled when the electric doorbell suddenly began to ring. At any other time he would have thought it was a prank by some of his students who had discovered his jealously guarded secret – his home address – because he was fearful of physical assault. But he guessed it was something to do with Gloria, and again he hated her because, even dead, she still came back to torment him. Before opening the door he raised the bottle to his mouth and let more of the wine flood down into his stomach. Then he stood up and drew back the two bolts. A tall man faced him, but he didn't seem at all threatening, and he didn't look like a policeman.

'Manuel Armengol?'

'Yes,' he replied, and cursed silently because his response sounded like a groan.

'My name's Ricardo Cupido. I'm investigating Gloria's death.'

The teacher looked down at the visitor's hands that hung motionless at his side, expecting him to produce a badge, an identity card – anything that might constitute a threat.

'Police?' he asked at last.

'No. I'm a private detective.'

Cupido expected to be asked who was employing him, but the other man simply moved aside to let him enter, as if relieved to know that he wasn't from the police. He offered him the armchair, having first removed the open newspaper. Cupido just had time to note the headline of the article that dealt with Gloria's murder. Then he became aware of the disorder: the unmade bed, the open bottle of wine on the table, and the absence of a glass. He could tell from his eyes and his voice that Armengol had been drinking. He waited while he took two glasses from a cupboard and had sat down in front of him before asking: 'Do you know how she died?'

'Yes. I happened to read about it a couple of days ago in an old newspaper. It was a dreadful surprise. Like a bad dream,' he explained. His teeth looked in bad condition, yellow like grains of maize, and his voice was hoarse, partly from teaching, but mainly from too much wine and too many cigarettes. He had the curious, watchful look of a hermit.

He raised the glass to his lips and drank. Then he lit a cigarette, and inhaled with deep satisfaction. He was one of those smokers who revive the desire to smoke in those who watch them.

'Who told you about me?'

'The lieutenant leading the investigation. Haven't they been to see you yet?'

'Yes, they have. At the college where I'm teaching. The officer was tactful at least,' he said. 'I thought that after giving them a statement it was all over.' He sounded dismayed.

'It's only just started,' said Cupido.

For several minutes Armengol remained staring at him in silence through the smoke from his cigarette, and wondering how he should interpret those last words. Suddenly, he said:

'For you lot I'm the perfect suspect: a lonely type who was besotted with her and had good reason to hate her.'

'*He's drunk too much to be talking like that,*' thought Cupido, glancing at the level of the wine in the bottle.

'Was it long since you'd last seen her?' he asked,

'A long time. A very long time. That was just around the beginning of the year, seven or eight months ago. I still had a few things of hers and I phoned her so she could take them back. We didn't see each other again. That portrait she did for me is the only thing of hers I've kept,' he said, pointing to a painting in which he looked ten years younger.

'Did Gloria paint that?'

'Yes. It makes me look ten years younger,' he said. Then, he added: 'There's nothing left now of what you see there.'

There were times when Cupido wondered what it was that induced some of the people he interviewed to make confessions to him – a person they hardly knew – with the same frankness with which they might talk to a priest. What led them to admit to being victims of an absurd confidence trick, or an adultery? Matters they wouldn't disclose to their best friend. He had arrived at the conclusion that they did so because a private detective is indifferent to the moral aspects of his assignment – and sometimes even to the illegal ones; he doesn't declare a person guilty like a judge or a priest, and he doesn't impose punishments. All he does is listen to, agree with, and take orders from his client – just like a prostitute. Always provided, of course, that they pay well!

'When she left me I knew for certain I was getting old,' the teacher went on.

Cupido was convinced he had drunk too much and it would only need one question for him to start on a recital of his misfortunes, and after such a long day, he wouldn't be able to listen to it patiently.

'Do you recognize this design?' he asked, showing him the drawing of the badge.

Armengol gave it a cursory look.

'No. I don't remember ever seeing it.'

It was the answer the detective had expected: the badge had been made some months after his relationship with Gloria had been broken off. The only clue they possessed didn't seem to be leading anywhere.

'It's a poor design, by the way,' he added. 'It wouldn't be difficult to improve it.'

'Do you paint too?'

'No, not now. I tried for a while until I realized that those of us who can't paint should give it up and resign ourselves to explaining art to others. That's how I got to know Gloria.'

The detective gave him an enquiring glance.

'In the course of the school year we take the students to one or another exhibition. Her gallery isn't far away, and last year we decided to go there, although once again I thought it would be futile because my pupils wouldn't have any interest in what they'd see. But when we went in and started looking at the paintings, even the most apathetic of them stood there without a word. They were astonished. I think it was the last time I managed to impress them. The artist was a young girl and she was standing there as well, watching our reactions. She was pleased I'd brought my students. We began to chat, and the next day I phoned to ask her if she'd come to the college and give us a talk about her work. Perhaps they might pay more attention to her than they did to me. You can guess the rest.'

'How long did it last?'

Armengol smiled ruefully, like a tramp who has had his plate removed when he's only eaten half his food. He refilled his glass before replying.

'About five months. Too long to be able to forget; too little time not to miss her.'

'Where were you on Saturday?' he asked suddenly.

'Sleeping,' he replied meekly, after remaining silent for a few moments. 'I'd had a bad night, and didn't feel well. I stayed in bed until the afternoon.'

Cupido noted the impatience with which Armengol raised his glass again, and he became eager to get away as fast as possible from that apartment that was as stuffy as a hothouse. His six days without smoking were beginning to bear fruit. He felt the need for fresh, clean air and a desire to get out into the street and look at pleasant, happy faces.

Seven

A week had gone by since Gloria's death, and Cupido had
returned to Breda with no firm conclusions and no clear ideas
about the next step in the investigation, but this didn't worry
him because he knew that, as always, patience was essential.
It was the others, those who had been in any way connected
with Gloria who were likely to be uneasy and waiting appre-
hensively for something to happen that would acquit them of
suspicion.

He got up late on the Monday morning and ambled slowly to
the Civil Guard barracks to talk to the lieutenant. Now that they
knew him there he wasn't kept waiting long at the gate.

'How did you get on in Madrid?' Gallardo asked.

'Lots of words, but nothing certain to go on.'

The lieutenant nodded slowly.

'I hate that city. I hate all big cities. Everybody's in a hurry
and nobody knows anybody else. It isn't surprising that criminals like to hide in them – or that we can never find them.'

The day before, Cupido had read in the local paper the latest
'news' about the crime: a press release issued by the provincial
governor which took a vaguely optimistic tone. But he knew that
when a spokesman for the authorities claims that an investigation is proceeding satisfactorily and all leads are being followed
up, the truth is they have nothing to go on and are stumped,
with no idea what to do next.

Something very similar happens in war reports: when a general asserts with confidence – and complacency – that fighting is progressing on all fronts, what he really means is that he hasn't won a single battle.

'Who did you talk to?'

'Anglada, again. Camila. The sculptor who has a house here. That extraordinary teacher, Armengol, who was one of the girl's lovers. Anglada's the only one with a perfect alibi for that morning.'

'We'd already checked that,' came the reply.

'None of the others have anyone who can answer for them. Camila says she was on her own in her art gallery all the morning. Sierra, the sculptor, was here in Breda, but claims he never left his house. Armengol apparently was asleep, probably because he'd got drunk the night before. He drinks too much.'

The lieutenant expressed agreement with everything Cupido said as he glanced through the typed pages in front of him. He stopped for a moment to light a cigarette, and offered one to Cupido. The detective was delighted to find he was able to refuse with much less trouble than a few days before.

'They told us exactly the same,' said the lieutenant, tapping the sheets of paper on the table to straighten them up. 'Exposito was also in Madrid that morning; we've got a detailed report from the laboratory where they took a sample of his blood for analysis. As far as those who live in Breda are concerned, there's nothing clear. The relations of the victim – ' He employed the cold, formal term that said nothing about her sex or her age and that Cupido refused to use as he sought for words that would better personify Gloria and help to prevent her fading away to become just one more component in the undifferentiated mass of the dead. ' – I mean the father and the son. They both tell the same story, but as they repeat it in exactly the same way they could both be lying. The warden, Molina, could also be lying when he says he took a different route that morning. This is going to be a tough case. We're right back at the beginning.'

'It's too soon to tell. They're all frightened now,' said Cupido.

'Frightened?'

'Fear is their worst enemy. It makes them distrustful of each other and reluctant to talk. Coming up against murder makes us all wary.'

Unlike the lieutenant, Cupido was in no hurry. He didn't have a time limit and he wasn't being pressured to act quickly by relatives or superiors, or by the press, which often confuses patience with ineffectiveness when commenting on the work of the official officers of the law. Patience had always been Cupido's strong point, and he had always known how to make good use of it.

'And the badge? Did you find out anything about that?'

'One or two things, both here and in Madrid.'

The lieutenant sat up straight. Ever since they had found the badge in the girl's clenched hand with the metal point stuck in the end of her middle finger he had seen it as the only firm clue worth following up. But so far it hadn't led anywhere.

'What things?' he asked brusquely.

'The girl's cousin had seen a drawing of the badge in a diary Gloria used to keep. He can't have been lying because he did an exact sketch of it in front of me.'

'Unless he knew the design because he had direct knowledge of the badge itself – which would be much more interesting.'

'Yes, if he'd been the only one.'

'Anyone else?'

'All of them. Or nearly all. That badge was well known in the circle of artists and painters who were close to Gloria, because she collaborated in the design and made all of them buy it to support the protest campaign. They were all familiar with it and had bought one or more, except for Armengol. But by that time they were no longer meeting.'

'You said a moment ago that the girl kept a diary.'

'Yes. And it could possibly clear up a number of things. Have you looked for it?'

'No. Nobody mentioned it to us. But that sort of item's normally the first thing we do look for. The Madrid police did a thorough search of her apartment. If they'd seen it they wouldn't have just ignored it.'

Having nothing more to say, the two men fell silent. It hadn't been much. Possibly the murderer wasn't even on their list of suspects. It was only the badge that had led them to believe that the crime hadn't been the work of a lunatic but of someone close to Gloria.

'They've completed the autopsy report. There's nothing there. There's not a thing that connects up with anyone, not even a thread under the victim's nails. Nothing at all,' the lieutenant concluded.

But possibly the way he spoke wasn't intended to express discouragement or a belief that the case wouldn't be brought to a satisfactory conclusion, but actually implied confidence in the man he was discussing it with. Possibly he – a military professional, accustomed to discipline and good planning, and who must have revered the uniform he wore and expected nothing but problems from those who didn't – was surprised to find himself talking in this way to a private detective who had done time in jail for smuggling. But circumstances had forced him into alliance with him, and even if it could never lead to true comradeship it was moving close to a feeling of trust. So far, neither of them had been quicker than the other at suggesting what they should do next, nor cleverer at analysing the few bits of information they had garnered. And undoubtedly it was that state of equilibrium that persuaded both of them to play fair.

'We'll have another go at the magistrates,' Gallardo spoke again after a short silence. 'It shouldn't be difficult to get permission to tap their phones. But I fear that won't get us far either. Everything tells me we're up against a lone lunatic!'

Eight

'I'll be frightened, staying here all on my own,' the girl said. She was about twenty-two or twenty-three, but had the voice of a spoilt child and a voluptuous figure emphasized by a very tight sweater and close-fitting jeans that were old, torn in places, and frayed at the ankles. Her black hair framed the soft, unblemished skin of her face with its first faint freckles caused by exposure to the sun during the day they had spent walking and pitching their tent.

The young man, who was about the same age, tall and strongly built, and wearing shorts and mountain boots, took her in his arms and held her close until he felt the arousal that her warm, passionate body never failed to induce ever since he had started going out with her barely a month before. His hands slipped down to grip her round buttocks tightly confined by her jeans, and pulled her pelvis against his own.

'Go on, don't be silly. I don't want to go either,' he said, kissing her lightly on the mouth and increasing the pressure of his fingers on the thin material of her trousers. 'It'll take me less than half an hour in the car. We can't leave the tent and all the other things here. They'd be stolen.'

'But there's nobody else here,' she protested.

'There's always somebody we can't see wandering through the forest,' he replied, with the obstinacy of a man who always knows best.

'We can get along without batteries,' the girl insisted, using her most kittenish and seductive voice, raising her face to his, and offering her mouth for another kiss while she caressed the back of his neck. 'We can go to bed early and there are lots of things we can do that don't need light...'

The young man felt the almost irresistible, tickling sensation of her fingers on his neck. He gave her an affectionate smile, but suddenly stepped back, and got into the car, a four-wheel drive, the ideal vehicle for those who want to disappear into the most rugged corner of the Reserve.

'I'll be less than half an hour,' he promised.

She remained motionless in front of the bright blue tent that stood out like a brilliant reflection of the sky on the dry, brown earth, and looked around like a lovely, frightened animal that suddenly finds itself a long way from its flock. She watched the vehicle disappear, raising a cloud of dust as it went, and listened to the distant sound of its engine even when she could no longer see it. Then, feeling very lonely, she took out a packet of cigarettes, lit one, and sat down on a large stone in front of the tent. She looked at her wristwatch and, with a sigh of resignation, settled down to wait for the half-hour to go by. She thought about her boyfriend and the way he had deserted her there, and promised herself that this was the last time she would go out with him. She wasn't prepared to remain alone in the middle of a forest in which they hadn't seen one human being since leaving civilization that morning. She wasn't prepared to give up cigarettes just because he disliked the smoke – and she resented the fact that he wouldn't kiss her when her lips tasted of nicotine! She wasn't prepared to eat out of tins or live on sandwiches and drink warm Coca Cola. And she wasn't prepared to walk twelve or fifteen kilometres along a goat track with sharp stones sticking into the soles of her feet, which had happened that day when they went to see those strange cave-paintings that she hadn't been able to understand. When she got back, her feet swollen, all she had wanted was to drop down and rest while he gave her a massage from her neck down to her feet, and yet she found herself having to stay on her own guarding their tent in the middle of a forest that had something menacing about it, on that day of all days, 1 November, All Souls' Day – the Day of the Dead. How she regretted agreeing to this misbegotten trip! She noticed a big, black ant investigating something between her feet. She raised one foot and squashed it furiously into the ground. When she raised her head she sensed that her surroundings had fallen strangely quiet, as if the whole natural world had caught her unawares as she committed that violent and gratuitous little murder, and mutely condemned her. It was then that she began to feel real fear, but refused to think about it because she knew that in that situation, once admitted, she wouldn't be able to control it until she was again surrounded by other people or her boyfriend had returned and taken her in his arms. She looked round to make sure that the silence wasn't caused by the approach of a predator. But not only was the silence complete, nothing moved. She was unable to suppress a shiver that made her teeth chatter. She jumped up, but saw nothing, and flinging away the burning cigarette end crawled into the tent. Her hands shook as she pulled up the zip on the entrance. She knelt inside, facing it, her eyes wide open, and her heart pumping violently, overcome by a panic more powerful than her will. She felt as if something in her bowels was forcing itself down, and the sphincter was barely able to hold it back. The low afternoon sun threw shadows of the branches of the trees on to the blue canvas of the tent, and the dim light inside was dappled with blurred anthropomorphic shapes. Suddenly there flashed through her mind that a week before, as she leafed through a newspaper, she had read about the brutal murder of a girl who had been walking alone through a forest. She couldn't remember exactly where it had happened, but guessed that it couldn't have been very different from where she was now. If someone wanted to attack her, there was nobody else for several kilometres around who would hear her shouts and come to her rescue. She recalled her boyfriend's words spoken only a few minutes earlier: '*There's always somebody we can't see wandering through the forest*' – but now they didn't seem just silly or tactless, but frightening and ill-omened. Again, she asked herself how she could have been so stupid as to accept his plans for this horrible trip with nothing more than a tent, when she should have insisted on their staying in a five-star hotel. She hated the parched, bone-hard earth which pressed against her knees, the smell of warm plastic, the weights they had to drag around with them, the odour of incipient autumnal decay, the boots that compressed her feet like the swaddlings of a mummy, the slugs that might fall on her head as she walked under the trees, the tiny insects she had spent the day battling with that always managed to get inside her clothes, especially the blood-sucking ones that would leave her skin irritated for a week. If these were the pleasures of hiking that had been praised so highly, then she had absolutely no wish to participate in them. She preferred more comfortable pleasures. She had agreed to come on this journey, tempted by what lovers have always enjoyed: hiding, just the two of them, in an isolated place where nobody could intrude while they indulged in all the delights of love. But it hadn't worked out as she had expected. As soon as her boyfriend came back she would insist on their immediately dismantling the tent and going to the beautiful hotel that looked like a castle that she had noticed as they drove through the little town where he had gone to buy batteries. Until he agreed she wouldn't let him touch her. She was instinctively repelled by her own sweaty body after their long walk, her hair thick with dust, and her lips dried by the sun and the wind.

At this point she discovered that the hatred she felt had dispelled much of her panic: anger had acted as a powerful antidote against the seeping poison of terror. She still had her fears, but had succeeded in reducing them to a reasonable level. Nervous habit made another cigarette essential. She searched through her pockets without finding one until she remembered having left the packet and her lighter on the stone where she had been sitting. With an effort she pulled up the zipper on the tent, telling herself that she was no safer in there and it did nothing to lessen her anxiety. Her friend would be back soon, and the two of them would be able to laugh at her exaggerated fears. She advanced on all fours, and put her head out through the opening, like a wary tortoise. She looked around but saw nobody. She remained like that for a few seconds without being able to suppress the acute feeling that somebody hidden behind the trees was watching her. She was a girl who wasn't in the habit of being on her own. She was always surrounded by girlfriends, or by boys and men who were attracted by her magnificent figure. She had learned to notice when they were gazing at her from the opposite platform of a metro station, or from where they stood at a bar, or through the dim light of a dance hall. At this very moment she was again aware of that impression of being admired, desired, and spied on that she was so familiar with. She listened intently, hoping to pick up the distant sound of the car's engine, but still she heard nothing. The most outrageous compliment, or the most direct and obscene proposition would have been preferable to the silence that surrounded her. *Why's he taking so long just to buy a couple of batteries?* she asked herself crossly. *Everything's closed. It's All Souls' Day*, she answered her own question. The sun would soon begin to sink behind the mountains. She went back to sit on the stone, flicked the lighter and, out of habit and quite unnecessarily because there was not a breath of air, protected its flame with her left hand. The cigarette glowed red as she took two deep, anxious puffs, and when she looked up again she saw the dark shadow that was descending on her, the implacable face, the moss green anorak, and, right in front, the knife with its curved blade that was approaching the level of her mouth. She knew what was going to happen and raised her hands protectively to her neck. As if it had foreseen that defence the knife found a gap between her fingers and plunged forward until it reached her throat. It stopped there for a moment as if relishing the sweet, hot blood before withdrawing. Then, like the mouth of a ferocious and famished animal, and without any more resistance from the hands that were thrust in front of her, it easily buried itself in her neck and, pressing hard, was held there until the pumping of her heart finally ceased.

A young Civil Guard, not much more than twenty, had come to his apartment and asked him to accompany him. 'They've killed another girl up there in the woods. The lieutenant wants you to go there right now,' he had said, standing in the doorway, not wanting to go in, and trying to assume the cool manner of one experienced in conveying bad news. Cupido had returned to his living-room where he had been eating his dinner, changed his shoes, and picked up his keys. He had caught himself checking his pockets, the gesture of a person who has forgotten something important but doesn't know what it is, and it took him a few seconds to realize he was looking for a packet of cigarettes. It wasn't the first time that old habit acquired over twenty years had bedevilled him, treacherously. He had gone ten days without cigarettes, and even though the desire to smoke seemed to have diminished he was still caught out by the traps and subterfuges that sought to undermine his resolve. It was like fighting an adversary who, although on the point of being beaten in a duel, isn't prepared to admit defeat, and from that moment on employs other, more subtle techniques based on a series of feints and tricks. He followed the Civil Guard out to his car, and they drove once more up the path to the Paternoster Forest. The policeman didn't have many details of the murder, and hadn't seen the body, because the lieutenant had sent him off to fetch Cupido as soon as they had arrived there.

The tent had been set up near water, one of the numerous, half-hidden creeks that the reservoir had created between the hills. The girl's body was next to the stone on which she must have been sitting when she was attacked, and it lay sprawled in that curiously shameless way that dead bodies have when they fall face upwards. Her bloodstained hands were raised as if she were praying, or asking for an explanation for the two enormous gashes in her throat. Her blood had ceased to flow, and was now congealing on the earth, having soaked down through the front of her sweater.

Cupido had anticipated that it would be a ghastly sight. On his way there he had been preparing himself for what he would be obliged to look at. He hadn't seen Gloria's body, but the information the lieutenant had given him combined with the photographs he had been shown had provided him with a clear picture of how her murder had been committed. Even so, he couldn't help himself shuddering. He had a feeling compounded of deep pity and a vague, fierce loathing as he gazed at the haft of the knife stuck in the girl's neck, the protruding eyes transfixed with horror, and the mouth – wide open – as if she had been gasping for breath like an asthmatic who fears he's being asphyxiated.

'Oh, my God!' exclaimed the Civil Guard who had brought him there and was standing beside him. His mouth became hugely distended, and he ran off down the bank. They all heard his retching and the sound of his vomit splashing into the water. The lieutenant turned towards him and gave him a deeply reproachful look.

Underneath the searchlights, a group of men was carrying out a minute examination of the ground. Cupido had never previously seen them engaged on this first and most painstaking part of the investigating process. '*There's no such thing as a perfect crime, only an imperfect investigation,*' he remembered hearing, and he had to admire the disciplined, ant-like co-ordination with which they scrutinized and smelled everything they found, exchanging notes in order not to get in each other's way or to duplicate their efforts as the work proceeded. One of them was photographing the body and every other significant object, another was sprinkling the canvas of the tent with a saffron-coloured powder for lifting fingerprints, others were stretching a yellow plastic tape around the area being examined in detail, while yet others moved about beyond this within a wider perimeter, searching with the aid of powerful torches any stone that had been moved, any piece of earth of a different colour so that the area it came from could be determined later in the laboratory.

The lieutenant stopped talking to a man in a white overall, and came over to him.

'I let you know about this so that you could come and see for yourself. This business is turning into a nightmare.'

'Same as last time?'

'Yes, looks like it. Same knife, same type of wound, and similar circumstances. The same killer.'

The detective looked at the tent; its plastic surface shone brightly under the searchlights.

'How did she come to be here after the other murder?'

'She wasn't alone,' replied Gallardo. He pointed to a young man sitting on a stone a little way off, his elbows on his knees and his head between his hands. He seemed detached from everything around, lost in the middle of a bustle of activity, the only motionless individual among a dozen men galvanized by this second bloodletting. 'He says they came here to spend a few days on their own. He left her alone for half an hour late in the afternoon to drive into town to buy some batteries they needed. Otherwise they wouldn't have had any light tonight. When he got back he found her like that. She was still bleeding. The lad knows something about mountain rescue and first aid, but he couldn't do anything for her.'

'Have you checked his story?'

'Yes. He's not lying. His statement agrees to the minute with that of the attendant at the petrol station who sold him the batteries. Apart from which, his receipt has the time of purchase printed on it. He should never have left her alone.'

'This may alter all our theories,' said Cupido.

'Yes. This death turns everything upside down. Possibly the murder of the other girl wasn't due to personal motives. I'm beginning to think we've got a lunatic round here somewhere. Either a lunatic or somebody who doesn't like visitors.'

'I'd agree if it wasn't for the badge,' Cupido cut in. 'Can I speak to the boy?'

'Of course.'

They went over to where he was sitting. As he heard them approach he raised his head and stood up. He stared at them. He seemed more stunned than distressed.

'Tell us everything right from the beginning.'

'We came to spend a few days here. We brought the tent so that we could be completely alone and wouldn't see anyone we didn't want to. During the day we left everything in the car down here near the water because we were going to camp here, and we climbed up to the caves with the paintings,' he explained. Every sentence was accompanied by a nervous movement of his hands as he pointed to the tent, the car, and the route up the mountain. 'When we got back here in the afternoon we took our things out of the car and pitched the tent. It was only then I realized we hadn't got any batteries for our torches and we'd be all night without any light. I decided to drive quickly into the town to buy some. She had to stay here to keep watch on all this because if we'd just left it somebody could easily have stolen it. After all, it wouldn't take much more than half an hour in the four-wheel drive to go and come back. I knew the route. She was a bit anxious and didn't want to stay here on her own but I convinced her that nothing could possibly happen. I should have listened – ' His voice broke, and he began to cry. Cupido and the lieutenant looked at him, wondering whether to continue with their questions.

'Why did you come to this area?' asked the lieutenant.

'I already knew it. I'd been here two or three times before, and it seemed the ideal place to be completely on our own.'

'Didn't you know that another girl was murdered here just over a week ago?'

'No, we didn't know. They've just told me. If we'd known we'd never have chosen this place.'

'Where are you from?'

'Madrid.'

'Did anybody else know you were going to be here at this time?'

'No. Nobody knew. It was a secret. We told our families we'd be with a group of friends. We've only been going out together for a month or so, and it was too soon to tell if... if we were going to get on together.'

It all seemed very logical. Obviously, it would be necessary to check that neither the girl nor the boy knew any of Gloria's acquaintances, in order to ensure there was no link, because, if there wasn't, then it looked like a coincidence. Gloria would have died because she had happened to be in that precise spot at that precise moment; and the same would be true of this girl. In that case it wouldn't make much sense to look further into their friendships and contacts. They would have to aim for a deranged killer, or people who were opposed to tourism in the Reserve and who could have picked on any likely victim. Unless, of course, someone had intentionally had that in mind in order to divert the investigation in other directions. Cupido still couldn't help thinking about the little badge.

'Did you see anyone at all during the day around here or in the caves? Did you pass anyone on the path up there?'

'No, nobody. Not a soul. From the caves we did see a vehicle a long way off but no one near us.'

They were calling the lieutenant, and Cupido followed him. For the second time in ten days the stretcher-bearers carried off the dead body of a girl whose neck had been slashed open with a knife. As he watched them at their task, behaving so impassively, the detective thought to himself that it doesn't take much for a man to get used to living with the consequences of violence.

'Either we catch him quickly or there'll be more murders,' said the lieutenant who stood beside him.

'Yes.'

'Once again we're right back at the beginning. And ten to one we won't get a single clue out of this one.'

Nine

It was a few minutes before eight and he was ready to open the metal door of the garage at the Base Depot as he did every morning. He was always the one to do this. The other two duty wardens and the men in charge of the feeding and care of the animals arrived later. They hadn't wanted to live in the houses that the management of the Reserve provided for them and had to travel in from Breda every day, but Molina didn't attribute their habit of arriving late to the time it took to get there, but to the sloth induced by city life. In the country, by contrast, there was an incentive to get up early, as if the multitude of tiny, noisy, busy animal life was offended by idleness, and made every conceivable type of noise to persuade shirkers to get out of their beds.

The Director of the Reserve put in an appearance once or twice a week, and never very early in the morning, not so much because his main offices were in the city but because he was a pale-faced townee little given to roaming through the countryside and he had an irrational fear of any type of insect bite. Now that the fire service with its helicopter usually on call for emergencies had been withdrawn for the winter, the game warden felt himself master of it all, like a minor monarch privileged to reign for six months of every year – the period of high winds and heavy rain, the time when the leaves fall, and all is quiet in the forest. When those October days came round in which he would be alone again he was elated by a feeling of liberty because, although he had no underlings to command, at least there was no one to give him orders that he would have to obey.

But that morning he was more tired than he remembered having been for a long while. He hadn't been able to sleep all night, and even the fact that he had made love to his wife when she was already asleep, ignoring her protests that he was rough and impatient, hadn't helped although sex usually left him relaxed and stress-free. It was only towards dawn, as the first soft light began to filter through the shutters, that he managed to doze off for a few minutes before the peremptory call of the dawn chorus obliged him to get up.

He had been able to cope with the consequences of Gloria's death and hadn't allowed that to interfere with his own interests and activities, or his peace of mind. But the death of this second girl that had occurred a couple of days before, on All Souls' Day, had gone beyond tolerable limits. As he put the key into the lock of the heavy garage door he looked behind him at the forest that fringed the open area; it looked as solid as a wall, and had fallen silent, as if every living creature in it was watching and spying on all his movements. The sliding bolt of the lock was jammed, and in forcing it until he got it to move he gashed his knuckle on a sharp, rusty protrusion on its metal shaft. He cursed quietly because that sort of injury to a joint was a nuisance; it could easily become infected and take a long time to heal. He opened the glovebox of his car where he kept a small first aid kit which consisted of tincture of mercury, distilled water, alcohol, some bandages, lint, sticking plaster, aspirin, and a needle and thread for stitching wounds. It was the basic kit issued to all units working in the Reserve after they had completed a first aid course. He had found it necessary to use sutures on injured deer, but never on a human being. He disinfected the wound with a splash of alcohol, and wrapped a plaster over it to stop the bleeding. As he replaced the first aid box he suddenly recalled another wound, and the blood of another person.

He had seen her descend the difficult path from the caves. Through his powerful binoculars he had observed every one of her movements: the way she brushed the hair back from her face which was wet with perspiration from the effort of walking, the care with which she stepped on loose stones, the slight movement of her breasts inside her sweater whenever she jumped over anything in her way. It was difficult to forget that girl, impossible to resist the temptation to spy on her with the impunity that distance gave – and with the justification of professional duty. After all, that was his job. He was paid to look, to observe, to keep an eye on the behaviour of everyone who penetrated his sector, the Paternoster Forest. He was vaguely conscious that this sort of activity pursued over many years couldn't fail to mark a man in ways that were very different from merely sharpening the skills he needed to do his job. It was the sort of work that could warp a man's character, and on more than one occasion he had indulged himself by prying on people to an extent that went well beyond his official duty and was not far removed from voyeurism, because he had learned that a person can reveal his true nature when he's alone; so he didn't so much check that visitors were observing the regulations of the Reserve as snoop on their more intimate moments – what they got up to when they thought they couldn't be seen. Spying on people for an hour from a long way off told him more than he could have gathered from a full day's conversation. Lying on a rock or leaning against the trunk of a tree, with his binoculars glued to his eyes, in a matter of minutes he was able to deduce the intentions, the fears, or the understanding of the forest and knowledge of the plant and animal life possessed by the person he was observing. Little by little, this habit had led him to be more daring, and sometimes to take considerable risks. There were times when he had seen hunters anxious to bag a specimen and prepared to pay heavily for the privilege, and he had gone ahead without either them or their accompanying warden seeing him in order to frighten off the deer or the bucks from under their very noses, to prevent them achieving an easy kill. This would increase their greed for a trophy which, later, he would satisfy at considerable benefit to himself. On other occasions he had followed groups of hikers with wolf-like stealth, convinced by what he had seen of them that they were going to trespass on those areas of the Reserve that were closed to tourists, and he would wait until they were in no position to deny their intention before challenging them. On yet other occasions, he had spied on pairs of lovers as they searched frantically for a space between the rocks or a hiding place in the bushes, and had watched all the intimate details of their love-making, listening to their gasps and sobs, while remaining just a few metres from their eyes and hands.

From his observation point he had followed Gloria for several minutes as she made her way down. The girl had taken a short cut to avoid the lengthy bends in the path which offered an easier descent, and at the last slope before rejoining the main track, when he was about to return to his four-wheel drive, he saw her stumble and stagger a few steps further and then fall sideways into a hard, dry ditch with such force that she must have hurt herself badly. Without stopping to think, he had run to his vehicle half-hidden under the trees round a bend in the track. It didn't take him more than three minutes to reach her. The girl was wearing linen trousers the legs of which were attached to the upper part by zips at mid-thigh which, when taken off, turned the trousers into a pair of shorts. She was painfully doing so. He braked sharply near her, jumped to the ground and asked: 'What happened to you?' – without thinking whether his words would reveal that he had been secretly watching.

'I fell over and something stuck into my leg,' she had replied, pointing to the side of her thigh but still without being sure whether the wound was serious or insignificant. Before trying to staunch the bleeding he looked around for what had caused it.

Then he spotted the small branch growing on the main stem of a cistus: it was splintered, as sharp as the point of a knife, and covered in blood. Gloria's glance followed his.

'It was that branch,' she confirmed, wincing, as if identifying the cause gave a better measure of the true extent of the wound than any explanation. He had knelt down to look at it more closely, and Gloria removed the red-stained handkerchief which she had pressed against it to stop the flow of blood. A fine stream ran freely down below her knee until it reached her sock which became soaked through. The wound was not more than two or three centimetres long but it was deep: the flesh had parted like a pair of lips. And given how difficult it was to stop the bleeding it must have penetrated a vein. The girl was becoming pale, her face drawn with pain, and he felt a compulsion to close the wound with his fingers, but didn't dare touch the skin around it because it was very swollen. The sight of blood struck a distant chord in his memory and it half-persuaded him to kiss the wound and, with his mouth, to suck out the splinters of wood and the dirt, just as he would have cleaned a poisonous snake bite. When he raised his eyes to hers he saw the confident look she gave him, like that of an obedient little girl who expects the adult to make the pain magically go away.

He stood up, saying: 'It has to be disinfected.' He went back to the car for the first aid kit he was required to carry in the glovebox. He knelt down again, placing it in front of him, quickly opened it, and took out the canister of distilled water and a square metal box from which he took two pieces of lint. He soaked them with water, but before applying them to the wound, and still holding them in his hand, he raised his head and said: 'It won't hurt, it's distilled water – ' as if he were asking permission to touch her before pulling the deep cut apart with the thumb and first finger of his left hand, and before cleaning out the dry dust, a small splinter embedded in the flesh, and the black specks of bark stuck to the sides. Again, he looked up to see her reaction, expecting that this cleansing process and the stinging sensation caused by the drops of disinfectant he had added would make her cry out, but all he saw was the totally docile expression on her face. The girl accepted his attentions without once complaining, trusting in the skill of his strong, dark hands, and the fact that he knew exactly what had to be done. She gave herself over to the expertise of the healing, almost caressing touch of his fingers. For his part, he had detected the slight tremors in her leg, the shudders that ran down the length of her long, supple thigh. *She's like a young deer. As warm and beautiful as a deer*, he thought, as he looked admiringly at the lightly tanned, unblemished skin that had no trace of veining and was covered with a fine down.

'It's clean now,' he said, when he saw that no trace of dirt remained in the wound or on its edges. He raised his head and mistook the tears that started in her eyes for relief. In fact, it was gratitude.

But the blood continued to flow, even if more slowly. While examining the wound he had realized how deep it was, and he knew that he ought to do something more drastic, and also more painful. The sharply pointed branch had pierced a vein or a secondary artery and it was vital to stitch it up to stop the bleeding completely. A sticking plaster would be useless, and the Breda hospital was some way off – at least twenty minutes down a hard, beaten-earth track which would bounce them around most of the way there. He had little experience in sewing up a wound. He had never done it on a human being although he had once watched one of his colleagues sew up a hiker who had been too fond of playing with knives. He had done it about half a dozen times to deer. He knew that technically there was scarcely any difference, that it was essentially a question of the hardness of the skin and the size of the curved needle and the suture he kept in his first aid kit – but much more delicate. The real difference lay in the wounded creature's resistance to pain and the coolness of the surgeon inflicting it. For the first time since he had spied her through his binoculars and seen her fall, he hesitated over the next step he should take. He put his hand into the box until his fingers found the little bag containing everything he needed. But then he stopped, uncertain whether to take it out. The needle would cause pain, pain would lead to protests, and her protests would make it impossible for him to continue. It was futile to attempt it.

I can't do anything to hurt her. I can't possibly hurt her, he said to himself.

He looked up again to see the docile expression which told him she was prepared to accept whatever he might do.

'I can't stop the blood. We have to get you to hospital. I think they'll need to put some stitches in,' he said as he got up from the kneeling position in which he had been all this while. He removed his belt, and used it to make a tourniquet halfway up her thigh, trying to apply just the right degree of pressure on the soft, smooth flesh which lay trustingly before him. He made no move to help her up, but waited until she was ready. Gloria simply leant on his shoulder, and hobbled the few steps to the four-wheel drive.

It took them less than twenty minutes to reach the hospital. He glanced at her frequently during the ride, watching how she fought against the feelings of sickness and dizziness, but fearlessly, and without complaining about the condition of the track. She wouldn't let him stop so that he could relax the tourniquet for a few seconds to let fresh blood flow down through her leg. She did that for herself. More blood streamed from the wound, but it didn't stain the seat because Gloria had placed her anorak underneath her leg.

She's like a young deer. As warm and beautiful as a deer, he repeated.

He was amazed by his own attitude. He felt like an adolescent. It was as if one of the wheels in his interior clock had had its normal functioning dislocated by the proximity of this girl, and had started to rewind, carrying him back to a time in his life before his feelings had become blunted.

After arriving at the accident department he waited outside until she emerged half an hour later. He had been right. They had put in several stitches after giving her a local anaesthetic. They had also given her a tetanus injection. The bandaged wound was no longer visible because she had replaced the detachable legs of her trousers. She limped slightly as she came out and looked around for him.

'Thank you for everything,' she had said, offering him her hand. She was still pale from loss of blood, but even more beautiful than before her accident. He was touched by the friendly contact as she held his hand longer than mere courtesy required.

'Where are you staying?' he asked, because he knew by her accent that this girl wasn't from Breda.

'In the Hotel Europa.'

'I'll take you there.'

The girl got into the car as he held the door open for her like a well-trained and obliging chauffeur.

When they stopped outside the great wrought-iron outer gate in the wall surrounding the hotel he had felt constrained to say: 'In spite of the accident you're very good at mountain trekking. No other woman would dare go all the way up there on her own.'

'Thank you again,' she had replied, gratified by the compliment and as if those words coming from one of the Reserve game wardens meant a lot to her. Then they parted.

His memory retained all the vivid details of that hour for many days. But while he had been hoping for a phone call asking for his name and to let him know her leg was getting better, he had begun to think he deserved something more than just simple words of gratitude. He wondered whether she would remember him, and if she would understand that in her case he had abstained from his invariable practice of insisting on a reward for his services.

Ten

It was nearly ten in the morning when Cupido parked his car on one side of the track, and set out on foot to the scene of the second murder. He guessed that it was two to three kilometres further on, but he would enjoy the walk.

He strode quickly along the earth track which was in poor condition, but was sufficiently clear for tall vehicles and four-wheel drives to get through. The early November sun filtered through the drooping branches of the pines that were interlaced above his head. The branches nearest to the track were white with dust, witnessing to the large number of vehicles that had driven through there during the past two days, whereas those deeper in the forest were still green. Some of the signs that prohibited hunting or the lighting of fires were holed by the bullets of frustrated hunters who had failed to bring down a running deer.

The temperature was pleasant in spite of the advance of autumn, and the clear sky gave no indication that there would be any badly needed rain. The deep and lonely woods on either side were alive with the songs of birds indifferent to the violence and fears that possessed human beings. Anyone who left the path and penetrated into the forest would trample over dry leaves, snail shells, and the corpses of dead insects, to find himself suddenly in another world that existed long before our civilization came into being. Just a few minutes into the depths of the forest, he would enter a virgin, unexplored territory loud with the sounds of animals that had the advantage of being aware of an intruder's presence without being visible to him. How many dead bodies lay buried in the forest, he wondered? How many stolen goods, arms, dead babies and other evidence of past crimes? The forest swallows everything, and hides it; the forest likes dead bodies – as much as the sea abhors them and throws them back on land. Possibly it does so because, every now and then, like an ancient, flesh-eating god, it exacts its tribute of blood, so that it can continue to preserve its solitude and mystery. A death from time to time is the levy that has to be paid so that young boys can go on dreaming that it is a place where monsters hide.

But men know that places that strike fear also contain treasures. When did they discover that fire and the crackle of wood burning in the flames, that became vital for their very existence, lay sleeping in the forest? Men enter or leave it according to whether they are drawn by its riches, or are terrified by it. They flee when they see shadows, but can't live without its bounty.

The forest had also provided the ideal setting for those two murders. As he walked, he recalled two very different theories. When he was in Breda's semi-rural environment he had the impression that the motive for murder was money and property – the fortune Gloria's family would inherit, or the lands Doña Victoria claimed as her own. His experience of Breda made him remember Machiavelli's harsh words: '*A man more quickly forgets the death of his father than the loss of his inheritance.*' On the other hand, while he had been in Madrid, he had ended up believing that the motive for the crimes was passion. These two theories contradicted deeply held beliefs about the causes of murder: that the spilling of blood for sexual reasons is of rural origin, whereas in the big city money is at its root.

He reached the area where the second girl had been murdered, and halted in front of the tape that cordoned it off. A number of officers were still searching for evidence with metal detectors, and they quickly saluted when they recognized him. The tent had already been taken down and removed to the laboratory. Soon, there would be no sign here on the banks of the reservoir that a crime had been committed; soon, the blood that had been spilled so profusely would have disappeared into the soil, washed away by the dew, or consumed by insects and animals. Soon, the exact spot would be forgotten, but the curse of the crime would spread to contaminate the whole of the Paternoster Forest.

He was baffled by this second death, and found it impossible to believe that someone from down there in the ancient town that everybody was now beginning to call a city could possibly be the murderer; that among the 15–20,000 adults between the ages of eighteen and sixty, there was one guilty person whom he had passed and chatted to dozens of times in the street, who got up every morning to go to work – although both girls had been killed on days when nobody worked – who went to bed each night confident that he or she would escape suspicion, although their sleep might be haunted by nightmares. Which way should he turn now if he was to continue the investigation? He had no idea. He had already taken all the steps that had occurred to him so far without getting anywhere. He had spoken to the lieutenant the previous afternoon, and this time they had been quick to check on the whereabouts of all those who had alibis for Gloria's murder for that Saturday ten days before, as well as those who didn't, and all of them had been found to be with another person. It was impossible for any one of them to have committed the two murders. Should he speak to Anglada and tell him he was throwing up the case because he felt it wasn't right to go on claiming his per diem charge when he hadn't made any progress to justify it? He decided to wait another couple of days until they had the autopsy results. If at that point they had no useful clues he would draw up a final account and send it to him. After all, he was like a day labourer – better paid, of course – but a day labourer nonetheless, who couldn't go on picking up wages if he spent the whole of each day sitting in the shade of a fig tree.

He decided to go back home. In his letterbox, among an enormous, and useless, mass of advertising material he found a single sheet of paper folded in half. He opened it and read the handwritten note: '*I've got something important for you. Come and see me. I'm in the Kasino.*' He closed the box, and without going up to his apartment, set off immediately for the Casino.

Alkalino was involved in one of his interminable games of dominoes, but as soon as he noticed Cupido he gave up his place, and came over to the bar.

'Two brandies,' he said to the barman.

They waited until the barman had gone away before beginning to talk.

'I believe it's an important fact. You'll be able to tell whether it's any use.'

'What is it?.'

'There was somebody else in the Reserve when the first girl was killed – a hunter who heard a shot. And he wasn't far from the place where she was murdered,' he whispered, in a conspiratorial tone, well aware of the significance of what he was saying.

'What type of shot?'

'A rifle or a shotgun.'

'Who told you?'

'No, I'm not going to tell you that. But I can assure you he's not lying. He's a comrade in the Party,' he said, as if there were only one party, and Cupido likewise had to be a member of it. 'My telling you this is conditional on not mentioning names. He doesn't want to make life difficult for himself, and with good reason: he hasn't got a permit to hunt so he does a bit of poaching on the quiet, and he was out there that morning.'

'How d'you know he isn't involved in the murder?'

'If he was can you imagine he'd have told me he was prowling around less than a kilometre from where she was killed?'

'No, he wouldn't have told you,' Cupido agreed. 'But why hasn't he talked about it before?'

'He's scared,' came the prompt reply. 'He got scared when he heard they'd killed the second girl. It's his small contribution to help clear it up. Everybody believes that if the murderer isn't caught soon there'll be more murders.' He was repeating Gallardo's own words.

'Why are you telling me and not the lieutenant?'

Alkalino shook his head as if he was pained by Cupido's lack of trust. He raised his glass, and with a quick flick of his wrist half drained it.

'Don't be so suspicious, Cupido. This character's already received one heavy fine for poaching some time ago. If he told his story to the Civil Guard, and even assuming they believed it, you know quite well that they wouldn't have any doubt about his reasons for being in the forest that morning. Besides which, confiding in you proves he hadn't anything to do with those two murders because, if he had, the last thing he would do would be to collaborate. Don't look for more complications than there are. He didn't find it easy to talk to me, and I'd put my hand in the fire that what he says is true.'

'All right,' Cupido agreed.

There was no reason why anyone should invent hearing a shot fired that morning, so accepting that, there were two possibilities: either it had been fired by the person who had killed Gloria, or there had been yet another person not far away. He rejected the first hypothesis – that it was the murderer who had fired – because if he had had a gun it would have been absurd to risk using a knife. That meant he had to find a fourth person, because if one had been in the vicinity, it was very probable he knew something that would incriminate somebody.

'Have you made much progress so far?' asked Alkalino.

'No. I haven't got anything definite at all. But I don't rule out the possibility that whoever killed the first girl knew her well.'

Alkalino looked at him closely; his gaze was penetrating.

'A few months ago,' he said, with one of those sudden changes of subject that were frequent in his conversation, 'I came across a little book that someone had thrown in a rubbish bin in the park, probably because they got bored with the heavy style and the fact that it hadn't got any dialogue. I picked it up out of curiosity and began to read it. I didn't understand everything it said, and yet I couldn't put it down. It dealt with a strange character who lived in the deepest part of a forest and killed with a single shot anybody who dared go beyond certain invisible boundaries he had marked out. I still remember it as if I'd read it only yesterday. It was weird. And I still remember the name of this one-man vigilante. Numa. His name was Numa. I couldn't get it out of my head, and I re-read the book trying to understand why he did it, who paid him to kill, and who he worked for. It came back to mind the other night after the second girl was killed. There's a Numa in every forest, a fanatic guardian who has just one mission: to make sure that the wild woods stay wild.'

There was a short silence while he drained his glass. Then he continued, almost solemnly:

'You're barking up the wrong tree, Cupido. The guardian of the woods is now on the alert. There'll be more murders.'

'So you don't believe any longer that Doña Victoria is behind all this?'

'No, not now. I saw her the other day as she was arriving from Madrid, and she was hardly able to get out of the car. Her ankles were very swollen, she was wearing heavy, black shoes, and she had to step out carefully before trying to walk. The old lady's aged a lot recently. I can't imagine her plotting to murder anyone.'

Cupido smiled. He was used to these abrupt changes of opinion. He was always grateful for the factual information Alkalino gave him, but never for his conjectures.

'I don't know how to thank you,' he said.

'You could always offer me another brandy. And one day I'll make sure I get the rest of what you owe me!'

He patted Cupido on the back and moved off with a full glass to continue his match with the players who had been calling on him to rejoin them.

As the detective left the Casino he thought about the difficulty he was in as far as this new piece of information was concerned. Up to now he had played fair with the lieutenant and hadn't concealed anything. But he had given Alkalino his word that he wouldn't mention this new disclosure.

'You can't come through here,' said Molina, approaching the window of Cupido's car.

The warden had stopped his four-wheel drive in the middle of the track to prevent him going any further. But that was just what the detective had hoped for – a chance to talk to him without his wife present because she would have listened to everything in silence but with a scared look on her face as if she was pleading with him to go away and leave them in peace. This was why he had entered a prohibited part of the Reserve without permission, well away from the Base Depot. It had also enabled him to check that it took Molina less than ten minutes to detect an intruder trespassing on the sector for which he was responsible.

'I know,' he replied. 'But I've come to talk to you.'

The warden stepped back so that Cupido could open the door and get out of his car. He noticed the plaster on the index finger of Molina's right hand.

'I thought you'd finished with your questions,' he said, his voice betraying a slight uneasiness.

'I thought so as well. But I forgot to ask you the last one.'

Molina put his head on one side. Uneasiness had given way to curiosity.

'That Saturday morning – didn't you hear a shot?'

'What shot?' he asked, clearly taken aback.

'A shot from a rifle or a shotgun, very near where the girl was killed.'

'No, I didn't hear any shot. I've already told you I wasn't here at the time. I was driving round another part of the Reserve,' he explained, nodding at the four-by-four that was blocking the track. 'If there was a shot, I was a long way off, and the noise of the engine would have prevented me hearing it,' he added.

Cupido kicked at the earth with the toe of his shoe before continuing.

'The report of a rifle shot must carry a long way in the Reserve. I thought perhaps you might have heard something and forgotten it.'

'I've got a good memory,' Molina replied, with an ironic smile.

'Tell me how you got to know Gloria,' the detective said, as if Molina's words led logically to that subject.

Molina looked at him with a bored expression, wondering whether to respond. He had already given a brief answer to that question and he wasn't under any obligation to repeat it, although he knew that the detective was working alongside the lieutenant. However, after reflecting for a moment, he said:

'It was just over a year ago, early last autumn. At any rate it was before 15 October which is when the helicopters withdraw for the winter. She'd come from Madrid with her boyfriend, the one you're working for now. They said they'd come out here from Breda in the morning in fine weather, but it became cloudy in the afternoon and the temperature dropped several degrees. We get those sudden changes here in the autumn. They felt cold and the boyfriend had the bright idea of lighting a fire to warm them up, although there are signs everywhere on the path saying it's illegal. We spotted the smoke immediately from one of the watchtowers and sounded the alarm. It wasn't far away. We went there by car while the helicopter was being got ready. Even so we were nearly too late. October's a tricky month. If the rains haven't started, everything's so hot and dry that just one spark can cause a catastrophe. Worse if there's a wind as well because that can be very strong. When we got there they were already trying to put the fire out. They'd lit it in a clearing, but it had caught some of the brushwood, and they couldn't control it. We smothered it immediately and the helicopter wasn't needed. The head of the emergency service was furious and wanted to lodge a formal charge because it had been so stupid. It turned out that it was the boyfriend who'd insisted on the fire although the girl had tried to dissuade him. Then Doña Victoria and her lawyer turned up because they'd heard the helicopter and seen the smoke. At that time they were still going in and out of the Reserve as if it was theirs because the final judgement hadn't yet come through, and nobody dared stop them. Surrounded by so many people the girl must have felt cornered, and I can still remember how she looked at us, obviously very sorry for what they'd done. We all left quietly, one by one. Just the way she looked at us was disarming. Those up in the helicopter continued hovering in order to see how it would end. And Doña Victoria turned on us, complaining that we were incompetent and a risk to the Reserve!'

'So Doña Victoria and the lawyer also knew her?' asked Cupido. Those two had denied doing so.

'Well, they certainly got to know her that afternoon. Doña Victoria and the lawyer stayed there after we went off with the boyfriend who had to pay a small fine in the office. Doña Victoria always used to ask for the identity of any person who entered the Reserve, as if she was the real authority. But even the old lady who's always suspicious of everybody must have been taken with the girl. I drove back there half an hour later to check that everything was in order, and I could see them still talking.'

'Did you see her again after that?' asked Cupido.

'I've already told you. I saw her around from time to time. Recently she'd been coming through more often. She'd obtained a permit from the management of the Reserve that entitled her to go into the prohibited area to paint animals and the scenery. On one occasion I had the job of guiding her to a particular site she was looking for.'

Molina's manner had changed in the course of the conversation, as if he were anxious to win the other man's trust.

'I think you're wasting your time with all this,' he said suddenly, in the friendly tone of someone giving advice. 'D'you want my opinion?'

'Yes,' said Cupido. It was the second time that day that he was being offered a theory.

'That girl should never have come on her own into the Reserve. Neither her nor the other one who was killed nor any other woman. The forest isn't a place for women on their own. The forest wasn't made for those who just want to *look* at it; the forest belongs to those of us who use it.'

The detective knew that Molina wasn't the only person who thought the same way. The twisted idea that it's the victims who are really the guilty ones is still widespread, as if they provoke crime, as if a girl who's raped is guilty because she wears a miniskirt, or every mountaineer who gets buried in the snow deserves the avalanche that falls on top of him.

'But you knew she was familiar with the whole Reserve.'

'I've already said it isn't a matter of being familiar with the territory; it's a matter of sex. D'you imagine a man would have been murdered?'

'Not in that way at least,' he replied. He had no idea where these remarks might lead but felt sure that something of interest might come out of them.

'Obviously not! No man would dare attack another one with a knife. The ground in the forest is littered with sticks and stones. It's only a woman who's likely to be attacked like that,' he concluded. He sounded almost irritated, and took a few steps back towards his vehicle, but then stopped, and went on as if it was a question he had given a lot of thought to: 'Any woman who walks alone in a forest is a potential victim; and any man who spies on her is a potential murderer.'

That made Cupido realize that he wasn't going to get much more out of him. The warden was the sort of individual who has more faith in actions than in words, although, in spite of that, he had talked freely throughout the interview. He wondered whether in what he had said, and in particular in his use of generalities without saying anything definite, he wasn't concealing something he knew. He had the feeling that his final words were coded in a way he was unable to understand. He could follow the meaning of every one of his sentences taken separately, but he suspected there was some sort of hidden warning in them that escaped him. Not wanting to miss an opportunity, he decided to ask him one last question:

'Where were you on Wednesday?'

Molina's face darkened. He was clearly irritated by this question coming after he had been so open with the detective.

'That's one time I couldn't possibly have heard a shot! I had the afternoon off and spent it in Breda. I've got at least twenty witnesses who can vouch for me,' he replied curtly, almost resentfully. 'Hasn't the lieutenant told you?'

Cupido knew immediately that he'd made a mistake. Molina was not as tractable as he had expected. After that last question with its veiled threat he shut up, turned his back on him, and set off in his four-wheel drive, raising a cloud of dust in his wake.

Cupido drove back, angry with himself for having been too precipitate. He had never been an impulsive interrogator, but on this occasion he had been unable to control his impatience.

This had rarely happened, because he always bore in mind Darwin's maxim, and he applied it to his own work as a useful antidote to impetuosity: '*To reason while observing is fatal; but how invaluable it is to do so later*.' When all is said and done, the word that characterizes two such different professions is the same: investigation. He had tried to go too fast, and Molina had drawn back like an angry snake, because he hadn't allowed enough time to gain his confidence.

He swore out loud as he realized it was too late to eat anywhere. He was very hungry but they wouldn't serve him in any restaurant, so on arriving in town he bought a couple of sandwiches and a bottle of Ribera del Duero and went back home. He didn't like drinking on his own, but by the time he finished the sandwiches he had already emptied his fourth glass. The craving for a cigarette returned so powerfully and unexpectedly that before he knew what he was doing he had searched through all the pockets of his clothes hanging in the wardrobe.

He felt the need to be on the move, to go out, and he decided to go and see Doña Victoria, even at the risk of disturbing her afternoon rest.

The maid didn't keep him waiting long. She took him into the drawing-room that he already knew, with the same light filtering through the net curtains, and the same odour of antique plate, and that atmosphere of sombre half-light typical of grand old houses where there isn't even a bowl of flowers. This time he had the impression that the room was even more cluttered with furniture and ornaments than on his previous visit. He wondered how many of the objects had been retrieved from the houses sunk beneath the water of the reservoir. He had heard it said that the beautiful wrought iron window grills had come from elsewhere, that when the El Paternoster village had been cut off by the slowly rising water as the dam filled up, somebody had made a number of expeditions in a boat and had looted various architectural features, decorative objects and traditional wrought ironwork that their owners hadn't been able to take away, or whose potential value they hadn't foreseen. Maybe this was what Doña Victoria had been referring to when she mentioned the trips his father had made for her in his old DAF lorry. Those trips were now beginning to have an air of piracy about them.

Without getting up, Doña Victoria offered him her delicate hand, mottled with age, and streaked with prominent blue veins. As he took it Cupido noticed the same oval gold watch on her wrist, the same familiar bracelet, her wedding ring, the same rather showy rings on her fingers that possibly she could no longer remove because of the swollen joints. Her looks had deteriorated, as if she had grown older in the week that had passed since their last interview.

After shaking hands he went over to the lawyer who was waiting near the window. The detective couldn't help looking at his lip: the cold sore had now developed a brown crust that made it awkward for him to talk. Exposito didn't wait for a sign from Doña Victoria before going to the sideboard and pouring out two glasses of port and a brandy.

'I knew you'd come to see us again,' said the old lady. 'When that other girl was killed I knew you'd come again to talk to us. You can't find any more obvious suspects.'

Cupido was pleased that it was she who began to speak as frankly as she had at his first visit. But this time there was sadness in her voice as if she was resigned to prolonging a battle she didn't want but which, once engaged on, she wouldn't give up until she won.

After serving the drinks, Exposito went to stand behind her chair, observing Cupido from between his swollen eye-lids and through powerful glasses, his hands resting on the high back of the chair as if it were an invalid's wheelchair, or like a bodyguard, in a pose that was more protective than the one he had assumed on Cupido's last visit.

'But you are largely to blame for that suspicion,' retorted the detective. 'The lieutenant tells me that on his second visit you refused to answer his questions unless he had a court order, and that he met with nothing but opposition from you.'

'The lieutenant's career record,' responded Exposito, with a disdainful look, 'still bears the consequences of a previous excess of zeal. A solution to this case would suit him down to the ground because it would help to improve his reputation. But he won't succeed in doing so if he persists in basing his rehabilitation on us!'

Doña Victoria raised her left hand to her adopted son, as if pleading with him for calm.

'What did he expect?' she asked. 'That we should be cooperating with him when he's been one of the most bitter opponents of our demands for restitution of the land that belongs to me? Do you know what his first question was when he came through that door yesterday?'

'No.'

'He asked him,' she said, pointing up to Exposito, 'where he'd been on that Wednesday afternoon at the time when the other girl was killed. He would have arrested him if I'd been the only person able to provide him with an alibi.'

The detective had already heard about this from the lieutenant: there were several witnesses who confirmed having seen him at the time.

'But I don't think you've come to ask us about that,' she added. 'I told you the last time you were here that you wouldn't be welcome if you simply asked the same questions as the lieutenant.'

'All right. But there's something else.'

'Tell me what that is,' she ordered.

The detective could see that both of them were now on their guard, unable to hide the tension caused by the long days during which they had been regarded as suspects. Exposito's knuckles were white as he gripped the top of the old lady's chair.

'The game warden told you…' Doña Victoria broke in.

'Yes.'

'We didn't think he'd remember. It was more than a year ago.'

'It seems that everybody finds it difficult to forget anything relating to that girl. They all remember perfectly the times when they've been with her,' said Cupido.

Doña Victoria took a sip of port and savoured it like a cat before swallowing and moistening the dry lips that had been soft and smooth when she had bestowed her last kiss on a little boy's dead body.

'Yes, she was very special. I also remember her well,' she said, raising her eyes as if she was looking beyond the net curtains. 'She isn't easy to forget. On the day of that little fire any other person would have become hysterical or tearful in the hope of eliciting sympathy and avoiding the heavy fine that their foolishness deserved. But that girl managed to convince us that she was genuinely repentant, if I may use that word. She had a knack for asking to be forgiven solely by the way she used her eyes, and without losing one jot of her dignity. More than that, she conveyed the absolute certainty that it would never happen again.'

All three remained silent for several moments, as if each one were mulling over the picture the old lady had conjured up.

'Besides which', she added in a low voice, 'she was very beautiful. The sort of woman for whom a man would be capable of committing any sort of stupidity.'

Cupido raised his eyes to Exposito, hoping to hear a man's version of the story. But the lawyer obstinately kept his head down, his myopic eyes fixed on the old lady's hair that was grey and fine like cobweb, with a straight parting that divided it into two equal halves, and done with an elegance that removed any suggestion of severity.

'Why did you lie? Why did you hide the fact that you knew her?' he insisted.

'To have mentioned it would have occasioned a whole lot of awkward questions from the lieutenant. And after telling him we didn't know her, we couldn't very well say the opposite to you,' replied Exposito. 'In any case, it wasn't an important matter. How important could it possibly be that we'd had a brief conversation with her one day?'

'None at all, if that's all there is to it.'

'Right. That's all there is to it.'

'Did you ever see her again after that day?'

'No, never. The next we heard of her was that she'd been murdered. We recognized her face when we saw her photograph in the papers.'

'I told you it was difficult to forget her,' repeated Doña Victoria.

Their habit of talking together, their identical stories – like a married couple acting in complete harmony – again suggested that they had agreed on the replies they would make to these questions. The detective had the impression that there was nothing more to be gained from the interview, that it was leading nowhere, as if they had anticipated his surmises and had prepared appropriate replies to his questions. He stood up and approached them to take his leave. Doña Victoria again offered him her hand, the palm facing down, in the old-fashioned way old ladies used in the past.

'You can come back any time you want to ask us anything,' said Exposito, with an irony that the detective couldn't fail to notice.

'Thank you very much indeed,' he replied, keeping up the bluff.

Eleven

Possibly not even the detective knew how right he had been when he said of Gloria: '*They all remember perfectly the times when they've been with her.*' He too remembered vividly every one of her gestures, every one of her words, every one of her glances... On the first occasion she had been the victim of an awkward situation; but on the second, she had been the angry and disapproving one. When the two of them had arrived on the afternoon of the fire, Gloria had been surrounded by a gang of Reserve workers who were reprimanding her and her boyfriend for having lit it on a windy day and in a dangerously vulnerable area. He had held back, refusing to take part in the chorus of recrimination which, a few minutes later, and once she had apologized for their stupidity, had melted away like a ripple on a calm lake. As he stood there he had wondered what would have happened if it had been he who had started the blaze. He had known for a long time that there was something about him – his physical appearance, his manner, his quick tongue, and his manifest air of dejection typical of individuals who have ceased to believe they will ever know happiness. It was something he was unable to overcome because he didn't know what it was that invariably put him at odds with those he had dealings with. His conviction that the rest of the human race was predisposed to be hostile towards him made him defensive. '*They wouldn't have forgiven me if they knew I'd done something like that, and they would probably have attacked me,*' he thought, recalling the four-wheel drive belonging to the Reserve authorities that he had set on fire one night with the help of Gabino. Watching how Gloria succeeded in deflecting the accusations of the wardens and the men from the emergency service who couldn't take their eyes off her, his feelings towards her were completely irrational, combining admiration with hate. Admiration, because everything about her – her beauty, her manner, the obvious love of life that radiated from her – seemed to predispose *her* to happiness; hate, because she personified everything that he lacked.

As always happened after spending days in negotiations and intensive discussions with other people, he had felt particularly lonely that Thursday when he returned from Madrid to the big Breda house. Too many people, too much time dealing with clients made him tired and tense, and he needed several days to shake it off. After the detective left, he had shut himself in his room, repeating his words: '*They all remember perfectly the times when they've been with her.*'

A week after that first encounter, he had still been unable to forget her. His previous experience of women had been limited to brief visits to prostitutes who worked from discreet apartments, because the idea of entering a brothel where he would have to wait his turn rubbing shoulders with other men who were priapic with desire and flushed with drink, filled him with horror. He would come away sad, unsatisfied, and feeling he'd wasted his money because he had let the woman take the lead and hadn't dared ask for what he yearned for: it was always too quick, professional and impersonal. He couldn't even stop them using dirty words when they were down on their knees, and he had never once managed to exact a modicum of kindness, unhurried attention, or tenderness. The encounter with Gloria, however, had given a new dimension to what he imagined a man might expect from a woman. On one hand he desperately wanted to see her again but, on the other, he was in no hurry to revive the feeling of wretchedness he knew this would cause. Before falling asleep at night he would dwell on that contradiction. He felt he could achieve so much: he had a prodigious memory and an extraordinary ability to organize his time; he was able to apply his exceptional intelligence to any branch of knowledge; and he was capable of an intensity of concentration that would have exhausted a chess master. However, he also knew that there was no woman to whom he could offer his potential. Apart, of course, from his commitment to Doña Victoria in her struggle to regain possession of the lands she had lost. There were times when he imagined himself as a cyclist with sturdy legs, powerful lungs, and a heart as strong as a horse's, but lost at a lonely crossroads in the mountains because there was no one around to show him the way and he didn't have a route map to indicate the road he should follow between the misty slopes on one side and the ravines on the other. There were nights, once he had managed to get to sleep, when he dreamed he had fallen into a deep, black well, was several metres below the surface of the water, and still hadn't touched bottom. He would wave his arms desperately in an effort to rise up, although he was fully aware that he would only be able to get out if first he sank down as far as the mud where he would find something – a ladder, a rope with a grappling iron – that would make it possible to climb back up to the top.

He had not succeeded in seeing Gloria again until two months later, towards the end of the previous autumn. At that time the struggle with the Administration had reached a peak of ferocity as they waited for the final court judgment and the confusion was so great that not one of the wardens dared stop them whenever they resolved to walk through the disputed territory, always accompanied by Gabino, the old and faithful tenant farmer who had never had any mistress other than Doña Victoria, a man approaching sixty, a skilful poacher and an expert on the rugged landscape of the Paternoster Forest since before the construction of the dam. He was still incredibly strong, and was capable of swallowing a whole loaf and a kilo of cold meat in an afternoon snack, and then digesting it like a boa constrictor. He had one indelible memory of Gabino: it had happened when he was a boy and the farmer was taking him for a ride on his donkey. They were passing a group of boys who wanted to open a garden gate but didn't dare because of a wasps' nest on its post; ignoring the risk, he had squashed it flat with his hand without incurring a single sting because the wasps couldn't penetrate skin that was calloused from thirty years of brute labour.

They had heard that that weekend, the last of the hunting season, the French ex-president, Giscard d'Estaing – a man who was very keen on game hunting – would be in the Reserve, attracted by stories of the quality of the trophies obtained there in recent years. Doña Victoria had decided that they shouldn't pass up the opportunity to heighten the tension and gain an advantage, faced with the uncertain outcome of the final negotiations. She had thought up a surprise that would shatter the protocol surrounding this important political figure, and cause a great commotion.

The night before Giscard d'Estaing was due to be there, Gabino and he had entered the Reserve a little after midnight – the hour when wolves come out in search of prey. The old man had led him along an ancient track forgotten since the flooding of the rich lowlands. It was possible to get along it at that time because the water level was still quite low. As they had foreseen, a huge stag had fallen into one of the snares the farmer had set the night before in a number of places he had chosen, based on his knowledge of the animals' favourite haunts and sleeping places. The stag lay on the ground, and made no effort to get up as they approached. Their first thought was that it was exhausted after a whole day trying to struggle free, but they quickly saw that it had twisted and turned so violently in the wire that it had broken one of its legs which was now bent double under its body. By the light of their torches they could see where the hair had been torn out of its rough pelt by the cable, leaving sores that were already attracting the attention of the first ants. He had felt a slight sense of guilt – those injuries were unnecessary. He looked at Gabino who was working away coolly, stopping from time to time to listen to the silence around them, untroubled by the dark. He wondered whether the old man had any opinion of his own about what they were doing, or whether he was simply obeying orders, restricting himself to these without questioning them. He always seemed the same, one day after another, as if he were made of stone. Nothing seemed to touch him. He was unfeeling, and as indifferent to the night as he was to the day. He, on the other hand, brought up from childhood to fight his battles in a welter of papers and documents, could feel his heart beating rapidly. He had never before been so deep into that part of the forest so late at night, surrounded by millions of animals, many of them hungry and poisonous. Even so, he wasn't frightened, and he persuaded himself that even if Gabino hadn't been with him he could have walked through there the whole night without feeling fear.

Before releasing the stag from the snare they lashed its legs together. Gabino then knotted a rope round the base of its antlers, and pulling its head to one side tied the other end to its tail so that it couldn't defend itself by butting them. The animal was transformed into a shapeless heap of hair and living flesh, with its antlers sticking out on top. They backed the Land Rover close to it, and between the two of them manhandled it inside.

They had already decided on the spot where they were to carry out the next part of the plan – very near the Base Depot where the hunters couldn't fail to see it in the morning as they went up the path to the hides. But the sound of dogs barking in the distance as they approached made them stop and go back to where they would run less risk. The imminent arrival of the

French politician in the Reserve had led to additional security measures being taken the day before, so caution persuaded them to go back a couple of kilometres from the place they had originally chosen.

The old man hadn't wanted to stay around much longer, and as soon as he thought they were safe, he stopped in a clump of holm oaks; he didn't want to use a torch when they got out of the car, his pupils having by then become accustomed to the dark, and the waxing moon gave enough light to help them in their task.

They lowered the stag to the ground and dragged it a few metres until it lay beneath a stout oak which had had some of its lower branches removed and stood open, like a candelabra. Gabino now began to work rapidly, without letting him intervene, as if this final part of the task required a decisiveness and cruelty that he didn't possess. Gabino threw a rope over a thick branch of the tree, and bound it round the animal's neck while he made him grasp the other end. He already knew what they were going to do, but now he knew how they were going to do it. The stag, unable to move, gazed up at them from the ground, its head twisted violently round by being tied to its tail, its eyes bulging with the stark fear that is common to all mammals. He saw the old man extract from a pocket of his trousers one of those knives with a wooden handle and a curved blade that are common among the country people of the region, and he heard the click as it opened. He also caught the words: 'Pull hard!' – but it wasn't until they had been repeated that he understood that they referred to him. He gave a strong tug on the rope but only managed to raise the stag's head. The pressure on its neck forced its tongue out of the animal's mouth. The rope didn't run easily over the branch because the rough bark made it a poor pulley. He tried again until he felt the palms of his hands burning as they were rasped by the coarse rope, but even so he was unable to raise it off the ground. The old man turned his head, and he imagined him looking at him, although it was impossible to tell in the dark, particularly as the old man's eyes were screwed up from years of squinting in the sun.

'I'll raise it. You'll have to do the cut,' he said, handing him the knife, with its blade open. Gabino hauled on the rope with brief, powerful tugs, and little by little the stag was hoisted into the air. It would have suffocated if it had been suspended only by the neck, but he had lashed the rope in such a way that it was also tied to the other rope attaching its antlers to its tail. In that way, its weight was distributed equally. He had decided that it shouldn't die by asphyxiation, but by hanging, in order to emphasize the human and ritualistic aspect of the killing. He understood then what he had to do without the old man having to give him any more explanations. He looked at the knife in his hand, its blade gleaming in the thin light of the moon as if it was made of silver. The stag, once it was well off the ground, struggled for a while, trying to escape, but this only served to tighten the pressure of the rope on its neck, so it stopped moving. Its head was facing down, and as it stared at them he couldn't help looking at the animal's eyes that were filled with terror.

'Now!' He heard the voice behind him. 'You've got to cut off its tail with one clean cut.'

He understood perfectly what would happen: when he cut the tail off, all the weight of the body would hang from the head, and the vertebrae in the neck would snap apart, breaking the spinal cord. It would be a quick and messy death, as the animal voided every bodily secretion. He wondered whether the animal guessed this, if its look of horror derived from its knowledge of what it could expect from human beings once it had fallen into the wire snare. He also wondered how many other deer or dogs the old man had killed to make him so expert in the process by which the operation had to be carried out. He raised his left hand and caught hold of the tail at the place where it was tied to the rope that supported half the animal's weight. His fingers felt something damp and sticky: the animal had defecated. *Just like a human being. It knows it's going to die*, he thought. It was more than an hour since they had, very cautiously, left the big house by the back door. He had been prepared, as always, to help in every way necessary, but had never imagined that in just seventy minutes he would find himself with one of those terrible, very sharp country knives in one hand, and the living flesh that he was about to slash through in the other, in order to kill a magnificent but helpless and terrified animal. His brief experience in earlier acts of sabotage had been confined to inanimate objects – setting fire to an official vehicle, or cutting through long sections of wire fencing. It was the first time he would kill something alive and breathing. This was work that had previously been entrusted to the old man.

'Nearer its arse.' Again he heard the voice behind him, and this time it was hard and decisive.

Obediently, he lowered the knife towards the base of the tail. He could feel the taut, warm flesh and the straining muscles and tendons, and he rested the blade on the skin, one centimetre from his hand, near his thumb.

'Cut – and then jump back as quick as you can so that it doesn't hit you as it drops,' he heard.

He took a deep breath, gathered all his strength, and waited for final instructions. But the old man, still behind him, didn't say another word. He was waiting to see blood. For a moment he thought he would insist on their changing places so that he would be the one to hold the rope now that the stag had been hoisted, but he could find no reason to refuse. He pressed the curved blade down gently until he found that it sliced through the first bristles with the ease of a barber's razor. Then, suddenly, he pressed down with all his strength as he drew the blade towards him, from its handle to its point. The tail was cleanly cut, and as he threw himself back the stag gave a violent shudder and remained suspended by its head. In this position, its eyes started out of their sockets, it gave several convulsions before finally hanging limp. He felt something damp and warm on his tightly closed lips, and before he knew what he was doing, licked them, until he realized it was the animal's sticky blood. He spat it out, and looked up at the gently swaying body. Gabino made no comment, not even of approval. He simply raised the body higher, and lashed the rope round the trunk of the oak so that it would stay there hanging high: a clear threat to anyone who saw it.

They returned as cautiously as they had come. He felt shaky and agitated like an adolescent, but at the same time proud that he had passed this test – killing a live animal in cold blood. Other boys of his age from his old village would have done the same thing fifteen years before. In a way, using that knife had seemed like a baptism, and the blood on his lips a communion.

Doña Victoria had given the maid the weekend off, and she was waiting impatiently in the house, unable to sleep, sitting in her high-backed armchair, on the alert for the sound of the Land Rover's engine which she could pick out from a hundred other car engines. Although this wasn't the first time he had taken part in other nocturnal activities that differed so greatly from his normal professional work, on this occasion the presence of the French politician made it especially dangerous. She had felt anxious and rather fearful as he set off.

When he re-entered the drawing-room which was lit only from the street outside, his boots covered in dust, and with small bloodstains on his shirtsleeves and around his mouth, she made him stand in front of her, and looked at him as if he was a son returning home after a long absence. Then she made him sit down next to her in the semi-darkness, and describe every detail, step by step. At last they went up to their own rooms to wait for the consequences that this venture would have, just a few hours later. Whatever the scandal, whatever the confusion it caused, anything would be preferable to the atmosphere of normality that the Administration was at pains to impose in the Paternoster Forest, as if they already owned it, and without waiting for the verdict of the High Court. The old lady and her adopted son had lost many battles, but not the war, and they clung to the hope of victory like a country on the verge of collapse that still has confidence in the deadly power of a secret weapon, the introduction of which is imminent and will change the whole course of the struggle.

What they didn't expect was what actually happened early the next morning when they made their way to the Base Depot with the excuse of having to hand in certain documents but in reality because they wanted to be present when the discovery of the stag was made, and to ensure that the authorities wouldn't be able to hush it up. Contrary to what they had foreseen, it was neither a warden nor a hunter who had come across it twisting slowly on the end of the rope. It was Gloria, who had a permit allowing her to go freely through the closed areas of the forest to paint her pictures. As soon as she saw it she had run back to the Base Depot to inform the wardens of her discovery. Doña Victoria and he were already waiting there to hear the news, but from a very different emissary. Gloria returned to the clump of holm oaks with the wardens in their vehicle, and they followed behind to the place which now seemed to him quite unlike what he had seen of it in the darkness of the night. They all stood stock-still, shocked by the spectacle of the carcass. A dog belonging to the wardens that had raced up behind them began to lap up the semen that the stag had ejaculated. Gloria asked them to take it down because she couldn't bear the sight, but Doña Victoria prevented them from doing so because she wanted the event to receive maximum publicity.

'Don't be in such a hurry, young lady. That stag isn't going to come back to life just by taking it down,' she said.

Gloria stared at them. Her look was so deeply disapproving that his cheeks burned with shame. He knew that he had blushed like a naughty schoolboy being chastised for cruelty to a bird, but she didn't notice because she quickly turned her back on them to express her contempt. His throat was parched, and he hesitated for several moments before obeying Doña Victoria's order to drive into town to look for a photographer.

On top of the painful death of the stag, on top of his feelings of shame, there was the futility of the whole episode: the French politician was kept well away from it, and news of this act of brutality did not become widespread.

When he went to bed that night, unable to sleep in spite of exhaustion, he began for the first time to have doubts about their strategy.

Twelve

He turned on the tap and stepped under the shower as soon as the warm water began to come through, letting it stream down over his head. He stood still for a few moments before picking up the gel and the shampoo to wash away the dirt that had stuck to his body while working out in the field, as he now did every evening, in the way snakes shed their skins in the spring. A thorough daily wash was something else he had learned from Gloria on one of those afternoons when he had helped carry her easel to one of the deeper inlets of the reservoir where the warden Molina had told her that bucks and does came down to drink in the early evening. For an hour he had watched her block in the main shapes on her canvas, carefully suggesting the outlines and areas of the water, the land, and the sky, leaving blank spaces until she could see the animals that would occupy them. They would only be visible for a few minutes on the other side of the little bay, and Gloria would have to fix the image of each animal in her mind so that she could break it down into its fundamental elements, and then reassemble it on the canvas in the same way that the first inhabitants of the region had drawn them on the walls of their caves. He had watched her in silence, overcome by her beauty as she sat silhouetted against the background of the reservoir and the little islands that had appeared in it now that the water level was so low. He was desperately in love with her – the hands that could paint with a skill he would never possess, the unruly wisps of hair at the back of her neck that had escaped from the band holding the untidy pony-tail high on her head, the soft curve of her hips that her loose, light trousers hinted at, her smile when she turned towards him that expressed warmth and gratitude for his help, always without a word being spoken because they didn't want the slightest sound to break the silence that was essential if the animals were to venture near them. However, whether it was because the deer had caught their scent, or because they hadn't had the patience of hunters who remain motionless in their hides, or for some quite different reason, the deer didn't put in an appearance that afternoon.

If it had been possible, he would have gone to look for them and drive them out from their hiding places towards the spot where Gloria was hoping to see them – anything that would make her take notice of him, her young cousin, whom she must have regarded with sympathy and compassion given his distressing poverty, his morose father, and the lack of opportunities for developing his talents in Breda: that lukewarm, detached compassion that never turns into real generosity.

Bored with waiting, and with a disappointed expression, Gloria told him: 'I don't think they'll come today. We haven't had much luck!'

He didn't know how to answer, but she didn't wait for him to do so, and began to fold away her easel and gather up her brushes. Then she walked down to the water's edge some fifteen metres away. He watched as she sat on a rock, her back towards him, took off her rough leather mocassins, and remained still for several minutes, engrossed by the afternoon silence and the light of the late sun as it hovered over the Volcan and Yunque peaks. He had never seen such a beautiful woman, had never imagined that love could be such a powerful emotion. He knew that, come what may, for the rest of his life he would retain the image of his cousin seated on the rock, her arms round her knees, the water close to her bare feet, in the evening light with

the mountains in the distance. The sky itself made its contribution to the scene as it alternated between reality and mirage:
violet-tinted wisps of cloud shaped like horses moved across the
sun creating in those moments a dreamlike atmosphere. If, one
day, he was capable of painting everything he could see now
gathered together in one single picture, he would never need to
paint anything else.

As if suddenly remembering he was there, Gloria had turned
her head, and said: 'I'm going for a swim. I hate feeling sweaty.
Do you want to come in or will you wait for me?'

Possibly, if she had only spoken the first half of her question,
he would have plucked up the courage to go with her into the
deep, grey, turbid water; possibly, he might have resolved to
master his cowardice and timidity, to overcome his normal ret-
icence and reserve, and not be embarrassed or troubled by
Gloria's naked and achingly desirable body; and not be worried
about what she might think of his body which had emerged
from puberty without yet being fully mature. He had reached
that difficult age, the last stretch that is more troublesome than
adolescence itself, when a boy no longer feels like an adolescent
but knows that he doesn't yet have the strength or the courage
of one who has completed the process of growing up.

'I'll wait here,' he replied.

He regretted his words even as he spoke, cursing his timidity
and the lack of daring needed to hurl himself head first on to the
smooth surface of the water, and swim after her, around her, and
beneath her naked body in the almost frightening depths of the
still, grey water. Knowing they were alone in the middle of the
reservoir he would be drawn by the pale gleam of her bare back
and the opportunity for playful touches that were the only way
he could get close to his cousin, since love itself was forbidden
by their blood relationship.

He averted his gaze as he noticed the self-assured way in
which she pulled her tee-shirt over her head, but he had a

split-second glimpse of her naked, bronzed, and graceful back. He didn't know what to do, and because of this, he turned his back on her and said: 'I'm going for a stroll – to see if I can spot a deer' – although he knew it was far too late, and the animals would already have settled down in their hiding places to rest and chew the cud, and that his words were no more than an excuse to hide the embarrassment caused by her nakedness.

'That's fine,' said Gloria.

As he walked towards the first row of pines, he heard the splash as she dived in from the rock. Only then did he dare turn and look back in time to see her head emerge to draw breath, and her arms, paler than the water, cleaving its surface with smooth, rhythmic movements. He still had time to change his mind, he thought, to undress, taking advantage of the fact that she was now a good way off, and to meet up with her again on the other side of that barrier to timidity and modesty that the shore of the reservoir symbolized. Everything would then be easier, both of them naked, but deeply immersed, and where their toes would be able to touch the slimy roofs of the submerged houses, both of them caressed and buoyed as if floating on a soft cushion. But he had continued to walk away, his eyes wet with tears of anger, with himself and – a sudden reversion to his father's fierce and ancient pride – with her, for having stripped naked in front of him as if he was still a mere boy. He let the tears trickle down his cheeks, and then decided to go back by a roundabout route, bending low, and hiding behind bushes and trees until he could lie down on the ground behind the first line of shrubs, a few metres to the left of where he had started from. The thirsty roots of the pines had risen near the surface, struggling for life beneath the dry top soil, like the veins under an old man's skin.

There was still that glow in the sky that a clear evening provides as a temporary respite before night finally falls. An almost full moon was now visible, casting its milky light. He parted the dry brushwood in front of him, and looked out towards the water. Gloria lay floating on her back, her arms outstretched, and facing away from him and, for a moment, this made him sense that she was waiting for him, that she was trying to persuade him to steal up on her, to take her by surprise or play a trick on her, because she couldn't have been unaware of his presence. But he knew he would never dare do that. He would remain hidden there, watching her in safety, with the harsh odours of the dry earth in his nostrils, hearing the little sounds of the forest growing fainter with the approach of night, and observing the brighter reflections of the moon on the surface of the lake. All his faculties were alert, and his heart was pounding against his ribs.

It was the hour when flies go to drink and the fish rise to catch them. A carp gave a great leap to seize an insect, and fell back, breaking both the silence and the smooth surface of the water. As if something had suddenly frightened her, Gloria turned, and began to swim towards the shore. He didn't move. He could feel his blood throbbing through every part of his body that was in contact with the ground. She emerged from the water at the place from which she had dived in, next to the rock where she had left her clothes, without making a show of – but without making any attempt to conceal – her magnificent naked body. All she wore was a pair of tiny white briefs that, soaking wet, revealed the dark smudge of her pubis. She squatted down and began to dry herself with a small towel she had brought with her, shivering slightly from the cold. He had had time to observe her closely, and never afterwards would he forget the sight of her wet skin, her gleaming, slender thighs, her breasts quivering with every step she took on her bare feet, and the dark, enchanted triangle between her legs.

Standing in the shower he felt the thrill of another orgasm course through his body. He was alarmed to hear his mother's weary but affectionate voice calling him from outside the door:

'Come along, son, hurry up. I need the hot water.' This brought him back to earth, back to their life of poverty, scarcity and scrimping. But he stayed under the shower for a few more minutes as he washed himself, trying hard not to forget the last images of that afternoon: Gloria dressing on the rock and calling him while he remained motionless in his hiding place. He didn't know why, but he had needed to experience the pleasure of making her worried, frightened even, to make her think he wasn't there, that he had disappeared; in other words, to make her understand that he was essential to her, even if it was only for a minute or so. He watched her comb her hair and then light a cigarette as she grew more anxious, and called him louder and louder.

When he had decided that enough was enough, he crawled backwards, trying not to disturb any bush in his way that might reveal his presence, and stood up only when he was well out of sight. He checked to make sure there were no traces of earth on his clothes or tears on his cheeks, and only then went down towards the shore.

'Where've you been? Did you go far?' she had asked, as he came in sight. He felt cheated by the realization that there was more disapproval in her voice than pleasure that he was back, but he replied gently that he'd seen some deer in the forest and had spent the time watching them. They picked up her brushes and easel and made their way to the place where they had left her car. He had avoided a futile argument by hiding from his father the fact that he had been helping her.

He turned off the tap, put on a bathrobe, went upstairs, and shut himself in his bedroom on the top floor of the house. It was a cold, sparsely furnished room, but it was the one place where he could be alone and do what he liked, a long way from the kitchen and dining-room on the ground floor. He locked the door, put on clean clothes, and before sitting down at the small round table covered with a plastic cloth, he climbed on a chair and brought down from the top of a high wardrobe a sketch pad in which he had done some charcoal drawings. From it he extracted a loose sheet of paper that bore a drawing of the face of a young boy: it was a portrait of him that Gloria had given him on one of the recent afternoons when he had been with her. He had helped her arrange various pieces of furniture in her old family house while they talked about painting. She had asked him if he had used up all the oil paints in the box she had given him and he had replied that he hadn't because although he felt he could draw quite well, he was finding difficulty in mixing the exact tones of the colours he wanted to use. To thank him for his help, and seizing a moment when he sat down to rest for a while near a window, his face lit from one side, she had asked him not to move. Picking up a pencil and a blank sheet of drawing paper, with what seemed no more than a few quick confident strokes she had sketched that portrait which he now kept as a treasured possession. He had hidden it from his parents, but often took it out to look at it with his bedroom door locked, in the way a wealthy collector contemplates, entirely on his own, a masterpiece that he can't show to anyone because it has been stolen from a museum. He would spend long hours staring at it, studying the number of pencil lines and their length, the ways in which she had suggested form, and the intensity of the shadows. It seemed to him that this simple drawing had the capacity of a great work of art to depict the reality of its subject better than any mirror. Gloria had succeeded in capturing his thin lips, his discontented, defensive look, his badly combed hair that had fallen across his forehead, wet with perspiration, and the taut wings of his nose which looked as if it had caught the very scent of her as she was drawing him. Even the tiny acne marks were suggested in exactly the right places. He paid particular attention to the eyes which reflected a mixture of timidity, surprise and longing. He wondered whether she knew how much he was in love with her. She had probably guessed something of this because she had incorporated in the drawing a suggestion of the tension that stems from desire combined with frustration. He wondered when he would learn to draw like that. Would he have enough time to make up for the lost years? Possibly now, with the prospect of all the money they should soon inherit. Gloria's inheritance. He turned the sheet of paper over and read the dedication she had written for him on the reverse: '*Don't look any further outside yourself. All the colours are there inside your eyes.*'

Suddenly, he raised his head to listen to the echo that the dedication brought back to mind like the sound of a distant bell in an abandoned monastery. He read it again, and then remembered Gloria's words about the hiding place of her diary that afternoon when she had come across him glancing through it. Once he saw that she wasn't annoyed by his inquisitiveness, he had ventured to say that she ought to take better care of it and not leave it open on a table. The exact words of her reply now came back to his mind: '*Nobody could possibly find it. Even if they were to open and close the doors of the hiding place they'd never see it. It would remain hidden.*'

He had thought deeply about what that meant, but couldn't see an explanation, and in the end had forgotten all about it. But now that buried memory came back, touched off by the words of the dedication that he hadn't read since before her death.

Although it was late, he put his shoes on and slipped quietly out of the house without saying anything to his parents. Five minutes later he rang the bell of Cupido's apartment. The detective was about to start eating his dinner on a tray. He offered the boy a beer.

'I've remembered something about the diary,' he said. His voice trembled from nervousness and the speed with which he had walked there.

'Yes?' said the detective. He hadn't moved a finger in connection with the investigation all that Saturday, and had spent the morning on various errands he been putting off, and the afternoon reading and watching a football match on television. He was waiting for the lieutenant to receive the results of the autopsy on the following Monday. He felt uncomfortable at losing a day, and David's unexpected visit was a welcome salve to his guilty conscience.

'I was at home looking at a portrait that Gloria did of me, and when I read what she'd written on the back I immediately remembered her words. She was talking about the hiding place of her diary. She said: '*Nobody could possibly find it. Even if they were to open and close the doors of the hiding place they'd never see it. It would remain hidden.*'

He looked at Cupido as if he expected the detective to provide the solution to a puzzle that he had been unable to solve. But the detective was equally baffled – both by the words themselves and by David's enthusiasm to help that had overcome his normally obdurate timidity and persuaded him to recount what he remembered. Once again, he wondered whether everything was really so spontaneous as it appeared to be, or whether there was some special reason for wanting him to locate the diary.

'Are you sure?'

'Yes. That's what she said: "*Nobody could possibly find it. Even if they were to open and close the doors of the hiding place they'd never see it. It would remain hidden.*"'

'And what did she mean?'

'I don't know. I just don't know.'

Suddenly, he had an idea and couldn't understand why it hadn't occurred to him before.

'Can we get into her house?'

'Her house here in Breda?'

'Yes.'

David was clearly taken aback, as if he had gone too far, and this visit to the detective might have consequences that he couldn't foresee. He hadn't been in the house since Gloria's death. It hadn't occurred to him that it might possibly become his property because his ambition, his real longing, was focused on the apartment and the studio in Madrid which had dazzled him when he had been there for the funeral of his military uncle, the one occasion he had seen the studio with the paint stains on the floor and the circular windows giving light that couldn't fail to provide inspiration, its luminous space, and the piles of canvasses leaning against the walls, the collections of brushes, and the big tubes of oil and watercolour paints that he would be able to use until they ran out.

'I think so. We've got a set of keys at home.'

'Can you get hold of them?'

'Do you mean now?'

'It's as good a time as any,' he said, although he was aware that it was already late. But he was afraid the boy might think better of it if he gave him time to reflect.

'All right,' he agreed.

They left the apartment together and drove to a point near Gloria's house where Cupido waited for him for about ten minutes. It was one of those streets that wasn't so close to the centre of the town for the houses to have been converted into a parade of shops, but nor were they so far out that they were likely to be knocked down to make room for new urban developments. The exterior was painted white, and he reckoned that once the internal work was completed, it would have a very respectable value.

David appeared round the corner, looking back as if he feared he was being followed.

'I've got them,' he said.

He opened the door without first having to try the different keys in the locks, suggesting that he had gone in quite often. Without any hesitation he switched on the lights and showed the detective round the ground-floor rooms. As in many houses built decades before, the front door opened directly into a long hallway, at the far end of which another door gave on to a spacious patio which gave light to the internal rooms. It wasn't a big house, but all the rooms were well lit. Cupido understood Gloria's interest in renovating it: it was an ideal place for someone who liked to paint. On the left there were two rooms, one with its window over the street, and the other with a window on to the patio. The first room was almost completely furnished, and he saw a chaise longue, a table with four chairs, and a piece of furniture with shelves that held small decorative figurines and books. There were also a number of paintings on the walls that bore Gloria's very legible signature, although their style seemed more uncertain and crude than those Cupido had seen in her studio in Madrid. He and David searched thoroughly, opening every single book, but without coming across a diary amongst them. She had used the inner room to store sketches that hadn't been successful, two easels, brushes, and every imaginable type of tube or pot of paint. The diary wasn't there either. They went up to the first floor. Only one of the four rooms, which had a balcony directly above the street door, was arranged as a bedroom. A big, old-fashioned bedstead with its head made of metal bars decorated with round marble knobs and still without a mattress occupied the centre of the room; ranged around it were a double wardrobe made of a beautiful wood, two small tables, and a chest of drawers.

The house would not have needed much to make it habitable, but it still lacked a few items of furniture and electrical appliances, as well as the warmth that only comes from being lived in. They looked in the wardrobe, but that was nearly empty: some summer clothing and country clothes. In one of the drawers there were items of underwear that embarrassed David when he saw them but didn't dare touch, as if there was something sacred about them. They went back down the stairs and out into the patio.

'Would you like one?' asked the boy, offering a cigarette. He had taken it out of its packet and held it up by the filter, not at all what an experienced smoker would have done.

'No thanks,' he replied. Since he had given it up it seemed to him that everybody else smoked and offered him cigarettes – men and women, old people and young, like the lad who now stood in front of him, with no thought for the fact that this automatic, polite gesture made it more dificult for him to forget the emptiness he still felt in the pit of his stomach, and the saliva that filled his mouth whenever he heard the word *cigarette*. David was still at that early stage when he could have given it up without much effort, the detective reflected, but he didn't want to say anything that might sound bossy – the last thing the lad would have expected from him. People start smoking out of admiration for a person on whom they model themselves. The catch with smoking is that once the initial impulse to start has passed – and the formerly admired role model has begun to seem ridiculous – the addiction has already taken hold.

They had locked the street door after entering, but suddenly they heard four or five quick, hard, and peremptory knocks. David glanced at Cupido in alarm; then, he dropped his cigarette, crushed it underfoot, and looked at his watch.

'Who knew we'd be here?' asked the detective.

'Nobody. But it must be my father if he's noticed that the keys aren't in their usual place. It's very late.'

Cupido went to the door and unlocked it. Clotario stood there, momentarily disconcerted until he saw his son behind him.

'What're you doing here? Who gave you permission to get in?'

'I asked your son to let me have a look round. I was hoping to find something that would help me clear up your niece's murder,' he replied in a conciliatory manner.

'And did you find anything?' the other man asked. His tone was ironic.

'No.'

'You shouldn't have gone to the boy. You should have come to me.'

'Would you have lent me the key?'

'No,' replied Clotario, looking him straight in the eye.

'Father!' broke in David from behind Cupido.

Cupido didn't turn to look at the lad because he was studying intently the enraged expression on the face of the old man who obstinately refused to give way to the youngster, to relinquish any of his paternal authority or powers of decision-making.

'Shut up, you,' he said. 'Get yourself home. We'll talk about this later.'

David hesitated for a moment or so, but in the end he went out into the semi-obscurity of the street, his head downcast, and without looking at his father who had moved slightly to give him just enough room to get through. Cupido guessed how ashamed the boy felt because, quite apart from the humiliation of being berated by his father, there was the fact that it had happened in front of him.

'I've already told you once you should be looking elsewhere because we don't know anything about the murder. You're being paid by that high-class gent in Madrid who was so keen to get hold of her properties and her money. If he hadn't been, he wouldn't have let Gloria treat him as she did,' said the old man once they were alone. 'He knows he won't get anything now, and he's only trying to get us mixed up in this murder so that he isn't.'

'No. I don't believe that's true. He wouldn't gain anything from it,' replied Cupido; but even so he began to wonder whether the lawyer might not have detected a possibility of inheriting by recourse to legislation relating to 'common-law' relationships.

Clotario looked at him for a moment before replying. 'Maybe he's pulled one over you as well. That lot all seem to be good at it. In the same way that Gloria cheated on him.'

He put one hand in his trouser pocket and scrabbled around for a packet of Kruger cigarettes, a brand that was so strong and rough that Cupido thought it had been withdrawn from sale. Then he took out a box of wax matches and struck one against the side of the box. The detective looked at his hands: they were broad and powerful, like great paws, and the lighted match shone between them like a thin and harmless thread. Its flame couldn't burn them.

It was his job to observe. And observation had taught him that in spite of concealment and dissimulation there was always one uncontrollable part of the body that revealed the real man. In the case of Clotario it was his hands that gave him away. As a consequence of a lifetime spent using farming tools he had difficulty keeping his hands open because the fingers invariably tended to close in a fist; they were short, blunt fingers that wouldn't have found it easy to dial the numbers on one of the old disc telephones.

The old man's hands brought back to his mind images he thought he had forgotten. Twenty years before, a group of young boys had been standing in front of a wrought-iron gate, not daring to open it because a swarm of wasps had made their nest on its post, drawn there by the warmth of the black iron when the sun shone on it. A farmer who was going by at that moment holding the reins of a donkey with a little boy on its back, stopped to listen to the boys who didn't dare open the gate, and with one clenched and calloused hand he squashed the hot wasps' nest between his fingers without the insects being able to sting him. When he opened his fist, he showed them the small, soft ball of wax, blood and venom.

Cupido watched the movements of the hand as it returned the packet of cigarettes and the box of matches to his pocket. He had to make an effort not to imagine how skilfully it might manipulate a shepherd's knife, and to concentrate on the old man's words as he went on.

'... they won't take it away from us. D'you hear me? They won't take it away from us.'

The detective gave him time to calm down before answering. He was familiar with that sort of proud, hot-blooded countryman who becomes progressively more heated when caught up in an argument, but can be easily calmed down with a few pleasant words spoken in a tone he is unused to hearing.

'I assure you it isn't my job to deprive anyone of any part of an inheritance that is due to them.'

His words were immediately effective. Clotario relaxed. He became thoughtful, and puffed deeply on his Kruger cigarette, although the expression on his face didn't change.

'Look, Gloria wasn't a bad girl,' he admitted. 'But her sort of life was very different from ours. And that's why she was a bad influence on David. Ever since he first met her he started grumbling every day we went out to work in the fields. We had an argument one day and he went so far as to say he'd leave home and go to Madrid and live on his painting as if it was as easy as that. Left to himself he'd never have thought of it. It was Gloria who put the idea in his head.'

Cupido recalled the old man's past life when, twenty years before, his young daughter had run off with the bullfighter who had turned up in Breda for the summer festival, and Clotario had gone after them on his mule, with a shotgun, determined to bring her back. But he'd returned alone, ten days later, having lost his gun, his mule, and his pride. But he still regarded himself as the protector of his clan with all the fierceness befitting the head of the family, determined to ensure that nothing like it would ever happen again.

'David's my only son and he's got to carry on working on the land. All my daughters have gone. David will now be able to do everything I couldn't. With that money he'll be able to buy up three times as much land as we've got now. Just take a look round the country here. All the land's up for sale, and none of it's being worked. He'll be able to buy a beautiful big house and all the machinery he'll need for the heavy work. This is the right moment now that all the others have pushed off – and before they come back, which they'll soon do. They'll have to leave the cities because everything we need comes from the land – food, water, and clothes. Everything. It takes a war to teach you what you can't do without!'

Cupido thought that this absurd and laboured diatribe might make sense in some distant future, but not now. The countryside would go on just being there, patient and unchanging, like an elderly, but famous, general who puts his trust in his monarch's summons as soon as the first drums of war begin to sound. In the meantime he rests his bones in oblivion, his only company being when other old soldiers or their sons come with increasing frequency to visit him in order to indulge their nostalgia or recall what their fathers have forgotten. He reflected that the taste for cross-country rambling was growing just as the old rural way of life was disappearing.

Clotario fell silent. For a few minutes he had recovered the pleasure of talking in that didactic and grandiloquent manner that long before had earned him the ironic sobriquet of *Legal Eagle*.

'But your son doesn't think like that.'

'He did until a year ago, when Gloria started coming here more often and told us she'd like to do up her parents' house. At first I was pleased for the boy to help her organize things. But then I found out that the two of them were sometimes going out together to paint in the Reserve. She was changing him, filling his head with those crazy ideas of becoming an artist and going off to Madrid. My daughters have left home and I don't believe they're better off for it. But David's place is here. I know him. He's my son and I know what's good for him, because when I was his age I made the mistake of wanting to get away from here. When I left home I didn't have my father's permission, and I had to return some years later very sorry I'd ever gone. Breda is a place you always come back to.'

Cupido was amazed to hear from the lips of a man so different from himself the very same words which he had used many times, like a curse.

'Besides which,' he went on. 'Do you really believe David would get anywhere as a painter in Madrid? They'd look down on him as an upstart. In any case, it's too late. He's got the stamp of a country boy. You can try to run away from the land, but the land doesn't let you go.'

With two puffs he quickly finished his cigarette and opened the door to throw it into the street, but the tiny butt fell inside the doorway and the old man simply trampled it under one of his dirty boots. When he lifted his foot, all that could be seen was a small dark stain on the floor and some crushed strands of tobacco.

'I'm not going to let my son make the same mistake I made. Everything's going in his favour to get all he needs. And I won't let them take away what's due to us,' he repeated firmly. 'My niece could have chosen to pass her money on to others, but she died without making a will. Even if she'd been a whore, even whores have families to inherit from them.'

As if to emphasize the force of his words, he stepped aside and ushered the detective through the street door first – as if he already owned the house.

As he opened the door of his apartment he heard the phone ringing.

'Ricardo Cupido?'

'Yes.'

'Marcos Anglada here.'

'I recognized your voice,' he said. He could hear a television in the background.

'Perhaps I shouldn't be saying this over the phone but I can't get away from Madrid for some days, and I've been thinking a lot about the murder of that other girl. It took place just ten days after Gloria was killed, and in the same circumstances. And it appears that a similar weapon was used.'

'Yes, and possibly it was committed by the same person.'

'Everything suggests we're dealing with a madman, a maniac – serial killings without any personal reason for them. He killed Gloria because she was there on her own in that precise place at that precise time.'

'You could be right,' agreed Cupido. He guessed what Anglada was about to say. He too had been thinking the same thing for the past forty-eight hours, but he wasn't going to help him make up his mind.

'I don't think there's any sense in you continuing with the investigation. I'd like you to give it up. Personally, I'm satisfied with what you've done, the way you approached the job, and the way you've gone about it.'

These words sounded very cool and familiar to the detective; they were the typical cant of clever men in positions of author-ity who have the right turns of phrase ready – made for every situation. But this was no reason not to be polite.

'Thank you,' he said.

'All we can hope for is that the police do their job properly and have a bit of luck. Once they get hold of the culprit I shall come forward with a personal indictment. Meanwhile, please make up an account of your fees. You can send it to me here in Madrid with the details of your bank account so that I can arrange payment. You'll get the money the same day.'

'Very well,' he replied curtly. Although he had reached the same conclusion, and had even thought of suggesting to Anglada that they should terminate the investigation, he felt a certain uneasiness. Anglada must have detected something in his tone because he immediately added: 'I realize that after all you've done, giving up now isn't an attractive end to it. But I believe it's the only thing to do.'

'I understand.'

'It's been a pleasure working with you. You're a good detective,' he repeated, as he was about to ring off. 'It's a pity it's worked out this way.'

Cupido would have liked to talk to him about certain details that were still in the air: the badge that Gloria had been holding in her hand, its pin stuck into her middle finger, and that almost certainly had been torn from the clothing of her aggressor, thereby linking her murder with someone within her circle; and the shot that had been heard that same morning. But it was obvious that Anglada had already taken his decision before phoning, and he wasn't the type of man who could be made to change his mind with vague suggestions. Accordingly, he said nothing. He would leave drafting a note of their conversation until the next day.

In fact, he got up much earlier than he usually did the following morning, and ate a substantial breakfast because David's visit and Anglada's phone call had prevented him having a proper dinner. He put on his cycling shorts and a sweatshirt, and took out his bicycle from where he kept it in the electricity meter room down in the garage. It was a beautiful machine with a light frame, and everything on it was made of aluminium. He hadn't touched it for a month, and he noticed the dust that had settled on the black saddle and the crossbar. He got on and started to pedal, slowly at first, stretching his muscles, and choosing the right gear to match the strength of his legs. A month without using it meant that it took him a while to get his rhythm back, but he left the city at a modest pace, passing the last villas, and the industrial buildings on the outskirts. He put it into top gear while he was still on the flat and found he could move with ease. His breathing was good, better than he had expected, and he was able to maintain that early effort. *It's because I've given up smoking*, he told himself. He felt good as he went along the main road that bordered the Reserve on his left for four or five kilometres.

He had gone up the first of the gradients that was fairly easy going, when he heard two shots that came from not far away. There must have been people out hunting, and it occurred to him that it was Sunday.

He had always liked cycling and had never completely given it up, although his rides had become more sporadic with time, and now he did only short distances – forty or fifty kilometres. Having given up smoking he was looking forward to enjoying more of these expeditions. It was a sport that held a lot of attractions, and anyone who went in for it could become adept. It wasn't as boring as jogging, it was less demanding, its scope was greater, and it provided a wider range of views across the countryside. And there was no need to be using one's legs all the time. Every route has its downs as well as its ups, and these help to give an occasional rest. At the same time it didn't require the long and tedious period learning the technique before it was possible to get pleasure from it that he had found with tennis. To him riding a bicycle was as easy as walking. Moreover, there was no need for another person to practise it with; it was equally enjoyable whether alone or with other people. And finally, he thought as he changed to a lower gear, as it wasn't a confrontational sport there was no need for all that drive and dash that were essential in adversarial games like football, basketball, or tennis. Every cyclist could set his own rhythm and goal, and move at his own chosen speed. Any cyclist could turn round and go back as soon as he felt that the effort was getting beyond him.

His back and wrists ached and his legs were stiff when he got home again, two and a half hours later. But he felt on good form. He lay down for a while to recover with a drink. He had done nearly sixty kilometres, but he felt that the sense of wellbeing more than compensated for the fatigue. He realized that in the last three hours he hadn't once thought about his work, and this had done him a lot of good. He'd have a word with the lieutenant to let him know Anglada had paid him off, and that he was giving up the investigation. He anticipated that the next he would learn about the case would be what he read in the papers. He got into the shower to wash away the dust and sweat, and stayed there under the very hot water for a full fifteen minutes, taking no notice of the warnings in the media about the need to conserve it. He turned off the tap, dressed, and set about preparing a really good meal. But then he heard the persistent ringing of his phone once more. After all the bad news that the recent phone calls had brought, the sound of the telephone bell seemed ominous.

Thirteen

He took his graduation photograph down from the prominent and privileged position it had occupied for years in the space on the wall between the two windows of his lounge. It was one of the first objects to be placed when he had come to live in this small but splendid apartment. While the walls were still bare, the first picture hook and the first blows with the hammer were dedicated to hanging that photograph in a place where visiting clients couldn't fail to see it. And he had derived great pleasure from looking at it, his eyes flicking over the hundred or so figures of his contemporaries lined up in orderly rows beneath the shield of Complutense University, their faces expressing hope and faith in their future careers; he would also study the features of the celebrated professors and lecturers, most of them well known for the books they had published and their frequent appearances on television and in the press – they lent a prestige to the photograph that went beyond mere official recognition of academic success. The photograph had filled him with pride and confidence in his professional qualifications, and had made him feel that he was supported by the powerful, if anonymous, collegiality of the Bar Association. However, now that he no longer needed to use the apartment for receiving clients because he had his own office elsewhere, the photograph had lost significance. In fact, it was getting in the way. He had no feeling of nostalgia as he stared at the heads of his fellow students, but turned his gaze towards his own face: he looked younger, proud and pleased with himself, almost smiling at the photographer, as if even in those early days he had predicted a brilliant legal future for himself – one that was completely at odds with the difficult circumstances he would have to live through as a result of the death of the only woman he had ever really loved. The portrait Gloria had painted of him would now occupy that position on the wall. He went into the bedroom and slid the photograph behind the wardrobe, in the space between that and the skirting board. Then he returned to the lounge and removed the brown paper protecting the portrait – he had had it framed with the most appropriate mount and moulding he could find – and held it at arm's length in front of his face as if it were a mirror, in order to study all its detail. He regarded it as the best of the many presents Gloria had given him, something quite special, because it came directly from her, made by her hands, a gift that came freely from her heart. He hung it on the hook where the photograph had been, carefully adjusted it until it was straight, and then stepped back to the far side of the table to look at it from there. That was his true face, a more faithful depiction of his inner self than the photograph that had previously hung there. It conveyed the same suggestion of a satisfied smile and the same firmness of the mouth as he withstood her gaze, but there were also shadows in the face, and the eyes had a withdrawn expression as if they hid something that was best not known. That was the difference, he thought: a photograph only shows what it sees on the surface, while a portrait searches for what lies beneath that surface. He sat down at the table facing it, where he used to position his early clients. He remembered so well the days when he had posed for her in that studio where from now on, according to the letter he had just received, nobody was allowed to enter until it had been established who was to inherit Gloria's estate. It had been a happy week, and he had been grateful to her for letting him penetrate her world, the world of her art, that she had jealously guarded. He hadn't entered it by means of a commercial transaction, but by her making this real portrait of him – a privilege she had granted to very few people. Each afternoon he had gone up to her attic studio wearing the white shirt chosen by her, and had sat quite still near one of the round windows while Gloria, standing all the time, began to set his face down on the canvas. She would observe him with rapid glances while her hand went backwards and forwards from palette to canvas, or she would remain still for several moments studying every tiny detail, the lobe of an ear, or a corner of his mouth, and then she would retouch something she wasn't satisfied with. For the first half an hour she would work away, only occasionally approaching him to lift his head that had dropped from fatigue, or to correct the position of a lock of his hair. During the first part of each session they spoke little. She would often smile as she looked at him, but wouldn't permit him to smile. However, towards the end they would both lose concentration – he, because he was tired from remaining motionless, and Gloria because she wasn't at all displeased to surprise him staring at her body: the breast that rose as she raised her hand towards the canvas, the thrust of her hip as she rested pensively on one leg – he having disobeyed her command to keep his eyes on the top of the easel. The result was that either one of them might be the first to break his pose; then, they would come together to kiss and caress. He would take his white shirt off so that it wouldn't be stained, and he wouldn't even give her time to wash the paint off her hands. He would remove her brush, and undo her smock to find, on the last of those afternoons, that she was wearing nothing underneath. They made love every day, as if that mutual and meticulous observation that enables the model to know the artist as well as the artist knows the model was an excitingly erotic prologue during which they had had time to think about what each of them wanted to do to every part of the other's body, what positions they would try, and which caresses would give the most pleasure and delight. They would throw themselves impatiently on to the narrow bed up there in the studio and quickly make love. Gloria was always the first to get up afterwards and she would cover the painting with a white cloth because he was strictly forbidden to look at it before it was finished. He had been somewhat concerned about what she was putting down on the canvas, fearing she had detected something about him that he couldn't see when looking at himself in a mirror. But he had always obeyed her, and it was only after Gloria had returned from the bathroom that he would get up to go and wash his penis which was stained with semen and, sometimes, with streaks of oil paint.

At last, a little more than a week later, Gloria had told him that the portrait was finished. She had waited until after they had made love before showing it to him, as if afraid that he wouldn't like it. But he had been deeply moved. The portrait was *him*, not just a reflection. After she had removed the cloth, it was as if she were saying: '*This is what I know about you,*' because it was full of unanswered questions, shadows, depths, nuances, and colours, blended like overlays that it would be possible to remove at some future time to reveal what was concealed underneath, just as expert picture restorers using X-rays can detect the first sketches of an earlier painting done by the artist before he decided on his final version.

That had been their last week of happiness. From then on there were moments, hours, evenings, and even whole days when they were happy, but never with the same sustained warmth. It wasn't long before that grotesque art teacher had become mixed up in their lives, and although he only found out about it some time later, Gloria's coolness, and his own jealousy, had begun to create a barrier between them. Like a mole he had started to burrow into her private life, spying on her, trying to catch her out when she described how she had been spending her time. But he did so in the certain knowledge that the more he tunnelled under the ground where she walked, the sooner the day would come when the earth would collapse beneath her and leave him crushed beneath it. But he couldn't help himself suffering from the illogical mistrust typical of lovers that becomes greater the more deeply in love they are. It was like being caught in a vast bramble bush: the more he tried to get free, the deeper the thorns pricked and tore at his flesh. One day he obtained proof, and there was no need to dig further; he stayed there, trapped in a subterranean gloom, feeling the repulsive and slimy touch of the worms of jealousy and humiliation.

From then on, nothing was the same. He had decided not to tell her that he knew about her deceit because if he were to act consistently with what he had always declared, he would have had to leave her. But he didn't want to lose her because he believed he still had the strength to escape from the pit of suspicion, and that she would gently cleanse him of the accumulated mire.

Later, when the ridiculous affair was over and Gloria had told him all about it, she had seemed repentant. Not so much for having been unfaithful to him but, he inferred, because she considered it a blunder that only concerned her. So what should have brought about an improvement in their relationship turned into yet another source of conflict, as if in talking about it the words she used had put the stamp of truth on what otherwise he might have been able to relegate to the level of a bad dream. Every time they got into an argument, he would end up reproaching her for it, although it bore no relation to the matter that had started their argument. When they finished making love, and he could watch her breathing softly and contentedly, he often wondered what was lacking in him that she had to go looking for it elsewhere: what did she get from others that his body didn't give her.

Even though there were days when he was very busy in his office and succeeded in forgetting all about it, the calm didn't last. When he was alone in his splendid, but cold, apartment because Gloria had a work commitment, and he turned and twisted in his bed, its memory would return to haunt him. He was convinced she admitted to less than the whole truth, and he imagined other lies and infidelities with other men he knew, and with whom he had tried to be friendly and generous. At those times he would do his best to contain himself, or he would have gone straight out looking for them, to confront them violently, face to face, in the hope of establishing the truth. He would spend several days without seeing her, pretending he had work that couldn't be put off, inventing clients who didn't exist, but a week later he would go back to her and spend every moment at her side, made ever more bitter by the realization that he had been incapable of keeping to the decision that common sense dictated. Those were days when he would go everywhere with her – to her gallery, shopping, out for dinner, to the cinema, until he could see that Gloria was becoming tired of his constant presence, although she never dared say so. If it happened that she had to attend a private exhibition, or had a commitment to which he wasn't invited, he came to believe that Gloria was inventing it, in the same way that he had done, in order to be free of him for a while. He thought he was turning into the type of man who is always cheated on, because his partner doesn't dare tell him that she finds him boring and irritating. As a result, failing to find a satisfactory solution, his self-torture had become more intense: what previously had been temporary, needling irritations that only needed a few days to go away, now seemed to crystallize into a permanent ache.

He wondered how he had been able to live like that. What devastating neurosis is able to make you love or hate somebody with equal intensity when these two sentiments are not only opposites of each other, but totally incompatible? Which organ or gland of the body is able to secrete both malice and passion all at the same time? These were the types of unanswerable question he had asked himself over a long period, and they had only generated new questions. Even now that Gloria was dead he was unable to find answers to them.

Fourteen

He raised his powerful binoculars and scanned the forest from right to left through the more than 180 degrees that his observation point allowed. Over the years, he had managed to pinpoint a number of strategic locations from which he could view all that sector of the Paternoster Forest for which he was responsible. He stood now on top of a rock at the summit of one of the many hills that marked the limits of the Reserve.

Every day he was on duty he drove along the same perimeter path in his official vehicle, carrying his standard issue rifle. He liked this aspect of his job, following the firebreaks that surrounded that part of the forest inside the metal fence that was too high for the deer to leap over. This circular route, instead of criss-crossing the forest, enabled him to assess the true extent of the Reserve, and it gave him a strong feeling of personal authority, like a feudal lord riding the bounds of his domain with a falcon perched on his shoulder, an earlier equivalent of the game warden's rifle. He had his home on this territory; he felt safe there, and it was where he gave the orders, which satisfied his tendency to arrogance. On the other side of the fence lay the outside world where he lost his supremacy and trappings of power. That was where that beautiful girl had come from, the one he had found so disturbing before she was murdered – although he had managed to keep his distance from her death without too much trouble, and in spite of persistent questioning by the Civil Guard lieutenant, as well as by that tall detective who seemed to know so much and had tried to put pressure on him. The murder of the second girl was more serious, because it greatly complicated matters and was giving rise to even more questions and suspicions. From now on, the price of his silence would go up.

When he had finished scanning his area of responsibility, he trained his binoculars on the main road bordering the Reserve, near its crossing with the path that led to one of the entries that had a cattle grid. No car was entering by that path, and all he could see was the small figure of a cyclist a long way off who was pedalling hard along the main road at that moment.

He returned to his car, satisfied that everything was as it should be, started the engine, and continued his tour. A kilometre further on, without getting out, he stopped again near the gate with the cattle grid that led to the path he had been observing. As usual, it was open to allow the Civil Guards and the lorries belonging to the clearance and reforestation teams to get through. The deer couldn't get out because of the metal bars of the grill over the ditch at the entrance. All was in order. He lifted his foot from the clutch and moved on, raising a cloud of dust in his wake from the dried-out track that forked away from the fence and extended into the interior of the forest because, from that point, the boundary followed the deep bed of a stream for three kilometres, and vehicles couldn't get through that. It was the most rugged and deserted part of the Reserve.

It was as he rounded a bend that he came across the car parked in the middle of the track with its engine running. He hadn't seen it enter the Reserve, and assumed it must have been there for quite some time. Presumably its owner had a problem because the bonnet was up, and all that could be seen of him leaning inside the engine compartment was the lower part of his body clothed in greenish trousers. He made as if to drive closer, but something – instinct, or his habit of observing intruders and the more troublesome type of tourist from a distance – induced him to brake ten metres from the car. Without getting out, he shouted:

'What's the problem?'

The other man couldn't have noticed him because he was screened from sight by the bonnet of the car and unable to hear above the noise of the engine.

He got down from his four-wheel drive, and advanced a few paces, still undecided between civility and mistrust, until he was only five or six metres away.

'What's the problem?' he repeated, more loudly this time. At first he thought he must have frightened the man because he suddenly stood up and turned towards him. Then he saw the balaclava that hid his face and the two barrels of the gun that emerged from beneath the bonnet. He jumped quickly to one side as he heard the report, but felt the shot smash into his left arm. The impact made him fall half-stunned into the ditch beside the track, but prompted by panic, his arm badly hurt, he began to run into the safety of the trees. His rifle was in his car, too far off. He got to the far side of the first tree trunk knowing that he had achieved the most difficult step, because the man whose face was concealed by the balaclava would have to get round the end of his car to be able to fire again, and this gave the warden a few moments' advantage. Those few seconds had run out when he felt the smack of more shots blasting into the tree behind which he was sheltering, and heard others whistling close to his head. He started to run for his life between the pines and away from the path. His lungs ached from the sudden violent effort, but as he ran he was cool enough to think carefully. If his enemy hadn't fired again it was because he was using a shotgun that needed reloading, as he had noticed before the man had opened fire. He must have stopped to reload. He called to mind the image he had of the lower part of the man's body as he had been leaning over the engine, and was sure he hadn't seen a cartridge belt on him. With luck he kept his ammunition in the car and this would give a greater margin of time for him to continue his flight or to find somewhere to hide.

He was caught up in a hunt in which he was now in the role of the deer. He had been through the process hundreds of times: he knew the animals and how their instinct for survival functioned. Now he had to remember their methods: where they went when they were wounded, which part of the forest they made for in order to hide, and what was the best type of camouflage. This knowledge was his only advantage against an armed man, and he was ready to put it to the test. Without stopping, he took a quick look back. The trees and the terrain's undulations already prevented him from seeing the cars and the path. Neither could he see his enemy or detect any movement of the bushes that would reveal where he was. It was just possible that he would behave like those unskilled hunters who give up the chase after failing with their first shots. But he dismissed the idea because in that case he would have heard the car drive off. He stopped behind a tree, completely out of breath, his back to its broad, protective trunk, and listened intently. He guessed it was three minutes since those shots had been fired. He couldn't be far off, and yet there was no sound. He would have had to go back to close the bonnet of the car and stop the engine before continuing the chase, because if anybody else chanced to pass that way and saw it open they might have stopped out of curiosity and seen the spots of blood in the ditch. That meant his enemy was coming after him. He thought of his own rifle and cursed his stupidity for being so rash after all that had happened in the last two weeks. With his gun in hand it would all be easy, very easy in fact, in spite of having only one arm with which to manage it. He was so tense that he jumped when he heard shots a long way off. '*It's Sunday*,' he muttered. It was a day when hunting was permitted, and nobody would be surprised to hear shots, nobody would come to help him, because on Thursdays,

Saturdays, and Sundays half a dozen of the wardens led small groups of hunters – or one man on his own, it was all a matter of cost – through the different sectors of the Reserve. His enemy had chosen the right place and the right day, and that cannot have been just by chance. The sound of shots echoing through the forest would heighten the rivalry of the wardens to ensure that each one's hunter bagged a prize animal, in the hope of receiving the substantial tip that had been agreed on in advance. He was filled with panic when he realized that in the area where he was – rough terrain with poor pasturage that attracted few animals – there would be nobody else apart from him and that individual armed with a shotgun and wearing a balaclava to hide his face. Wounded and unarmed, he felt as defenceless as a rabbit far from its burrow. '*All right. If I've got to be the deer, at least I'll give you a run for your money,*' he muttered, pressing his damaged arm against his side in an attempt to staunch the increasing flow of blood. He peered round the tree and looked back. He saw the upper twigs of some bushes move rather more than a hundred metres behind him. So long as he could maintain that distance between them the shotgun wasn't a serious threat. He wanted to draw a deep breath, but the pain in his arm prevented it. He had passed that way, and his pursuer who was following the trail of his blood would have to look in front, and then down at the ground, and this would slow his progress. Maybe that wouldn't worry him unduly if he hoped that his victim's loss of blood would bring him to his knees. But the warden didn't need to follow any particular trail and should be able to move faster, at least until the weakness caused by the haemorrhage sapped all his strength. *The blood. I must stop the bleeding so that the bastard loses the trail.* He had entered an area where the undergrowth between the trees had been cleared, which made it a bad place to stop. A little further ahead there was another low canopy of shrubs which would pro-vide greater protection, and between them he could see the shiny, grey surfaces of big, fat, granite boulders resembling huge wine vats. Having got his wind back he began to run faster, and it was only as he crashed through the first bushes that he heard the sound of shots and saw the torn leaves floating down around him; the sound was like hail falling, and was soon followed by another report. The other man had begun to catch up on him as soon as he could actually see him and didn't need to follow the trail of blood. But now that he could stoop and continue running between the broom and cistus shrubs he would regain the advantage. The bushes hadn't grown too close together, and he was able to move ahead without being seen. *I'm not dead yet*, he told himself, in order to keep his spirits up. At that very moment he experienced his first dizzy spell, and was on the point of falling. He would have to stop soon to do something to slow the bleeding; he wouldn't stand a chance of escaping if he went on losing blood every time he put his weight on his left foot as he ran. Galvanized by fear, he pressed the palm of his hand against the wound and continued to move as fast as his legs would go. The ground was beginning to slope down which lessened the strain. Suddenly, he arrived at the dry bed of a stream: there wasn't a drop of water in it, not even a pool where he could snatch a drink. His throat burned with thirst. He took off the jacket of his uniform because he was beginning to feel unusually hot. As he stretched his left arm in order to pull down the sleeve, the pain became more intense. Fear had prevented him from paying much attention to it, but now he felt an acute spasm that travelled from the elbow to his neck. In order not to lose heart he told himself that in the past he had put up with even greater pain than this caused by the slugs in his arm. He raised his head and looked back, listening. He heard nothing. Even so, his persecutor couldn't be far away, and it wouldn't be long before he reached the dry river bed. He started to run again, knowing that the other man wasn't going to give up his relentless pursuit. More than a battle of wills, it was a battle between the determination of the pursuer and his powers of resistance. He knew perfectly well that this wasn't a case of having bumped into a poacher who had reacted with an attempt to eliminate him in order to avoid complications. He had been waiting for him on that track. The open bonnet of the car designed to conceal him, the balaclava that hid his face, and the shotgun at the ready all spoke of a meticulously prepared plan. He thought he knew who it was, but couldn't understand why he had needed to disguise himself. He heard more shots from a hunter's rifle, and these sounded less distant now. Rescue depended upon reaching a warden or a hunter who would help him, or lend him their rifle for a few minutes. But he couldn't waste any more time before stopping the flow of blood. He crawled on all fours into a thicker patch of bushes. Squatting there quietly and without his jacket, his back felt cold, in contrast to the heat that the wounds were generating in his arm. He removed his leather belt and tied it round the muscle of his upper arm. As he did so there flashed through his mind the recollection of that same belt made into a tourniquet round Gloria's smooth and lacerated thigh. He was opressed by a confused and bittersweet memory. Then he shook his head, and the instinct to fight for survival triumphed again. He pulled the belt tight and wound it round twice so that the buckle coincided with one of the holes in it. The blood stopped flowing. This enabled him to take a better look at his wounds. There were five small holes: two in his forearm, one in his elbow, and two others a bit higher up his arm. If he got out of this, they would all heal without after-effects. The most painful was the damage to his elbow where the lead shot had penetrated the joint and dislocated the bone, but it hadn't broken it as he had thought at first. It wasn't too serious because his pursuer had used small slugs, which suggested lack of experience with firearms and uncertainty in his aim. Someone more experienced would have used bullets. But that amateurism wasn't matched by the persistence with which he was hunting him down. He knew that the man wasn't going to leave his work half finished, unless he could prove himself to be the more skilful one. Hidden in the shadow of the bushes, gathering his strength, but again assailed by thirst, he remembered his own habits as a hunter. Once he was sure of catching up with his quarry he never abandoned the chase. He would pursue it without bothering about fatigue, hunger, or thirst, knowing that he mustn't lose the advantage gained, and swayed by feelings he couldn't define: superstition, pity for the creature that was suffering, or his inability to accept the idea that the animal should be allowed to continue living in the forest with a piece of lead lodged in its body. He pricked up his ears again, peering through the branches. Nothing. No movement. No footsteps. He put his jacket on trying hard not to disturb a single twig that might reveal where he was. The pain returned as he put his arm through the sleeve, but it was lessening now, as if the tourniquet held back the pain just as it held back the blood. Now he would be able to run without leaving a red trail behind him. He took several deep breaths. He felt better although still very thirsty. He started to slip away on all fours between the thickets towards the far edge of this dense patch where he would be able to start running again towards the area where he had heard the shots fired by the hunters. As he reached the edge of the patch he raised his head and saw in front of him a wide area that had been cleared and replanted with small pines from whose branches there already hung the silken tents of processionary caterpillars with their sharp poisoned hairs. He raised himself like a sprinter waiting for the starting gun when he heard footsteps to his right, on the very edge of the patch of thickets. He stared up in terror and saw, at the level of his eyes, the two parallel barrels of the shotgun and, above them, the balaclava helmet that hid the man's face, with two holes for his eyes which didn't even blink as the finger pressed the two triggers, hurling him into oblivion.

Fifteen

It was the lieutenant who phoned him with the first details of Molina's death, but by that same afternoon a storm of rumour and gossip had burst upon Breda. Cupido was sorry he was no longer on the case. He had to resist the temptation to get involved and to start all over again questioning those individuals who had been connected in any way with Gloria.

Although an official news blackout had been decreed, everybody in town knew all about the death within a matter of hours, and also knew that it was no accident. Everybody assumed that this murder was somehow linked with the deaths of the two girls. Molina had not been hired to accompany a hunter on that Sunday; he had gone out alone, and his vehicle had been found with its door open in the middle of the track. Bloodstains on the path indicated that he had been wounded there, and had then been pursued and finished off with two shots that had blown half his head away. Some hunters had come across the trail of blood, and by following this had soon found him.

The detective recalled with more bitterness and sadness than he could have foreseen the warden's words to him: '*That girl should never have come on her own into the Reserve. Neither her nor the other one who was killed nor any other woman. The forest isn't a place for women on their own. The forest wasn't made for those who just want to look at it; the forest belongs to those of us who use it… Do you imagine a man would have been murdered?*'

But someone had murdered him. Molina had not been a woman contemplating the beauties of the scenery, and yet someone had killed him.

It had happened near the fence that separated the Reserve from the main road, and very near where he had been cycling that morning. The detective guessed that the shots he had heard, and had attributed to hunters, were the same ones that had killed the warden. He interpreted this coincidental timing as a sign that the case now concerned him personally, that it was his case, and that he was the only one who would be able to solve it. Moreover, he was convinced now that Molina had died because of something he had seen or heard, something he knew – possibly connected with the shot that had rung out on the morning of Gloria's death. This was a vital piece of information that lieutenant Gallardo knew nothing about, and that Cupido couldn't pass on because of his promise to Alkalino. Cupido was sure that all the evidence pointed to the truth of his theory. Nor could he believe that a poacher was responsible for this latest homicide: no poacher would have let himself be caught in a car in the middle of a dirt track, and nor would he have been so furious that he would have undertaken such a long and systematic pursuit. Someone had gone there with the intention of killing the warden and had waited for him in that exact spot – and this gave the case an entirely new dimension.

Curiously, Breda was more disturbed by this latest crime than by the two previous ones, in spite of the innocence, the youth, and the sex of the first victims. The difference was that they had been strangers, whereas Molina had been one of them. Besides which, they felt a greater familiarity with the method of killing – a shot from a gun, rather than a knife to slash a girl's throat. Nobody dared admit it, but many of them were afraid. Since the second girl had been murdered nobody went alone into the fields near the Paternoster Forest, nobody walked through it, and nobody spoke loudly.

There were a few who threatened to go on armed patrols through the Reserve on the pretext of protecting their daughters and their girlfriends, citing the need for exemplary and summary justice: if they caught the criminal they would string him up like a dog from a branch of an oak without more ado. And it is probable that they would have done so, given the opportunity, because their nonchalant attitude towards the deaths of the two young, beautiful and innocent girls, who were nonetheless strangers, had given way to feelings of outrage over the death of one of their number. It was the other face of the ancient character of the town – a taste for using a sickle to cut down an ear of corn – which surfaced whenever a feeble excuse justified it. But by listening carefully, the cautious scraping of heavy bolts and the sound of padlocks being fastened could be heard in the town at night because its inhabitants were convinced that the warden's murderer was one of them.

'Put it on the table. And give me a glass of port.'

'Yes, madam.'

The pretty maid's black hair was neatly combed, and she wore a spotless white uniform – although hers was the sort of spotless appearance that arouses a suspicion that what lies beneath may not be quite so spotless... She left the cup of camomile tea on the low table, went to the sideboard, and returned with a glass and a bottle of port. She filled it to the very top with the dark, viscous liquid, turned away to put everything back in its place, and left the room without a sound. The old woman didn't thank her and didn't even murmur an acknowledgement. She was very tired. When she looked at herself in the mirror that morning her face had been deathly pale after a sleepless night and she had had a severe headache; she looked as if she had aged two years in the past two weeks. She had lost so much weight that the maid had been ordered to take in the seams of the black dresses she always wore by a good two centimetres. She had noticed for some time that her body seemed to be shrinking and her joints becoming more and more inflamed. Although until then she had paid no attention to the discomfort, she was no longer able to ignore the severe pains of arthritis.

She watched the way the wisps of steam rising from her tea became thinner and thinner. She told herself she should drink it before it got even colder, but the strength needed to lean forward to pick up the cup and saucer in both hands in the way she had been taught as a girl was almost beyond her. She closed her eyes, sighed, but finally decided to make the effort. The camomile tea tasted stale and flavourless, so she put it to one side and raised the glass of port to her lips. She took a slow and refreshing, but noiseless, sip, in the way priests drink communion wine. The alcohol immediately gave her a comforting feeling of internal warmth. Then she slowly stood up, looking distrustfully at her swollen arthritic ankles and her feet encased in their heavy, black shoes, and walked over to her bureau, a beautiful piece of furniture made of chestnut wood. She opened an album, and glanced quickly at several pages of black and white photographs: a child less than one year old photographed in various poses, a weak-looking man with a moustache wearing a dark suit who stared directly at the camera, and a very beautiful woman carrying the same baby whose little head just appeared above the arms that cradled it while the man placed his right arm over the woman's shoulders in a protective pose. From between the pages she took out an envelope bearing a foreign stamp featuring the blue flag with stars of the European Union. She walked wearily back to her chair facing the window, sat down, and placed the letter on her lap. It had arrived three days before, on the Friday, and she had read it so often that she knew it by heart. At least her memory wasn't failing her yet. She had a real terror of those illnesses that don't harm the body but attack the soundness of the mind. She didn't fear physical pain but was afraid of what might happen to her body when she was no longer there, when her mind had gone, and all that remained would be mere flesh and blood, and if Octavio were to disappear nobody would know who it really was. '*No, I haven't lost my memory. Everything lies in the memory*,' she murmured. However, her words weren't dictated by defiance, but by doubt and resignation. She still hadn't shown it to Octavio because she knew it would cause him even more pain than it did her. After all, she had brought him up to fight their battle, and had trained him to put up with temporary setbacks in the expectation of ultimate victory. She had ensured that he would devote himself solely to that struggle. Now, she was aware of how much harm she had done him, how much he had had to sacrifice, and to what terrible depths she had made him sink. Too late, she realized that if a person's life is dedicated obsessively to one single objective and that objective isn't achieved it is as if that person's whole life has been a failure. *Poor Octavio, what demands I have made on you!* She lowered her eyes to the letter, and read *The Supreme Court of the European Community* without moving her thin, compressed lips, and without a flicker of expression crossing her face. She had known from the start that it would be a long and difficult struggle, but had never had any doubt about final victory. She had carefully followed previous rulings of the Supreme Court, such as the one concerning the La Encomienda estate which had ended favourably for the Duchess of Alba, and the ridiculous series of judgments in the Rumasa affair pronounced over more than fifteen years that had still not been finally resolved, and others in which there had always been cause for hope. At the same time, she had shut her eyes to those items of news that appeared from time to time concerning old women who had only won their cases against one or another ministry long after they had been dead and buried for several years. She had always shielded herself against despair in spite of knowing that in litigation of this type the struggle is inevitably an unequal one, and the powers that be are the last to tire of the matter because civil servants move on and are replaced by fresh ones, whereas the private individual is alone in his or her battle against authority. Octavio had often repeated that they would win, that in the end they had to win. But now, after this last defeat, there was nobody else they could turn to for help. She felt her eyes starting to water, but there was not one real tear. Many years had gone by since she had been able to cry. Since the death of her little son when he was less than a year old, she had become empty, dried up. The pain of that death had been so intense that, from then on, the idea of weeping for any other reason would have seemed shameful, shabby, a cowardly way of cheating and suppressing a hurt that couldn't be washed away with tears. She hadn't even cried when her husband, who had been unable to bear the tragedy, had died shortly after their son. She felt a gentle hand on her shoulder and another that caressed her fine, thin hair, like cobweb, that she washed and combed repeatedly every morning, and gathered up in a neat chignon. She didn't have to look up to know who it was, or to hear him speak, to know that he had already read the heading of the letter as it lay on her lap and had guessed its contents. That was why his caress was so unhurried and his other hand lay gently on her shoulder, feeling the bones that in those last few weeks seemed to have become more angular.

'They've beaten us,' she said quietly, trying to hide her unbearable sorrow, her gaze lost in the distance beyond the net curtains where the brilliance of the midday sun flooded the street.

Octavio bent down to pick up the letter, and she saw then, close to her tired eyes, his pale face slightly damp with perspiration, his eyes sunken from years of constant study peering through the thick lenses of his glasses, the typically swollen eyelids of a student, the wings of his nose quivering with anxiety, and the last traces of the cold sore on his lower lip. She heard the rustle of the paper as he unfolded the letter to read its contents which, in a few lines, not only dashed all their hopes, but also revealed with sudden and painful clarity her deep debt to him; above all, a debt that he would never remind her of. She had begun this fight of her own free will, but she had drawn him into it without him giving him any choice in the matter.

'They've beaten us,' she repeated. 'They've finally beaten us.'

She watched him as he placed the letter on the table, walked over to the window, and stared out, turning his back on her. That was what she had made of him: a prematurely aging man, his back bent from spending too much time poring over papers; a sad and lonely man, irretrievably incapable of being able to attract a wife. He should have been living with a young girl, but he was living with an old woman; he should have been going to bed every night to enjoy the warmth of a young woman, but he slept alone. The maids she engaged to work in the big Breda house provided no more than a second best relief which could never replace what he really needed. The first time the evidence of her mistake had struck her, like a flash of lightning, had been when she saw how awkward and speechless he had been, like an adolescent, in the presence of Gloria. It was then that she became truly aware of the degree of deprivation to which she had subjected him. And the fact that she had not recognized it until then was no excuse.

'There's nothing more we can do now,' he said, so suddenly that Doña Victoria nearly jumped.

She didn't reply immediately, hesitating while she chose the only words that might express a degree of hope.

'There is something more we can do,' she contradicted him. 'We can work to keep what we still have.'

She watched him wheel round and look fixedly at her through his thick glasses, amazed that she was able to accept defeat with such fortitude. As he was in the habit of doing ever since he had developed his cold sores, he pushed his lower lip up over the other one in order to obviate discomfort or contact with the scab, and this accentuated his expression of despair and anger. Looking at her, he thought that if she agreed to sign the documents surrendering her claims, it would be because she imagined that a final defeat in the courts would be even more painful. 'She's frightened for my sake,' he said to himself.

'We'll leave this town. We'll go away and never return,' she said. All her old anger was revived, and the words burst out forcefully, as if fighting was the only thing that kept her alive.

'We've got too much that ties us to this place,' he protested mildly, with a sweep of his hands that took in the house itself, the wrought-ironwork seized before it was lost in the waters of the reservoir, the ornaments that brought back so many memories, the subtle ways in which a beautiful house and its occupants become attached to each other. They also pointed towards the graves on the little hillock in the Paternoster Forest.

'We'll come back once a year to visit them,' said the old lady who had guessed what he was thinking. 'But we'll leave here for ever. This town is full of enemies.'

Sixteen

Two days after receiving Anglada's phone call, Cupido had still not been to see the lieutenant to tell him he was no longer working on the case because his client believed the murderer to be a lunatic, or sadist, who had no personal connection with Gloria, and therefore it didn't make sense to go on spending time and money on the investigation. He knew that once he presented himself again in the Civil Guard headquarters and informed Gallardo of his dismissal, he would no longer have any involvement in the case, and there would be no going back to it. That was why he had delayed his visit. Underlying his indecision there lurked a secret desire to find out more about Gloria, in the hope that a sudden metamorphosis would transform her before his eyes from a woman of many mysteries into a girl who had acted from coherent and transparent motives.

It's always the same, he thought, you dig into the more intimate aspects of a person's life and reopen old wounds in order to identify the virus that has infected them or the poison they're secreting. You retrace the steps that go from the victim to his or her tormentor. In the final analysis, it's the thirst for knowledge. As if we were all born with an innate instinct for detection which is almost as powerful as our other basic urges, and must be linked to fear of the unknown and the search for what we call truth. Coming up against a problem has always provoked men to want to solve it.

So the detective delayed taking a decision because, in addition, everything he saw, heard, or read made him more reluctant to abandon his enquiries. The day before, as he was walking past a hardware store he had seen in the window a knife similar to those used in the murders of the two girls. Through the glass he saw a hundred shiny, steel knives of all shapes and sizes: knives were available to anyone. He walked on, but then turned back, stopped in front of the window, and looked intently at the weapon he had never noticed before, until he saw that the shop assistant had observed his interest and was looking at him as if his behaviour was becoming suspicious. Later that evening, while he was rereading *Romeo and Juliet* in the belief that the beautiful classical text would divert his attention away from present-day events, he found to his surprise that Shakespeare had made reference to cold sores four centuries earlier:

> *O'er ladies' lips, who straight on kisses dream;*
> *Which oft the angry Mab with blisters plagues,*
> *Because their breaths with sweetmeats tainted are.*

Even these words read in an old play reminded him that he had left his job unfinished. He very much feared he would be unable to rest before he had discovered the truth and buttoned up the case. To replace X the unknown with a name, he told himself, was the only way to put it behind him for ever, the only means of transforming a nagging worry into a distant memory.

He was in this mood when a Civil Guard rang the bell of his apartment on the Tuesday morning because the lieutenant wanted to see him immediately – and Cupido knew the lull was over and he was back on the investigation.

They entered the gate of the Civil Guard headquarters without being stopped, and arrived at the office block. The Guards he passed all looked anxious and bad-tempered. He guessed that this was due to the three murders which, without warning, had shattered the comfortable provincial existence they had become accustomed to, far from the violence of big city life with the constant feeling of insecurity and fear of terrorist outrages. They had grown fat and lazy while their reflexes had become slow. Suddenly, it was their turn to have something to worry about, to work overtime caged up in barracks on twenty-four-hour shifts, in readiness for any disturbance, or to investigate any reported sighting of a man on his own, or a woman, in or near the Paternoster Forest. The lieutenant kept them on twenty-four-hour duty, whereas over the past fifteen years the only public service that had been truly active in Breda had been the Fire Service during the summer months because they had to be on continuous alert to prevent fires breaking out in the Reserve.

The lieutenant was seated at his table. It was a week since they had met, after the death of the second girl, and it seemed to Cupido that these three crimes had made him more alert than usual. He looked on particularly good form – leaner and darker. Or maybe that was just the impression conveyed by his civilian clothes. It was the first time Cupido had seen him out of uniform.

'Doesn't look as if you're working very hard for your money,' said Gallardo, by way of a greeting.

'Nobody works if they don't get paid,' he retorted.

'Has Anglada fired you?' The lieutenant sounded surprised.

'On good terms. But he's terminated my contract.'

'When?'

'Two days ago. Sunday. He said that the murder of the second girl made it obvious it was the work of a lunatic or a sadist. I drew up my account and sent it to him. His arguments are logical; there's no question about it,' he concluded, concealing the deep irritation and disappointment he felt. It was the first time he had had to give up a case without finishing it, and the prospect of empty days ahead was made worse by the vacuum he was leaving behind.

The lieutenant shook his head from one side to the other.

'And what are you doing now?'

'Just getting bored. Why did you ask me to come?'

'I wanted to invite you to come on a visit with me.'

'Who are you going to see?' He spoke too quickly to suppress the unusual tone of eagerness in his voice.

'Molina's widow. You may not be under contract any longer but I think we can probably let you come along for the ride!' He said it jokingly, but it was too forced to be convincing or to raise a smile, or to make believe that he wasn't thinking about what he had been unable to put out of his mind for the past three weeks: three murders in the depths of the forest.

'Does she have anything to do with all this?' he asked with surprise.

'We don't think so. On the Sunday when her husband was killed she was in the Base Depot dishing up a meal for a bunch of hunters.'

They left the office and got into a patrol car. Gallardo didn't want anybody else with them because he wanted to avoid any suggestion of intimidation when they saw the woman who now lived on her own in the forest with her two children. That was also the reason why he wore civilian clothes.

'We're no better off now than we were at the beginning,' he said, once they had passed the Chico Cabrera fountain and were on their way towards the foothills of the Reserve. 'In a case of murder you always hope the murderer will have left some evidence, one little clue that may not mean anything on its own but, put together with others, makes it possible to construct a complete picture. But in this case every murder just adds more confusion.'

A quick, dark object flashed across the earth track, like a shot from a gun, about ten metres in front of the car, leaving a trail of dust hanging in the air behind it, and disappearing between the oaks as rapidly as it had appeared.

'The only happy creatures now are the animals, the deer and the wild boar, like that one,' he continued. 'Look around. What a wilderness!'

It was a fact that they hadn't seen a single individual as they drove along, they hadn't heard another human being, and there was no indication of any person being there. The forest had reverted to its normal state of eternal and ungovernable menace. News of the three murders had spread well beyond the region. They had been mentioned in the national press, and a television team had visited Breda to make a film that was due to be shown one evening in a programme about acts of violence. The fear of being murdered in the forest was now widespread – not even the game wardens were free of it – and it was acting as a powerful deterrent to visitors. Through the windscreen they could see the lonely forest, as if newly created, dense with oak trees, pines, cistus shrubs and broom, above which hovered the birds that were always poised to swoop on their prey. It seemed incredible that in barely three weeks this had been the scene of three murders.

'D'you know anything more about Molina's murder?' asked Cupido.

'We're working on three different hypotheses. The first is that he caught the person we're looking for unawares and that he or she killed him before he had a chance to defend himself. That would suggest that our unknown uses a knife for preference but also carries a shotgun of a type that's very common and anybody might have in their house. The second is that he came up against a poacher who wasn't prepared to face a prison sentence or pay a heavy fine. But we know something that makes that unlikely: it was Sunday, a day when hunting's permitted. Nobody with an atom of common sense would dare enter illegally on a day when half the Reserve is thick with hunters who hold licences and wardens who are guiding them around. But we're not dismissing that one, and we're working on it.'

'And the third?'

'The third assumes that this was a personal or professional matter. Hatred or revenge. Molina wasn't the sort of character who made himself liked, but we haven't been able to find anything that would give us a lead.'

It was obvious that the lieutenant inclined towards the first of his three hypotheses, the only one to which he had made no objection.

'I too believe that somehow or other it all links up, that the individual who killed Molina is the same murderer, but using a different type of weapon on a different type of victim. Molina was tall and strong, and it wouldn't have been as easy to cut his throat as it was in the case of the two girls. The question is whether they met by accident, or whether he went out intending to attack the warden.'

The lieutenant looked away from the road ahead and stared at Cupido.

'You're thinking too much about this case not to be still working on it.'

'Yes. I can't get that first girl out of my mind. I shut my eyes and try to imagine each one in turn of those who knew her being her murderer: from Doña Victoria to Anglada himself, from that sculptor friend of hers to her relatives here. And when I indulge my imagination I can't help thinking that the death of the other girl was a sort of decoy to distract our attention. Even Molina's death may have a simple explanation,' he said, measuring his words carefully. He wasn't prepared to go too far.

The hoarse bellow of a distant buck echoed above the noise of the engine. It was answered by an even more powerful bellow.

'Have you checked what all the others were doing at the time the warden was killed?'

'Yes, but that hasn't clarified anything. Every one of them who didn't have an alibi for the first murder has an unbreakable one for at least one of the other two. And so on. We've cross-checked their stories over and over again, and all of them have witnesses in the case of at least one of the murders. I can show you the papers in the office if you like.'

'No, from what you say it isn't worth the trouble,' said Cupido despondently.

They could see the Base Depot at the end of the track, the hangars for the fire engines – now closed, the small office building, the high surveillance tower, and the houses for use by the wardens. Molina's widow was still living in one of them. For some days, or even weeks to come, no one would want to tell her that she had to move out, but she already knew she would have to go as soon as the brief period that was the local government's concession to charity ran out.

They parked in front of her house, and as on Cupido's first visit, the woman came out immediately she heard the sound of the car. She wore mourning, but not even her black dress could hide her shabby appearance. She would have been an attractive woman if she hadn't allowed neglect to get the better of her. The lieutenant was the first to shake her hand and offer the conventional words of condolence, which she acknowledged while looking at them with disquiet. The four- or five-year-old boy appeared in the doorway, and from there he gave an expressionless glance at the two visitors, and then directed his gaze towards the official car.

'Did the sergeant sort your papers out for you?' asked the lieutenant.

'Yes, all of them. He was very helpful.'

'Can we come in?'

'Of course,' she said, pointing towards the house.

The front door led straight into a living-room floored with tiles made of baked clay; the walls had been painted white but this was turning yellow near the ceiling and black on either side of the fireplace. It had a generally dirty appearance. Next to a piece of plywood furniture could be seen a few cheap prints of hunting scenes, their frames and glasses thick with dust and fly droppings. The little boy who had no interest in grown-ups' conversations had gone back to watch a programme of cartoon animals on the television. The younger child must have been asleep behind one of two closed doors. The detective guessed that these led to badly aired bedrooms with unmade beds covered with an excessive number of blankets. The kitchen could be seen on the other side of the room as well as a passage that probably led to a backyard. A table, one or two chairs with rush seats, and two imitation leather armchairs made up the totality of the furniture, and it was all pervaded by the same air of careless disorder, with breadcrumbs that hadn't been brushed away, stains from spilled liquids, and a myriad of tiny forest insects feeding on the remains of a meal.

'Would you like something to drink? Beer?' she asked.

Both Cupido and the lieutenant accepted the offer. The woman went to the kitchen and returned a moment later with two small bottles, two glasses, and a dish of cut slices of a dark, dry sausage.

'Is this venison?' asked the lieutenant as he tasted a piece.

'Yes, venison.'

The woman sat on an upright chair, her knees pressed close together, and watched them chew the tough but delicious meat helped down by long draughts of beer. She didn't join them however, possibly because she had acquired the habit of remaining on the fringe of conversations about work or hunting trophies, or while Molina recounted anecdotes to his guests.

'Is there anything else you need?' asked Gallardo.

'No. I think everything's all right. The sergeant took care of all the paperwork. All I'm waiting for now is for them to tell me when I have to leave the house.'

She didn't appear much affected by the death of her husband. Possibly she wasn't. The detective calculated that between her widow's pension and the orphan allowances she would get for her two dependent children she would receive in total about eighty-five per cent of the wages Molina had earned while he was alive, and that wasn't at all bad. And maybe she was happy also to know that she would now have money in her own right as well as being free of a man who can't have been either a particularly pleasant husband or a very supportive father. When all's said and done, he thought, it might prove difficult to find a married couple in which one or the other of them hadn't at some time desired the death of the other – although nobody would dare confess it, because parricide, like rape, betrays the most murky depths of what can be seen in the mirror, is socially repugnant, and anyone who perpetrates it is regarded as a monster. However, if it were possible to kill simply by using imagination or dreaming of it, the world would be full of widows and widowers.

'Do you have any money problems?' he asked, although he knew the question was indiscreet and the woman might refuse to answer.

'Not at the moment. He had another bank account, and he'd been putting money aside,' she said.

Her use of the singular pronoun sounded a little odd to the detective and the words struck a chord with him.

'Didn't you know your husband had that money?'

'He never told me anything about it. He must have been keeping it for the children,' she said, with the need that all unfortunates have to explain a sudden stroke of luck, as much as anything to justify the fact that the money has been gained by honest means. 'Also, they've given us a guarantee that we can keep the money in that account. With some of it I'll be able to buy a little house in Breda. And my son can go to school,' she said, pointing to her elder child who remained absorbed by the fast-moving action on the television screen.

'Have you given any thought to what I said?' the lieutenant intervened. 'Anything you can remember that might help us? Anything that happened in the past?'

'I've tried to think, but there isn't anything. Nobody benefits by his death.'

Except his murderer, thought Cupido. He had the feeling the woman didn't want to have anything more to do with the investigation; she was talking to them as if she was at confession, to finish with it once and for all, to forget it, and to carry on living without either remorse or happiness. Just possibly, once she was back in the town and had daily contact with other women she would begin to take better care of herself, and would feel the need to improve her appearance and attract another man to her bed.

The lieutenant drained his glass and put another round of sausage in his mouth. Cupido didn't wait any longer to ask:

'What weapons did your husband own?'

The woman turned towards him. Her eyes held an anxious expression, but they didn't look as if they had shed many tears; her hair was more or less the colour of straw, but it seemed almost colourless.

'He had the rifle they gave him because of his job as game warden. I handed it back myself yesterday.'

'Nothing else?'

'He also had an old shotgun. He hasn't used that for a long time.'

'Can we see it?' asked the lieutenant. He didn't know what Cupido was aiming at with these questions, but guessed that it could be important.

'I don't remember where he kept it. It must be hidden somewhere out there at the back. Because of the children,' she explained, looking at the boy who continued to be engrossed by the television cartoons, and so carried away by the vertiginous speed of the images that he was unbothered by the voices of the adults.

'We'll help you look for it,' said the lieutenant, getting up from his chair.

The woman led them to the back of the house. They went through the kitchen and emerged into a concrete-paved patio with earth borders along the walls, although nothing was planted in them. A small shed with a metal door stood against the far wall. The woman took down a key from where it hung on a hook high up, and opened it with ease. They were met by the powerful smells of sausages, leather and dried fruit seeds. She moved to one side and the two men took a step forward. They stopped to let their eyes become accustomed to the dark. The woman slipped between them, opened a small side window, and the room was illuminated by a bright shaft of sunlight which revealed the uses to which it was put. It was somewhere between a storeroom for old bits and pieces and a larder. They saw two rods suspended horizontally from the ceiling from which dangled a number of venison sausages like the one they had been offered. Cupido went over to where there was a third rod: the skins of two bucks were hanging from this one to dry out. He stroked the outside of the skins which felt hard and smooth, and then the inner sides that were like cardboard from the salt, and possibly also urine, that had been applied to them. He looked back. While Gallardo searched for the shotgun the woman only looked at him as his hands caressed the pelts of the dead animals.

'The hunters give us those,' she said, again feeling the need to provide an explanation. 'When they manage to shoot an animal many of them don't want the body. They'd get him to remove the head, put it in a bag, and take it away to decorate their houses. And they give us the carcass if they're feeling generous,' she added, pointing to the skins. 'It's only the head that's worth anything to them.'

The detective suddenly recollected having heard Alkalino use the same or very similar words when he was talking about the poacher whose name he wouldn't reveal: '*What's really valuable is the head.*'

The lieutenant opened a wooden bin, and after rummaging through some old hunting clothes took out the gun that was wrapped in a blanket. It was a double-barrelled repeater. He opened it carefully, but skilfully, and from where he stood Cupido could see the smooth way in which its greased hinges turned. The lieutenant raised the open gun to his nose and sniffed it several times as if he was imitating a wine expert. He looked at Cupido and nodded. In that moment the detective knew what they had to look for as soon as they left that house.

Gallardo leant over the bin again and pulled out five cartridges held together by an elastic band that would fit on to the butt of the gun. Cupido had seen that way of carrying ammunition before, because it was used by some Civil Guards at checkpoints on main roads. The band made it easier to load the gun quickly without the need to raise a hand to a cartridge belt across the chest or round the waist, but he guessed that that wasn't the advantage it had for Molina, but the ease with which he could hide both gun and ammunition if he ran the risk of being caught. There were many clues here, all pointing in the same direction.

'Is it long since your husband used this?' asked Gallardo.

'Yes, I told you so. A very long time. He always carried his official rifle when he went out,' she replied. Perhaps she wasn't lying, and that was why she hadn't bothered to conceal the existence of the gun. Maybe she had simply believed what her husband told her.

The lieutenant put the gun back where he'd found it and went over to examine the pelts. He too was unable to resist feeling them, as if the skin still retained the warmth from when it had covered a living body. He was waiting for Cupido to take the next step. He didn't know the significance of what they had found and was scarcely able to contain his impatience to ask him.

They returned to the living-room and took their leave of the woman.

'I'm sorry I haven't been able to help you,' she said, but her tone suggested that this didn't bother her greatly. Both men suspected that she didn't have many regrets about the death of her husband, and in fact may even have been pleased by the unexpected benefits of her new situation.

They had hardly started off in the patrol car when the lieutenant said angrily:

'I'm not going to let you pull a fast one and leave me in the dark. What were you trying to prove by looking for that shotgun?'

It was the first time he had heard him speak in the way he had always imagined a lieutenant of the Civil Guard would speak when deeply involved in a difficult investigation, so he wasn't intimidated by the high-handed tone. His only problem was to find the right and convincing words in his reply. From the moment the woman had put the beer and plate of sausages in front of them all his actions had been directed towards trying to prove a theory that had come into his mind. While they were still in the house he had been convinced that everything fitted neatly together, but now, faced with the probability that the lieutenant would play devil's advocate, he wasn't so sure. He feared he had been carried away by intuition when one of the first things he had learned in his profession was that intuitions were worthless; what was needed was a scientific approach in which every theory had to be demonstrated to be true, and the only correct way of proceeding was by means of rigorous, logical deduction, and not by jumping to conclusions. He tried to make his answer sound plausible:

'As soon as I saw that plate of sausage something occurred to me that I hadn't thought of before.'

'Molina would never have taken the risk for a few kilos of meat,' the lieutenant said, shaking his head vigorously. 'A Reserve game warden hunting illegally? If he'd been caught the punishment would have been twice as harsh as if he was an ordinary poacher. And he'd have lost his job. Everything the woman said is right. I've seen for myself how some hunters take the head and leave the rest of the carcass for the guides.'

'I know. But that doesn't alter anything.'

The lieutenant looked at him without lifting his foot from the accelerator.

'Is there something I don't know?'

'Yes,' replied Cupido. He knew that the time to speak out had arrived, and he couldn't conceal his secret any longer without seriously hampering the investigation. 'But if I tell you what it is I need a guarantee that you won't involve the person who told me in any way.'

'That's not in our agreement,' the lieutenant answered with asperity.

'And I assure you I don't want to change it. But I had to make a promise to someone. In any case, the names themselves aren't important.'

The lieutenant was silent for a while in order to make Cupido fully aware of the enormity of his demand and the problem he had in accepting it. But finally, he agreed.

'OK. No names and no more questions than necessary.'

'On the morning Gloria was killed there was somebody else besides her and her murderer in that part of the Reserve. In fact, there were at least two other people. One of them was a poacher. He'd been waiting for sight of a prey without moving from his hiding place from early morning onwards, not very near where the girl was killed, but not very far away either. I don't even know his name, but I do know he isn't lying when he says he heard the report of a rifle or a shotgun round about ten o'clock that morning, because by admitting he was there he's putting his neck at risk.'

'A gunshot? Who fired it?'

'A fourth person, because I don't believe that the person who used a knife would also have been carrying a gun and would have shot at anything because that would have risked drawing the attention of a game warden or of frightening the girl a few minutes before killing her. There was somebody else there,' he repeated.

'Molina?' asked the lieutenant. He had quickly realized which names were important and which were superfluous.

'Could be. He never gave us a clear answer as to where he was at that time. All he said was that he was following a different route, more towards the interior of the Reserve, but there's nobody who can vouch for that. We've all thought of him off and on, and just now when I saw that venison the idea came back to me more forcibly. That's why I needed to confirm he had a shotgun.'

'It was well oiled, in good condition, and had been fired less than twenty days ago, even though the woman told us he didn't use it.'

'There's no reason why she should have known. I don't think Molina was the type of husband who'd go and tell all his little secrets to his darling wife. But it's perfectly logical he should use it for hunting – assuming it was he who fired that morning – because if he found himself having to get away quickly and abandon his catch, the poaching couldn't be pinned on him because the sort of ammunition a hunter uses is quite different from that supplied for use in his official rifle.'

'He could have fired it for some other reason.'

'Target practice?' suggested Cupido with heavy irony.

'All right,' agreed Gallardo. 'It all fits up to that point. But I can't see him risking the loss of his house, his job, and his gun licence for a few kilos of meat, because he must already have had more than enough with the two carcasses that had been given to him.'

'But Molina didn't shoot game on the sly for the sake of food,' the detective explained. 'Not even the poacher who heard the shot that morning was hunting for food. That sort of hunting is ancient history. The poacher who was hiding in the forest was hunting in order to get a head, a trophy, not for the meat. I'd been told that, but I didn't see the significance of it until the woman repeated it a few minutes ago: "*It's only the head that's worth anything to them.*" Molina wouldn't risk everything for the value of the food to himself, but for the value to others of ostentatious decoration. Our conversation with that woman was very illuminating. Remember her words: "*He'd put a bit of money aside.*" "*He*", you notice, not "*We*". So all we have to do now is check out what I'm saying, and then we'll find that everything slots together: the meat, the pelts, and the shotgun that's been fired recently... Saying they were presents from grateful hunters was just camouflage. A perfect cover for his commercial dealings in trophy heads. Do you know how much people are prepared to pay for them?'

'No.'

'Between 200,000 and 500,000 pesetas* depending upon the number of branches and points on the antlers and their height. And even at those prices there are more buyers than sellers. There are plenty of *nouveaux riches* who've bought themselves nice, shiny, new hunting equipment and kept the spaces above the fireplace in their smart chalets free for trophies, and aren't prepared to go home empty-handed after their first hunting trip. And Molina's here on hand to provide the solution.'

They both stayed silent, mulling over Cupido's words. He had sensed that it should have been possible to piece together these apparently unrelated facts during their visit to the widow. And now, talking it through, he had seen how to do it.

The lieutenant seemed to be waking from a dream as he said: 'It does all seem to fit, but it's still only a theory.'

'But it's the only one we've got that explains a gunshot that Molina must have heard but said he hadn't, and the existence of an old shotgun that's been fired recently.'

* Between approximately £770 and £1,925.

'We don't know anyone who might have bought a trophy head from him, and we don't have any trophies.'

'Because Molina couldn't keep them in his deep freeze,' he replied, becoming progressively more confident that he was on the right track. 'Nor is it necessary for the buyer to return to Madrid the same evening with an enormous stag's head dripping blood over the upholstery of his lovely Mercedes. He can ask for it to be cleaned up and prepared, to be picked up a few days later. There are places in Breda that do that sort of work.'

They were nearing the city, but instead of entering it by the most direct route to his headquarters, the lieutenant continued along the main road towards the commercial area. He had understood. The basic question remained in the air – what did all this have to do with the previous murders? – but it made no sense to go into that until they had made the next step forward.

He parked the car in the restricted parking zone, and after displaying a ticket that would give them a couple of hours, they went into a café to order drinks and look through the yellow pages of the local telephone directory. They found the addresses of four different shops and worked out the shortest routes for visiting them. Cupido would deal with the more central area, and the lieutenant would do the other two.

They met up again half an hour later. Nobody had commissioned work in the name of Molina in any one of them, but they had both made the same discovery as a result of their separate enquiries. There were only two workshops in Breda that carried out taxidermy. Two of the four shops belonged to the same family business which had its own workshop, and the lieutenant had checked that there was nothing there to give them a lead. But the other two shops didn't have workshops and used a private taxidermist. Cupido hadn't learned more than this, but the lieutenant had been given the address.

This turned out to be a small and unobtrusive shop, situated on a ring road where there were few other businesses. There

was nothing in its narrow, and not very clean, window to indicate that taxidermy was carried out there because all that could
be seen from the street were mouldings and a few framed pictures. But as soon as they went in they were assailed by the powerful odours of alcohol, ammonia, and varnish. The walls were
hung with paintings and prints alongside stuffed birds, weasels,
foxes, and a variety of stags and fallow deer heads. On the untidy
shelves there was a jumble of every kind of china, wood, and
alabaster ornament and figurine, both new and second-hand. It
was one of those shady types of shop that looks as if it probably
belongs to a fence who is willing to buy or sell anything without
asking too many questions about where it has come from.

Behind the counter, a tall man, very bald, and with bulging
blue eyes was in discussion with a young man with long and
dirty hair, his clothes almost in rags, and standing with his back
to them. The shopkeeper saw them enter, gave them a quick
appraising look, and seemed quite suddenly to increase his offer
to the youth, as if anxious to close the deal as fast as possible.

'OK, I'll give you 3,000. That's my final offer.'

His customer, realizing he had gained ground, continued to
haggle feebly. The way he dragged out every syllable seemed to
be the consequence in equal parts of contempt and exhaustion.

'The paint and the canvas alone are worth more than that.
You've got to make it 5,000. You'll be able to sell it for 20,000. I
had to slog at it for a week. It's a great painting.'

To make his point he picked up from the counter a canvas
measuring 40 by 60 centimetres on which was depicted a
vaguely human figure nailed to something resembling a cross
that floated between clouds that seemed to be made of open
mouths displaying rows of teeth. The young man looked at it as
if enraptured by his own artistic talents. It was clear he suffered
from the common habit of confusing self-delusion with genius.

He became aware that there were others standing behind him
and turned his head, still holding up the picture. He saw the

cold, impatient, and indifferent looks on the faces of the two men as they contemplated his masterpiece. He immediately decided to speed things up and without another wasted word accepted the offer.

'OK, 3,000.'

The shopkeeper took a wallet from his pocket and extracted three notes. The artist snatched them and, in a flash, disappeared through the door.

'Yes?' said the shopkeeper when they were alone, regarding them with a mixture of curiosity and suspicion.

'We've come to pick up some taxidermy work you've been doing,' said the lieutenant. 'It's in the name of Francisco Molina.'

'Have you got the ticket?'

'No,' said Cupido.

'Molina. Francisco Molina,' repeated the lieutenant more insistently, with both hands placed flat on the counter.

'Molina... I don't remember that name at all,' came the reply. The shopkeeper took a notebook with ruled lines out of a drawer and read the list of orders in hand, stooping very low over it as if he was short-sighted. 'What sort of work was it?'

'Two heads of buck to be cleaned and stuffed.'

'No, they're not down here. You've come to the wrong place,' he said, shutting the notebook. 'I don't do that sort of work directly for the public. I only do it when it's commissioned by other shops. You'll have to ask them.'

'We've already done that and they sent us here,' said Cupido. He knew that this was their last chance, and if Molina had been working a racket with trophy heads this was the place he would have brought them to be prepared. It was a hole-in-corner outfit that wouldn't bother with invoices, and the owner wouldn't question where the goods came from or where they were going.

The lieutenant picked up the painting of the crucifixion which still lay on the counter.

'What's your price for this?'

'Do you like it?'

'Yes. It's a masterpiece.'

'I can let you have it for 6,000*. It's a real bargain at that price.'

'Yes,' agreed the lieutenant, continuing to look admiringly at it. 'How d'you know it wasn't stolen?' he asked abruptly.

The other man gave a forced smile as he replied.

'Oh, no. It wasn't. It can't have been.'

Gallardo took out his wallet as if about to pay, but what he put before the eyes of the frightened shopkeeper was the special identity card that showed he was a Civil Guard lieutenant.

'All I've seen you do is buy a picture without knowing where it's come from, and I'm sure that this dump of yours is full of shit of this kind. D'you want us to look for the heads ourselves, or are you going to go straight back through there – ' He gestured towards the back room and spoke without raising his voice. ' – and show us the heads Molina brought you to work on?'

For an instant Cupido thought the lieutenant was taking too big a risk with that threat, because it was just possible that all his hypotheses were wrong, and the skins really had been presents from grateful hunters, as Molina's wife had said. Gallardo had given way to an impulse just as he had two years earlier, and he couldn't afford to risk another blot on his record. He gave a deep sigh of relief when the shopkeeper closed the shop door and led them into the back room. On a long carpenter's bench they saw an armature made of wire and plaster standing ready to be covered with the dried skin of a greyhound that was suspended from a hanger. Also on the table were pieces of coarse canvas, lime, and a shoe box full of glass eyes of different sizes and colours. The man drew back a dirty curtain that

* About £23.

concealed a deep metal shelf on which sat the head of a buck: its fur gleamed, its great antlers had been polished, and its brilliant glass eyes seemed to observe them with a mocking stare for having taken so long to find it.

'Only one?'

'Yes, only one.'

'When did he bring it in?' asked the lieutenant.

The man looked at the label attached to it, and read out the date: it was the Saturday on which Gloria had been murdered.

'Do you remember the time?'

'It was late that afternoon. I'd already shut the shop, but he called me at home.'

'Did you know him?'

'Yes. He'd given me other jobs from time to time.'

'How long do you reckon it had been dead?' he asked, pointing to the head of the buck.

'Only a few hours. It was easy to clean out.'

Cupido and the lieutenant looked at each other. They knew now who had fired the shot that had shattered the silence of the Reserve on that Saturday morning.

They returned to the shop. Its owner followed them, downcast, and fearful of the consequences for him of this affair. But the two men went over to the door without a word, so he pushed in front to open up for them, and only then said:

'What should I do with it?'

'Keep it for a fortnight. If you don't hear from me by then, sell it and give what you get for it to the local orphanage. I shall check on that,' said Gallardo curtly.

Later, over a beer, the lieutenant said: 'You should have told me everything right at the beginning.'

'I couldn't tell you something I didn't know,' responded Cupido. He felt he had done his job properly and was unworried, although clearing up this particular matter didn't seem to take them any nearer to solving the murders. *For now, at least,* he said to himself, because it was possible that on the following day this discovery might prove relevant to something even more important. He knew that there comes a time in any investigation, once all the available facts are known and all the suspects have been interviewed, that it tends to get stuck in a rut, and it is only by small steps forward that things begin to lead slowly towards the truth. They were already convinced that Molina's death hadn't happened by accident or as a result of a personal vendetta, but as the result of a bloody and determined pursuit that had led to his elimination: silencing him had been vital to his murderer because he had known something that was deeply damaging to him. The question now was why it hadn't happened earlier. Several weeks had elapsed between Gloria's and Molina's murder. That led them to guess at blackmail, and the game warden's unexpected, secret hoard of money also pointed in that direction. Molina had been hunting very close to the scene of the crime and must have seen or heard someone, but they were no nearer to guessing who that person was. Nor did they know how they would find out.

'If we don't get him soon there'll be more murders,' said the lieutenant. 'This type of madman tends to repeat himself.'

'It could be that Molina's murder is the last for a while. The murderer must have been very frightened to have killed him in that way, because he ran tremendous risks.'

'Or maybe he's come out more confident as a result,' the other replied. They weren't optimistic, in spite of the day's good work. 'The only certainties are that in a drawer in my office I've got two knives, there've been three murders, and we know little more about them than what the pathologists were able to tell us.'

Seventeen

He struck three blows on the chisel to force its shiny, bevelled blade between the wood of the trunk and the bark. Starting work on a sculpture was always a special moment, just as the first chords of a symphony must seem to a composer, or the first words of a novel to an author. The speed and depth of the blows matched the tempo of his inspiration, his choice of tools suggested how it would be shaped, and his raw material dictated the surface appearance of the finished work. Several days before he had come across a holm oak that had fallen on a stretch of irrigated farmland. It must have been dead for some time, probably because of an excess of water round its roots, and this was the perfect moment to start work on it: it was dry enough not to shrink, crack, or warp, but had not yet been damaged by damp, the sun, or insects. He had looked up the owner from whom he bought it at what was an inflated price for an ordinary tree trunk, but a ridiculously low price in relation to what he should be able to produce from it. The lower part was broad; it narrowed, and was slightly twisted in the middle, suggesting a waist; and the upper part, once its branches had been lopped off – an easy task – hinted at shoulders and a head tilted to one side. He was delighted with his find, and also because it proved that he had recovered his artistic insight without which he would probably have walked straight past it without spotting the possibilities it offered. That recovery had coincided with the death of Gloria, as if her disappearance had enabled him to cast off her influence. He remembered that while working on his metal sculptures he had never asked himself if what he was doing pleased him, but if it pleased her. But attempts to work in this new medium under her influence had led to disaster and now, at last, he wouldn't hesitate to admit this to anyone. Most of his work in metal had been mediocre, and it was while working with Gloria that he had come to recognize his limitations. He wasn't really capable of creating something out of nothing, out of a void; he needed an existing solid material on which to exercise his talents. He wasn't inventive in an abstract sense, he could only draw out or transmute whatever shapes were already implicit in his raw material, whether it happened to be a tree trunk or a piece of stone. He had to admit to himself that that was the real difference between a truly talented artist, able to fashion a world and a style of his own, and a more or less competent craftsman. He belonged in the second category – with those whose corpses create the fertile soil from which every so often there springs the glory of real genius – which Gloria would have become. She had tried hard to drag him up to new and vertiginous heights, but he had lost all clarity of creative thought. It was she who had convinced him to work in metal when his inclination was to use stone; it was she who had impelled him to work with volumes and empty space, when all he was really good at was sculpting a solid material, with the result that what should have been a gainful increase in skill had only resulted in self-torture. Now that she was dead he was alone and free, and in a matter of a few weeks had rediscovered the agreeable sensation of clutching a chisel in his hand. The first strip of bark came away under the pressure of the sharp steel blade with a sound resembling an almost human groan. He felt a small shiver of pleasure as he laid the clean wood bare, the flesh of a tree that would have bled its sap had it still been alive. He stroked the slightly porous inner surface which still had dark fibres attached to it like tendons on a bone, and through the tips of his fingers he sensed the satisfying feeling of power that he had never experienced when working with metal. That tree trunk had matured in the earth over three or four centuries, full of life and strength, and he could now reshape it as he pleased; he could transform it and polish it until he had converted it into something quite different from its original, natural form. So different from metal. And so different from what Gloria had wanted. For a whole year he had made advances to her without receiving anything in return other than kindness, understanding and a modicum of affection, that was far from giving satisfaction, and left him increasingly frustrated. Even then he would have preferred a frank negative to end it all for good rather than vague phrases such as '*It isn't really possible*', '*There's Marcos to consider*', '*I think we'd risk spoiling everything*' – all of which seemed to leave the door slightly ajar, and give some hope for the future; but they filled him with uncertainty because they didn't amount to a forthright rejection of him personally, but were based on factors external to the two of them. Only once, for a few minutes, he thought he detected a possibility of penetrating the friendly barrier she interposed between them. It had happened one afternoon three weeks before she died, when she had gone with him to the forge to help him weld the last pieces for his exhibition. She had arrived at the agreed time, and Luzdivina, the owner of the forge, was already waiting for them. The fire was lit and spluttering with red, blue, and greenish sparks like a swarm of fireflies. Luzdivina was a tall woman and still strong in spite of her age; she was fairly plump, but working with iron, and sweating permanently from the heat of the fire helped her keep obesity at bay. Her parents had given her that unusual name* because she had been born during the evening when the electric lights were first switched on in Breda.

---

* It meant literally: Divine Light.

Her father, the blacksmith, who cared for the hooves of half the horses in the town had watched fascinated as the little pear-shaped globes suddenly lit up – while many of the other inhabitants, led by an unbalanced and easily terrified ex-soldier who had seen the results of exploding gas-shells in the trenches of northern France ten years before, had fled into the woods at the very moment when the lights were due to be switched on, convinced that the bulbs would explode, hurling fragments of glass at the unwary who stayed to watch. It was Sierra's grandfather who had taken the necessary measures in Madrid to have the power station built, and from then on there had been close links between the families of the exiled politician and the simple blacksmith who had been dazzled by the splendour of technical progress. They were ties of respect and esteem that it had been easy for the sculptor grandson to renew when he needed to use the forge for his sculptures. Luzdivina treated him like the son she had never had, and seeing him arrive that afternoon accompanied by such a beautiful girl brought a gleam of delight to her eyes. Without bothering about the sweat that was beginning to pour down her face she had held Gloria by the shoulders, kissed her, and looked closely at her. Luzdivina was approaching seventy but seemed less, as if the heat and the work kept her young and always put a touch of colour in her cheeks. Although she must have been receiving her old age pension she continued to do little jobs in the forge – soldering the broken stem of an antique lamp, repairing small agricultural implements, sharpening billhooks – not so much for the money as out of loyalty to a craft that was doomed to disappear, with all the illogical persistence of those fanatics of old-fashioned methods who continue to defend their efficiency even when the tools and techniques they once helped to develop have become obsolete. '*I see you've brought somebody to help you,*' she had said, smiling at Gloria. '*Yes, and I'm sure it'll all come out better today,*' he had replied, thinking that of all types of manual skill, that of a blacksmith is the one most usually displayed with other people around, sometimes because the heat of the fire attracts those who suffer from the cold, and sometimes because those who have nothing better to do know that their help will be welcome when it comes to lifting a heavy piece of iron. *'The fire's ready, and you've got all the tools you'll need here,'* Luzdivina had said as she left them to it. Once the two of them were alone they had put on heavy gloves and picked up the pieces of iron – round bars like those used for window grills, and sheet metal in varying widths – and after checking his designs they had started work. Gloria's gloves were too big for her, but he had insisted she protect her hands from the rough edges of the metal, and also because they would prevent ash getting under her fingernails because once ingrained it can take a week to remove. He had plunged the iron bars into the coals that had been heated to 1,000 degrees; they had thrown out a stream of sparks while she watched admiringly as he took out the first pieces which, before, had been black and grey and now were a bright cherry red, put them on the pointed end of the anvil, and with hammer blows moulded them into the shapes suggested by his sketches, with a tap between each blow to deaden the vibrations, and to give himself a split second to think about where and with how much force he should strike the next blow. She had helped him by indicating the necessary curvature for each figure, by adjusting the air flow in order to maintain the heat of the fire, and by holding each sheet of metal with pincers while he hammered it. Glancing at her he had seen how the vibration of each blow reached up as far as her face creating a tiny, but delectable, movement in her cheeks and lips. Her face glowed with the heat and physical effort, and she was so beautiful in her leather apron and light grey shirt that he could scarcely contain the desire to take her in his arms. Later, he regretted not having done so because if ever there had been a good opportunity it was during that afternoon when they were working together on his sculptures, that afternoon of smoke, hot iron, and blazing coals that had raised the temperature of all their senses, during those fleeting moments when she had been watching him, admiring the precision with which he moulded on the anvil the iron that was as red as a cherry and as malleable as Plasticine. The four sculptures he forged, welded, and shaped that afternoon were also the only ones in his exhibition that he considered, weeks later, to be successful, as if her presence and her suggestions had for once inspired him. But he had made no advance to her because he was afraid of appearing weak, and feared hearing once again that gentle but firm negative that he had heard from her lips so many times before. He had concentrated on his work and allowed his feelings of desire to die down with every blow of his hammer on the anvil, sensing how the vibrations ran up his arms, his neck and his face, and seemed to bounce against the top of his head, and then fade into whichever part of his brain harboured despair. In that final moment, he knew he would never possess her, and while he was striking the last piece of metal to flatten it into a thin plate that he planned to model into a deer, he recognized that he had to do something to forget her, so that her image would no longer lie in ambush behind his every thought, every word and every dream. Quick, red sparks leaped up from the iron, and he thought she had taken a step backwards to avoid them, but when he raised his head he saw that she was looking into his eyes and that it was from him that she was retreating, as if suddenly she had become frightened by the excessive passion with which he had started to beat the metal into shape. He lowered his arm, down which sweat was pouring from his armpit to his wrist, and holding it with pincers plunged the glowing metal sheet into the butt of water to cool it rapidly. That abrupt cessation of fiery heat seemed to coincide with what was happening in his brain, as he finally realized that Gloria would never belong to him. In the same way that the iron had still been soft and in a condition to be moulded by the artist but had suddenly hardened in the water, so his hopes died that afternoon as he understood the sham he had been living. He rubbed a handful of steel wool over the surface of the metal plate to clean it while he tried to explain to himself the origin of the obscure satisfaction he had felt on perceiving that frightened expression on her face.

When their work was finished, they had sat down on a rusty iron bench and remained silent for some moments, both of them tired and tense, gazing at the pieces of iron that were no longer just pieces of iron but four stylized shapes that could have been torn from the walls of the cave in the mountain. He had wanted to say something to her about the results of his work, but couldn't think of anything: he didn't have a clear thought in his head. He had merely exclaimed: '*Now I need at least a litre of beer*' while taking off his gloves to wash his hands. Then he had gone out to a bar nearby from which he returned with several cold cans which they drained in order to wash away the smoke, the ash and the taste of iron that had gone down their throats. It was not long before night began to fall. Around them, the forge seemed full of the shadows of hard and threatening objects, all of them capable of inflicting harm.

They had gone back to look at the sculptures. There were a few more loose pieces to be welded on, but this was work he could do without needing either assistance or advice. The flat metal sheets and the tubes had taught him a lesson. It was only while he had been exerting himself physically on these sculptures that he had been able to establish a brief supremacy over Gloria. He had felt strong and effective wielding the hammer, accepting her suggestions for accentuating a curve here or lengthening a longer section there. But the invention of completely new shapes, the truly creative aspect was entirely her territory, from which he was banished. It had been hard to accept this, and as they had been sitting on the iron bench drinking cold beer he had asked himself whether Gloria's silence, coinciding with his, wasn't due to the same realization. Perhaps she had regretted suggesting they work together since he had shown himself incapable of rising to her level. He had been aware of a deep feeling of depression catching him by the throat. He was surprised to find that he had made so many discoveries about himself in so short a time. Just a few hours one afternoon had been enough to make the long journey from desire and self-delusion to the acceptance of reality and, finally, renunciation. He felt that weeks rather than hours had gone by.

Eighteen

The house was rectangular in shape and its front faced the main road and the bridge over the river. Its sobre appearance was in keeping with the architectural traditions of the region: thick stone walls, small windows to keep the inside warm in winter and cool in summer, a balcony over the front door, and a sloping roof with Arabic style tiles. It gave an impression of solidity, but also of probably being damp, like many other houses in Breda, partly because of the choice of site and partly because of the depth of its foundations. At the same time, its isolated position in the middle of a field gave it something of the appearance of a hermitage, with a small bell high up the wall next to the door by which visitors could announce their arrival, a lightning conductor, and an old, rusty and useless weather-vane in the shape of a cock, as well as a farm building alongside where swallows built their nests under the eaves.

Emilio Sierra's grandfather had had it built very near the river sixty years before, during the early years of the Republic, in the hope that other local families in the town would follow his example and build themselves second houses not just for the pleasure of being close to the river but also to enjoy a summer temperature that was several degrees lower than in the town itself. But nobody had followed him. The people of Breda had preferred to remain rooted in their town houses, as if they were by nature gregarious, although most of them lived for years without exchanging a single word with their neighbours. And as far as the advantages of water were concerned these same people, whose origins lay in the surrounding mountains and forests, maintained an Olympian disdain for regular personal hygiene that was almost as great as their panic at having their sense of modesty shocked by the sight of thighs and navels that hadn't seen the sun since they were babies in arms, bared and displayed in the public bathing areas on the banks of the river. The house, in consequence, had remained isolated in that central region of the Lebron River. Almost thirty years later, after the dam had been constructed in the deep valley in the mountains making irrigation possible, the new country houses that were built were no longer above the course of the river but close to cultivated plots that depended upon an extensive network of irrigation channels that brought the water almost to their doorsteps.

Cupido entered the precinct of the property that was demarcated by a fence of unpainted metal poles with spikes, and as the bell beside the door didn't have a rope to pull, he walked round the side of the house, guided by the sound of hammering from somewhere at the back. Turning a corner he saw the lean-to where Sierra was working. He had raised the large trunk of the holm oak on to a big bench and was removing its tough bark with a hammer and chisel. As in his Madrid workshop, a candle burned in a sconce.

Cupido raised his voice in greeting and the sculptor wheeled round in surprise. He hadn't heard him above the noise of his hammering.

'Come on over,' he said, removing his protective goggles. 'It's taken you a long time to come and see me!'

Cupido noticed that he was less brash than he had been during their first interview in Madrid. He seemed calmer, almost cordial.

'I'm off the job so I don't have an excuse to badger people any longer,' he joked.

'Wasn't Anglada paying you enough?' he asked with a laugh.

'He paid me what we'd agreed on. But after the murder of the second girl he didn't believe any longer that Gloria was killed for personal reasons.'

'And you still believe the motive was a personal one?' asked Sierra, looking closely at him. 'And you've decided not to give it up.'

'I like to finish what I've started. Would you leave a sculpture half-finished?' He pointed at the heavy tree trunk that lay across the bench.

Sierra threw his head back and laughed.

'A half-finished sculpture? Lots of them! I've left dozens unfinished. I always give them up halfway through if I lose inspiration. And even those I've finished I often think I should have done more work on.'

'That's the difference between your work and mine. I can't rely on inspiration from the Muses. Only logic.'

'Aren't detectives guided by intuition any longer?' His tone was ironic, but it remained pleasant.

'No, and I don't believe they ever were.'

The sculptor hung up his hammer and chisel on a wooden board attached to the wall, where they remained silhouetted, like tools in many repair shops. Then he blew out the candle. In another corner of the shed Cupido noticed a couple of jointed puppets, one male and the other female, that seemed to stare at him with stupid expressions on their old-fashioned faces.

'I thought you were working in metal,' he observed.

The sculptor glanced towards the oak trunk and its tough, strong, rich wood.

'I always come back to wood. Particularly when I get my hands on material like this which is already dry and won't split. It's a wonderful survivor of those immense forests of holm oak that irrigation has ruined. So tough, noble, almost eternal,' he said, giving it an affectionate smack as he might the shoulder of an old friend or the flank of a horse. 'Do you know how old it is?'

'No.'

'Three hundred, maybe four hundred years. It would be unforgivable not to make something really good out of this.'

The detective recalled the spindly, twisted metal figures, the disastrous exhibition and the bad reviews.

'There are times when I think that you people here don't really appreciate the good things you have around you. It needs someone from outside to point them out.'

'Maybe.'

'D'you know what Hesiod said of holm oaks more than 2,700 years ago?'

'No.'

'He said it was the tree the gods had planted for the happiness of good men. And he was right. Everything about it is good: its shade, its roots, its wood and its fruit. There isn't one season of the year when it doesn't provide some benefit to both man and beast. Besides which, it doesn't burn easily when it's alive.'

He tugged at a small filament of bark that remained attached to the wood. The detective wondered what had brought about this change of attitude. Now that he had put aside his arrogant manner the sculptor was pleasant and thoughtful, as if the wood touched him with its humility and warmth.

'It isn't easy to find a trunk like this one. You have to wait a long time. If you were a sculptor what would you do with it?' he asked suddenly.

Cupido considered the thickness of the trunk, the slight narrowing in the middle, and the soft curve to one side. He had no idea from what part of his mind or memory his response emerged, but he replied: 'A mother and child.'

Sierra's look was approving.

'Yes, a mother and child,' he agreed. 'It may not be a very original subject, but that's one of the things I learned from

Gloria: I had to find out where my own powers lie, and what my limitations are. Even now that she's no longer with us I've learned my last lesson from her.'

Cupido followed him to the house and entered an enormous living-room furnished with a mixture of dark and massive antique furniture with fat, turned legs, and narrow, slender shelving made of metal and glass. Cupido couldn't see even one of the stylized metal sculptures that had been the product of his work with Gloria. On the contrary, there were several empty stands, and others that supported figurative sculptures and busts. There wasn't a single drawing of her on the walls, as if he had tried to suppress not only his memories but the fact that she had ever existed.

Sierra went to the kitchen and came back with a bottle of wine and two glasses which he filled without even asking if that was what Cupido would like to drink.

'I've reached the conclusion that Gloria would never have suggested collaborating with me if she'd foreseen the unsatisfactory work she would get out of me. I never made one metal sculpture that was worth the effort when I was trying to respond to her vision. What I mean is: reproducing the cave-paintings in three dimensions. I was simply following her lead, either copying her directly or trying to reproduce her ideas in sculpture. She must soon have realized that it wasn't working out, but she didn't say anything. I'd have preferred it if we'd talked it through. I suggested doing so once or twice but Gloria always avoided the subject. But the harder she tried to ignore the disparity the more the distance widened between her work and mine. It was as if her inspiration grew as mine diminished.'

He took a long drink of wine, and rolled it round his mouth before swallowing it straight down as if trying to clean or freshen his tongue in preparation for what he wanted to say next.

'What I hadn't expected was that even after her death I would go on learning from her. Now that she's no longer with us all that talk of future joint exhibitions has collapsed like a statue made of sand. I could never bring myself to confess to her that I was only good for figurative work, and that I lost all my powers as soon as I approached any form of abstract art.'

The detective looked round the room and understood perfectly what he was saying. The sculptures there, almost all of them carved in wood, and some of them in a shiny black material, were possibly less ambitious, and displayed less of an attempt to surprise than his metal ones, but they combined naturalness with a distinctly individual style. By contrast, in her paintings done in the Reserve, Gloria had gone much further. There was a personal philosophy implicit in these: a hymn to the hardness and fertility of the ground, respect for earth's bounty, the rich animal life it supports, and the conviction that a deer living on the mountain makes it pregnant with mystery. Her paintings displayed nostalgia for a lost paradise. *He, on the other hand, is a social creature. Although he seemed very shallow the last time we met, he's obviously a man who needs the company of others*, he said to himself. In the relatively few days since the fiasco of his exhibition in Madrid he seemed greatly changed. He had swallowed his pride, as if his profession as an artist justified all previous contradictions. Cupido didn't ignore the possibility that this might be nothing less than a carefully thought out diversionary tactic: it is difficult to imagine someone who expresses gratitude towards the victim being capable of her murder. More loose ends in the tangled web, he thought. But he was confident he would soon make the right connections that would throw light on the mystery.

Sierra must have interpreted his glances round the room as a search for something, because he said: 'I've put away the pictures I got from Gloria. For a while at least, until I stop feeling her presence around me. However, I can show you something that'll interest you.'

He drained his glass, stood, and went up a single flight of wooden stairs leading to the upper part of the room that had been built as a gallery. He came down a moment later holding a videotape.

'I couldn't remember if I had it or she did, but a few days ago while I was putting her pictures away I found it in a corner. You'll like it.'

He switched on the television, tuned it to the video, and returned to the sofa with the remote control. A beautiful view of countryside that Cupido knew well glided slowly and smoothly across the screen. It showed the narrow stretches and the twists and turns in the Lebron River where it is held back by the dam. The shot had been taken from the high ledge with the caves, and the detective had to admire the steady hand of the person who had taken it. The four years he had spent in the Film Institute made him appreciate the smoothness of the pan. He was thankful that the photographer was not like those tourists who think that a camera has the same ability to capture a vast panorama as quickly as the human eye – and can reduce the whole of the Canary Islands into a fifteen-minute film!

'Who did this?'

'I did,' replied Sierra, without averting his eyes from the television screen.

The camera stopped panning when it reached the figure of a girl who, with a smile and a wave of her hand like a professional guide, invited spectators to follow her along the narrow ledge which, a few metres further on, led to the mouth of the cave. The detective sat bolt upright. It was Gloria. It was Gloria, and now he could see her as if she were alive, the way she moved, the radiant smile that showed to perfection her exquisite red lips, looking so much more lovely than in the still photographs he had seen of her and which hadn't been able to capture more than one facet at a time of her remarkable beauty, nothing more than a single expression. There she stood before them, filling the screen with her arms outstretched, lighting it from within every time she smiled with a spontaneity that combined sensuality with innocence.

The following sequences, shot inside the cave with the inadequate natural light augmented by a small battery lamp attached to the top of the camera, showed the detail of the paintings: the deer, some isolated, others in groups, the stylized human figures always depicted in profile as they hunted the deer, the arrows flying across the stone of the cave wall like raindrops. These images brought back to Cupido's mind the memories of afternoons when he, with a number of other boys, had climbed up there. They would sit on the ledge, their legs dangling over the void, drinking rough, heavy wine that made them stumble on their way home. Then they would enter the cave, and sometimes urinate over the paintings to make them stand out better. The red oxide would turn to a more intense red which gave greater precision to the outlines of the figures. Years later, he had wondered whether these sporadic sprays of urine to which they subjected the paintings hadn't made them deteriorate, but nobody seemed to have noticed any ill effect, almost as if adolescent urine had rather surprisingly contributed to their enhanced preservation. In those days, clambering up to the caves for the first time was a sort of tribal initiation rite, and until he had gone through it no young boy was admitted into the ranks of the adolescents. And later, as night began to fall and the sun sank into the Volcan crater, they would return to Breda in silence, feeling they had seen and experienced something they were unable to comprehend: that they had changed from who they were before going up there and contemplating those paintings to become wiser, and less childish.

'We made this video so that we could study the details of the paintings more closely to help us work up our variations on them.' Sierra's voice brought him back to the images on the television. 'Gloria had it for a few days, and then she passed it on to me as if she'd already learned all she needed to know.'

A few moments later, the camera left the cave interior and returned to the ledge outside. Sierra had begun to photograph Gloria again in spite of her protests. But then she had sat down to look at the view, and allowed the camera to make a searching examination of her whole body until coming to concentrate on her profile and its halo of hair. Lost in admiration of the view she seemed almost happy, without a worry in the world, and with no premonition that she would soon die near that very spot.

'She was very beautiful,' the sculptor whispered.

'Yes,' was all the detective found to say.

'I phoned her at the hotel that Saturday,' he added, suddenly. 'I thought I'd go with her on her walk. I had to talk to her. I was going to ask her to cancel the exhibition.'

'How many times did you ring?' asked Cupido.

'Twice, but I probably didn't insist strongly enough.'

Another tiny detail that I know now and which doesn't lead anywhere, he thought.

The video had ended, and the screen went blank as it scrolled to the end, but Sierra didn't switch it off.

'Did she mention anything significant to you? Did she say if she was going to walk up there with anybody else?'

'No. She was going on her own as she had often done, and she didn't want me to go with her. I told her we had to talk about the exhibition,' he explained. He gave a despondent look, and added: 'You know how that ended. A week ago I came to Breda and left it all behind.'

'You haven't been to Madrid since?'

'No.'

'And last Sunday – were you in Breda?'

'What does that mean?' he replied slowly, as if trying to detect a trap.

'The lieutenant will be asking you what you were doing on Sunday morning – when the game warden was killed.'

These words seemed to make Sierra ill at ease, but he hid this by making a face at Cupido as if to indicate that he wasn't at all happy at being considered a suspect. After talking so freely to the detective and showing him the video, he hadn't expected the type of question that suggested continuing suspicion.

'He's already asked me. I went for a walk in the country. That was the morning I came across the tree,' he said, gesturing towards the shed.

'Did anybody see you?'

'I don't think so. Although, out in the country, you can never be sure somebody isn't watching you.'

'So you haven't got an alibi for that day,' said Cupido, trying to ensure that his tone of voice didn't sound harassing.

'No, and I don't need one. Not having an alibi isn't proof of guilt. You're the ones who have to prove your accusations,' he replied sharply. But he seemed more sad than angry.

'No, don't get me wrong. I don't accuse anyone. That's the job of the police and the magistrates,' said Cupido mildly.

'What's your job then?' asked Sierra sarcastically.

'It's different every time. It depends upon who's paying me.'

'And this time? You told me that Anglada's sacked you.'

'Not sacked exactly. In his opinion there isn't anything to work on. Anyway, I haven't given it up yet. I don't like leaving work unfinished. I've told you that already.'

The videotape came to the end with a click and began to rewind. As if this was a signal for him to leave, Cupido stood up and went towards the door. From there he asked: 'Were you lovers?'

'No. I lied when we were talking in Madrid. I thought that a rejected lover always runs the risk of being regarded as a suspect. But Gloria always rejected my advances.'

Without knowing quite why, the detective was pleased to hear those last words. It also occurred to him how different Gloria was according to which person was describing her – each one's image of her was distorted either by cowardice, by love, or by the intention of discrediting her. He left Sierra with the same feeling he had begun to have for some days: he felt drowsy and slow-witted, as if he'd just woken up after sleeping for a month and was unable to deduce the underlying truth in anything he saw or whatever he was told.

While he drove slowly home the thought struck him that all the individuals who had been attracted to Gloria had been loners. Or they had become loners after her death: Sierra, Marcos Anglada, David, Camila, Octavio, Armengol. As far as he knew not one of them had a stable relationship. In one way or another, almost all of them seemed to have depended upon Gloria emotionally, and once she disappeared the only link between them was loneliness. During her life, Gloria had been their only support and centre of gravity, in the way the central rod of an umbrella supports its spokes. Now she was dead there remained only tattered black cloth clinging to spikes that were capable of inflicting damage.

He went up to his apartment, and when he had sat down, bored, to eat some leftovers from the previous day, he realized he was irritated with himself. He emptied the remaining half bottle of Ribera del Duero he had kept in the fridge, and by the time he reached the coffee stage found himself obsessed yet again by a longing for a cigarette, although he thought he had overcome this. He wondered what the explanation was for this sudden fit of unjustified bad temper, and stopped short when it occurred to him that it was Gloria who was the cause. She had revealed to him too his own lonely condition. His brief, occasional adventures were of no importance, as if by now he was incapable of real passion; these escapades involved slightly more than just sex, but fell far short of love. Had they not occurred, nothing fundamental would have changed in him. They were encounters that happened at convenient times, each one giving a few moments of pleasure, and then almost disappearing from memory, like pale shadows. He couldn't even remember the names of many of his women; and not even their faces in some cases; only physical sensations. But all of them, in one way or another, had provided a break from solitude and the feeling of contentment that for him always followed the act of love. It was quite some time now that he had been living in a state of self-imposed continence. Gloria had made him remember all the chances he had let slip through his fingers: not always having to eat alone, not having a child of his own – because that would never happen now, not having a profession that wouldn't provoke so many doubts and anxieties. He realized that his memories of the really good things in his life dated back at least fifteen years. It was too long not to end up relapsing into depression and nostalgia.

Without giving his stomach time to assimilate the food and wine, he put on his cycling clothes and went down to the garage. He unlocked the padlock and mounted the bicycle. He hadn't used it since the day of Molina's murder. As he went up the stretch of road where he had previously heard the shots, he looked with misgiving in that direction, as if the huge, silent expanse with its millions of oak trees and pines where millions of animals lived was still unexplored territory, as threatening as it was fascinating. He changed into a higher gear, prepared to sweat it out. A bit further on he turned off the main road, and on to the road bordering the northern slope of Yunque Mountain, which, in winter, was blocked by snow and landslides. A climb of fourteen kilometres, with scarcely a flat stretch. He began to pedal slowly, trying to maintain an even rhythm like Induráin whom he had frequently watched, but after fifteen minutes he was already beginning to feel the strain.

Feeling very tired, he soon went down to his lowest gear, and the speedometer hovered between nine and eleven kph, the slowest speed that kept the bicycle upright. At that rate it would take him another hour to get to the top. He knew by then he wouldn't make it, but he clutched the handlebars tightly, clenched the muscles in his lower back, and for a few minutes found the strength to carry on. He set his eye on targets in the distance – a tree, a curve in the road, a pile of rocks – bent his head and pedalled until he reckoned he should have reached them. But he was wrong each time, and whenever he raised his head it was to see that there was still some way to go. He calculated that he was halfway to the top. The road was beginning to deteriorate, and every rut in it made the effort greater. The surface was rough and hard, and the dry earth threw up a fine dust that caught his throat. He began to feel his legs trembling as if they had turned to jelly, and that somebody had ripped his lungs out of his chest. The palms of his hands hurt from gripping the handlebars so hard, and the drops of sweat on his forehead streamed down over his eyebrows. When he saw the sign indicating that he had reached kilometre ten of the climb he decided he had done enough. At least he'd got that far. He turned slowly round, pulled up the zip of his anorak to protect him from the rush of air and then freewheeled faster and faster down the slope. But he had to slow down: he was too tired to let it go so fast, to hold tight on the handlebars, to concentrate on steering round bends, or having to brake hard. He stretched his legs one after the other – which his knees gratefully acknowledged. He had a distinct feeling of blood coursing smoothly again through the arteries and veins. Thick phlegm came up into his mouth from the very bottom of his lungs as a result of his efforts, and he spat it out distastefully to one side. *The remains of the nicotine*, he thought. It took him fifteen minutes to ride down the ten kilometres, and then he coasted the last fifteen kilometres to Breda. When he reached the door of the garage he felt well, fully recovered and regretted not having made a bit more effort to get to the top. He believed that happened to all keen cyclists.

He wheeled the machine to the two-metre-square room that housed the electricity meters. It had a sliding door set into its brick wall, constructed this way in order not to have a door opening outwards on to the narrow space where cars passed, or inwards where it might have damaged the meters. He leant the bicycle against the wall and took the small padlock key out of a back pocket of his anorak. Possibly because his fingers were wet with perspiration or stiff from gripping the handlebars until just a moment before, the key slipped out of his hands. Without bending down, but watching it fall, he heard the three metallic, almost musical clinks it made, like a little bell, as it bounced on the concrete floor and came to rest in the narrow aperture into which the sliding door fitted. He swore and bent down to pick it up. But he couldn't see the key. It must have slipped a few centimetres into the gap between the double wall. He tugged at the door in the hope that he could pull it open further, but this didn't work. He knelt down and peered through the two-centimetre gap that the door left on each side. The poor light in the garage didn't penetrate it, and he could see nothing. He stood up and thought for a moment of leaving the bicycle without its padlock so that he could go up, have a shower, and forget this tiresome little problem. Tomorrow he would buy a new padlock. It would be sheer bad luck if someone came in and stole it during the night. He gave a last look round, and then spotted on top of one of the highest meters a small torch that must have been there for use in case of difficulty. He took it down and, although it was covered in dust, checked that the battery still had enough strength to light the small bulb. He pointed its yellow light into the slot and saw his key some fifteen to twenty centimetres inside, beyond the reach of his fingers. Nor would any of the tools he carried under his saddle for repairing punctures be long enough to reach it. And he couldn't see anything else around that would help. But now he'd found it he had to get it out somehow. He looked at the rail fixed on the upper part of the doorway. The door itself slid along this by means of two runners until it came up against a small stop or buffer that was held in place by a simple Phillips screw. Something flashed through his mind, but recognition of its significance was so fleeting and faint that he didn't immediately realize its relevance. He took out a small screwdriver from his car tool kit and slackened off the screw holding the stop. This enabled him to slide the door a little further, which was enough for him to be able to put his hand in and pick up the key. Without the thickness of the door between the double wall there was a space of about eight centimetres: a hiding place where no one would dream of looking because the purpose of a door is to open and shut to conceal or reveal the interior of a space, not so that something can be hidden inside it. That was the moment when he remembered the exact words Gloria had used when talking to David: *Nobody could possibly find it. Even if they were to open and close the doors of the hiding place they'd never see it. It would remain hidden.* He remembered the double sliding doors in her apartment, and in that instant was convinced that, in there, in a similar place, but cleaner and easier to get at, 250 kilometres from the garage where the little key of his bicycle padlock had by chance fallen, there, in that locked apartment, lay the diary.

Nineteen

The very next day Cupido was in Madrid. In spite of impatience having made him sleep badly he was up unusually early and left Breda at nine. Two and a half hours later he left his car in a parking place near Anglada's apartment. From there he phoned him, but hung up before the answering machine worked all the way through its message. If he couldn't speak to him personally it wasn't going to be easy to get into Gloria's apartment again. They'd already searched it together and found nothing. Besides which, Anglada was a lawyer, and now that the detective was no longer working for him he might come up with a dozen legal reasons for not getting himself more deeply involved in the matter.

To pass the time he went for a coffee, read the paper, and strolled round the neighbourhood. Even in the capital he was conscious of the effects of the drought. The gardens and the lawns were yellow. The acacias had lost their leaves early and their thorns were more sharply pointed than ever, and many bushes had shrunk down in the flower beds to conserve their moisture.

At one-thirty he made his way back to the apartment block. As nobody answered Anglada's door bell, he decided to wait in the entrance hall, and he sat down in one of the deep armchairs ranged along one side. By four o'clock Anglada still hadn't arrived, but the wait had not been excessively tedious because he had enjoyed watching the comings and goings of a wide variety of characters: a bustling individual carrying a Samsonite briefcase in one hand like a letter of recommendation who wore a double-breasted suit and expensive shoes; a prostitute who had a taxi waiting permanently at the door; her clients, lonely types who came in looking furtive and suspicious; a girl who had been out jogging; part-time cleaning women; handsome and elegant elderly gentlemen who displayed no surprise at all by what went on around them.

He knew by then that Anglada wouldn't be returning for lunch but would have eaten in a restaurant not to waste time, and as he reached this conclusion he realized that he too was getting very hungry. He had more appetite, and was eating more since he had given up smoking. He'd already put on a kilo or so, but this didn't worry him because he had always been slim, and it wouldn't show. In a bar on the other side of the street, from which he could still keep watch on the main entrance to the apartment block, he ordered a ham sandwich and a glass of beer. After this he had a coffee and stayed there for a while longer in order to delay returning to the lobby opposite. But by a quarter to five he was back in the armchair, still waiting.

He saw him arrive on foot, a briefcase under his arm. Cupido got up quickly and hurried up the stairs to the second floor before Anglada could notice him. As the lawyer came out of the lift looking for his keys he caught sight of the detective leaning against the wall, and looking weary as if he had spent a long time in the same place and the same stance.

'You here?' he asked, with no attempt to hide his surprise.

'I've got something else to ask you for.'

Anglada looked at him suspiciously, as a banker might look at a beggar who approaches him on the corner of the street.

'Yes?' he asked, without making a move to open the door.

'Can we talk inside for a moment?'

He could see that his request was not welcome, but the lawyer reluctantly agreed.

'Is there something new?'

'No. That's why I've come to see you. There's nothing new, but I still think the diary contains information that could clear up a number of things.'

Anglada sighed, raised his hands, and dropped them on to the back of a chair.

'Are you still going on with all that?'

'Yes.'

'Who are you working for now?' he asked. His eyes couldn't help revealing apprehension made more acute by pessimism, presumably because of the many days that had elapsed since the murder, and the lack of success in Cupido's investigations.

'Nobody,' replied the detective. He didn't find it easy to explain but made an effort to sound convincing. 'I can't get this business out of my head, and I can't accept that there's no solution to it.'

'I thought for a moment you were coming to ask for more money.' He smiled. 'Just for a moment. Then I remembered your way of working, so it doesn't surprise me that you want to continue with the case on your own account. You're not a lawyer. You'd never make a good lawyer, though you're a good detective.'

Cupido accepted this judgement without interrupting. He needed all the goodwill possible for what he was about to ask for.

'You ought to forget this job once and for all,' continued Anglada. 'I've got more reasons than you have to remember her every single day, but every day I make an effort to put her out of my mind. That murder was committed by a maniac, a lunatic. The later murders show there was nothing personal about it.'

'I'd like to have another look for the diary,' Cupido insisted.

Anglada shook his head.

'A waste of time. We've already made a thorough search and we didn't miss a thing. That diary isn't in her apartment or her studio.'

'Let me try once more. Just once. Nothing will be lost by doing so. You owe it to her,' he said. He felt slightly ridiculous and melodramatic as he brought out these last words, but he knew they would be the most difficult ones for the lawyer to rebut.

'Is there something new that leads you to believe the diary is hidden in the apartment?'

'No,' he lied. He no longer had any obligation towards Anglada.

'I can't let you have the keys,' he said, shaking his head again. 'I haven't got them. I had a letter a few days ago from a firm of lawyers in Breda. It was a nicely written letter – as from one professional to another. Those extraordinary relations of Gloria down there have started proceedings to obtain her inheritance. It seems they're in a hurry. So until that's cleared up, nobody's allowed in there. The apartment and the study are legally barred to entry. They didn't specifically ask me for the keys, but even so I sent them back by return of post.'

He opened his hands to indicate that they were clean and empty, that he was holding nothing back, but Cupido wasn't sure whether to believe him. Nothing would have been easier than to have made copies of the keys. He couldn't see him giving up all Gloria's possessions so meekly: her jewellery, paintings, personal letters, objects that had belonged to the two of them, and all those intimate items that are part and parcel of living together. He glanced up at the walls of the apartment: there was still room for more pictures. But he also sensed that there was something different about them. The living room furniture was still in its usual places, the kitchen was still spotless, and everything was still neatly arranged.

He stood up and Anglada accompanied him to the door.

'Let me know if anything new crops up.'

'Of course.'

Armengol's apartment was halfway on his route to the Gallery. He wasn't confident of discovering anything from him, but he wouldn't lose much time in trying.

He rang the bell twice and waited more than a minute. As he heard no movement inside he pressed the button again, mechanically, before turning away to go back to the stairs, not greatly disappointed because he hadn't expected much from the interview. Then he heard footsteps that were muffled, but not furtive, and were approaching the door. He looked up at the peephole through which he knew Armengol was looking at him, and waited for the door to open. He wore a blue towelling bathrobe that was too heavy for those early November days which were still warm and dry. His hair stood on end as if he had been stretched out on his bed or the sofa, possibly sleeping, although the television could be heard from somewhere in the apartment.

'Come in,' he said, stepping to one side.

The detective went into the small living-room, on the left of which could be seen the tiny kitchen that was only one and a half metres wide. The forty or fifty square-metre rented apartment was all the teacher's salary would run to after handing over the amount he was required to pay for the maintenance of his two children at the end of each month.

It was as dirty and untidy as before: there was clothing draped over the back of one chair, two empty beer bottles and several ashtrays full of cigarettes that had been smoked down to the filter on the table; the floor was unswept, and the furniture was covered with a coating of dust that had accumulated from neglect.

'Sit down,' he said, pointing to an armchair, and revealing his bad, yellow teeth, that resembled grains of maize. 'I've got some beer. Would you like some?'

'Yes. Thanks.'

Cupido watched him from behind as he bent down in front of the door of the fridge: the bathrobe looked as if it was a long time since it had been washed and was fastened round his waist with a cord; he wore slippers and black socks which came up to his calves revealing parts of his thin, white, hairless legs. Either Gloria hadn't looked closely before going to bed with him, or he had gone downhill quickly in the year since his separation and desertion, and had become a different man, sad and old. The black socks he wore at home added to his dirty, pathetic appearance. *It won't be long before he becomes really ill. Drink, cigarettes and living alone are burning him up, and he'll go out like a light*, he thought, looking at the almost empty fridge. There was half a cheap loaf, something dark that could have been cold meat and a dozen cans of beer. It was at the far extreme from the aura of strength, success, cleanliness and care of himself that emanated from Anglada. Two very different men who for a time had shared the life and the bed of the same woman. It wasn't easy to understand her, as Camila had said, although the contradiction might possibly be explained by an intense desire to explore every aspect of life, to sample all its extremes – to taste flavours that differ so much from each other that when taken together their differences are even more contrasted, like a person who fills his mouth with oysters and lemon juice in the same moment.

'Have you got more questions you forgot to ask me last time?' he said, his voice husky from heavy smoking. He held two cans of beer in his hands, but hesitated before opening them.

'I've come to ask you for something.'

'I haven't much to give,' came the reply, his voice expressing both distrust and discouragement.

'Do you still have keys to Gloria's apartment?'

'The apartment where she lived?'

'Yes.'

'Why d'you want to know?'

'I need to get in there.'

'Why don't you ask Anglada?'

'Because I'm no longer working for him.'

He stared at him in surprise, but didn't ask the reason. He snapped open the cans of beer and gave one to Cupido without offering a glass. There was nothing friendly in the gesture; it merely expressed a weary indifference.

'There was another murder similar to Gloria's, and Anglada believes both were carried out by a lunatic. He saw no sense in continuing to spend money on a private detective.'

'But you still believe it was someone who knew her?'

'Yes,' he replied without hesitation.

'And you're going on looking although nobody's paying you.'

'Yes.'

He made a face and shook his head implying that for once he agreed with Anglada, and wished the whole business could be forgotten.

'What d'you hope to find there?'

'Her diary.'

The detective noted how he suddenly became defensive, and although he had learned not to place much trust in the facial expressions of people he interviewed, the signs of fear and suspicion that appeared on the other's face were too obvious and unexpected not to be taken seriously.

'Did you know about it?'

'I'd forgotten it, but now you mention it I do remember Gloria telling me about it on one occasion. I think she used to note down anything important that happened to her. Is that why...?' He stopped, as if suddenly realizing that his own privacy might be breached, and possibly in a not very pleasant way. What might Gloria have written about him? Not in the early days when she still liked him, when she was persuading him to take up painting again, and when she talked to him about her dreams for the future, but in the last weeks when boredom, impatience and a total loss of desire had suddenly come over her.

'Yes.'

Armengol shook his head several times.

'No. I never had keys to her apartment. And even if I did I wouldn't give them to you,' he concluded, firmly and obstinately.

They looked at each other for several moments without a word, the detective surprised by the man's sudden and unexpected opposition – as if he were reacting for the first time to the threatened destruction of the last defences round his private world and his pride with a fervour he wouldn't have believed possible.

'You've no right to violate her private thoughts,' he said bitterly, trembling from his head to his feet in their black socks, the elastic tops of which cut into his thin, white, almost hairless calves.

'I've no intention of violating Gloria's private life – only her murderer's.'

'It won't bring her back,' he riposted. He stood up, and added: 'Now go away. I can't and won't help you in anything like that.'

The detective obeyed him in silence. As he heard the door close his mind was full of doubts.

The gallery had closed to the public at nine o'clock, ten minutes before he arrived, but Cupido could see from outside the bunch of keys dangling from the lock of the door and the lights that were still on, illuminating an exhibition of pastel landscapes of middling quality. He gave it a quick glance and thought that this was more saleable material than Gloria would have liked. But now that she was no longer there, her partner, working alone, seemed to be betting on safe sales rather than taking risks with less conventional material. He saw Camila go through the office door at the back of the gallery, and wondered for a moment or so whether it was worth going in. He didn't expect she would be able to help him. Besides which, he was tired, it had been a long day, beginning with his drive that morning, quite apart from the two unhelpful conversations. On the other hand, this could be a good moment to talk to her, because there were no customers around. He pressed the bell which was placed high up on the frame of the door. Camila's head appeared, and she looked towards him. Recognizing him immediately, she walked smartly over to the door, her high heels tapping across the floor.

'I never expected to see you again,' she said. She was wearing less make-up than the last time they had met, just a few light touches of eye-shadow and lipstick, which gave Cupido the impression that she was now using make-up less as a defence against unwelcome familiarity, and more as a deliberate seduction technique. Because, he thought, women employ make-up as a means of declaring publicly what they want or what they fear – their intentions, or as an expression of their insecurity.

'There's something else I have to ask you.'

'Are you still involved in the investigation?' she asked with surprise. 'Marcos told me the two of you had given it up.'

'He has, but I don't like leaving a job unfinished. My reputation would suffer,' he added with an ironic smile.

They were still standing in the doorway. Camila nodded towards her office, and said: 'Wait a moment. I'll close up, and then we can go and talk somewhere else. Somewhere quiet.'

She switched off the light, and for a second or two Cupido could see nothing until his eyes grew accustomed to the dark. Without moving away from the door he heard her footsteps approaching, and then he was just able to make out her excellent figure, and he also caught a subtle waft of perfume that suggested she had renewed it before coming back to him.

'Have you had dinner?'

'No.'

'Let me invite you then. This has been a wonderful day for sales, and I've nobody to celebrate it with,' she confessed.

'I'd be delighted.'

She locked the front door, and turning round, gave him a warm smile.

'When everything's gone well this is the very best moment of the day. Once everybody else has gone home I can lock the door and leave my work behind – and the smell of oil paint and varnish.'

Cupido looked at her in some surprise, because her words did nothing to conceal an openly commercial attitude towards her job, which was more than just different, it was at the other extreme from Gloria's idea of it.

'We'd better take a taxi,' she added. She sounded like one of those pleasant and protective women Cupido had quite often got to know when visiting cities with which he was unfamiliar. Fifteen minutes later they were sitting opposite each other at a table in the Restaurant Viridiana. They had already started on a third glass of wine each before the waiter brought their first dishes, and still the detective hadn't told her the reason he had come to see her. And nor had she asked. They had begun by talking about Gloria, and the little they knew about her death, but then had moved on to the gallery and the different artistic tastes of the two women, and it finished with Camila describing how the gallery had come into her hands, as if she had an interest in giving him her side of the story. The legal agreement between them had stipulated that the property couldn't be split up and there was a clause stating that in the event of one of them wanting to sell out at some future date, the other would have the first right of purchase. In that way, the spirit of continuity in which they had set it up would always be maintained. For the same reason they had decided that if one of them disappeared unexpectedly, her half share would pass automatically to the other. Neither of them had direct descendants who might inherit it. Gloria only had her relations in Breda, and Camila some brothers and sisters she rarely saw.

'It was Gloria who suggested we put that clause in – it would never have occurred to me, although I immediately agreed to it,' she explained. 'It simply expressed the confidence each of us had in the other, because nobody imagines they're suddenly going to disappear. It's always other people who are going to die. In any case, it would probably have been me because I'm eight years older than her.'

'Was she always an impulsive person?'

'Almost always, except in her painting. She never thought too much before doing things, although afterwards she'd spend hours analysing them. She loved running on quicksand. But she had a guardian angel who looked after her.'

'Except the last time,' said Cupido.

'Yes, except the last time,' she repeated.

'Was she also like that with her friends?'

Camila raised a piece of meat to her mouth, and savoured it before replying.

'She sent men mad. They all fell in love with her.'

'Why? What was so special about her?'

'First of all, she was very pretty. I can't explain it easily but she still had something of the adolescent in her face – a balance between light and shade. There were two types of attractiveness in her that seemed to contend with each other, as if she waited for the man to make up his mind in favour of one of them, knowing that she held the other in reserve for another occasion. I imagine that must be very bewildering for a man.'

'I understand,' said Cupido. He knew what she was trying to say. The first time he had seen a photograph of Gloria he had been fascinated by the childlike fullness of her lips, while her cheekbones had seemed to attract the light. He had observed that in infancy the expressiveness of a face lies in the flesh, whereas in maturity it's in the bone structure, and finally, in old age, the most telling feature is the skin with its network of lines and wrinkles. Gloria had arrived at the second stage without losing the best of the first.

'And secondly, she knew how to behave with them like a woman deeply in love, but without actually being in love. And when a man reaches the age when it's no longer quite so easy to pick and choose, there's nothing more seductive than to see a woman in love with him, don't you agree?'

'Yes, I do. But didn't that sort of behaviour create problems for her?'

'With whom?'

'Anglada. But not only Anglada. With all of them. No man likes to discover one day that the woman he believes is really in love with him has been leading a double life behind his back.'

'It wasn't always like that, but certainly it did sometimes create problems for her. All you men are the same in that respect,' she said, raising her glass and taking another sip of wine. Then, she added: 'That's what led to my divorce.'

The detective looked at her in some surprise because it wasn't the first time when talking about Gloria that she had made a point of referring to her own experience, as if she feared being left out.

'I didn't know,' he said. He couldn't say quite why, but he had never thought of her as having been married. He glanced at her left hand on which she wore a profusion of rings, but there wasn't a wedding ring among them.

'It was a member of your profession who contributed to the break-up,' she explained, assessing Cupido's reaction to what she was saying.

'How did that happen?' he asked out of curiosity. He noticed that their bottle was empty and motioned to the waiter to bring another.

'My ex-husband hired a private detective to obtain proof that would make our divorce go through easily. I was going out with an artist who had an exhibition in the gallery. It didn't last long, just long enough to discover that it was a flash in the pan and wasn't going to lead anywhere. My ex also had a lover, so I didn't worry about my little adventure until a few weeks later when it was all over and he presented me with a demand for divorce and some ghastly photographs to justify it. I'd thought that what was happening between us was simply a minor crisis in our relationship that would soon blow over, as it does with so many people. After all, he too was enjoying himself away from home. But I couldn't do anything about it. We broke up and my life changed completely. It wasn't a happy time. To be separated in that way when it's the other person who insists on it is depressing, above all when you find out that he wasn't in the least upset by my affair and only made use of it to make it easier for him to obtain the divorce. As you must know, everybody's careful to hide from the wife the fact that the husband is having a fling while you're still together but can't wait to tell you all about it once you're separated. Anyway, from the gossip going around I know now that he was divorced again not long after. I've been more prudent since then.'

She was silent for a few moments but Cupido waited for her to go on with her story. He knew that silence on his part could often bring people to talk more freely than questions did. She wasn't the first woman to tell him about the break-up of her marriage, but she was the first to talk about it almost with indifference, while revealing little ill will towards her unfaithful and contentious ex-husband, or seeking sympathy for her own misfortune. *She's tougher than she looks*, he thought. *There's a lot of strength behind that delicate make-up and perfume, just as it's the most fragile-looking sea-shells that make the hardest fossils!*

'It ended badly and neither of us was wholly guilty or wholly innocent. The only individual I came to detest, only briefly but intensely, was the detective he'd hired for the job. He was loathsome. I had to meet him twice in the lawyer's office. It seemed to me a repellent job – at least that particular aspect of it – ' she explained, lowering her eyes, ' – watching and snooping round bedrooms. That's why I was surprised when we were introduced. You look so different. I can't imagine you taking dirty photographs for a divorce case.'

You'd be wrong, thought Cupido, but he didn't say a word. He had done it twice, and each time had avoided meeting his victims. He had limited his role to obtaining the evidence by the most discreet means possible, and without agreeing to a personal meeting. Even so he hadn't be able to shake off the uncomfortable feeling that he was contributing to a prosecution without granting the accused a chance to defend himself.

The mention of his work reminded him why he had gone to see her. Their conversation, and the considerable quantity of wine they were drinking had almost made him forget it.

'Do you have keys to Gloria's apartment?' he asked.

'Yes. I've still got a set at home. I forgot to give them to Marcos when he picked up her personal things. Do you need them?'

'Yes. I want to look for her diary.'

'Haven't you found it yet?'

'No, but I believe that what she wrote in it should clear up a number of things. Anglada has no right to touch anything there until the question of inheritance has been sorted out,' he said, forestalling what was likely to be her next question.

'It's a bit late now. Can you wait until tomorrow?' she asked.

'Of course I can,' he responded readily. He had guessed a few moments before how the evening was going to end, and the prospect was far from displeasing. He had become fastidious with the years, and had now reached the age when he didn't go to bed with just any woman, refused to drink poor wine, and he wouldn't read a book simply because it happened to be to hand. But Camila attracted him more than enough to arouse his desire and to lead him to ignore the gulf between them.

She had already settled the bill by the time he came back from the cloakroom. They left the restaurant and took a taxi to her apartment. In contrast to the other apartments he had seen in the last few weeks – Anglada's, Sierra's, and Armengol's –

each of them designed for one person only – this one was big enough to house a family. The sofa in the living room was designed for three people, there were three bedrooms, and it had a general air of spaciousness.

Camila took out two tall glasses, put ice cubes in them, and poured a generous quantity of whisky into each.

'Do sit down,' she said.

When she returned from the bathroom a few minutes later, the detective sat with his head resting against the comfortable back of the sofa, his eyes closed. He didn't hear her, but felt her hands placed on his shoulders from behind at the same time as he became aware of her perfume.

'You're tired,' she said.

Cupido placed his right hand on hers and drew her towards him; she came round the end of the sofa and sat beside him. It was just a few minutes before, after coming up to her apartment, that she also knew how the evening was going to end.

'A little,' he replied.

She leant over towards him, and they kissed slowly, while their hands began the caresses that each expected of the other, and their lips parted from time to time to whisper the familiar words of love-making.

'Come to the bedroom,' she said.

The bed was very big. On one of the side-tables he saw a pair of reading glasses on a book: *Games Of Later Life* by Luis Landero. On the other table was a little box of pills that he didn't recognize. He guessed that she didn't sleep well, and when she did it would be a disturbed sleep, making her get up and walk about several times during the night.

He didn't stop kissing her as he helped remove her blouse. She seemed impatient when he raised his head to undo the complicated fastening of her black bra because she unhooked it herself with a quick movement of her fingers. They sat on the edge of the bed, half-naked, caressing each other's bare skin, and kissed again. She was the one who seemed to be in a hurry, and asked him to undo the belt of her skirt. *It's a long time since she last went to bed with a man*, thought Cupido. *Probably even longer than it is since I last had a woman.* Camila nibbled his lips in the way a hungry man nibbles a slice of bread. They fell back on the bed to make it easier to finish undressing, and, without a word, smiled at each other as they removed their last items of clothing. Cupido slipped his hand up between her soft, smooth thighs until he reached her vulva. The hair was trimmed short, and he could feel the wetness between the folds. Camila bent over his stomach and fondled his penis, helping the foreskin to retract. Then she took it deep into her mouth, and ran her lips up and down the shaft while his hand lingered on her raised buttocks. She continued until she heard him whisper, 'That's enough,' before lifting her head. She had recognized the taste of that first drop of moisture which indicates a full erection and signals the start of the coming effusion of semen. He lowered his hand again to the triangle of short, dark hair, until his middle finger touched the warm, moist nub. She remained still and compliant while he caressed her, in anticipation of the pleasure and release that he was about to bestow on her.

Twenty

If she didn't get up soon she wouldn't get to the gallery on time
– but this was one morning when she didn't care. Still lying
under the sheet, she began to stir, stretching like a cat, and lux-
uriating in the warmth that the bed still retained. On the pillow
close to her she noticed one short, dark hair, and smiled as she
thought about the man whose head it had come from. It had
only needed those few hours together for her to fix a clear image
of him in her memory, and to know that it would be a very long
time before she forgot it. If she closed her eyes she could reconstruct him: he was about thirty-five, very tall, with clean-cut
features and profile, although he gave the impression of not
knowing how to make the most of his good looks. He never
allowed himself a broad smile, as if something secret and deeply
buried in his past prevented him doing so. However, when it
looked as if something might be bothering him he never seemed
unduly concerned. He appeared calm by nature, but by no
means impassive; he was sceptical, but not pessimistic; his way
of dressing was too casual for her taste, but she was in no doubt
that if he were to wear formal clothes he would look as elegant
as a prince. She had known very few men like him, and could
well understand the feelings he was able to arouse: men would
want to be like him, and women would consider him a challenge
to their powers of seduction. He hadn't stopped kissing her all
night, and now, as she ran her tongue over her lips she recalled

his lips which had tasted of wine, but not of tobacco. He had been a good lover, an outstanding lover, who had known how to combine the delicate precision of fingers that resembled those of a miniaturist painter with the primitive strength of a stone-mason. While he caressed her he had made her feel that her buttocks and hips were tight, firm and smooth like burnished steel. Although from the very first kiss she had known she was in the arms of a skilled and experienced lover, she was overjoyed to find that there was a little touch of tenderness in the way he made love. There was only a suggestion of it, but for a woman like her it satisfied her need to be sure that it wasn't just a matter of sex. He was also very handsome. She would have loved to see him again, but he lived so far away, and he seemed so self-sufficient. She stretched again, rejoicing in the sheer luxury of physical satisfaction, and as she tensed her legs she was aware of a slight but agreeable discomfort. She smiled as she realized she would feel that tiny irritation for the rest of the day, because it would make her remember the wonderful night. Then she sat up, folded the pillow behind her back, and leant against the head of the bed. From that position she cast her eyes around the room: the bedspread lay crumpled on the floor and the shade of the bedside light had been tipped forward towards the box of sleeping pills that she hadn't needed; her shoes were placed side by side in their usual place near the bed, but one of them was upside down, and she could see the gleam of the metal point of the high heel; her blouse and bra had dropped down on the other side, and her skirt lay crumpled on the chair where he had thrown it from the bed. Somewhere or other she would find her panties. But of him there was no trace; he had left nothing behind except her sense of well-being that comes from sexual satisfaction, and that one short, dark hair on the pillow, and she looked at it again happily, like an adolescent on the verge of tears at the sight of a lock of hair from the head of the boy she loves. She hated disorder, whether it was at home or in the gallery –

and that had occasionally sparked friction with Gloria – but the disorder in her bedroom filled her with delight. Basically, and in spite of her elegant and apparently aloof appearance, this was what delighted her about the act of love: intense desire and a violent explosion of passion. If she took so much care of the way she looked – her exclusive designer clothes, her meticulous make-up, the chestnut tints in her hair, the perfume that was regularly reapplied – it was to differentiate herself from the many divorced women she knew who seemed unable to avoid giving the impression that they had given up, let themselves go and were helpless. She hated the idea that anyone might think of her in that way, although it was known that she was a divorced woman and had been dropped several times. Her relationships with men had always been difficult, both before and after marriage. *They're so selfish they prefer to break off an affair rather than change a single one of their own habits*, she told herself. How different Gloria's life had been. She hadn't been lying when she told the detective the night before that all men had fallen in love with her. Even he had insisted on asking her what had been so special about her, and had put such emphasis on this that anyone might have thought that Gloria was seducing him too from beyond the grave, because instead of interrogating her in the way she expected from a detective – *Where was she on such and such a day? At what time? Who had she been with?* – his questions had been aimed at getting to know about Gloria as a person, as if he was more interested in her than in her murderer. She lay down again in the bed with a smile of triumph and revenge on her lips. Gloria hadn't been there yesterday evening to deprive her all over again of the admiring glances of a good-looking man who had happened to come into the gallery. She had waited so long for this that there were times when she had come to believe it would never happen. For the past two years Gloria had been the centre of attention while she had been relegated to the second rank. She had found it intolerable when all the bouquets of roses that used to arrive in the gallery were put on Gloria's desk, and every phone call that had nothing to do with the business was a personal one for Gloria. She had always had to make a special effort to assert herself, because what came naturally and easily to Gloria she had had to struggle hard to emulate. However, now she was dead, it had all become surprisingly easy. More than that, she had begun to adopt some of Gloria's characteristics – gentle playfulness, an easy smile and colourful clothes. Although she had long since known their value, she had never dared use them herself while Gloria was alive, fearing that it would look as if she were parodying the other girl who would certainly have noticed what she was doing. She had even become more at ease in her dealings with artists and customers. She had often heard it said that a woman must never appear eager with a man she has just met because nothing will frighten him off more quickly than too much eagerness, but she wasn't sure she had always been able to hide it. Or was it that they detected it in various little nervous signs, and once in bed with her they retained the advantage either by behaving passively, or by getting carried away so quickly that they never bothered with the foreplay that would allow her to enjoy total pleasure in the assiduous way the detective had done that night. She had gone through such a bad patch after her divorce that she had begun to suspect she was mistaken in believing that she needed men to satisfy her. If only she had known Cupido just a few months earlier, and what had happened a few hours ago had happened then, she would have avoided the embarrassment of that night with Gloria! From then on she had lived with a deep feeling of shame that had only disappeared with the girl's death. As they almost always did after inaugurating a new exhibition, they had gone out to dinner with the artists. On this occasion they were two very young painters who hadn't put together a large body of work but what they had produced was interesting. They had sufficiently distinctive styles for their pictures to be displayed in the same room without inviting invidious comparisons, although there did seem to be a subtle affinity in their themes and locations. In fact, it was they who had suggested a joint exhibition. Gloria was delighted with their styles, and it was this exhibition that had given her the idea of working in parallel with Emilio Sierra, one of them using paint, and the other metal sculpture, basing themselves on the same theme: the cave-paintings about which she always talked with enthusiasm. At first, Camila had had doubts about the idea because their work didn't seem particularly brilliant to her, and probably wouldn't sell very well. But as there was nothing better around at the time she gave her agreement. Even if sales turned out to be modest, they would always be able to keep at least one of the paintings – the donation of a work to the gallery was a basic condition for being accepted – and if the two young artists had genuine potential it would make a useful contribution to the growing private collection they owned jointly and that already included works by artists who had gone on to greater fame. They hadn't been long at the table before discovering that the two painters were homosexual, and soon after that it was made very plain to them that they were lovers, as if they were proud of a way of life that she had always believed to be at odds with the rest of society. Gay couples had always made her feel nervous. She observed them closely, trying to guess which one played which role. She wondered whether to be born a man but to function as a wife wasn't likely to be a permanent torment to him. But these two seemed not only content, but extremely happy. They lived together, and assured the women that their relationship was a stable one, rejecting the notion of immaturity and impermanence that she had always believed to be commonplace in such relationships. They were drinking heavily, to the point where their ancedotes became blatantly scabrous, but they told them with great humour, using words that would have sounded unacceptably obscene coming from anyone else.

Gloria laughed loudly and joked with them as if she had known them all her life, like friends meeting again after a long separation. It was while they were drinking whisky in a pub on the Paseo de la Castellana that, rather drunk, and smiling broadly, they confessed their great secret: in reality they were not two different artists each one producing his own paintings because both of them worked on the same paintings from start to finish. The only exception to this came before they began, because it needed one or other of them to think up the subject and the way it should be treated. At first she thought they were joking and were teasing her about her knowledge and percipience as a gallery owner, but then she felt she had been swindled, and would have liked to get up and leave before they could say another word because they looked so pleased with themselves and their absurd trick. But Gloria seemed delighted with the extraordinary situation. During the next round of whiskies she thought she detected something ambiguous in what one of the artists was saying, hinting that the two women were lovers too. She suspected that it was characteristic of gays to believe that everybody else is gay in an essentially gay world. For a moment she again felt irritated, but only for a moment. Gloria would never cease to surprise her. But then she also entered into the spirit of their game, pretending to accept their amusing and equivocal situation: two men and two women who were couples, not linked, but separated by the difference of their sexes. It was the sort of mischievous game that Gloria often enjoyed and which she too decided to play that evening with a hitherto unsuspected display of bravado. She didn't even refuse the line of cocaine that one of the artists divided into four equal parts on the shiny surface of his credit card. They had gone on to a discothèque and then to a male strip-tease club where the two men were allowed in with them although entry was normally restricted to women, before ending up in a dive frequented by gays of both sexes – one of those night spots that reaches its most lively pitch not long before dawn when the night has sorted out the revellers and got rid of those who are weary and unenthusiastic, and those (like herself) who always have to get up early in the morning. To her surprise she didn't feel uncomfortable there, nor did she feel like an impostor out of place among so much shouting and laughter. She had laughed with the others, and possibly rather louder. Completely at her ease, she had leant on the shoulders of both artists, and at one moment put an arm round Gloria's waist keeping it there rather longer than was necessary, to show how happy and self-confident she was. This was the game they had chosen to play, and she was happy to join in. She had the stamina to carry on in spite of the late hour, her feet didn't hurt although they had been dancing with scarcely a break to sit down, and her head was clear, notwithstanding the wine and the whiskies, as if the line of cocaine she had sniffed had eliminated the negative effects of the alcohol. It was a long time since she had enjoyed a night like it, and she was surprised to find that dawn was breaking when they left the club – she could have sworn it wasn't nearly so late. The two artists walked off arm in arm, thoroughly drunk, having lost all interest in the two women. As her apartment was quite near and it seemed that the taxis that worked at night were returning home empty and the day service hadn't begun she had invited Gloria to go back with her. '*Come and sleep at my place. Tomorrow's Sunday so there's no need to get up early.*' Gloria had accepted willingly, bored with waiting for a taxi, and possibly because she would be able to avoid being woken up too early by an impatient phone call from Marcos Anglada. Once in her apartment they found that the sun that was beginning to blaze through the tall windows was blinding, and they hurried to close the blinds. She felt rather drunk standing there in the dim light of the bedroom, as if the dark had an intoxicating effect that the daylight outside had almost neutralized. Tired, and still giggling as they reminded each other of some of the more amusing moments of the night, they had dropped half-undressed on to the big bed to sleep together, because they couldn't be bothered to look for sheets to make up the little guest bed in the other bedroom. As soon as she fell into a horizontal position everything seemed to go round in circles. She had to open her eyes in order to put a stop to the merry-go-round of bright lights and images that swirled around in her head. She was bewildered, and unable to focus clearly on the sounds, the colours and the objects about her. Only one image was fixed in her mind with absolute precision: Gloria, stretched out on the bed beside her wearing only her underwear, asleep, defenceless and breathing evenly, her face turned towards her, her hair streaming across the pillow and with the sheet covering the lower half of her body. She shut her eyes again to banish the disturbing temptation that fluttered through her mind – and also down through her loins – stimulated by the long night of alcohol, cocaine, the behaviour of the two artists, the strip-tease, and the gay club they had visited last. She felt a desire to caress Gloria and to be caressed by her. But when she lowered her eyelids, the sickening, giddy feeling returned, as if she was travelling on a train moving at vertiginous speed with everything whirling past – the almost deserted morning streets, the vague outlines of couples kissing, parks, fields, lonely woodlands of the type that Gloria loved to walk through... until she fastened her eyes on the one goal she could clearly discern: Gloria's exquisite body lying so close beside her on the bed. Gently, she placed a hand on the girl's hip. She held it there for a moment, but then, made reckless by the whisky, her inability to sleep, added to the moistness and the throbbing sensation she felt between her thighs, but sensing also that she was not being rebuffed, she slid her hand beneath the sheet towards the other girl's pubis. That was the moment when Gloria had opened her eyes. They didn't express amazement or weariness so much as indifference. She didn't speak, she didn't push her hand away, nor did she move aside. She simply stared at her for a moment, more puzzled than upset, before closing her eyes again, pulling the sheet up to her armpits, tucking it round her, and then turning over with her back to her. It was an unmistakable gesture of unconcern, not even disdain, not even rejection strong enough to persuade her to get up and go away, merely a desire to be left to go on sleeping in peace. Camila, on the other hand, was fully awake by now. She could hear the noise of Sunday morning traffic as people made their way out of town, and the muffled murmuring of the faithful, with their thick ankles and bowed heads scurrying to early Mass, not one of them suffering as she was from the burning sense of shame that was beginning to come over her. She managed to get to sleep briefly after turning her own back on Gloria who continued to slumber peacefully and almost defiantly, without moving a muscle. It was ten o'clock when she got up and went to the bathroom where she vomited, kneeling in front of the lavatory, and making an effort to be as quiet about it as possible. She had a strong sensation of ice on her tongue and fire in her cheeks. She showered, dressed and went out into the street, without knowing where she was going, after leaving a note for Gloria stuck to the door handle with a magnet: '*I've left you a set of keys on the table. Please lock up when you go. I'd arranged to have lunch with my brothers.*' This was a lie, but she hadn't felt strong enough to face her when she woke up and to talk as if nothing had happened between them during the night. Talking was what she feared most – that Gloria would bring the subject up and make her confront it, and wouldn't accept the tacit pact of silence and blackout that their night of drunkenness and other excesses made appropriate. She didn't feel inclined to justify what she had done, and certainly not to discuss openly what had occurred. It had been like a dream, exactly the same as a dream.

Early on the Monday morning, they arrived at exactly the same moment at the door of the gallery. Gloria had greeted her with her customary smile, as if she remembered nothing – or wanted to put it out of her mind, or at least was uncertain whether that particular incident belonged to the real or the dream world – and she had said: '*I think we overdid it the other night. I'm sure I'm going to have a hangover for a week.*' After that they got down to their normal work routines. Gloria had never mentioned the incident again. But Camila retained a deep residue of shame which resurfaced whenever an untimely word stirred it up…

But now at last, the memory of it was dead and buried. What she had needed was a night like the one that had just ended, because apart from the consummate pleasure she had experienced, the thrill that had coursed three times through her from her head to the tips of her toes, the detective had managed to make her feel that morning that she was once again in harmony with her own body in which she had begun to notice the first signs of aging. She took a small mirror out of the drawer of the bedside table and looked carefully at her face and neck, searching for the smallest trace of his lips or teeth, but there wasn't a single blemish. On the contrary, she looked so lovely she was barely able to recognize herself. *It's men's kisses that keep women looking beautiful*, she spoke into the mirror, amazed that time seemed to have receded, leaving her several years younger. This morning she would paint her lips with a brighter lipstick, put on earrings that were at least ten centimetres long, and the shortest skirt she possessed. When she went out into the street she would walk with a straight back and more of a swing to her hips; the tapping of her shoes on the ground would be more self-assured, because nothing gave her greater confidence in her physical attractions than a perfect night of pleasure. And once she arrived at the gallery, unlocked the door, raised the blinds and switched on the lights… all these little actions that the day before had been empty, mechanical gestures would be given new meaning and significance by her renewed physical awareness and wellbeing.

Twenty-One

He opened the door of the apartment with the keys Camila had given him half an hour before. She had stayed in bed, and after showering he had returned to the bedroom, kissed her on the lips and said: '*I'll be seeing you*,' trying not to let his words sound like a final farewell.

Gloria's apartment was dark, and only one partly open shutter on a far wall let narrow strips of daylight through. He waited for his eyes to adjust before shutting the door behind him. Then he groped round the wall for a switch, pressed it, and the hallway was flooded with light. He remembered the exact layout of the apartment, having searched it thoroughly for the diary in the company of Anglada, and he knew he should go to the right. He switched on the chandelier that hung from the living-room ceiling and saw in front of him the sliding doors that stood open, its two leaves deep inside the cavities in the double wall, just as he had remembered them two days before in his garage in Breda. He called back to mind the words that David assured him Gloria had used when she found him leafing through her diary: '*Nobody could possibly find it. Even if they were to open and close the doors of the hiding place they'd never see it. It would remain hidden.*' He walked over and grasped the handle of the right-hand door. It slid smoothly along the rail set into the top of the frame until it came up against the stop in the very centre. A butterfly screw fastened the stop to the rail, but it was so small that nobody would have noticed it unless they knew exactly what they were looking for. And nobody would have thought it concealed a hiding place – it was so simple. Not even a tool was needed. It took him no more than a moment to loosen the nut with his fingers. He moved the stop towards his left, and then pulled the door again. This time it moved further along until the detective stopped it. It ran smoothly and without a squeak, which seemed to him a good omen. The gap in the wall into which the door fitted was about eight or nine centimetres wide, and the light of the chandelier failed to penetrate it. Cupido looked around and chose an adjustable table-lamp with a glass shade. He plugged this into the nearest socket and pointed its light towards the gap. There was nothing there apart from dust, fluff and a few dead insects on the floor.

He carried out the same process on the left-hand door, and by shining the light into the gap on that side he was able to make out a thin plank almost at floor level that fitted neatly into the gap and served as a sort of shelf. There was a book on it inside a sleeve which he was immediately convinced was the diary. He pulled the plank towards him. Behind the book there was a tall, narrow box made of lacquered wood with the Air Force badge etched on its front. Before opening the book he poked around inside the box. It contained a handful of military decorations and several pieces of jewellery, amongst them a pearl necklace and a set consisting of a diamond ring and earrings. He deduced that this hiding place hadn't been thought up by Gloria but by her father, because he couldn't imagine her keeping valuable jewels anywhere except in a strong room in the bank. It was probable they hadn't discovered the diary before because they'd been trying to work out what Gloria might have done with it, rather than following the thought processes of a dead military man. All Gloria had done was to take advantage of a hiding place that in their lifetime her parents would have regarded as safe.

It had taken him less than a minute to get into it, and he imagined that she would have been even quicker. Once he knew what had to be done it was an incredibly simple operation. He assumed that she didn't hide the diary there when she was alone in the apartment, but only during those periods when she wasn't writing it up, or was travelling and didn't want to leave it where anyone might find it. After all, putting it in and getting it out was no more trouble than using a drawer, the key of which would in any case have had to be hidden somewhere.

He looked around and decided to sit on one of the upright chairs at the dining table. The light from the chandelier fell directly on him. The quarto size book was inside a sleeve which had a gap to reveal a label on its spine that had one word on it: DIARY. It was silk-covered, with highly coloured floral motifs printed on a black background, like a Manila shawl. He didn't try to read any of it immediately but turned the pages over quickly to give himself time to stop his hands from trembling. It was three quarters full, written in the clear, neat hand that he had already noticed in the signatures on her paintings. It was the hand of a very young woman, as if even in her handwriting she kept those elements of innocence and childishness that Camila had observed in her face. He glanced rapidly at one or two drawings inserted here and there in the text, impromptu sketches which she may have decided to put in so that they wouldn't be forgotten, or reflections of a state of mind for which she didn't need words. He turned back to the first page. It was dated during the summer of the previous year, fifteen months before her death:

Tuesday, 26 July
We buried Father yesterday. The ceremony was short and simple,
just as he would have wished. Short and simple, but without giving
the impression that we were merely disposing of a dead body such as
you sometimes get at funerals, especially when it's the culmination of

a long drawn-out decline, or one of those illnesses that ends up with the house full of medicines that everybody knows are useless, and bedlinen that smells like a shroud. Papa had worn a uniform for half his life, but he had never enjoyed the ballyhoo of march-pasts and military parades. So I rejected all the suggestions made by his old comrades, and there was no brass band and no medals and flags draped over his coffin. We were quite a small party, forty to forty-five people. Everybody he would have wanted was there, his friends both military and civilian, and his relations: his brother – my uncle Clotario – and David, my strange teenage cousin who never stopped staring at me to the point that was both embarrassing and tiresome.

When they put the coffin in the topmost niche and the priest finished his reading, they all looked at me as if they expected something from me. It was a dreadful moment because I didn't know what I ought to do or say. In spite of the fact that the past few weeks during which he went rapidly downhill had been long enough to drain me of grief and to get used to the idea of him dying, it was only in that last moment of waiting and silence before the first brick was placed in the niche to cast the first shadow on its interior that I realised I was now utterly alone.

On the way back I began to remember things I'd forgotten about Papa. It was as if his death had reversed the chronological order in my mind. His last months already seemed remote although they were so recent but, against that, my earliest childhood memories of him came into focus: riding on a horse with him holding me by the waist; our first summers in Breda, now so distant; the special smell of his uniform, and its rough feel when he kissed me before going out in the morning... These are memories I'm going to guard jealously now they've found their way back to me by a secret route, and I'm never going to lose them again.

At home, later, when I looked at the armchair where he always sat I stopped thinking about myself. The sight of his personal things erased all the self-pity that everybody had been talking me into with their sympathy and their trite words of condolence. They ought to forbid the convention that death obliges one's relatives to profess a respect that almost nobody feels. It was Papa who had died, eaten away by cancer in spite of his battle against it. I console myself with the thought that he's not suffering any more, that he'll like the niche where he lies now, in the sun, on the very highest of the upper rows, right next to Mother. It took them over a year to reserve that place. He had always loved the open air, so much so that he couldn't bear the idea of being buried in a grave. If there is anything after death, they are now together wherever that may be.

Marcos, Camila, Clotario and David came back with me and wandered round the apartment without knowing what to do or where to sit because they didn't dare occupy a place on the sofa or sit on a chair in case they looked like intruders in places where he used to sit. Although they were very kind and offered to help, they seemed to me like shadows who, at that time, were simply in the way. I would have preferred to be on my own. I heard Marcos and Camila in the kitchen making coffee and talking quietly, like conspirators. When I went to the bathroom I saw from the door into the corridor that Clotario had gone into Papa's study and was looking bewildered in front of the framed panel where he hung his medals, like a boy scout who covets what he could have obtained but didn't, because he was too cowardly or too incompetent. I don't like to judge him harshly, but in the few seconds I was watching him that was the impression he gave me. Then, when I went back into the living room David was looking closely at my paintings, and although his eyes also seemed covetous this was quite different − less concerned with material things. I've seen something like it in certain collectors in the gallery who are tempted much less by the financial value of a picture than by its artistic value. Marcos and Camila were still in the kitchen talking very quietly. I wondered what they had to talk about, what any of them were doing there, what they wanted. I'd have liked to have been entirely on my own to grieve over Papa's death, and not to feel that they were taking over the territory of a king who has just died, and that I was just one more of the chattels of his inheritance.

Cupido went through the next pages one by one, searching for
the capital letters of names he would recognize. In this first reading he was concerned only with what was directly relevant to the
investigation. A little further on he stopped at another date:

Friday, 5 August
As this diary isn't written for anyone else to read, I haven't any rea-
son to lie. And as I'm not in a court of law I don't need to defend
myself. In these pages I can be wrong without anybody correcting
me. And I can be hard, pretentious, cruel, unjust, outrageous,
romantic, or silly without having to regret it later. If only I'd dis-
covered before the pleasure this diary gives me, and these moments
during which all pretence is cast aside because it isn't necessary.

Thursday, 27 October
That art teacher who visited our gallery with his students to see the
exhibition of my paintings rang me this morning. I imagine he must
have told me his name but I didn't remember it and felt a bit awk-
ward not knowing who I was talking to. He wanted me to go to his
college tomorrow to give a talk to his students about contemporary
art. I refused at first, because it was all a bit rushed, and also because
I didn't believe I'd be able to talk to a class of teenagers for whom
anything to do with an art gallery must seem very dull. But he con-
vinced me in the end. And at last I got his name clear – Manuel
Armengol – and we agreed on the time and the main points I should
put over. What finally decided me was his confidence in me, although
he doesn't really know me – it was blind faith, and you can't let that
down. Besides which, instead of assuring me that I wouldn't have
any problems with his students, he suggested I should actually make
my talk a challenge to them – turn it into a sort of duel between them
and me. At the other extreme from a pompous lecture. It didn't take
me more than three minutes to agree. It was the first time a teacher
had brought his students to see one of my exhibitions, and this
made me rather curious about him. When I put the phone down I

remembered his visit yesterday. I'd liked the shy way he behaved, which he only lost when he talked about painting. He had a rather dubious appearance – worse for wear and a bit of a nonentity. Why is it that I, and so many women, are drawn all at the same time to two opposite extremes – brilliant success and hopeless failure. Marcos with all his self-confidence, his excellent physique, and his style belongs in the first category. This Manuel Armengol looks like a perfect example of the second. We'll see what happens tomorrow.

Friday, 28 October
My talk at the school went better than I'd expected. The youngsters asked me a lot of questions that I answered, I think, accurately and with a touch of humour. Even Armengol – everyone calls him that and I think I shall do the same – was surprised how well they reacted to what I said. I left the school with a feeling of euphoria that stayed with me all that night, during the dinner he invited me to, and all the time we were having a drink afterwards before he plucked up the courage to suggest we went to a hotel. I agreed to go with him because although he's married I didn't see that as a reason not to.

I believe that from the very first time we go to bed with a man we really know a lot about him. Armengol seems to waver backwards and forwards between lucid thinking and lack of balance, a blend that can be very creative for an artist. However, although he used to paint he never managed to give visible form to his visionary ideas. He's an odd person, but he attracts me. He behaved the same way in bed. He went from being very gentle and affectionate to being really rough. It was an unusual combination and it brought me to the very peak of pleasure.

Monday, 31 October
From time to time I like to bet on outsiders.

Cupido raised his eyes. He understood now why Gloria had chosen that hiding place for the diary. It was too intimate to let anybody else read it.

Sunday, 27th November

Back in Madrid, feeling tired.

This morning I got up very early. I'd planned to do a landscape of a small hill in the Reserve that is covered in holm oaks, forming a perfect cone like a witch's hat, and stands on its own surrounded by low land. The locals call it Trigo Hill. I wanted to get there early, soon after dawn, when the land is slowly waking from its night's sleep, when the animals emerge from their lairs to sniff the air, and the trees raise their heads and haven't yet closed up their leaves to avoid evaporation in this long drought. At this first hour of the morning, everything comes alive, from the tiniest ant to the unsociable and timid deer. Everything moves, either to hide away or to search for food. And that's the moment when the land is exposed and vibrant and I wanted to capture it then and compose it all into a picture. I was walking along very near the hill and as I pushed through a cluster of broom, I saw this thing with horrible clarity just two metres from my face. They'd hung it by the neck in the way they still hang men in some countries and in wartime. Its head was horribly twisted and one of its antlers was caught in the thick rope as if it had made a last attempt to escape by attacking the rope as it tightened round its neck. Its eyes were dilated with terror, its long, thick, whitish tongue hung out of its open mouth, and the first flies were beginning to crawl over it. Its face still bore a look of pain suggesting that it had been subjected to lengthy torture before it died. Its tail had been cut off and thrown on the ground nearby, and a stream of coagulated blood hung like a stalactite from the stump, leaving a big, dark stain on the ground. A dribble of semen hung from its penis, the end of which was red and tapered like a small carrot. It was all so horribly gratuitous that I was nearly sick. Who could have dreamed up that way of killing a stag without the excuse of needing it for food, and not even for the grotesque reason that they had wanted the head for decoration? It was so cruel, so unnecessary, that that individual must suffer from some sort of insanity – which he possibly doesn't even realize himself. I turned round and hurried back to the Base

Depot that wasn't far away. They would know who might have done it and how to find the person responsible.

The image of that stag hanging from the thick branch of a holm oak kept flashing vividly through my mind as I walked. In spite of the evocative nature that it might have in a picture I knew I'd need time before attempting it so that the cold-blooded viciousness with which it had been killed – hung by the neck and with its tail mutilated – shouldn't influence me when I took up my brushes.

A few minutes later I heard furious barking coming from the dogs in the Base Depot, but I didn't stop for them. I went straight away towards a group of men – two game wardens and three Civil Guards – who looked at me in astonishment. As I came near I saw Doña Victoria come out of the office. She's the old lady I met on the day of the fire, and with her was that strange lawyer who was at university with Marcos and who treats her like a solicitous son or a protective bodyguard. I learned later that they'd gone there to sort out some sort of legal matter connected with the lengthy litigation in which they're involved over the Reserve. According to what she told us on the afternoon of the fire it concerns the ownership of some of the land.

I told them about finding the hanged stag. The policemen were obviously dumbfounded, and all they could think of was to ask me to produce my identity card. Fortunately I'd got it with me, which isn't always the case, and with that lack of initiative that comes from excessively strict discipline only then did they decide to call up a senior officer over their car radio to ask for instructions. Apparently, an important foreign politician was out hunting in the Paternoster Forest that day, which was the reason for their being there, keeping a watch out for trouble. We got into their car and I directed them to the exact spot. Doña Victoria and the lawyer followed after us. We all stared at the stag that was swaying slowly on the rope in a light breeze, but not one of them could make up his mind whether to cut it down, as if they didn't want to get their hands dirty, or as if they'd come across the body of a dead man and nobody was allowed to touch it in case they left some mark that might implicate them or confuse the investigation. One of the wardens' dogs that had run up behind the cars stopped next to us, panting. Then it sniffed the stag, and after looking back as if asking permission it began to lick up the drops of semen, and nobody stopped it. 'It's got to be taken down,' I said. 'It doesn't make sense to leave it like that.' One of the Civil Guards who had a stripe on the arm of his uniform and seemed to be in charge of the others hesitated for a moment, but then took a step forward. Doña Victoria told him to stay where he was. Her voice was curt, harsh and domineering, very different from the way she had spoken to me on that other occasion. 'No. Not yet. Don't be in such a hurry, young lady. That animal's not going to come back to life if it's cut down. It's important that everybody should see what goes on in the Reserve.' I gave her a look that was deliberately disapproving. Neither she nor the lawyer seemed in the least upset by the horrible death of the stag. Quite the opposite: they seemed delighted to have something to throw in the faces of their enemies in that ludicrous battle of theirs. The Civil Guard looked at her for a moment, but by then he had decided to cut it down, and he went over to the tree. It was the lawyer's voice that stopped him again with a threat that he couldn't avoid taking notice of: 'You're about to destroy the evidence of a crime.' The Guard went to his car to consult once more with somebody, but I found the prospect of another wait intolerable. I turned my back on them all and walked off taking no notice when one of the wardens offered to give me a lift in his car. I couldn't stand the sight of swarms of flies arriving to crawl all over its tongue – or that hungry dog. It seemed to me that at any moment the dead body would begin to smell and contaminate all the onlookers with its stench and putrescence.

Saturday, 7 January
I'm sure many people hate Christmas and New Year celebrations, just as many dislike Carnival, and many of the inhabitants of Pamplona dislike the San Fermin bull chases, and many village

people dislike their awful local 'fiestas' which are just an excuse for all types of excess. And I also believe that others don't dare admit it because they're afraid of being called bores or bigots. If a fiesta is a time of freedom, the first requirement is not to force those who don't want to participate into doing so. I say this now that the Christmas holidays are over because I didn't enjoy them at all. It was the first year without either of my parents. I'd always spent them with them, or with Papa after Mother died, and the loss of both of them upset me so much I had no wish for a substitute. Then Marcos turned up with a complete programme: a few days with his family, and New Year's Eve just the two of us. When I suggested that what I really wanted was to go away on my own to one of those big foreign cities where I didn't know anybody, he had such a fit of jealousy and bad temper that in the end I accepted his plans. It would have been better if I hadn't because it wasn't exactly a happy time. I didn't feel comfortable with him, and although he didn't say so, I know he was thinking that there's somebody else in the background which explained my indifference. To make things worse, one day here in my apartment he picked up the phone and it was Armengol. I had to lie that it was a business call, but I don't think I was very convincing.

What people call fits of jealousy, those outbursts or sudden attacks of fury that finish with tears and forgiveness, aren't dangerous. If only this were true of Marcos then I think he could control his jealousy. As it has happened after other arguments we would have ended up making love and all his anger would have melted away in an orgasm, in the way a lump of sugar melts in a glass of milk. The damaging thing about Marcos's jealousy is that he never lets it be seen. He keeps it hidden, and it would really frighten me if one day he were to let it burst out because he could hurt me. I believe that jealousy brought into the open can turn a relationship into an inferno, but jealousy that remains hidden turns a relationship into a desert.

Saturday, 8 April

I've brought this diary with me for the first time. I'm writing it up while staying at the Europa Hotel in Breda. I feel good here. I like the décor because, unlike the national Paradors and other hotels of that type, they haven't gone in for that anachronistic practice of putting bits of medieval armour in every corner and tapestries all over the walls.

I've also brought a little table that I don't need in Madrid and a dinner service I don't use there. Although it's not complete, it is pretty with its tiny designs of fruit and it goes well with the house. I've been to see it again. Once the repairs to the roof and the sanitary system are finished it won't need much more for me to be able to live in it. I'll have to have it rewired throughout so that I can install the essential items of electrical equipment. My visits are becoming more and more frequent as if, now that my parents are no longer around, the place draws me to come here as powerfully as it drove them to leave it.

Even now, in spite of the extreme drought the Reserve is beautiful. The scenery, the water in the reservoir – although the level has dropped so much – the birds of prey in the sky, and so many animals all around manage to create a place of such beauty that even this terrible drought that has gone on for four years can't diminish. It's April, but the land is thirsty and hard, and it doesn't seem at all like spring. Only in the inlets on the edges of the reservoir where the level of the water has gone down anything between eight and ten metres are there narrow strips of fresh growth like green fringes round the blue of the water, separating it from the brownish yellow of the earth. There were a few April storm clouds moving across the sky, and suddenly one of them released a heavy shower. It was a very special moment, magical, like a baptism after so much time without rain. The whole forest fell quiet, listening to the sound of the raindrops. The leaves of the plants and shrubs that were curled up on themselves, and coated in dust accumulated over four years, opened out like thirsty men in a desert who, in a sudden shower of rain, open their mouths to drink the water before the sand swallows it up. It was beautiful and terrible all at the same time because the magic didn't even last for the five minutes that I sheltered under an immense oak. All the flowers opened looking up into the sky, anxious, like infatuated lovers: their leaves seemed to gleam and they showed off their best colours for a few moments to seduce the heavens with their display. Then the cloud moved on like an impotent or scornful lover, and the earth closed down again, dry and unsatisfied, disappointed and thirsty.

The suddenness with which colours appear and disappear, and the stark contrasts with no transitional tones between them, suggest a number of possibilities for paintings that I'd like to study in more depth, once I've finished my series of cave-paintings. I went back up there today, and sat in front of them for an hour on my own, looking closely at them. On the way back I had a little accident which fortunately didn't have any serious consequences. In order to avoid the wide zigzags in the path I took a short cut down; it was a steep and difficult route because of the shrubs and loose stones, but it would have saved me a lot of time and considerably reduced the distance. As I was going down a little slope to get back to the path I tripped over something, and staggered a few steps until, unable to keep my balance, I fell into a dry, hard ditch. The cistus bushes had been cut back on both sides of the path in order to prevent fires spreading. When they do that there are always five to ten centimetres of woody stems left sticking out of the ground, which go as hard as iron when they dry, and quite often if they're cut at an angle they become small but dangerous stakes that wound quite a few deer. There have even been times when these tiny stumps have slashed the tyres of cars. I learned this later from Molina, the game warden. I had the good luck to see him drive up in his official car, and in uniform, not long after I'd picked myself up with a very painful wound in one thigh. It was a deep gash caused by the dried out splinter I'd fallen on.

It's the second time he's turned up when I've had some little difficulty in the Reserve, like the day when Marcos and I let a fire get out of control. I was grateful to him for being there this afternoon because I was frightened, with that special fear that is caused by any little accident that happens when we're alone in the middle of the countryside and a long way from any possible help. Now, while I write this it has occurred to me that it may not have been purely by chance that this angel of a warden has twice put in an appearance just at the right moment, but I reject the idea as nonsense. After all, it's his job to keep an eye on people doing silly things and to help anyone who goes into the area he's responsible for.

He had a small first aid box in his glove compartment. He helped to stem the bleeding, disinfected the wound, and put a piece of lint and a sticking plaster over it for protection. As it continued to bleed, he made me get into his car and brought me to the hospital here in Breda where they put in five stitches.

I'm writing this in the hotel with my leg stretched out on a chair in the position that makes the wound least painful. I hope to be able to drive back to Madrid tomorrow. This will have cut my weekend in half.

I'm thinking about the warden. In spite of a certain brusqueness in his manner, and the odd way he looked at me, and the roughness of his hands as he disinfected the wound, he managed to convey a comforting sense of security – that having him around you'll never bleed to death!

Sunday, 16 April

Hello, secret, hidden, lazy diary.

Sunday, 21 May

It's Sunday night and I'm writing this in bed. I've still got a headache and a hangover which, as always, puts me in a bad temper. Marcos rang this afternoon to ask me out, but I told him I wasn't well. I had no wish to explain why, so I invented some trivial excuse which didn't convince him. He was annoyed and rang off, and now he's probably imagining the most extraordinary things. But how could I tell him about last night's binge with the two gay artists, *the line of cocaine, the visit to the strip club, and how we laughed our heads off until dawn? And he, who doesn't drink or smoke, and is so proud of himself for not doing so! It's days like this that I wonder how we get on so well together much of the time, given that we're so different.*

I'm thinking about the working method of those two artists – both together on the same canvas. I'm trying to think of another example, but I can't. I couldn't possibly work that way myself, but the idea came to me this morning of suggesting to Emilio that he should develop a series of sculptures using the same themes as I am, based on the cave-paintings. Early artists already had the same sort of idea when they made use of the edges, hollows, and corners of stonework to reinforce the mass of their figures. I'll call him tomorrow to discuss it when my head's a bit clearer. Just at the moment I can't get the memory of Camila's extraordinary behaviour out of my mind. We got into the same bed at her place because I couldn't be bothered to come back here. I was beginning to drop off when I felt her hand on my hip. It stayed there for a moment, and then it moved down towards my genital area. I was surprised and opened my eyes and looked at her for a second or so. I wasn't shocked that she was doing it because I'm too old to be shocked by anything to do with sex. Maybe I had unintentionally led her on while we were joking with the artists and entering into the spirit of their game. But it surprised me very much because I would never have imagined it of Camila. It has never come into my head to make love with a woman. I get all the physical pleasure I want from men. Possibly I should have talked to her then, but I was so tired I just closed my eyes and turned over as if I hadn't noticed. I hope that's what she believes. It's the simplest solution.

Camila baffles me at times. I feel sometimes that they all look to me for love. And now Camila as well! I can't satisfy them all.

Once again the detective lifted his eyes from the diary and remained thoughtful for several minutes. After the night he had spent with Camila whom he had left only a few hours before, what he had just read caused him as much surprise as it had Gloria. He was convinced she hadn't been pretending in bed with him. However, this diary was revealing how so many of them were liars. That was also true of Doña Victoria and Exposito when they told him they hadn't seen Gloria again since the day of the fire, whereas only a short time after that incident they'd been arguing with her over the body of the hanged stag.

He would have liked to stay there with all the time in the world to read through the whole diary with its fund of daily, personal observations that revealed the mind of the woman who had written it, but he was anxious and in a hurry. It was the same feeling he had had that night, driving across the frontier in his old DAF crammed with cartons of contraband cigarettes under cover of a pile of beehives; that special feeling of anxiety and tension caused by something you know to be illegal. He had no right to enter somebody else's property, and if anyone were to turn up – Anglada because his persistence had made him suspicious, or an employee sent from the notary's office – he would have no valid excuse for being there.

He continued turning the pages. He was still unable to stop his fingers trembling. Gloria hadn't written in her diary every day. There were sometimes gaps of a week or two. He stopped suddenly as he came across a sketch of the badge that he recognized from the paper he still carried folded in his wallet. He'd looked at it often enough not to need to compare them to know they were identical.

Wednesday, 14 June

I had a visit in the gallery this morning from a group of young people in their early twenties. Someone had told them about me after the talk I gave in Armengol's college. They belong to an ecological group and are organizing a campaign against the French nuclear explosions in the Pacific. They'd come with a number of design ideas but couldn't make up their minds between them. They wanted my opinion, as if I were an expert, when the truth is that that overblown fashion for slogans and designs that lasted for about ten years seems to me to have produced nothing more than an insignificant load of pretty bits of trivia. I objected and tried to refuse, but they were so enthusiastic about their protest movement and had such confidence in my 'expert' opinion that it wasn't long before I gave in. I shut the gallery door and we sat down in the office to see what they had brought with them and what they were trying to put over. In the end we combined two ideas in one and the final design came out more or less like this:

Camila arrived before we'd finished. She saw that the door was closed in spite of the time and was rather angry, but had the delicacy not to say anything to me in front of the youngsters. She waited until they'd gone before scolding me for not paying more attention to the sales side of the business. I know she's absolutely right because the most recent exhibitions haven't sold well and the gallery isn't growing as fast as we had hoped. But I wasn't at all happy because she said it over and over again even though I'd admitted I was in the wrong. She seemed very tense.

Saturday, 1 July
I went to the reservoir with David today, hoping to see deer, but they didn't play fair and failed to turn up to have their portraits painted. I had a swim before coming back. There are times when I feel sorry

for him: he's so much in love, but it's out of the question. He has a gift for painting, judging by the few bits of his work I've seen, but he hasn't anybody to help him develop his talents. He's always there when I need him, but I forget him the rest of the time.

Saturday, 16 September

What is happening with Marcos?

This afternoon I bought myself the big bunch of roses that I've got now in front of me in the studio. I put them in a vase, opened the windows and the last of the summer sun streamed through the three of them, flooding the room with light. I was so delighted with this that I began to paint an idyllic woodland scene with more flowers than trees, more of the tiny and the ephemeral than the durable. After a while Marcos came in. He didn't even look at my picture. All he could do was fix his eyes on the roses and ask me before anything else: 'And who gave you these?' I looked at him, quite taken aback by his manner and, in order to prevent any misunderstanding, I put my brush down, put my arms around him and kissed him. I shouldn't have done it because I didn't really want to, and was only trying to remove any basis for his suspicions. Kissing, which is a marvellous stimulant to love can become sheer poison when the one you love guesses that you're doing it for a reason other than affection. Marcos received my kisses without another word, but from time to time he looked at the roses as if he wanted to throw them out of the window. The whole afternoon was ruined. After that I couldn't make a correct brush stroke or mix the right colour. Then he went away and I kept on repeating the question I asked myself at the beginning: What's happening with Marcos?

Tuesday, 19 September

I'm reading through the notes I've made during the last few weeks. I'm surprised to see that there's nothing very happy in them, as if nothing has occurred that has been nice enough to want to write about. I sometimes think I only have recourse to this diary when I want to offload matters that are bothering me. And yet, I should much prefer it to be the other way round – the joy and pride I feel when I've finished a good painting, the wonderfully contented feeling I have after making slow, satisfying love, little anecdotes that when I reread them in fifty or sixty years' time when this blue ink will have faded and the white paper turned yellow will make me smile. But if I lie – what's the good of a diary?

Saturday, 30 September

He frightened me yesterday. But fear is not an innocent emotion. The fear I felt is the price I have to pay for everything that has happened before. It all began with a silly argument: what was the best route to the house of some friends who'd invited us to dinner. I've been there a dozen times before, and he didn't even know where it was. Marcos was driving but he didn't take any notice of my directions. We got lost and arrived late. The dinner passed off more or less well, but on the return journey the atmosphere changed again and our argument became more heated. Although it was clear that he too was in the right about the route we took, neither of us would give way. I wouldn't admit it immediately, and he refused to accept anything I said. We both got very cross, and raised our voices in a way we've never done before, like those married couples who are full of resentment and contempt for each other but still can't make up their minds to split up. I was deeply wounded by the words he used when it would still have been possible to curb the dispute: 'And now we'll see if we can still play happy families after all that's been going on!' I know he was referring to Armengol, because he doesn't know about certain other little matters, and I regretted having told him about it in a moment of weakness in bed. I should have listened to Camila who is so shrewd, always so calculating, when she told me that infidelities should always, always, always be denied, and when it's been shown that you're lying, denied again. The most reasonable thing for us would be to break up while we can still do so in an amicable way. But I'm so illogical that I love him even more now, and I feel he's essential to me.

To go back to our argument: there was one moment, as I was get-
ting out of the car, when he squeezed my arm hard grabbing it just
above the elbow. That was the moment I felt afraid. But I knew
instantly that I couldn't let him see it because, in spite of the pain,
that would only have made him increase the pressure of his fingers.
The weaker women are when they are frightened the more powerful
and threatening men become. I believe it's fear that makes us vul-
nerable quite as much as physical weakness. I don't want to lose
Marcos, but neither do I want a relationship in which one gives the
orders and the other has to defer.

Tuesday, 3 October
At last, when I woke up this morning I was able to remember in
detail the dream I've had several times, but which so far has always
eluded me before I could fix it clearly in my mind. When the alarm
went off I stayed in bed without moving and without opening my
eyes, recapturing every one of the images which I don't know
whether to call a nightmare or not because, although they don't pro-
duce a strong enough sense of panic to wake me up in the middle of
the night, they do leave me shivering and bathed in sweat.

I was driving a train through a country that was divided into two
zones by a civil war, and I had to take people across the front lines.
The horror, however, didn't come from the bombs exploding outside
but from the passengers: they were all lepers, starting to become
paralysed, and losing pieces of their flesh. They had been thrown out
of hospitals to make room for the large number of wounded soldiers.
After I managed to get to the other side – the Red Cross was painted
on all the carriages – the generals there refused to accept my train-
load of sick people in any hospital, claiming they were completely
full, although I knew that it was really their fear of contagion that
made them refuse. They made me turn round after giving them some
food – sackfuls of crusts of bread hurled through the carriage win-
dows. I drove the train back across the battlefield towards the zone
from which I had started out, but I got the same reception on that side

and they made me go back again to the other zone. Nobody was preventing me from getting off and abandoning my convoy of sick people, and I don't know why I couldn't do so. Flocks of birds of prey had appeared in the sky, following in the wake of the train, in the way dolphins follow big ships at sea. They hovered, impatient for the pieces of flesh that flew out of the windows from time to time, and famished, they threw themselves on them. Or they stopped for an hour to devour a corpse that the other passengers had thrown out with obscene and deafening shouts when one of their number died; and then the birds caught up again with the train by following the railway track. Over and over again they made me turn and go back, turn and go back, turn and go back, without letting me stop anywhere.

I know that this dream has some connection with my present state of nerves and irritability, because it tends to recur at times like this when I'm tense and anxious, but I can't begin to explain it. I don't want to use this diary as a sort of psychoanalyst's couch, but what is certain is that all this week I have felt like quarrelling with everybody. With Camila who becomes less concerned as the days go by about the quality and coherence of the work we exhibit because she is only concerned to make money – although that's not the only thing we agreed on when we opened the gallery. With Marcos who doesn't say anything, but I know what he's thinking. With Emilio who has shown the first signs of aggressiveness towards me that before he only displayed towards others, as if I was responsible for his increasing inability to create a sculpture worth looking at. He conveys all the signs of being a male chauvinist who refuses to give way to a woman who runs faster than he can.

I often feel I'm surrounded by useless individuals who weigh me down and get in my way, but at the same time, I can't get rid of them without leaving a trail of corpses behind me. Bother! Now I've gone back to my dream although I promised I wouldn't try to interpret it. I'd like to paint that train in a really big picture, in one of those gigantic baroque triptychs that fill the whole wall of a hall in a palace.

Maybe I'm harming them, but I can't help that unless I stop being the person I am. I should love to rest beside someone who would lie there quietly with me for two full hours. Two hours without any obligation to talk.

Wednesday, 4 October

If one day, when I'm dead, somebody reads this diary, I shouldn't like it to be a child of mine. Children are the worst judges because they insist on perfection in their parents and it takes them a long time to forgive their faults. On the other hand I shouldn't mind if it were my grandchildren who read it because they would do so with that amused tolerance with which they look at old photos of their ancestors. Or even an unknown person who reads it out of curiosity but also with understanding, and who, when he reaches the last page is sufficiently intrigued to look for a portrait of me in order to see what I look like.

Monday, 16 October

I've just spent a sad and boring weekend in Madrid. Now I've decided. Next weekend I'm going to Breda again. On my own. I need it now more than ever. And I've told Marcos.

Tuesday, 17 October

I met Armengol quite by chance today. It's six or seven months since I last saw him, and in the street in the light of day he looked six or seven years older. He hadn't shaved properly, his clothes were creased, and he had that air of abandon about him that used to trouble me, and now that he lives alone it seems to have become accentuated. I really didn't want to, but I agreed to go for a coffee. As soon as I looked him in the face for a second or so, he took that as meaning that what was in the past could be started up all over again. His tone changed and he began to relapse into personal matters and reminiscences that made me feel very uncomfortable. That affair now seems so far off. The extraordinary thing is that he still thought there was room for hope. I refused to meet him again another day – 'for a little talk'. I told him that with all the work I had I didn't have the time, and next weekend I was going away.

I don't feel guilty, and I don't feel sorry for him. All I feel is the sort of awkwardness that invariably develops between a person who solicits favours and the one who refuses.

Wednesday, 18 October

Today we inaugurated the exhibition of Emilio's sculptures. Fewer people than we'd expected, and the sort of reiterated lukewarm praise that always masks disappointment. I'm afraid it's not going to be a success.

Thursday, 19 October

I really am going to break off with Marcos. We've had another argument, and again I felt frightened. Why doesn't he just leave me if he can't come to terms with what's over and done with? Why does he carry on with me, being delightful one day and overbearing the next? He came to the studio today when I wasn't expecting him and without phoning first, as he always does when he knows I'm painting. Yesterday, we made marvellous love. Afterwards, we got into the bath together and washed each other, our backs, our legs and our toes until we became so lustful all over again that we did it in the water, like sea creatures. He was charming, delightful, affectionate, taking his time over every stage of every caress. Sex is the oxygen of love: it washes it clean, purifies, and renews it. There can be sex without love just as there's oxygen in the desert that nobody benefits from. But you can't keep up a loving relationship without those healthy moments of physical pleasure, just as there can't be life on the moon.

I thought that yesterday would have put a stop to the squalls in our relationship that had gone on for too long, but today I realized it was more like that special last meal granted to those condemned to die. This afternoon in the studio his ugly mood was even worse; he was rude and he spoke to me very roughly indeed, as if he considered that yesterday he had been weak, and today he was irritated by his own weakness. I can't, and don't want, to have to put up with these violent swings of mood. I'd have liked to save our affair. I know that I've recovered the feelings I used to feel for him after they've been dormant for some months, but I can't give him my love if he refuses to accept it.

I told him I'm going to Breda this weekend on my own and I don't want anybody with me. I also said that both of us had to give some thought to our relationship and decide whether it's appropriate for us to go on together. He gave me an extraordinary look, and then he stared at the painting I'm working on, the last of the cave series, as if there was something in it that had to do with him. Suddenly, I understood: he's thinking about Emilio. It's always these fits of jealousy that cause his changes of mood. I remembered mentioning yesterday that Emilio was due to come to the studio today to pick up the sketches he had used for his sculptures. But he didn't come. Marcos came without warning, thinking Emilio would be here. The fact that he wasn't should have cheered him up, but in him jealousy works in a ridiculous way. Some jealous people only seem satisfied when they have proof that their suspicions were correct.

I've never believed in the idea that possessive, jealous men are attractive, and even less in that false justification put forward by some people that they are jealous precisely because they love their partners so dearly and identify confidence on the other's part with indifference.

Now I'm on my own, and the afternoon has been ruined where painting is concerned. I've come down to the apartment, taken this diary out of Papa's hiding place, and begun to write. Instead of hating him for our row upstairs, I'm inclined to pity him.

I've stopped for a moment, still holding my biro. I don't know if I ought to go on writing about all this. If I reread it one day, it will all come back to hurt me.

Friday, 20 October

I made a very last effort today to save my relationship with Marcos. And I failed. Although I told him yesterday I was going to Breda, last night I decided we ought really to go together. It's a long time since we had two days on our own, as we used to. Something always comes between us: a visitor, a phone call, an urgent job that has to be finished. I know he doesn't love it as much as I do, but he does also quite enjoy physical exercise and walking. I thought that if he agreed to come with me up to the caves, and we talked, we'd be able to clear away the useless burden of what's past but which is getting on top of us. I'd have shown him the cave-paintings to prove to him that when I base my work on them it isn't Emilio imposing the theme or inspiring my pictures, but those magical phantom men who drew on those walls with their fingers smeared with pigment. These phantoms are more real than those he nourishes in his mind, because they were the beneficent and civilizing result of human attempts to communicate: men stop and talk beside a blazing fire, having broken away from the nomadic horde, and then they settle down as a tribe.

And possibly he would come to understand how vital painting is to me and would at last stop using that sneering indifference with which he still talks about my work as if it's just a hobby I could give up without regret.

I phoned him to suggest this and he agreed to come here. But as soon as he came in he didn't even give me a chance to explain why the qualities I associate with that countryside are real. He stared at me without a word, but with that closed look on his face that so often makes him unapproachable.

It was the look of a man I don't really know, although I got an inkling of it when I was doing his portrait. Its main feature now is contempt. Then he said: 'No. I've got to see my doctor tomorrow. I want him to do some analyses for me.' I asked him if anything was wrong, if he felt unwell, thinking for a moment that possibly his cold and stand-offish attitude was due to some problem he was hiding from me. But he answered so abruptly, brusquely even, that it was just a routine check-up, that after that it was I who didn't want to go on talking. I stood up and went to the bathroom so that he wouldn't see the tears I couldn't hold back. When I returned he had gone.

Cupido stopped reading and stared into space, thinking through the implications of that last paragraph. There was half the answer to the question he had been asking himself for the past three weeks. He reread the last few lines, and then continued.

It's all been useless. However pleasant I've tried to be with him the more he rejects me. Marcos is consumed by a sick and destructive malice which gets worse day by day. This afternoon he was like a bundle of dry tinder that would burst into flames at the merest touch. I didn't dare go near him. I find it impossible to understand how something that happened so long ago can go on festering in his mind.

I remained alone, not knowing what to do, but I could sense shadows invading my home and closing in on me.

I'm going to Breda. I'm always happy there.

The detective closed the diary. The remaining pages were blank. Now that he knew what had happened everything seemed painful, sad, and cruel. To kill for so little. Those last words of Gloria's: '*I'm going to Breda. I'm always happy there,*' that were so full of hope and pointed a devastating contrast with what awaited her only a few hours later in the silence of the forest. He knew now who had killed her, and he thought he knew how, but he had no way of proving it. Raising his head he looked round the enormous living-room divided in two by the sliding doors. Being alone, without Anglada this time, he couldn't resist wandering through the apartment once more. It all remained the same: the paintings on the walls, the layout of the furniture, the depilating pincers next to the little mirror, the unfinished crossword in the last newspaper, the cold silence of

the electrical appliances. He opened the wardrobe in her bedroom and gently fondled Gloria's blouses, Gloria's coats,
Gloria's trousers, the not very valuable items of jewellery she
kept in a small wooden box. In the bathroom a stuffy smell was
beginning to overpower the perfume of the soap that was starting to crack in a ceramic dish. He opened a bottle of scent to
smell its delicate fragrance. Although he had never met her he
felt he had come to know her well, in the way a man and a
woman do who live in distant countries and have started up a
correspondence, knowing they are never likely to meet. He was
familiar with her face, he could close his eyes and reconstruct
her: he knew her favourite colours and scents, her likes and dis-
likes; he knew her paintings that explained her vision of the
world. All that was lacking, he thought, was the sound of her
voice. He went back to the living room, to the piece of furniture
in which, during his first search with Anglada, he remembered
having seen a number of video cassettes labelled with the details
of her art exhibitions and the names of places she had visited.
These tapes lay next to her photograph albums. He hesitated for
a moment, thinking. Something came back to his mind, and he
turned his attention to the photograph albums. Somewhere in
these there had to be the other half of the solution to the mystery. In strict order, and still trying to contain the trembling in
his fingers, but impatiently nevertheless, he turned over the stiff
cardboard leaves, looking carefully at every photograph. He
knew what he was looking for because during that first search he
had registered the fact that it was unusual to see Gloria and
Anglada pictured together, just the two of them, as if there had
never been a third person available to take their photograph.
Otherwise there was always someone else in the photograph
with them. He found what he was looking for in the second
album. It had been taken in Anglada's apartment, a single photograph that didn't seem to be part of a series, as if it had been
used to finish off the film, or as if somebody else had taken it for

them. They sat facing each other on opposite sides of the office table in his apartment, and they were shot in profile. Their arms lay on the table and they held hands, looking at each other, and smiling as if to underline their impatience at being kept apart by the table. It had been taken at a time when they must have been happy. In the background, in the gap between their heads, in the space on the wall between the two windows, a hundred minute and featureless heads regarded them impertinently from the graduation class photograph. The detective's eyes narrowed to help him concentrate on those tiny heads on the wall behind the two happy lovers. *Almost the same age, the same degree, the same city. Probably the same faculty. That's what he had changed when I was in his apartment yesterday. He'd put Gloria's portrait of him in place of this photograph*, he thought, remembering that he'd been conscious of a small modification Anglada had made to the pictures on his walls. He studied it intently, but it was impossible to make out the detail in the faces because they all looked alike and were out of focus, nor could he read the dark row of spidery letters beneath them. He rummaged through the other drawers without worrying any longer about the noise he was making until he found a magnifying glass. This increased considerably the size of the details, but even so the poor focus and the small size (nine by thirteen centimetres) made it impossible to pick out anything for certain. He sighed with relief when he saw the transparent strips of negatives all numbered and in perfect order. He held them up to the light of the chandelier, afraid that that particular photograph had been taken by somebody else and wouldn't be there.

But he found it at last, at the end of a strip that he drew out of its plastic sleeve without touching the emulsion with his fingers. He recognized the silhouettes of Gloria and Anglada. In the negative they had white hair, grey skin, and their mouths looked toothless like the mouths of the dead, making their faces reminiscent of skulls. His four years of studying still and cinema photography had taught him everything that a negative can reveal if it is skilfully handled in an enlarger. He wrapped the strip in a sheet of paper and put it away in the inside pocket of his jacket. He was convinced he was right.

Twenty-Two

Her life was dragging on too long. Now that there was nothing left to fight for, both the days and the nights seemed endless. The final ruling by the Luxemburg Court had closed the last door on hope. If she were suddenly stricken now and were to fall dead on the ancient, polished tiles of the floor, nothing in the world would change. Only Octavio would miss her. For a while he would feel distressed, and possibly vulnerable, but in the end he would benefit from her death, freed from the weight of obligations with which she had burdened him. Sitting at the dressing table in her room, she looked at herself in the oval mirror. The extensive ageing process that had begun three weeks before – the day she had heard about Gloria's murder – was advancing rapidly. The glass cast back at her the image of a sick woman. The pallor of her skin and the dark blotches had become accentuated. It's curious, she thought, how freckles that are considered to be signs of good health, energy and sunshine in childhood, turn into grim omens of necrosis and cancer in old age. Besides this, she was having difficulty in preventing one eyelid from drooping, and her lips trembled like those of an old dog. How little remained of the woman of forty years before who had been strong, full of fight and determined to break the absurd conventions of the dictatorship which had ruled that the only public sphere in which women had a role to play was the Church! She put tiny drops of the French perfume she had been using since she was fifteen on the lobes of her ears, and for the first time in her life wondered whether that wasn't superfluous now – a vain and pointless affectation. '*No, not yet. There's still Octavio,*' she muttered. For his sake she had to keep up appearances as well as she could. She had made him sacrifice so much in all these years. She had forced him to endure an arduous journey across a barren desert with the assurance of arriving one day in a distant Promised Land, but when they arrived it was to find that the pomegranates and the bunches of grapes were no more than a mirage and that sterile, poisonous wasps had invaded the hives. Since he was a child she had made him tread barefoot through the sand when they should have been lingering at the oases along the way, the waters of which are made to be drunk at his age. She was now the one guilty of his thirst.

She rang the little silver bell and waited for the maid to help her down the stairs to the living-room. She had lost confidence in the strength of her knees and swollen ankles to negotiate the steps, her feet crammed into the narrow shoes with their little heels that she had always worn, because even at home she had never allowed herself to wear soft slippers or to wrap one of those horrible black, grey, or brown shawls over her shoulders as many old ladies do, where they only collect dust and dandruff. She put her arm through the maid's, and welcomed the feeling of security that the girl's strong, young muscles communicated. At the same time, she was conscious of the erotic warmth of her breasts and the way they gave a little bounce at every step. The girl was twenty-two, with black hair and eyes, a pretty face, and a firm, voluptuous figure. Not one of her maids lasted much more than two years in the house, and one of the conditions imposed on all who applied for the job was that they should abide by that term. She had no doubt they guessed what the other condition was before accepting, which meant that it was never necessary to spell it out. As to the rest, they received extremely good wages without being overburdened with work.

It was part of their job to keep the house closed up but well looked after when she and Octavio were in Madrid, to perform all the usual domestic tasks, to observe meticulously all the old-fashioned forms of behaviour, and to be on call twenty-four hours a day for any eventuality when they came for the weekend or for longer stays, which never exceeded a hundred days a year in total. Her two years would soon be up, and this girl had begun to show signs of impatience: she paid less attention to Octavio when serving his aperitif, and was beginning to skimp on her work. Before leaving for Madrid on a recent Sunday, Doña Victoria had put a coin under her bed, and when she returned the following Friday she found it in the same place in spite of having told the girl to clean the room thoroughly. She could imagine that when she had the whole run of the house to herself she would stretch out on her bed dreaming visions of wealth and a soft life, trying on her jewels and using her perfume, rummaging through her drawers, and looking at every object hoping to find evidence to confirm the rumour circulating in Breda which claimed that half the things in the house had been obtained illegally. Furthermore, she was becoming too familiar with visitors, in particular that tall detective, and from her earliest childhood she had learned that the more familiar they were with visitors the less respect maids had for their employers. It would soon be time to look for a new girl.

Old age had made her wise and given her time to observe things – she knew that the first to show indifference had been Octavio himself. Since Gloria had appeared in the Reserve he had begun to look down on the servant girl, and since her death he had revealed a frank rejection of all women. She wasn't his mother, but after so many years together she knew his likes, his fears, his desires and his weaknesses. That was why she was the best person to protect him. That was why she hadn't refused to receive that detective with the unusual name, Cupido, and had welcomed him into her house. It was better that Octavio should be questioned in her presence rather than caught on his own in the street. Cupido was the dangerous one, not the Civil Guard lieutenant who talked and put his questions in the way agents of the law are taught to do, because Octavio knew perfectly well how to defend himself when faced with the cold language of the law courts. The danger lay in the detective and his very human method of putting questions that never seemed to conceal a trap or a threat.

They reached the living-room, and the maid helped her into her armchair.

'Would you like me to bring you something?' she asked, with a solicitude that she hadn't shown in recent weeks, as if the girl too had noticed the atmosphere of anxiety and fear that had begun to pervade the house.

'Yes. Bring me a glass of port,' she said.

The maid went over to the sideboard and took out a pair of two identical glasses and the bottle, filled one glass and silently withdrew.

She didn't try to pick it up until she heard the door close because she didn't want the maid to notice her trembling hand. She sipped it slowly as if it was an agreeable medicine, and without removing the glass from her lips to give herself time to moisten them with the sweet, aromatic wine. She replaced it on the table empty, and sat back in her chair, looking at the afternoon light that acquired a yellowish tint as it filtered through the lace curtains. '*The colour of a shroud*,' she whispered to herself. She listened to the sounds in the street: the distant shouts of children playing, the murmur of two women – probably old – deep in conversation as they walked past, and from time to time the noise of a car engine. She knew that the detective would put in an appearance some time, but she didn't know how long she would have to wait. She felt her eyes stinging from having kept them fixed so long on the brilliance of the window, so she put her hands over them and closed their lids to protect them from the light. She was beginning to forget things that had happened that day, but remembered with exactitude details from the past. Now, without knowing why, her memory chose to torment her with the image of the eyes of the hanged stag that had bulged like those of a rabid dog. Even that act of cruelty had proved to be futile, either as a threat or to create a scandal. She recalled Gloria's face which had expressed two emotions: pity for the animal, and fury directed at the perpetrators of the killing. Everyone had been on her side. Even Octavio had begun to doubt the effectiveness of their strategy, upset by Gloria's protests and by the sympathy that most people feel for these animals of the wild, and she was the only one who had had the strength to counter the girl's demand that the stag be cut down – as if that was likely to bring it back to life! It had all been very disagreeable. And to cap it all, there had been that dog, a mongrel, with its famished appearance and protruding bones, that nobody had dared chase away because they are always wary of the reactions of a hungry animal when separated from its food. She had never agreed to have pet animals in her house. They had always seemed to her a weakness of hysterical women and an additional source of work, dirt, fleas and ticks. She believed that all animals, like people, had to earn their keep by hard work or the production of food. She despised those individuals who love their pets more than they do their neighbours...

She had fallen asleep, but had no idea how long for. But it had been long enough to have a dream in which she saw herself sitting paralysed in her chair, her head against its back and unable to open her eyes. But she saw herself from the outside, as if her eyes had left her body to observe her from afar. She took a deep breath and wondered whether the type of vision she had recently been experiencing wasn't a first warning of serious illness, and possibly death. They were recurring with ever greater frequency. She dozed during the day, but at night it often took her a long time to get to sleep. On the other hand, there were nights when she fell asleep as soon as she got to bed, but then woke up, confused, a few hours later and stayed awake for the rest of the night surprised at how many hours there were to dawn, as if her aching body had had too much rest already. This had happened on the Saturday Gloria was murdered. They were in Madrid, and she had heard Octavio go out very early, much earlier than usual. She had looked at her watch which said half past six. She had stayed in bed, her eyes open, thinking that he probably had work to catch up on in his office before going to the clinic where he was due to have some medical tests carried out that morning; or maybe he hadn't been able to sleep either – insomnia doesn't only afflict the elderly. She hadn't considered it important until the following Monday when she heard that a girl had been killed in the Reserve, 250 kilometres from Madrid. She knew then that they would come to interrogate them because it was known that everything that happened in the Paternoster Forest was of concern to them. She had asked him what time he had left the apartment and Octavio had replied that he had gone out at half past eight just as he did every day. She had listened to this lie without contradicting him because she was convinced that he would never have dared kill a soul. Not only was he incapable of such wickedness, he didn't have the courage for it. Apart from which he had shown her the results of the analyses the next day which indicated that he was clear of any medical problem and also indicated, she recalled, the time when the specimens had been taken for analysis: half past ten. This proved that what he said was reliable because he wouldn't have had time to go to Breda and back – although there remained the shadow of doubt regarding the two-hour discrepancy that morning. It vouched for his movements where the Civil Guard lieutenant and the detective were concerned, and avoided any difficulties that might have arisen if he hadn't had an alibi – that ugly word – but she told herself that it hadn't been necessary to lie to her. Her anxiety had increased when she learned the identity of the victim: Gloria, the beautiful girl who had so fascinated him in their brief meetings. However, she didn't want to ask him any more about it. Whatever happened she would protect him from the world. He was like a son to her, and she wasn't prepared to throw him to the wolves.

The light through the window had become less intense. A large fly had found its way in attracted by the warmth of the house, but in no time at all it was buzzing against the windows trying to escape from the gathering gloom. '*It'll soon be winter. You ought to be dead,*' she muttered as, exhausted, it stopped moving and lay in a corner. She looked at the time on the oval gold watch she had worn for forty years. It was late for Octavio not to have returned. The sun would soon set, and he had only gone out for a coffee after his siesta. He knew scarcely anyone in Breda, and there was no good reason for him to be so late. She leant her elbows on the arms of the chair and sat up straight, trying to hear if there was any sound in the house. Maybe he had come back while she was dozing and hadn't wanted to wake her. But she heard nothing. She picked up the little bell and rang it. The maid appeared immediately.

'Has your master come in?' she asked. She still employed all the old forms of speech that she had learned before everything changed and wasn't prepared to use the more informal terms that had come into use.

'No, madam.'

That was the reply she had feared, and she remained silent, not knowing what else to say. The girl waited near the door.

'That's all. You can go. Tell him to come and see me as soon as he arrives.'

Her fears grew stronger as the shadows deepened. She didn't want to switch a light on, as if the darkness would sharpen her hearing in readiness for when there would be steps coming down the street and the sound of the front door opening. '*My poor boy*,' she murmured. It was so long since she had last cried that she was taken aback by the tears she felt running down her cheeks. She quickly wiped them away, because Octavio might arrive at any minute, and she didn't want him to see her like that. Or perhaps he wouldn't come. Perhaps the only person who would appear through the door would be that odious Civil Guard lieutenant to inform her that he had been arrested on suspicion of being involved in the murders. '*No, it's not possible*,' she whispered again. Octavio had been in Madrid the whole of that Wednesday afternoon when the second girl had been killed. And yet, those two hours... She would have liked to know the truth, but she didn't want to question him because any doubts that arose between the two of them would be worse than an accusation.

Twenty-Three

Night had now fallen, but she wasn't going to eat anything before he arrived. Dining together was a custom they had always scrupulously observed, not because she had ever practised the emotional blackmail used by many mothers who go hungry and refuse to go to bed but always wait up for their troublesome children who enjoy staying out late, but because in a relationship that could never be truly one of mother and son, to share those moments strengthened the bonds she considered essential in her concept of a family. Guided by the faint light of the street lamps, she poured herself another glass of port to allay her hunger. While her tongue savoured the smooth, sweet wine and she still held the empty glass in her hand, she heard the front door open. By the sound of footsteps in the hall, she knew he had returned, and that he was alone. She wiped her eyes again so that he shouldn't see she had been crying. She heard him approach along the passage and open the living-room door. There was no light on in the room, and as he wouldn't be able to see her he would be wondering where she was.

'Octavio,' she called from the shadows. Her voice was as gentle as she could make it.

He stepped forward to switch on the light. The antique bronze lamp with its crystal drops cast the brilliance of its six lamps on the grey head of the old woman, dazzling her. But she preferred that, because the sudden contraction of her pupils would explain any tears visible in her eyes.

'What were you doing in the dark?' he asked in astonishment.

'I fell asleep.'

He bent down to give her a light kiss on the cheek, and looked closely at her, like a doctor examining a patient.

'You shouldn't sleep during the day,' he complained fondly. 'Because then you can't sleep at night.'

'I know. Where have you been?' she asked. She had caught the smell of whisky on his breath when he bent down to kiss her. And yet he never drank, apart from the one glass of port he would take with her in the afternoon.

'Oh, I've just been strolling round,' he answered vaguely.

Doña Victoria didn't want to press him further. She turned back to look at the blackness of the window. They were very long, these November evenings. She needed to go to the bathroom after sitting for such a long time without moving. She rested her elbows on the arms of the chair and made an effort to get up but was surprised to find that for the first time in her life her legs refused to obey her, as if they too had gone to sleep, although she didn't feel any tingling sensation. She tried to hide it, but Octavio had already noticed her helplessness and he gently helped her to her feet. Doña Victoria thought she had never needed him more than she did in that moment.

'Don't ever leave me,' she said, giving way to a weakness she had always spurned, as befitted the last descendant of an ancient provincial family that, without being noble, had never lost its good name, had never borrowed money, had never needed to buy its meat, and had never engaged labourers to work on its lands other than the sons of its own farm workers.

The old woman left the room and Octavio remained alone, looking round at the furnishings and ornaments, and thinking that from now on, as they had finally lost the battle for possession of the forest, and as there was not even a chance of coming to a just and amicable agreement between the winners and the losers, it made no sense to come so often to Breda. All they had there was that house and a few small fields on which Gabino supported himself. He would have to get down to working longer hours in Madrid as a lawyer, since their financial resources had been nearly exhausted in the expectation of ample compensation at some future date, and they would even find it difficult to retain a maid to keep house for them throughout the whole year.

Doña Victoria was returning to her chair when they heard three loud knocks at the front door. They looked at each other for several moments without a word, both fearful of what this visit portended. They heard the maid's quiet footsteps, the sound of the door opening, and the distant murmur of a voice they both immediately recognized.

'It's Senor Ricardo Cupido.' The maid's words confirmed what they already knew, and she waited for their reply.

'Do you want to talk to him?' asked Doña Victoria.

'I don't think we have any option.'

'Tell him to come in.'

Doña Victoria went to sit in the armchair she always used, as if the high back would protect her from the dangers she anticipated from this latest visit by the detective, because he couldn't possibly have any more questions to ask, and his appearance now could only mean that he was coming to give them answers to some of the unknowns. She was aware of Octavio moving to stand behind her. She sensed his hands resting on the upholstered back of her chair, very close to her head with its fine, grey hair, like cobweb. For the first time she couldn't tell whether he did so to protect her or whether it was in response to the sort of fears that make a person want to hide.

From there, from the shelter of the chair, the two of them watched as the maid opened the door, stepped aside to make way for the detective, and withdrew when told she was no longer needed.

Cupido addressed them as politely as he had done on his previous visits, but they noticed the agitation in his voice.

'Cognac please, Octavio,' said Doña Victoria in an effort to pretend that everything was the same as before, that they had nothing to fear – her usual attitude of incredulity and indifference to anything from the outside world that threatened to disturb their lives.

The lawyer poured two brandies and another small glass of port for her. All three took their first sips to delay the start of the conversation, as if not one of them knew how to begin.

'Do you still have some questions to ask us?' asked Doña Victoria at last.

'No,' replied the detective. 'No more questions. Today I've come to give you some of the answers.'

'Please begin,' she said. Her voice was still haughty and defiant.

'I'm waiting for another person to join us,' said Cupido.

Octavio and the old woman exchanged a disbelieving and questioning look.

'What do you mean?' asked the lawyer.

'I have invited to this house the last witness we need. He's already been seen on the road and should be here in a few minutes. He has a very powerful motorbike.'

Cupido noticed Exposito give a quick glance at the telephone, but he didn't make a move towards it.

'How dare you?' Doña Victoria cut in furiously. 'How dare you intrude on our privacy in this way?'

The detective looked her straight in the eyes, ignoring her anger, the lips that trembled like those of an old dog, and the sound of her quick, heavy breathing.

'Leave my house immediately,' she commanded. 'I should never have let you in. I knew from the start that you were the one we had to beware of.'

'That's all right,' said Cupido. 'I'll wait outside in the street.

As soon as I go you'll start wondering what I know about all this, and what you're going to have to defend yourselves against from now on.'

He hadn't taken the first step before they heard two quiet knocks at the front door, as if he had been no more than the emissary of the main guest. This was what he had been waiting for, and he kept quiet in the knowledge that this knock totally changed the situation and obliged his reluctant hosts to reconsider their order to leave. All three listened to the maid's hushed footsteps as she went to the door and exchanged a few whispered words with the person outside.

'A gentleman is asking for you, sir,' she said, returning to the living-room and addressing herself to Exposito. 'He didn't want to give his name.'

The lawyer made as if to go out into the passage, but before he could do so Cupido took two photographs out of his jacket pocket and placed them on the small table beside the glasses of brandy and port.

Exposito and Doña Victoria leant over to look at them. In one, Gloria and Marcos Anglada appeared seated at a table opposite each other, holding hands, and smiling. In the gap between their heads could be seen the distant and unfocused image of a graduation photograph. The other, very grainy print was a greatly enlarged detail of the first: it depicted one of the faces in the graduation photograph, and had been drawn out of the negative in the way a fossil is extracted in an archaeological excavation. It was the face of a man looking five or six years younger, as well as paler and thinner, but perfectly recognizable. The face betrayed tension and nervousness in front of the camera, but underneath, and in spite of the indistinct letters it was possible to read his name: Octavio Exposito Blanco.

Cupido waited in silence for their reaction. The lawyer looked at Doña Victoria as if it was to her that he had to explain himself.

'What are you trying to prove with this?' he asked, but his voice was no longer as steady as a defending lawyer's needs to be if he is to convince a court of law of the innocence of his client.

'Nothing yet. But I don't think you should keep an old university friend waiting outside the door any longer.'

'Tell him to come in,' said Doña Victoria to the maid. The anger she had felt earlier was giving way to perplexity and fear. She had lost her fortune and her family's lands in interminable litigation. All she had left was Octavio, and she was beginning to suspect that she now risked losing him too. The detective realized that the old woman didn't know the whole truth. He knew she would defend Exposito against any peril, and she would defend him all the more determinedly when she knew the nature of the peril. To protect him she would pledge everything she still possessed – the house and its contents – and would devote all her efforts to doing so before leaving this world.

The tall, athletic figure of Anglada appeared in the doorway. He didn't seem perturbed, just distrustful in the presence of Cupido and Doña Victoria. This wasn't what he had been expecting. He wore black leather trousers that were appropriate for a motorcyclist, and a long-sleeve check shirt over which he had a jacket also made of leather. The crash helmet he held in his hands, the way he was dressed, and his untidy, sweaty hair contributed to his forceful appearance, and lent him a new, aggressive air.

'He's the one who sent the message telling you to come,' explained Octavio, pointing to the detective.

Anglada looked at him with fury and contempt, as at someone capable of revealing a jealously guarded secret out of stupidity.

'There's no reason to go on hiding it,' said Cupido. 'You two have known each other for many years, since you were both students at university.'

He stooped over the table to show him the two photographs.

'If you hadn't substituted the graduation photograph, possibly I wouldn't have noticed. But that change-over wasn't in keeping with the brilliant lawyer who takes pride in his talents.'

'I've never hidden it,' said Anglada with an open gesture of his hands and forcing a smile to his lips. 'We studied together and we knew each other. There's nothing odd about that. What are you trying to prove? What are you getting at?' he asked. From the moment of his arrival he had become the dominant person in the room, like the principal actor in a classical tragedy who thrusts into the background the chorus and the secondary characters, as soon as he appears on the scene. Exposito seemed to accept this, but Doña Victoria watched with disbelief the unthinking gesture with which he put his helmet on the table without asking her permission, and the energetic way he was walking about in his big, dusty boots – in that house where everything was usually so calm and sedate.

'There's something else as well,' said Cupido.

'Have you found the diary at last?'

'Yes. And half the truth is in it.'

'You mean that after she died she wrote down the name of the man who'd murdered her!' joked Anglada.

'No. That wasn't necessary,' replied Cupido mildly, and with no trace of sarcasm. 'Gloria was murdered by two lawyers who were at university together, who lived in Madrid, who knew Breda, and also knew her habit of walking alone along the paths through the Reserve and the routes she was in the habit of taking. One of them had been her boyfriend until a few days before her death. I suspect the other one would have liked to be. They murdered her, and later, in order to confuse the investigation and at the same time exert pressure on a matter connected with the ownership of the Paternoster Forest, they killed the other girl. In that way they led people to believe that both murders were committed by a lunatic. Later, they killed the warden

Molina because he knew too much. They'd worked it all out in meticulous detail. Not for nothing were they lawyers who knew everything to do with the ways of the law. To provide perfect alibis for themselves they depended on each other. Nobody knew they were friends. And did they by any chance exchange notes when they were studying at the university?'

Exposito didn't reply. He remained silent but wary. Anglada managed a broad smile.

'And we used to copy off each other during exams!' he said in a provocative tone, still convinced he was invulnerable.

'They depended on each other,' repeated Cupido, 'in the way creeping plants look for support. These two brilliant lawyers worked it out together, and both made the mistake of believing that the other was reliable. But in fact they each let the other down, and now they've fallen flat on their faces. The sum of two nothings is still nothing.'

'A pretty little speech. A fantasy story about heroes and culprits,' said Anglada. 'But I'm afraid this is the real world, Mr Detective, and the only thing that matters here is proof, and nobody's going to admit to anything,' he added, looking round at Exposito and Doña Victoria, his eyes gleaming with fury at having had their secret exposed. 'It's true we knew each other – you've shown that by your clever trick with the photograph, but that doesn't prove a single one of your theories.'

'What proofs do you have to support your accusations?' Doña Victoria spoke for the first time. Her voice had recovered its natural authority which made it unnecessary for her to raise it.

Cupido turned to her. Faced with Exposito's silence and Anglada's sarcasm, the old lady was the only person with whom he felt obliged to carry on talking. He had to tell her the whole truth clearly and in all its detail. This was the final moment, and he always found it the most unpleasant in any investigation. He had never liked making direct personal accusations, and would always have avoided them if possible. In most cases he found the investigatory process a fascinating exercise, but it was always the final outcome that made him say he hated his work.

'Your adopted son killed Gloria.'

'Go on,' she ordered, sitting up straight in her chair. 'But if you are unable to prove your accusations I shall take legal action against you for slander and I shall ensure you are never permitted to work any longer in your disgusting profession.'

'Your adopted son killed Gloria,' he repeated. 'And not because he happened to meet her by accident in the middle of the Reserve, but because it was premeditated. He'd thought through exactly what he was going to do. On that Saturday morning he left your house in Madrid earlier than you said, perhaps because you were asleep and believed what he told you, or possibly because you were lying. Old people don't sleep well, and they wake up at the slightest noise.'

He waited for a response or a protest from one or other of the three, but not one said a word.

'That hour and a half, or possibly two hours,' he continued, 'was all he needed while a cast-iron alibi was being created to prove he was very busy in Madrid during most of the morning, having a blood test done in a clinical laboratory, and paying for some purchases with his credit card in El Corte Inglés. It was all a lie. In reality he was riding a powerful motorbike on the road to the Reserve, towards the one path that Gloria was bound to take in order to get up to the caves with the paintings. It was quite by chance, during a transport strike in Madrid, that I learned something that Anglada had kept quiet about: he had a motorbike. Camila, Gloria's partner in the gallery, was surprised he hadn't used it the day I was there to avoid the traffic jams. I forgot that detail at the time, but later I understood why he hid it. That morning, while your adopted son was waiting hidden in the bushes near the path, it was Anglada disguised in his glasses and his clothes who used his credit card to make a few purchases, and who gave a sample of blood for analysis in the clinic. Of course, before that he had had time to attend a court hearing before a judge and surrounded by a crowd of potential witnesses who knew him, which meant that nobody would doubt he had been in Madrid all the time.'

Cupido sighed, and took another sip of brandy. His system craved a dose of nicotine to go with the alcohol, but he resisted this without too much difficulty.

'It isn't necessary to go into all the brutal details of the murder, except to mention that they made one small mistake, and something else happened that they couldn't have foreseen. Their mistake was to let Gloria snatch the badge that was pinned to his clothing. This made us think that the murderer must have had some connection with her. What was completely unforeseen was the gunshot not very far from where she was killed.'

Cupido and Doña Victoria noticed the exchange of glances between the two lawyers – an involuntary reaction to this disturbing piece of information.

'If it was the mistake with the badge that forced them to commit a second murder in order to demonstrate that it was all the work of a sadist and to bring pressure on a legal action – because any bit of countryside where serious crimes have been committed has a curse on it and nobody who's keen on rural tourism will dare walk through it – it was the unforeseen event that made it necessary to kill Molina. The warden was on the prowl in the same area that Saturday morning, but not because of his official duties. He was an ambitious individual and very fond of money, and there were times when he acted on his own account. He would hunt stags in order to have their heads prepared as trophies that he would sell for a good price. There are a few details that I don't know, but the whole business is so serious that a few details aren't important at this stage. I imagine they caught sight of each other, each of them having committed a crime, and their paths crossed unexpectedly as they were both hurrying away.

The warden couldn't say a word because he'd have lost much more than his job. Both had to keep quiet, and that suited them both. But as the death of a girl is more serious than the death of a deer, Molina was well paid for his silence. In the meantime, Anglada had engaged my services so that no one might doubt his desire to have it all cleared up, even his desire to avenge Gloria's death. He took on an obscure provincial detective who would get hopelessly lost in the jungle of the capital when he went to Madrid searching for the origins of the badge. He got rid of me ten days later, soon after the death of the second girl, because he didn't need me any longer. They reckoned everything was neatly buttoned up. But there's always a problem. Molina must have become very nervous after the second murder. That hadn't been included in the price of his silence. This detective and the Civil Guard were beginning to close in on him. Now his silence commanded a higher price. So he had to be killed as well, but not with a knife this time. He was a powerful man. Not long before, he told me it was only women who were attacked in that way, because the ground in the forest is full of sticks and stones with which a man can defend himself. They used a shotgun. Not long after this the detective discovered something that suggested a possible hiding place of the diary. Of course, he's just a little provincial, but he does like to finish his jobs, and it often happens in his investigations that once he's assembled all the evidence, he begins to have doubts: how much has he established for himself, and how much has he been prompted to believe? He suspects that right at the beginning he was led astray, and now he's no longer working on the case, he begins to see the light. Discovering the diary revealed everything.'

Cupido fell silent. It was proving to be a lengthy monologue and he was tired; his words weighed heavily on him. But he continued, still addressing himself to Doña Victoria.

Pointing to Exposito he said: 'He's the one who killed Gloria. Anglada killed the other girl. As both of them had solid alibis for the morning of the first crime, and it was thought to be almost certain that there was only one murderer who used the same method twice, no suspicion attached to them. Anglada was believed when he said that on the afternoon of the second murder he had been at home on his own, getting drunk. Everybody sympathized, and nobody could prove the contrary. Where Exposito is concerned, you and your servant in Madrid knew that he had been there all the time.'

'You say we had alibis. We still have alibis,' riposted Anglada, still smiling. But not finding support from anyone else in the room his smile was becoming even more forced.

'No, you don't any longer. You two both belong to the same blood group, a small coincidence that you knew you could use to advantage. But you slipped up on one thing you hadn't foreseen. You're both good lawyers, but you're not doctors.'

Cupido noticed the two men suddenly become more tense and they now listened to him with an anxiety bordering on fear.

'Although it's Sunday today, the lieutenant has been able to obtain a copy of the results of the blood test done in the name of Octavio Exposito, whereas in fact it was you who gave the blood for analysis,' he said, turning to Anglada. 'The day before, you had told Gloria that you weren't coming with her to Breda because you were going to a clinical laboratory to have some tests done. It was basically routine and couldn't in any way compromise either of you because it was a simple analysis and check for antibodies, and you probably believed that neither of you had anything wrong with you. All you had to do was give a little blood to prove it. You also knew that laboratories destroy blood samples used for simple tests in forty-eight hours, and although a group of boys found Gloria's body earlier than you'd hoped, there was no chance of doing any more work on them. All you did was to ask them for the results that would support your alibi: the blood group, which is always provided, the haematocrit and leucocyte counts, and a check for antibodies.

As it turned out, the analysis showed that the blood was normal and there were no antibodies.'

'And what does all that mean?' asked Exposito. His voice trembled, and there was panic, not only in his eyes behind their thick glasses, it suffused his face.

'It means that the blood didn't come from you. You do have antibodies in your system because of the herpes virus that caused the cold sore on your lip. But that didn't appear in the analysis.'

A hush fell on the room, as if it were empty, as if even the venerable old wooden furniture had stopped creaking, and the wind outside didn't dare disturb the lace curtains at the window. It was all over.

Cupido took a photocopy of a sheet of paper bearing the stamp of the Madrid laboratory from his jacket. Exposito didn't move; as far as he was concerned it wasn't necessary to prove where it came from or who it belonged to. But Anglada went over to the detective and snatched it out of his hand. He ran his eyes over the words written there, deciphering the technical terms that had ruined their whole scheme, the meticulous web they had spun, secreted by hate and greed. The detective looked at Exposito. His lips were now free of the infection, but they were trembling, his mouth was twisted – not as a result of scar-ring left by the virus as it withdrew into its winter quarters where it would sleep and grow stronger, like those terrible species of omnivorous ants, until a new stimulus awoke it and launched it into another painful eruption on his lip – but from anguish, shame, the recognition of defeat and panic.

Cupido felt depressed and tired, as he always did when he had solved a case and at last understood the motives that had led to the crime; but he made an effort not to let himself be carried away by pity because he was only too familiar with the skill of some criminals who manage to make themselves look like vic-tims when their luck changes. He believed that evil acts in the same way as herpes inside a person. Just as the virus lies dormant and indestructible in the body until revived by illness, anxiety, or intemperance, and bursts out again painfully, so evil lies dormant in the mind until brought to the surface by hate or unhappiness. Both are immune to any kind of therapy and coexist with the infected individual all his life.

Anglada raised his eyes from the sheet of paper, and looked towards Exposito and Doña Victoria as if seeking their help. Then he began to stride backwards and forwards across the room as if the walls hemmed him in, and Cupido wondered whether he wasn't looking for some sort of weapon. He was the strongest of the three and seemed to be the only one refusing to accept defeat. Whereas the old woman was bewildered by the revelations, and Exposito sat with bent head, his hands gripping his temples, Anglada seemed about to leap to the door like a cornered wolf searching for a way of escape. His leather jacket and trousers made him look particularly threatening. Cupido wondered why the lieutenant was taking so long to arrive as they had agreed he would come in ten minutes after Anglada. He had extorted the concession of a delay out of regard for Doña Victoria, and in exchange for passing on to the Civil Guard everything he had discovered about the case. Pity had made him feel he had an obligation to extend this minor courtesy to her and to be the one who would recount the full story without using legal jargon and without the presence of uniformed police and photographers. He knew that after having killed, a murderer ceases to think of his victim, brushes aside all feelings of remorse, and thinks only of himself, of saving his own skin, escaping conviction and not being trapped. He was afraid that Anglada's reaction would be to turn violent if he thought that nobody else knew the truth. Even so, he was surprised when he heard Doña Victoria ask in a harsh voice:

'How much do you want to keep your mouth shut?'

She had raised herself up again in her chair, ready to fight a new battle now that Exposito no longer had the will to do so. In doing so she reversed the normal order of things that when two generations live under the same roof, the younger one is full of drive and ambition and the older one is full of fears. Cupido looked again at her wide open eyes, her tensed neck, and her face that stubbornly rejected defeat and the loss of the most valuable thing left to her.

'How much do you want to keep your mouth shut?'

'No,' he replied. He would have liked to add that it was only for her that he would even have considered keeping quiet. He didn't have an atom of sympathy for the two lawyers.

'Who else knows all this?' asked Anglada, at last able to express the words that must have been choking him. 'Between the two of us we'll give you enough money to retire for life. Now, does anybody else know?'

For a second Cupido thought of Molina. He must have received a similar offer – and believed it.

A shout and a dull thud of something falling in the passage outside cut short his reply. Gallardo suddenly threw the door open. He stopped short, taken aback by the apparently calm atmosphere in the room where he had been expecting to see a scene of violence. Behind him they saw two Civil Guards gripping Gabino by the arms. He was handcuffed, and he raised his hands to his nose to wipe away the blood that was running down to his mouth.

The lieutenant went straight to Anglada without looking at the detective. He addressed him by his full name, and while another guard handcuffed him he pronounced the formal sentence of arrest, careful to comply with the strict form of words. Anglada did not lower his gaze as if even in that moment he wasn't prepared to appear humiliated – as if such a thing was foreign to his nature.

Everyone in the room wheeled round to stare at Exposito as they heard the first sob. His eyes behind the heavy glasses were bathed in tears, and one of them ran down until it hung from his chin, making him look ridiculous. He got up from the chair where he had been sitting with his head in his hands, the same hands that had wielded the knife, and walked the few steps that separated him from Doña Victoria, indifferent to all the others in the room – Anglada, the lieutenant, the detective, and the guard who stood hesitantly near him with open handcuffs – all except the old woman who sat immobile in her chair. He knelt down in front of her and, racked by sobs, buried his head in her lap. Cupido knew that Exposito's tears wouldn't move her, and her eyes would stay dry. He couldn't imagine her ever crying. On the contrary, he saw her as one of those people who are irritated by the tears of others since they deny themselves that consolation. Doña Victoria smoothed his hair without allowing either her eyes or her hands to betray any sign of weakness, to show that he could still count on her fortitude. Then she raised his head and made him look at her so that he would never forget what she was about to say, and the full significance of her words:

'You are my son.'

Exposito calmed down, like a wrongdoer who has suddenly received a formal pardon. He stood up, and obediently let the guard put the handcuffs on his wrists. Then they all left except for Cupido and Doña Victoria, still seated in her chair, endeavouring to summon the strength she would need for what was still to come – a harder, longer, more painful battle even than the one she had fought over the past twenty years.

'I believe I shall loathe you for the rest of my days,' she said at last, without looking at him, without looking around, her eyes not focused on anything.

'It will be easier for you if you do,' he replied. He sincerely believed in the truth of his words; they were dictated by the sympathy he felt for this hard, but also frail, woman, as he thought that the most terrible and repugnant aspect of a murder lies not only in the pain of the victim and the victim's family, but also the pain felt by those close to the murderer because, in spite of their own innocence, they are tainted and scarred by his crime.

'How long?'

'Twenty to twenty-five years. If all goes well they'll let him out at weekends after anything between eight and ten years. And soon after that he'll be permitted to sleep out.'

'I shall go to see him every day of the year. I have nothing else to do with my life. I shall wait for him until then.'

Cupido advanced to the door, shut it softly, and went out into the street. He began to walk, leaving behind the ancient stone walls of the house, the antique furniture and its aged and desolate owner.

Twenty-Four

The land began to resonate like a drum. The first drops, as big as marbles, struck him on his back and thighs, and on his helmet which amplified their noise. He had gone out that afternoon for a cycle ride although the weather forecast had threatened rain, because autumn would soon be over and the winter cold would reduce him to a state of indolence. Besides which, after four years of drought – the most terrible he could remember because it didn't only damage the crops but also the very fibre of the trees – he had ceased to believe that clouds in the sky meant rain. Over that whole period he had often watched them glide across the sky and disappear without releasing a single drop, leaving the ground even more thirsty and disappointed than before.

But it had come at last, drenching everything around, bouncing off the tarmac and creating puddles everywhere, to the extent that it was difficult for the narrow tyres to keep their grip, even more so in view of the slippery film of mud and oil that the first rains always produce. He leant further forward over the handlebars, changed down a gear, and concentrated on staying upright. The downpour became heavier, and five minutes later it was impossible to carry on. He noticed a country house not far off the road and walked the bike over to it to take shelter in its porch. He waited half an hour, but the storm didn't abate. Dense, storm-tossed clouds converged and blotted out the sky.

The freshly saturated earth gave off a smell like that of solder, or of red-hot iron when it is suddenly cooled.

In spite of the cold that was beginning to penetrate his soaked tee-shirt and shorts, he knew that this was the right time for the rains to start. The storks, swifts, and swallows were flying off, and the first signs of autumn were apparent: tiny olives like goat droppings, reddish chestnuts, their spines hard and prickly from lack of moisture, tiny mushrooms like round eggs, and all those fruits that would ripen in the cooler air. Now, with all this water, everything would change. The sap would well up through the trunks of the trees, and their leaves, washed and shiny as glass, would open again. As they walked, the workers in the fields would be happy to feel the weight of mud on their boots. A million flies would die.

Bored with waiting, he mounted his bicycle again as soon as the rain began to ease. Feeling stiff, he pedalled slowly along the road avoiding the deeper, water-logged holes, but reached his garage without mishap. As he passed the first houses he saw people standing at their windows, smiling as if they were witnessing a wonderful and long-forgotten spectacle. There were mothers with small children in their arms who held their hands out through open windows so that they might experience the unknown sensation of water falling from clouds.

He had a long bath in very hot water, stretching his muscles, and regretting the lack of a companion to rub his back and neck that ached from his crouched position over the handlebars. He dried himself on a clean towel, and walked naked through the apartment, another of his habits – a result of living alone, like his gloomy, hurriedly eaten meals, and his other habit of falling asleep at the wrong hour of the afternoon which left him unable to get to sleep at night. He went to the built-in wardrobe in the hall where he kept his overcoats and winter clothes. He chose a light sweater to put on over his shirt, noting the slight odour of camphor, as well as enjoying the pleasantly itchy feel of the wool on his neck and arms that heralds the approach of cold weather. He looked at himself in the wardrobe mirror, and although he was pleased with his appearance – tanned and standing tall as a consequence of so much exercise like a late holiday-maker recently back from a long vacation – he couldn't help being conscious of the emptiness in his life that always assailed him when he brought a case to its conclusion, just as he used to feel in June during his student years when classes were finished and exams over. It was that disconcerting sensation of not knowing what to do with so much free time in spite of the numerous projects that had been held over for when that time came. He was withdrawing into himself after days that had been crowded with questions and answers.

As he put a jacket on he noticed the bulge of something hidden in the inside pocket. He pulled out a nearly full packet of cigarettes. This discovery surprised him because it was little more than a week since he'd searched through all his clothing for a cigarette. He gave a satisfied smile, took a deep sniff at the sweet-smelling tobacco, and put one of the cigarettes in his mouth. He looked at himself again in the glass with the cigarette dangling from his lips, but the mirror reflected an image of him that was both obsolete and incongruous. He threw the whole packet in the rubbish bin and went out into the street.

He arrived at the Casino carrying an umbrella to protect himself from the rain that was still pouring down. Alkalino was talking to two other men, but hurried over as soon as he saw him, as if he had been waiting for him.

'What a crazy way to lose a million!' he said. 'I'll have to treat you today.'

He called the waiter over and, without asking Cupido what he would like, ordered two glasses of brandy as he jabbered away about something to do with the rain and the cold.

'A great job you've got!' he added. 'You think they're going to pay you for finding out the truth, and then when you do they don't! You ought to get another job.'

'If I did I wouldn't have so much time for chattering with you,' he retorted with a laugh. He was grateful to Alkalino for the information about the poacher who had heard the shot, and this was the best way to say it. Alkalino would have rejected conventional thanks. Besides, he was right about the strangeness of his job: in spite of the written contract he held, he couldn't very well go to the prison and insist that Anglada pay him the million pesetas they'd agreed on for finding out who had murdered Gloria!

'Now it's your turn to talk. I suggest that today I pay and you do the talking,' Alkalino said, indicating once again how skilfully he could dispose of a glass of brandy.

'What do you want to know?'

'Everything. Who killed the first girl?'

'Exposito. Anglada covered him with a perfect alibi until Gloria's diary revealed its one weak point: she had asked him to come to Breda with her that weekend and he had refused on the grounds that he had to have a blood test done. He wasn't worried about telling her that because he knew she was going to die the next day. But it was Exposito who claimed he'd been to the clinic. They chose one of the best known in Madrid that deals with lots of people every day. Anglada put on heavy glasses like Exposito's, possibly a wig as well because he has his hair cut very short, dressed like him, and went in his place. Anybody there might legitimately claim they didn't remember him, but nobody would have dared swear in court that it wasn't Exposito. They have the same blood group. As they'd expected, the analysis didn't turn up any problems, but in fact that was their second mistake: the analysis should have shown that Exposito carried antibodies of the herpes virus. Anglada killed the second girl. One good deed deserves another! Exposito was still hoping those murders would somehow prevent the final expropriation of the Paternoster Forest, because no visitor would ever dare walk through it. They worked together just like the crocodiles and those birds that pick their teeth for them.'

'Did Doña Victoria know?'

'No, but she may have suspected it.'

'And Molina?'

'That was Exposito again because he had perfect alibis for the two previous murders. He used an old shotgun they kept in the house.'

'But why did they kill him?'

'It was he who fired the gun your poacher heard. He was dealing illegally in stag trophies. He came across Exposito that morning, understood exactly what he'd done, and demanded money to keep quiet. They gave it to him, but he was already a marked man. By the way, thank your poacher from me. He was a great help.'

'I told you before he would be,' boasted Alkalino. There was a pause as he thought of something else he hadn't understood. Then, he said: 'Were these lawyers really such good friends?'

'An unusual type of friendship, a sort of mutual understanding between individuals who suffer from the same disease. The lieutenant has dug everything out of them. He's been very clever at getting them to accuse each other by telling each of them that the other is accusing him of being the prime mover in the murders. Apparently, Exposito was the first to come out with something on the lines of: "*I'd even commit murder to get those lands back.*" A statement like that falling on ground already made fertile by spite can quickly bear fruit; it starts up a chain of events that isn't easy to stop. If Exposito made the first step without knowing where it would lead, Anglada made the next two, and made the other man follow him. They'd been in the habit of working together when they were students.'

'Like the birds and the crocodiles,' repeated Alkalino.

'Exposito helped him more than once to get through the more difficult exams. At the same time Anglada was one of the very few students in their year to befriend him. They were such different characters that they got on because they didn't compete. If Anglada drank, Exposito was as sick as a dog; if Anglada screwed half the girls in their year, Exposito didn't even try because he was sure he'd get the push; if Anglada travelled abroad, the only journey Exposito ever made was from Madrid to Breda. In other words they were like two different faces of the same coin.'

'Yes, but in the end they were each as bad as the other!'

He still had more questions and Cupido was quite prepared to clarify every detail that Alkalino would later flaunt as privileged information in order to confute the extravagant rumours that tend to circulate about any crime; but before Cupido could continue, he said:

'I can understand Exposito's reasons for murder. In fact I pointed out to you that you'd find the solution down that road, but I can't begin to understand Anglada's motives.'

Cupido took a first sip of his brandy.

'We've all got a weak spot that we're sensitive about, but when it doesn't happen to be our weak spot we find it difficult to believe that another person is willing to commit murder for so little. Gloria had been unfaithful to him several times, and he knew it. But they had only been brief affairs at a time before his relationship with her had become steady and serious. But quite recently, in a moment of weakness she told him about an affair she'd kept up for two or three months with a very odd and unsavoury individual which, in his eyes, made her deceit even more humiliating. I too have difficulty in understanding why, at that moment, Anglada began to react so violently. I imagine he's the sort of man who takes care that a hurricane doesn't destroy his house, but when it's blown over and one small hinge falls off a door he caves in, incapable even of picking it up. Everything he'd suffered in the past came back to haunt him because he no longer had the strength to resist it. He couldn't stop loving her, but he wasn't able to put up with this new deception. He was in that situation, struggling between forgiveness and hate, but probably knowing it was hate that would get the better of him when he happened to meet Exposito one day in a law court in Madrid. They'd already seen each other once in the Reserve where there'd been a small fire and had nodded to each other, but in the confusion that followed they didn't have time for more. But in Madrid they went off to a restaurant to chat about the past and the work each of them was doing. Exposito described the problems they were having in their litigation regarding the Paternoster Forest – the same area that Gloria often visited. He and Doña Victoria feared that final expropriation would turn the whole forest into a national park, and they were determined to do everything legally possible to prevent an invasion by hikers and tourists. At the same time they were making various threats and attempts at sabotage. The first idea that they should work together grew out of that lunchtime conversation. Having met Exposito, everything he'd imagined in his worst nightmares, in the moments when he felt most tormented by jealousy, began to take shape as a real possibility, of actually being feasible. They met several times after that. Both being lawyers they knew it would have to be very carefully planned, and with no risk to either of them. They quickly made a plan, and it seemed to them convincing. If Anglada had had any doubts up to that point, he soon put them completely out of his mind because of his desire for revenge.'

'We're all better at remembering insults than the good turns we've received,' said Alkalino, looking up at Cupido. His eyes were narrowed, serious, and thoughtful. He picked up the fresh glass of brandy he had ordered from the waiter with a wave of his hand, and with a quick flick of the wrist emptied the drink straight down his throat, savouring its aroma as he did so.

'Once again it's the old story of love and deceit. It happens all the time. Human beings aren't very original. Always the same old emotions in every new generation, the same old belief that they're doing something nobody else has ever done before.'

'Like dreams,' said Alkalino. 'We believe something new's happening to us every night, but we only need to wake up to realize they're always the same old nightmares.'

'That's right, the same old nightmares.'